AN ACT OF NATURE

A NOVEL IN THREE PARTS

M. WILL SMITH

Published by Red Frog Publishing a division of Red Frog Media

Visit our website at www.redfrogpublishing.com

First published in 2021

Photo/Art of Nuclear explosion by Romolo Tavani (Licensed under iStock)
Cover Design by Becca C. Smith

ISBN 978-1949877397

Printed in the United States of America

Dedication

The document has been professionally produced by my daughter Becca C. Smith and without her it would have continued to lie in state, gathering dust. Proofreading was by my patient and loving wife Carrie, whose background as a legal secretary helped guard against mistakes, bad English and bad writing.

FOREWORD

The world changed forever near the end of the Second World War. Mankind developed the ultimate people-killing weapon, the thermonuclear bomb. It was not just one country that was racing to develop this weapon, but it was one country that demonstrated its devastating power to kill people. As time went on, more and more countries became 'nuclear powers'. Stockpiles of these weapons grew. These bombs were each hundreds of times more powerful than the first one, so the destructive power reached unimaginable heights. Despite treaties and other actions aimed at limiting the growth of both nuclear weapons and the countries that had them, the world's nuclear armament grew. Rationalized as a deterrent to war, it was argued that these stockpiles were necessary to warn others not to cross the line as these weapons actually work. They are not a placard with a warning sign. They are the deadliest weapons the human mind could ever have created. They are not spears. They are not guns. They are not fighter jets. They are weapons of war that can vaporize a city in a single flash, erasing the lives of millions of men, women and children instantaneously. And, we are humans, so mistakes, miscalculations, misinformation and sheer ignorance is spread evenly among nuclear nations. Setting off a nuclear war is far from unlikely.

Our reality is that despite our intellectual achievements, we are still members of the animal kingdom. As such, we have animal instincts wired into our bodies. Are we capable of containing these animal instincts that have allowed us to survive over the eons to become the climax species of the world? Survival of the fittest brought us from surviving the beasts that sought to eat us, to now having to survive members of our own species. We now have the power to literally erase our foes from the face of the Earth. But our foes are our fellow humans, not cockroaches. By erasing our foes we are, in effect, erasing a part of ourselves. Is this survival instinct simply the desire to survive as our ancestors did, or does it point to our uniquely human teachings and the beliefs that we fervently foster, whether they be ideological or religious? Do the teachings themselves derive from the requisite for survival?

This book tells three connected stories about how things might play out if, in the distant future, we slip from our lofty perch as humans and fail to stop ourselves from killing one another with weapons that we specifically developed for the purpose of mass annihilation.... of ourselves. What happened as our inner animals sought to eliminate other animals of our species, when survival must be winning, because losing was death. But winning was also death. And as the smoke cleared after the ensuing war, some survived with enough capacity to do something. What could they do in a world laid bare, with much of its population dead or sick and dying? Were they somehow winners just because they survived? What indeed would they have won? No, they were the undertakers, left only to pick up the pieces and observe the suffering while trying desperately to keep it from happening again.

The catastrophic event assumed in this book was the result of a fatal combination of nature's instinct to survive and the intelligence that nature gave us to survive with. This intelligence catapulted our species to the top of the food chain, while at the same time allowing us to develop potentially conflicting beliefs as well as create monstrous weapons capable of mass annihilation of competing beliefs. We then fought to the death over which belief was right. In the end, what did it matter which belief was right? It was only for those who were left to survive as best they could.

ALMOST FREE

BOOK ONE

M. WILL SMITH

Chapter One

"It is the call," said Luke looking off into the dense gray blanket that had begun to roll in from the ocean over the meadow where the children sat before him. The orange buds of California poppies sprinkled the green in the background. In the distance there was a tall structure with a light on top that flashed through the descending gray as it turned. Momentarily, a horn echoed into the cool damp morning air. Its tone starting higher, then gradually lowering to a bone-shaking throb.

"We hear this from the village," said Sarah from the front row after holding up her hand and Luke pointing to her.

"Yes, I know, it means I now must go to The Tower," said Luke. He turned his head and stared out toward the flashing light as the thickening gray began to engulf them.

"Well, actually, it's no big deal because it sounds off almost every day this time of year, and besides, it's purpose has been obsolete for a very long time," said Jake who was sitting next to

Sarah. He then quickly raised his hand, but only after he had spoken, which was against the rules of the school. He winced as he looked up at Luke whose head was turned away at the time. Luke now turned and scanned the sea of small faces looking for the offender. He saw Jake who now held his head down.

"What we do is the way of The Message," said Luke after a momentary pause, bringing the palms of his hands together beneath his chin.

"I just wanted to know why it is important since it's just a rotating light and a horn that used to warn ships a long time ago," said Jake. He had started to raise his hand, but only after he had spoken. He winced again, knowing he had disobeyed. He waited to be reprimanded.

"You must raise your hand to be recognized before you speak, young Jake," said Luke taking a step forward and wagging his finger at him. "This behavior of yours must be controlled. We must always follow the rules of conduct." Jake had lowered his head again, and now nodded.

"It calls when the gray matter descends," said Luke, again looking out over the sea of young faces. Jake looked up and raised his hand to reply, but Luke looked down at him and shook his head. Jake's hand came down.

"That's just fog," Jake muttered quietly. But Luke heard him and glared at him for a moment.

"Now...." Luke began, then paused a moment, concerned now about how much Jake knew. The children should not know any of this, and, as the teacher, he would have to deal with it. However, at the moment, he was supposed to go to The Tower. It was his job. He would deal with Jake later.

"The class will go back to the school until I return from The Tower,"he said, pointing to two carved stone pillars guarding an entrance that was dug into the hillside. The pillars were now just visible through the blanket of gray. Behind him the piercing sound of the horn began again, thundering its blare as the children seemed to vibrate in its wake. He turned his head slightly and nodded. He then pointed again to the mound with one finger and held his other hand out in a waving motion as they rose almost in unison and began filing back up toward the entrance. He stood watching them through the gray until finally, one by one, they disappeared through the thick wooden door. A few stopped momentarily to look back at him as he stood with arms folded, watching. As the last one entered, he turned and walked into the gray mist that Jake called fog. Of course it was fog, thought Luke. The horn blared almost every day this time of year. But in all his years of teaching, no child had ever shown the knowledge that Jake had just displayed. The children should not know what he knew, so obviously he had acquired restricted knowledge from somewhere. It would have to be books since there was no electricity in the village to play a memory card. But where did he get the books? Across the fence? That would present a major problem. So when he returned to the school, he would have to question Jake to find out.

Going to The Tower was a routine he had repeated many times over one hundred eighty years, ever since he had become a teacher. It was part of an act for the children. It was a job that he had to perform or he would lose his immortality. He taught The Message to perpetuate a kind of religion that Chandler had cooked up to control the behavior of the village. As he walked, he thought about his tenure at the school. Despite being forced to do what he did, he did love teaching. And the rules of The Message did keep the villagers in compliance with the dictates of the Controllers, who were a mysterious civilization that somehow survived the great war and were now imposing rules on survivors. They had informed Chandler about these rules and how everyone must adhere to them. But neither he, nor Chandler's other assistant, Ed, had ever seen nor heard from this mysterious civilization. It was Chandler who said that someone contacted him with this warning. After that, Chandler created his religion, and dubbed the lighthouse 'The Tower'. He also produced a large book called 'The Message' that laid out rules of conduct for a village that was living out in the forest when they arrived after the war.

Luke's role was to teach the children the rules of The Message. Children from the village had to come to school in the spring once they reached their tenth year, and would attend school through the summer. They would do this for three years. His mission was to indoctrinate them into The Message and its rules. The children would walk to school in the morning and return home in the afternoon after school.

As Luke approached The Tower, he went over in his mind what Jake had said. It was all true, and the teacher in him made him wonder if he could somehow incorporate this new knowledge into his curriculum without Chandler finding out. However, reading books was a serious fracture of the rules that were spelled out in The Message. Outside knowledge was dangerous and no one from the village was allowed to access outside knowledge. So now, Jake had somehow acquired this forbidden knowledge and Luke was not sure how to deal with it. A feeling of confusion swept over him and he wondered what he was going to do about Jake as he crossed the bridge to the lighthouse.

He stopped when he reached the green door to the lighthouse and looked up at the silver disk rotating inside the clear dome. Jake was right, it was a warning to ships of long ago. And long ago no longer existed. Now, the lighthouse was being used as an icon for Chandler's religion. It was now The Tower. He knocked.

"Come in Luke," came a voice. He heard the click that unlocked the door and he entered.

"Good morning," said Luke after closing the door behind him.

"Someone has reported rumors about one of the women," said a tall man sitting on the stairs that led to rooms up in the lighthouse.

"This cannot be condoned," came a baritone voice that seemed to emanate from above. Luke turned to the control console. The head inside a glass bubble atop a metal box now turned and looked at him.

"What cannot be condoned?" asked Luke.

"We don't know the details yet, but it could be a second pregnancy," said Ed from the stairs.

"Luke, you must remind the children the fate of anyone breaking this rule," the voice from above continued. "You must tell them that the man who impregnated her will be punished and forever banished from the village."

"I know," said Luke.

"Exceeding the limit of one child per couple at this time

5

must be enforced," came the voice.

"Yes, with banishment of the offending father," said Luke.

"For a first offense," came the voice. "A second offense is the pit."

"Yes, I know, I'll remind them," said Luke, glancing at Ed who turned away.

All violations of rules of The Message were reported by someone among the faithful in the village. So someone had found out about a possible pregnancy and reported it to Ed when he showed up for his evening briefing at the village in his grotesque costume. Ed was the dreaded Helper. Today, Chandler's order to Luke was about teaching the children about a second child and how violators are dealt with. Luke knew all about the penalties. He had known about many that had occurred. He didn't like the punishments because he thought they far exceeded the crime. But teaching was his job, not enforcement of the rules. That was Ed's job. So he would keep doing what he was supposed to do as he had for countless decades.

"Go now Luke," the voice concluded. Luke nodded and walked outside, crossed the bridge and started up the trail back to the school. He entered the door to find Jake speaking to several other children. This was an act that was strictly forbidden at the school. No child shall take it upon himself or herself to command an audience of more than one other child while at school. As Luke entered, all eyes fell upon him and Jake shrank back with his shoulders turned in. He knew he had disobeyed again since he already knew that rule, having already violated it yesterday. Luke stared at him for a moment before he spoke.

"Before we begin our lessons young followers, I must speak

privately with Jake," he said, pointing at Jake then motioning toward a door to his left. He waited for Jake to reach the door before he followed him in. Luke closed the door behind them.

"How do you know what you know?" asked Luke as he pointed to a chair and Jake sat down.

"I just do," said Jake, looking up at him and beginning to shake since he knew that reading books was forbidden, and that is how he knew what he knew. Luke studied Jake's face. He had arrived the day before with Sarah and had immediately begun to break rules. Both were there for their first year. Jake appeared to be extremely bright and clearly had acquired knowledge from somewhere. Someone in the village had apparently had access to books. In all his years, no child had ever read a book, or worse, passed information from a book on to others. But here it was, and it had to be a book.

"Do your parents speak to you of these things?"

"Uh…no," he replied.

"Life in the village must be simple, Jake."

"What do you mean?"

"Only thoughts of food, shelter, having children like you and living by the teachings of The Message….nothing other than that."

"That doesn't make a lot of sense to me," said Jake.

"It's a violation of the rules of The Message, Jake, so it does make sense," said Luke.

"Maybe to you, but….." he began.

"Did you get this knowledge from books which you know are forbidden?"Luke questioned, in a much louder and a threatening tone, with his brow furrowed and his shoulders raised. The one large candle in the room behind him created a dark, ominous silhouette of him against the wall. Jake shuddered in fear, glancing first at the door, then into the darkened corner of the room. There was no way out. His mind reeled.

"I did," said Jake, finally.

"Where did you get these books?" boomed Luke's voice, even louder this time.

"I can't....." Jake began.

"It was across the fence wasn't it?" Luke guessed, knowing there were four women who lived there and they likely had books in those abandoned research facilities where they lived.

"Yes," Jake nodded.

Luke closed his eyes. Crossing the fence was another forbidden crime against The Message. His mind reached back to remember the four women who lived across the fence. He had come here with them and they had settled there. Chandler, himself and Ed settled inside the fence. But how would Jake get across this fence? It was an impenetrable barrier with a powerful electric current. It had been used to contain political prisoners before the war two hundred years ago.

"I saw another Tower in the books," Jake blurted out while Luke was in deep thought.

"You mean lighthouses," said Luke.

"Yes, lighthouses, and there were many of them long ago," said Jake.

"I know, but you should never have been allowed to read, because it carries a very severe penalty," said Luke.

"I know, banishment forever," said Jake.

"Yes," said Luke.

8

"There is so much to learn in the books," said Jake

"I know, but villagers cannot read books......The Message is clear," said Luke.

"Well, needless to say, I crossed the fence and read many books," said Jake.

"How did you get across?"

"I crawled under where a creek had washed out a gap."

"Who did you meet over there?"

"Ellen."

"Ellen, right," said Luke. Yes, Ellen was one of the women. He knew her. He knew all the women there. They were immortalized together over two hundred years ago.

"So you know Ellen?" asked Jake.

"Yes, but that doesn't matter, you have shattered two sacred rules, reading books and crossing the fence," said Luke, now staring at Jake in silence since he did not know who else knew about this. Should he tell Chandler and see Jake and possibly others severely punished? He shook his head.

"Are you going to turn me in?" asked Jake.

"I don't know," said Luke as he now focused on the ceiling.

"I won't tell anyone," said Jake.

"Does anyone else know about this?" asked Luke.

"Yes, I brought books back for others and taught them how to read," said Jake.

"How many others?"

"I don't know, maybe five or six."

"Five or six....that's a lot.....and people talk," said Luke, now more calmly as his mind was now swirling with the realization that it was too late to cover it up.

"My mother might have known, but didn't say anything," said Jake.

"What about Sarah?"

"Yes, of course, she reads, and her mother does too."

"Where are the books now?"

"I returned most of them."

"Most?"

"Some were shared and are still in the village."

"They are?"

"Yes."

"OK, well, I think it's way too late to hide this little infringement of the rules," said Luke. "You realize that if you're caught you could be punished as a multiple offender since others were involved."

"What happens to multiple offenders?" asked Jake.

"They are thrown into the pit....well, that's what is supposed to happen, but I happen to know that nobody is ever killed," said Luke.

"OK, so, just banished for life," said Jake.

"Yes, and the place you'd be sent to for banishment is quite comfortable," said Luke.

"Have you been there?" asked Jake.

"No, but my friend Ed, the Helper, has told me about it."

"Your friend is the Helper?" asked Jake.

"He dresses up in costume, but he's actually a very nice man," said Luke, shocked that he was being totally honest with this ten year old.

"Well, that's encouraging, but I feel I have done nothing for which to be punished," said Jake.

"You really haven't, but there are rules that the villagers are supposed to obey," said Luke, knowing that Chandler's rules were wrong. And being banished forever even to a fairly nice place, away from your family and friends, is too harsh just for reading. The rules were wrong. Reading was a good thing, not a bad thing. So how can he now subject Jake to any type of punishment? Faced with what had now happened for the first time ever, he had a decision to make. And his decision would involve not only Jake, but himself.

"Reading helps me know things, a lot of things, and that makes me feel good inside..... powerful, not guilty," said Jake.

"I know that," said Luke, shutting his eyes and holding his head back.

"Will your friend Ed come and take me away?" asked Jake.

"Yes, that's the routine for offenders," he replied, even though he wanted to explain why Ed meant no harm to anyone, and even though he was dressed in a grotesque costume, he was just doing a job he neither liked nor believed in, but was being forced to perform.

"What about the others I've given books to or helped to read?" asked Jake.

"They'd be banished too if they are caught," said Luke.

"So, as teacher, it's your job to tell your friend Ed or the guy in The Tower," said Jake.

"Yes, it's my duty," said Luke.

"But will you?" asked Jake.

"Well, the reality is that this guy in The Tower will eventually find out," said Luke. "And there are people in the village who report those who break the rules." Luke backed toward the wall and finally settled onto the bench, then looked back at Jake.

"I suppose you're right about that...... we're busted," said Jake.

"You are, but I guess it was inevitable that someone would eventually cross the fence and find books to read," said Luke.

"And now it's happened," said Jake.

"Yes it has, so tell me some of what you learned in the books?" asked Luke, sensing the profound change that was about to occur in his life. Right now, he just wanted to be reminded of a past he had left behind two centuries ago. From this day forward, everything would be different for both him, Jake and the village. He could not see Jake punished, so his life as a teacher would be over. Chandler would cancel his immortality. But Ed could continue to enforce the rules of The Message and carry out his non-punishments, at least for a while.

"There was a time, long ago when there was a world in which we did many more things," Jake began. "There were people inside metal containers called cars that moved around fast taking us great distances. And flying machines that whisked people quickly, even great distances. There were tall huts called buildings where people lived and worked. And there were live pictures on screens that carried stories about everything to all corners of the Earth."

"You know a lot," said Luke, wondering how many books Jake had read. It had to be many.

"Yes, I know about a lot of things that are unknown to the villagers," said Jake.

"I remember what you describe," Luke nodded, as his mind reached back to when he lived in this world Jake spoke of. This was a world before he went to work for Chandler and brought here to work as a teacher. It was a world before the big war.

The war that laid the planet bare, with few survivors. Modern conveniences were destroyed. People were left to survive, competing for what was left. Before the war, Chandler had been one of several who created ways to achieve immortality. Luke and Ed, along with the four women across the fence, and a number of others, had been immortalized using a method developed by a woman named Shannon. With Shannon's procedure, one had to be near an activation device in order for it to continue to work. Only one activation device came to this area. It was for Ed, himself, and the four women across the fence. Chandler had his own immortality solution which left him in a unit that was not very mobile. Chandler took possession of their activation device, and warned that he could turn it off anytime he wanted to. They never found where he had hidden it so they were literally at his mercy with regard to their immortality.

When they arrived in this location, the four women moved into two abandoned research facilities outside the fence. Chandler, Ed and Luke moved into this old lighthouse. The electrified fence that had been used to contain political prisoners before the war provided power to it. The prison complex was located on the other side of the hill eventually became the home for those banished for violating the rules of Chandler's Message. Unknown to Chandler, Ed could not see anyone hurt so he established the prison complex as home for the banished.

Luke was assigned to be the teacher for Chandler's religion. He would teach the children about The Message. Once Chandler's religion was established, Luke moved out of the lighthouse into an abandoned underground bunker in a nearby hill. One room became the school and another Luke's residence. Ed remained in the lighthouse. He crafted a grotesque costume for his role as enforcer, called The Helper. He was a very large man, nearly seven feet tall, so his massive stature was part of his threatening character.

After the effects of the war had dissipated, some twenty years after the war ended, a woman contacted Chandler and spelled out the requirements of what Chandler began calling the Controllers. Apparently, some country had survived the war with enough capacity to establish worldwide rules intended to keep what remained of civilization from ever conducting a war again. These were what Chandler called the Controllers. The village, because of its size, was a target of these rules and the primary subject of concern to the Controllers. Chandler was told that the Controllers had satellites to enforce their rules. So Chandler decided that he would enforce these rules locally to avoid being under the Controller's thumb. So he created his religion with its Message, and dubbed the lighthouse "The Tower." Luke was assigned to teach the children and Ed to enforce the rules. It was difficult at first to achieve compliance, so Ed had to threaten them with a gun, but over the decades the villagers complied with just Ed's appearance. Today, all Ed has to do is show up and no one dares challenge him.

But now, Jake, a ten year old from the village, crosses the fence and gains access to books. This was an epic event so now everything will have to change. As Luke listened to Jake recite excerpts from the wealth of knowledge he had acquired, it was obvious that Jake had used their dynamic reading mechanism which allowed him to consume the content of a book in minutes instead of hours or days. He had clearly read a great number of books. So obviously the women had used the fence for electricity as Chandler had, because the dynamic reading mechanism needed power to deliver the recorded content to an individual.

"The women I met across the fence told me they were made to live forever. It's called immortality when you live forever, even though I don't think that living forever is possible. But Ellen says they have lived there for nearly two hundred years, and that's a very long time. I think you must be immortal too."

"I am," said Luke. "For you to know as much as you do, you must have used their dynamic reading mechanism."

"They called it their rapid reading device," said Jake.

"Yes, there were different brands."

"I did use it, and was able to read many books," said Jake.

"Did anyone else cross the fence and use it?" asked Luke.

"No, they only read the books that I brought back for them.......so, what will you do with me now?" asked Jake.

"I have to decide," said Luke. He stood and opened the door, then walked out leaving Jake sitting inside on the chair.

"Children, I am going to my chamber for a little while," said Luke. "You will stay here until I return." With that he slowly walked to the main entrance and out into the fog.

All eyes now turned to the open door of the room where Jake and Luke had gone. As they watched, Jake came out looking a bit dazed. He searched for Sarah among the students. She was his best friend and someone he very much needed to see now. This was not just because she had read books with him and was subject to punishment like him, but because she was who she was. She was someone even closer to him than his parents. He had heard Luke say he was leaving, and heard the door close, so Luke was not there in the classroom. Everyone continued to watch him as he walked over to Sarah.

"We need to talk," he whispered, motioning her over to the corner of the room. The others looked at one another as the two went to the corner.

"We have to leave immediately," he whispered.

"You mean go back to the village?" she whispered back.

"No, we can't go back there."

"Why?"

"Teacher Luke knows we read books."

"You told him?"

"Yes."

"OK, but we can't just leave, can we?..... won't someone stop us?"

"Teacher Luke won't," Jake replied quietly.

"He won't?" asked Sarah, loud enough for the others to hear.

"No, but we need to leave immediately," Jake whispered, holding his finger over his mouth.

"Alright, but where will we go?" Sarah whispered, looking apprehensively at Jake but feeling a closeness with him that she always had. There was a clear trust between them. They were now in trouble together for reading books, and books had a special place in their lives. If books were outlawed, she knew she would have to find some way to find them and read them anyway. And she knew Jake felt the same way. She trusted his judgement and she knew he trusted hers. But now, because he knew much more about what was going on than she did, she looked to him for what to do next.

"I have a plan," Jake whispered, pointing to the door.

"I know, we're leaving, but what if we're caught?" she asked.

"Let's not worry about that right now," he said confidently as he started for the door. Sarah followed. He cracked the huge door open slightly and peered out. He then looked back at the children. They had stopped chatting and were all watching the two intently. Sarah nudged him while pointing out the door. Jake nodded, then opened it and they shot out together, quickly disappearing into the dense fog.

Chapter Two

"Other than just leave, do you have a more complete plan?" panted Sarah as they rushed down a narrow pathway beneath a canopy of trees. Fog flowed past their faces with its cool damp hand as they ran.

"Sort of," said Jake over his shoulder between breaths as they were now racing in full stride.

"Sort of, meaning yes?" she asked.

"Sort of yes," he replied.

"Do you think they'll come after us," she panted.

"I don't think so, but we have to go fast just in case," he replied.

"How far is it to your 'sort of yes' plan?" she asked.

"Sort of yes is Ellen's place where I found the books, but I'm not exactly sure how to get there."

"I see, but it's across the fence."

"Yes, that much I know, so we'll have to cross the fence."

"Will we cross where you crossed before?" she asked.

"No, I think that's too far from where we'll reach the fence from here, so we'll have to find another place to cross," said Jake.

"Are you sure we can find another place?" asked Sarah.

"No, but don't worry, we'll find a way across," said Jake.

"Do you know the way to the fence from here?"

"I sort of know."

"Sort of know isn't know," said Sarah.

"If we go south, we'll end up at the fence," said Jake.

"Do you know how to go south?"

"Yes, I think so."

"All right then, 'I think so' will take us to 'sort of yes'?" asked Sarah.

"It should," he replied with a laugh.

"OK, I won't add 'it should' to 'I think so' and 'sort of yes', but you said you crawled under the fence before," said Sarah. "But maybe we can climb over if we can't find a place to crawl under?"

"Well, it's electric and it will kill us if we try to climb over," said Jake.

"I haven't read about what electric is yet, but I'll take your word for it..... we won't climb over," she replied.

"That's right, we can't touch it, whether we go under it or over it."

"Maybe I can read about electric and other things after we get across the fence."

"You can, but for now, just remember to never touch the fence."

"I'll remember, but what if we can't find Ellen's place once we get across?"

"Quit worrying, we'll figure things out when we get across."

"I know we will because we can't go back to the school and we can't go home," said Sarah.

"That's right, so let's hurry!" he shouted when he noticed she was beginning to lag behind.

"By the way, how do you know the direction to 'sort of yes'?"

"I studied maps at Ellen's."

"I'm not sure what maps are."

"They're pictures that show you where to go."

"There are pictures of how to get to places in my books....so are those maps?"

"Yes, they're probably simplified versions of maps."

"I'll just follow you."

"Now......there should be a departure point going south up ahead where the wooden bridge crosses a creek. Do you remember that bridge from when we came to school?

"Yes."

"OK, so according to the map, an old road runs parallel to the trail, and it's fairly close to the bridge. I thought that might be a good place to depart the trail and go south," said Jake.

"But I don't remember seeing a road near the bridge when we came to school, do you?" asked Sarah.

"No, so I hope the map is correct."

"So do I....by the way, what exactly is a road?"

"It's what cars used to travel on," said Jake."

"I've seen cars in my books."

"You learned a whole lot more than others from the books you read. You're the fastest learner I know."

"I love reading."

"Ellen will show you a super fast way to read and we'll do a lot more of it once we're safely across."

"I trust you, Jake."

"I trust you too, Sarah, and I'm very glad I have you as my best friend."

"I'm glad I have you too, Jake."

"OK, here's the bridge," said Jake as he walked onto it, and stood for a moment looking up to his right. Sarah did the same and pointed.

"That's why we couldn't see the road, it must be up there," said Sarah.

"Yes, the terrain was not shown on the map," said Jake.

"So we'll have to climb up there," said Sarah who stepped off the bridge and started toward the hill.

"That's right," he said as he jumped off to join her. They began grabbing shrubs and anything else they could grab. After a difficult climb up the slope, they finally reached the top and walked through the weeds to a clearing. They were now standing on a wide, flat surface with multiple cracks where grass and brush had taken root and now stuck through. Some of it was waste high. The road disappeared into the fog in both directions.

"So this is the road," said Sarah.

"Right, and that's south," he pointed.

"I'm concerned that if the Helper or teacher Luke follow us, and we're not able to cross the fence, they'll catch us."

"Teacher Luke will not come after us to take us back, but I'm not sure about the Helper," said Jake

"So, you think teacher Luke is on our side?"

"He is," said Jake, as they stood in the road for a moment to catch their breath.

"Why are you so sure about that?" she asked.

"Because he knew what I told him was true, even though it was completely opposite of what he was teaching in The Message."

"And?"

"And I wouldn't be surprised if he follows us..... not to catch us and take us back, but to cross the fence to freedom with us," said Jake.

"Do you really think so?" she asked.

"Yes."

"OK, then maybe we'll see him on the other side."

"I believe we will."

"Well, just in case he decides to do otherwise, or the Helper comes after us, let's keep going," she replied, pointing in the direction Jake had indicated.

"You're right," said Jake as he began to jog down the road, weaving around the larger plants. Sarah was close behind.

"From what I heard others say about what they learned at school, the rules in The Message don't make a lot of sense to me," said Sarah.

"Well, the rules were created for our village by the guy in the lighthouse to conform with rules that he said were called for by the Controllers."

"The Controllers?"

"Yes, teacher Luke told me there was a country or society out there that had established these rules that everyone on Earth must follow."

"Earth?" asked Sarah.

"A globe in space where everyone lives," said Jake.

"Boy, I do have a lot of catching up to do," said Sarah.

"You will," said Jake.

"I don't understand why they would need these rules."

"Well, two hundred years ago there was a war and most of the people in the world were killed," said Jake. "Ellen told me that."

"OK, so these Controllers survived and now make everyone else who survived follow their rules," said Sarah. "Why?"

"To prevent another war?" asked Jake.

"That makes sense.......OK, so our village didn't voluntarily choose to live under these rules," said Sarah. "The guy in the lighthouse set them up. Otherwise the Controllers would come here to enforce them?"

"I think you've summarized it quite well."

"Then the Controllers didn't actually create The Message. The guy in the lighthouse did," said Sarah.

"Yes," said Jake.

"These rules prohibit books because books tell the villagers about our past, right?.... so I assume it's bad for us to know about our past?" asked Sarah.

"That sounds a bit stupid, but I guess you're right," said Jake. "Maybe they don't want anyone else in the world to become educated so then they can't figure out how to kill one another."

"Wow.....well, there's obviously a lot we don't know."

"I just don't think it's right to prevent people from learning," said Jake.

"I agree....and banning people from their family and friends just for learning is definitely wrong. "

"Teacher Luke agrees," said Jake.

"So this war happened two hundred years ago?" asked Sarah.

"Yes, and everything we read in the books at Ellen's was written before that war," said Jake.

"Then everything that happened during the war and after the war is yet to be written," said Sarah.

"Correct."

"When did this guy in the lighthouse come here?" asked Sarah.

"After the war. He came here with teacher Luke and his friend Ed, the Helper," said Jake.

"But that means they're all over two hundred years old?" asked Sarah.

"They're immortal," said Jake.

"Immortal?" asked Sarah.

"They were made to live forever," said Jake.

"No one from the village lives forever, and we don't live forever," said Sarah.

"We're mortal, which is how everyone comes into the world, so someone has to make you immortal," said Jake.

"Is that in the books?" asked Sarah.

"It is."

"More for me to learn."

"Ellen and her three friends from across the fence are immortal too," said Jake. "They arrived here at the same time teacher Luke did."

"It's going to take me a while to catch up," said Sarah.

"We both have a lot of catching up to do," said Jake.

"But a lot of what I'm learning tells me that what is happening here in the village is definitely wrong," said Sarah.

"Yes, and it's something that has to change," said Jake.

"I agree, but how can we ever do that, we're just kids?" asked Sarah.

"I don't know, but when I crossed the fence and read books, I exposed the village to reality for the very first time, which will blow up The Message....and with it, the Controller's rules..... game over."

"Game over?"

"That's right, because if Teacher Luke leaves as I believe he will, there's no teacher...... ergo, no passing on of The Message, and eventually a breakdown in enforcement of the rules."

"Ergo?....you're using weird words..... but I think that right now we have to look out for ourselves," said Sarah.

"That is not only true, Sarah, but it's very wise," he replied. "Our immediate concern has to be getting safety across the fence."

He took her by the hand as they hurried down the road together, tripping at times on the tall grasses. A short time later they saw a break in the fog and soon emerged into the sun where they stood for a moment taking in its warmth. Eventually, they came to a rise where they could see far ahead. The sky was a deep blue and to their right in the distance was the vast expanse of the Pacific ocean. To their left, green hills stretched to the horizon with wisps of blue smoke winding up from the green where their village was located.

"What is that ahead in the distance?" asked Sarah, pointing to what appeared to be a large structure peeking through the trees.

25

"It looks like Ellen's place but I don't think it is."

"How do you know it isn't?"

"According to the map, the road doesn't come to the fence near Ellen's place."

"Well, maybe someone else lives there."

"I think it's Ellen's other two friends," said Jake. "She mentioned another place like theirs where the other two lived."

"What is that in the far distance?"

"It looks like a giant silver box or something," said Jake.

"Were there a lot of people living out there long ago?"

"That's what the books say, but everything in the library happened before everything out there was destroyed, so I don't know what happened....maybe some people are still living out there."

"At least we can read about what it was like before things got destroyed."

"Yes, once we get across the fence."

"Wait..... look, is that fuzzy thing through the woods the fence?" she asked.

"Oh, right, yes it is," said Jake.

"How far to it?" asked Sarah.

"Not far."

"Good, because I'm getting hungry."

"Didn't you eat breakfast?"

"I don't like breakfast."

"OK, well, we can get food and water at her friend's place once we get across the fence."

"Let's go," said Sarah who started running.

"Wait for me," he replied as he started after her. Eventually he caught up and they raced along together.

As they drew closer to the fence, its sheer size became more apparent. It was ten feet tall with barbs on top. Its grid of wire mesh stretched across the road and wandered into the forest on either side. They stopped before it, looking up at its imposing presence.

"Jake, whatever happens, I won't blame you if it doesn't turn out like you've planned."

"Don't worry Sarah, we'll make it across and everything will be fine, you'll see."

"OK, so you crawled under the fence before......so maybe we should look for gaps underneath."

"There was a creek running under it where I crossed, and that's what washed away the soil and created the gap."

"Maybe we can find another creek."

"That may be our only chance to crawl under," he replied.

"Why can't we just cross where you crossed?" asked Sarah.

"It's that way," he pointed. "But I'm pretty sure that's a long way through the woods, and with no trail, that could be tough going," said Jake.

"But at least we know we can cross there."

"It's much shorter and faster to cross here and time is of the essence."

"So let's start looking," said Sarah.

"Which way, right or left?" asked Jake, who was studying the forest on either side.

"Well....actually.....what I was thinking, instead of looking for another creek to go under, maybe we could climb over on these trees," she said, pointing to their right. "That tree down there is much taller than the fence and has limbs that touch limbs of a tree on the other side."

"What?.....oh, right, I never thought of that," he nodded as he started walking in that direction.

"We could climb the tree on this side and go across on a limb, then grab a limb on the other side and swing down," said Sarah, as she followed close behind.

"That's a great idea, and I think the tree you spotted might just work," said Jake.

They went down into the forest toward a large tree whose limbs seemed to be intertwined with a tree across the fence. They ran to its base and began to climb, helping each other as they went up. Jake took the lead and was working his way along a large limb that extended over the fence. He stopped for a moment, trying to locate a suitable limb from the tree on the other side. From the ground the limbs had looked closely intertwined, but up close it turned out they were not well matched, and too small to support their weight.

"I'm not sure if we can get to a limb that's big enough to climb out on, but I think we can get far enough over the fence to jump across," said Jake. "Then, maybe we can grab something on the way down."

"Well we're already up here, so if that's what we have to do, that's what we have to do," she replied.

"I know, but it's a long way to the ground," he cautioned.

"True, but there are a lot of bushes down there, so maybe we won't hit the ground as hard if we land on them," she replied.

"You're right, they should cushion our fall, so I guess it's what we have to do lacking any other options."

"OK, so let's do it," said Sarah, pointing.

"I think you're a lot better at directing this crossing than I am," said Jake who turned and smiled back at her. She again pointed to the ground, indicating that he should jump now. He looked down, then nodded.

"Look, we wouldn't be here at the fence at all if you hadn't figured out how to get here," she shrugged. "But now that we're here, you have to jump."

"I know," he replied as he stood looking down.

"Not next week."

"Alright, I guess I'm the Guinea pig," said Jake, staring at the thicket below.

"Is that the same as a sacrificial lamb?" she asked.

"Not quite since I'm hoping to survive, whereas a Guinea pig just gets roughed up a bit," he replied. "A sacrificial lamb usually doesn't survive."

"Guinea pig works."

"Alright, so stay where you are until I jump because this limb is beginning to sag, and we don't want the branch to touch the fence."

"I'll wait here until you're safely in the bushes."

Jake nodded and eased forward until he was almost across the fence, then he stood upright and turned his head toward Sarah.

"I may try to land on my back since I don't want to hit the brush with my face," he said.

"Great, just do it sometime today," she replied.

"Yeah right....OK!......aaaaaaaaa!" he yelled as he leaped. As he flew through the air he twisted around so he was facing the sky. But he hit harder than expected as he tore right through the

29

thorny blackberry bushes to the ground, landing with a thud and knocking the wind out of him. He lay in the thorns trying to catch his breath with a thousand needles pressing into his back, arms, neck and everywhere else.

"Are you all right?" asked Sarah as she scooted forward to position herself for her leap.

"Sort of.....but these are sticker bushes and I can't really move right now, so try not to land on me," said Jake.

She could see Jake lying on his back in the hole he had punched in the bushes. As she looked for a place to land, she spotted a limb on the tree across the fence and thought she could grab it on the way down. She aimed for it and leaped as assertively as she could with her hands extended outward. On the way down she was able to grab the limb with one hand and clung on tightly until she could grab it with the other hand. The limb allowed her to smoothly swing to the ground just beyond the briar patch to a soft landing on her feet.

"What happened, I didn't hear anything....are you down?" asked Jake, when he was not able to see her.

"I landed quite nicely on my feet," she replied.

"No way!" said Jake, who was trying to sit up to see as he grimaced in pain.

"I just grabbed a limb," she replied.

"So you land on your feet without a scratch and I land in the sticker bushes ripped to shreds," said Jake as he managed to get to his feet and eventually pick his way out of the brambles. By the time he reached Sarah, his hands, cheeks and torn pants were ample evidence of the damage the thorny bushes had done.

"You're a mess, and stained with blackberries and, oh my,

you're bleeding too," said Sarah, who brushed a few blackberry leaves from his shirt. She then wiped a trickle of blood from his hand with her finger.

"Well, the good news is I'm alive, but I'm not sure for how much longer," said Jake, with a little laugh as he removed a blackberry limb that had followed him out while attached to his pant leg.

"Here," said Sarah who pulled a bit of cloth from her pocket and placed it over the scratches on his forearm.

"This bush is full of ripe berries and I'm hungry," said Sarah who began picking the plump purple berries and stuffing them into her mouth. Jake watched her continue to paint her face and hands with the berry juice and began to laugh, but he soon joined her. Sarah stopped stuffing blackberries for a moment to observe him with his torn pants, bleeding arms and blackberry stained hands and face.

"Wow, when we get to someone on this side of the fence I'm not sure what they'll say when they see you," said Sarah.

"Well, you're quite a sight yourself," said Jake. Her face and hands were smeared heavily with blackberry juice.

A short time later they started walking through the forest, working their way back up to the road which they now followed. The road passed by the structure that they saw from up on the hill and was much easier than picking their way though the underbrush of the forest. Eventually they spotted a building through the trees and soon they emerged in front of it. It was very large and curved, with a series of glass facades on each of its four stories. At the end nearest them was a stairway to the first level.

"There are trails everywhere, so someone must live here," said Sarah.

"I know, so let's go," said Jake, pointing.

"You said Ellen's friends must live here?" asked Sarah.

"Yes, and according to that map, this is the only other structure, so it has to be where they live," said Jake as he downed one of the last berries he was still carrying in his cupped hand. Sarah watched him and snatched his last berry, popped it into her mouth, then smiled. He looked at her with her painted face and hands and started to laugh. She joined him in laughter as they raced toward the stairway.

"Shouldn't we announce our arrival?" asked Sarah, as they reached the stairway.

"Let's find a door first," said Jake. Sarah nodded and started up the stairs.

Before them on the first level was the first curved window that extended the length of the building. It was tinted dark so they could not see inside. They walked along the window looking for an opening. They found nothing, so at the end they went up another staircase to the second level. Again, they walked along the window looking for a door. Finding nothing, they went on to the third level where they finally came to a break in the glass facade. Jake pushed his fingers in and pulled sideways. With some effort, it opened enough for them to enter. Sarah, who was right behind him, grabbed his shirt in an attempt to hold him back, but he towed her into a large room that was darkened from the late afternoon sun by its tinted glass. Desks extended as far as they could see in both directions, but it was otherwise empty. They stood for a moment as their eyes adjusted to the dimly lit room. It was warm in the room and was a pleasant relief from the coolness they had felt for most of the day.

"Should we announce our presence in case someone is here?" asked Sarah.

"I'd first like to rest a minute, I'm very tired," said Jake, who leaned back against a partition, eventually sinking to the floor. Sarah watched him before sliding down beside him. They were soon both asleep.

Chapter Three

Luke paced his room, his mind spinning with the enormity of what he was dealing with. A ten year old boy had crossed the fence for the first time in the village's history and brought back books, then shared them with others. This literally shattered the rules for both crossing the fence and reading. And now he was faced with the truth about who he was and what he had been doing for the past hundred and eighty years. What this boy was learning from the books was of course true. Luke knew that. He had always known that. So the inevitable realization was that he had been promoting a lie for all these decades. Promoting it under the threat that he would lose his immortality if he didn't. So now, faced with having to make a decision for what to do, he had to choose between his fate and the truth. Was it now time for this charade of Chandler's to end in the name of truth and honor? Perhaps it was.

Timing was critical. It seemed virtually impossible for this event to remain a secret much longer. Someone in the village would eventually report it. And, more immediately, Jake could not return to the village. He must again cross the fence, but this time for good. And there was no time to lose. Luke had to act quickly and decisively. Yes, by choosing truth, his role in this lie must end immediately. His career as a teacher will end now and he must leave. Perhaps he could cross the fence where Jake had crossed to acquire the books. It may now be his only realistic option. Perhaps Jake and he could cross the fence together. Yes, because Jake knew the way.

He sat at his table and stared at the large book that was The Message. It was a book and the villagers were forbidden to read. They were asked to take for granted what was in the book. For the first time in countless decades, he would choose conscience over threat. Reason over suppression. Despite the fact that he would lose his immortality, he felt a clear sense of freedom. The only downside of what he was doing was that the rules of the Controllers would still remain. Chandler's religion was just a local effort to enforce their rules to keep them away. But the Controllers would still be out there, watching from their satellites. Of course these Controllers, as Chandler called them, may not even exist. After all, no one, not even Chandler, had ever actually seen them in person. And even if they did exist at one time, perhaps they no longer existed, or no longer enforced their rules. But the bottom line was that he could not report Jake and therefore he must leave. Whatever happened with the Controllers could not be worse than enforcing Chandler's rules. Ed would continue to enforce the rules as he always had. But there would be no teacher and Jake will have disappeared, exposing the book and fence crossing episode and possibly a number of villagers. This was a major event and one that Chandler would not be pleased about.

Luke stood up and walked to the small portal that was his window and stared out at the green grass. Sunshine created patches of light as it peeked through the clouds. The sun was shining on the grass, turning it into a silvery circle that glowed so brightly that the light blossomed before him as if to beckon him outside. He smiled. He will leave. He had made the right decision.

The children watched as Luke returned to the classroom and stood quietly looking among them. He searched from one corner of the room to the other.

"Where is the child, Jake?" he asked. None of the children spoke. They just watched him in silence.

"Anyone?" he asked, looking around. There was no reply.

"Did he leave?" he asked. One small face in the front nodded.

"Come child," he said, waving his hands for her to come forward. "It's alright," he said softly when she didn't immediately come. Finally, after looking around, she slowly made her way toward him, fear in her eyes, her lip quivering.

"When did he leave?" asked Luke, in a calm and soothing voice, much like he did when teaching.

"A long time ago," came the tiny voice, almost in a whisper.

"How long after I left here did he leave?" he asked.

"Right after," she nodded. "And....."

"And what?" he coaxed when she hesitated.

"And Sarah went with him," she said.

"Sarah," said Luke, stopping to think. Wait, why Sarah?

What did she know? They had come to school together, so they were friends. So she may also have read books. Jake decided he must leave immediately, and since Sarah was a co-conspirator, he took her with him. They could not return to the village because they knew they had been caught and would be punished. So they had to cross the fence. Jake knew friendly faces there, and he knew how and where to cross. But Luke did not know how to cross and had hoped that he and Jake could cross together. Nonetheless, he must leave and cross the fence. And he must do it alone. Once across, Luke knew where the four women lived. It was south from here at the school. The sun comes up in the east, so he oriented himself and pointed south.

The children were staring at him as he worked things out in his mind. The girl was still standing in front of him looking up, waiting for the next instruction as the children in his classes usually did.

"You may go back with the others, child," he said softly, putting out the palms of his hands and pushing the air in front of her. She turned quickly and ran back to the others.

"Class for today is over, so you may go home now. But I want you to be ready for lessons tomorrow morning," he lied. There would be no lessons tomorrow, or any other day. Because he would be gone for good. He turned and walked out the door. The trail to the village went southwest, but mostly west, and it was the only trail, so he started for it, knowing that eventually he would have to leave it to travel south.

As he set out, he looked for evidence of where Jake and Sarah left the trail to go south. After a while he became concerned that he would not be able to find it, or that he had somehow missed it. He stopped to rest on a wooden bridge wondering if he should retrace his steps and look more carefully. He held onto the bridge's rail and looked down into the creek. A salamander drifted beneath him in a pool of crystal clear water. Reflections of the hillside were visible on the surface and something caught his eye. He looked up toward the hillside where he saw fresh dirt and a dangling fern frond. The marks were fresh, so it had to be Jake and Sarah! He stepped quickly off the bridge and went to the base of the hill. He saw two sets of footprints and the unmistakable gouges made as a result of climbing up the hill. Luke looked for a foothold and began to slowly work his way up. Going was difficult and Luke was nearly exhausted when he finally reached the top. He stumbled through the brush to a flat, hard area that extended off in both directions. A road. Wait, he vaguely remembered this road. Yes, this is the road that leads to the fence and continues beyond it to one of the research facilities where the women live! He nodded to himself, then started off in that direction.

Luke was not conditioned for a long hike. For too many years his routine had been relatively passive and he was not in very good physical condition. After more than an hour he was nearing total exhaustion and was thirsty and hungry, so he sat down on the side of the road to rest. He could hear the trickle of water in the near distance, so he groped his way through the tangle of weeds to a puddle of clear water where he fell to his knees and drank. He then found a soft place among the underbrush to sit down, tucked the heavy material of his clothing around him and lay back. He was soon asleep.

Much later, he awoke with a start when he heard movement

nearby and opened his eyes. It was now almost dark, with the pale light from a half moon casting shadows through the brush. Something scurried away when it heard him move. How long had he slept? He did not know and wondered how far it was to the fence. It was about five miles or so to the fence from the lighthouse he recalled from his distant past. He had already traveled much of that, so it couldn't be too far. He arose and stumbled out of the weeds and onto the road which was just visible. He started out again and before long came to a hill where the road started down. Downhill was easier so he began walking faster and it was not long before the fence loomed just ahead. When he arrived, he stopped and looked up at its dark silhouette against a darker sky and wondered how he would get over it. The fence is high voltage, so no one must touch it. Perhaps he could find a place to go under. How did Jake and Sarah get across, if they arrived at this location? Jake had crossed before, so he would know how. So he would follow their tracks, if he could find them in the moonlight. He scanned the area on both sides of the road and discovered that the tracks went down into the forest to his right, so he followed them.

Under the forest canopy the moonlight cast dark shadows and Luke had to go onto his hands and knees to find the footprints. He crept along, sometimes on his knees, sometimes walking crouched over to see the ground. Eventually he came to the base of a large tree. The footprints seemed to end there. He looked up at the tree to see that its limbs extended over the fence, touching limbs from a tree on the other side. He went beyond the tree to see if the footprints went on, but they did not. So they must have climbed the tree and crossed over on the limbs. Sure, why not? For two ten year olds, it would be easy. But he was not a ten year old and not nearly as nimble. In fact he was not sure if he could even climb the tree. But this was his only option, so he had to try. Slowly and clumsily he made his way up the trunk, carefully securing handholds and footholds and then straining to advance upward. It seemed forever when he finally reached a limb that appeared to extend over the fence. He slowly began to crawl out on it. As he moved forward, his weight made the branch sag dangerously close to the fence. A leaf touched the fence and sent sparks shooting up at him. Even both children together were most likely lighter than he was he thought as he lay still on the branch contemplating his next move. He was now directly over the fence, so perhaps his only option now would be to jump across if he could get to his feet without falling, and also without pushing the branch down onto the fence. He had to do it because there were no other choices. He had expended most of his energy just getting to where he was. So he would either fall and die on the fence from electrocution, leap to his death on the other side, or somehow make it across safely. There was no going back. He very carefully got to a kneeling position on the branch, retaining his balance using surrounding limbs. Then, he very slowly stood upright. He crept forward a few baby steps, held his breath and leaped. As he flew through the air he held out his arms to grasp whatever he could. But his hands caught nothing but leaves and he belly flopped into a thicket of sticker bushes, leaving him barely conscious. He lay in the bushes gasping for breath and in pain. Thorns from the bushes sent a million points of anguish to his brain, while stars danced inside his eyelids. It was several minutes before he was able to open his eyes and longer still before he made any attempt to get up. On his first attempt, he fell sideways into the thorns, only to get another round of painful pin pricks. Still stunned and struggling to breathe with countless thorns piercing his face, arms and ankles, he was finally able to stand. He stood for a moment in stunned and painful silence, before stumbling forward. Blood trickled down his face and hands, and thorns continued to dig into his legs through his pants. But he kept moving until he finally emerged from the blackberry bush. He was across! Through the pain he smiled. Keep following the road. Yes, he remembered, it led to one of the abandoned research facilities where the four women lived. He began walking away from the fence and back up to the road which he then followed in almost complete darkness.

Eventually Luke came to a clearing where he saw the white facade of the facility. He remembered it from two centuries ago. It had to be where Jake and Sarah went, since there were no other structures that he knew of nearby. He spotted the staircase and started for it with renewed energy. After going through the same route that Jake and Sarah had followed to the third floor, he came to the doorway that was now open enough for him to enter. Inside, it was inky black and not aided at all by the moonlight. Unable to see anything, he sat down with his back against something. Thoroughly exhausted, he fell asleep.

Chapter Four

Luke awoke when he heard a noise. He opened his eyes just as a light came on and he held his hand up to shield against its brightness. To his right, a short distance away, huddled together and asleep were Jake and Sarah. Across the room, standing perfectly still was a woman. He rose slowly to his feet, wincing in pain, and squinted to focus on the face of the woman.

"Virg?" he asked.

"Oh my god.... Luke?" asked Virg, cocking her head a little and blinking.

"Yes, Shannon's immortality party," he replied, trying to focus on her face.

"Holy shit, that was many moons ago.....and when we came here, you and Ed went inside the fence with Chandler to that lighthouse," she replied.

"Yes, I became his teacher," he smiled.

"His teacher, OK, I'm not sure what that is, but you came

across the fence with these two?" she asked, pointing to Jake and Sarah who were now awake and beginning to get to their feet.

"No, they came ahead of me," he replied.

"Wait, are you Jake?" asked Virg, taking a step closer.

"I am," said Jake.

"And this is?" asked Virg.

"Sarah," said Jake.

"Let me guess, Sarah is another book reader, and, as I understand from Ellen, you aren't supposed to read books over there, so you had to run away too," said Virg.

"Yes," said Sarah.

"Well, Jake, you're kind of famous on this side of the fence," said Virg.

"I didn't know I was famous," said Jake with a shrug.

"So what was the penalty for reading?" asked Virg.

"Banishment from the village forever," said Jake. "Two offences, supposedly death, but teacher Luke says they never did that."

"Banishment for reading....really?" asked Virg.

"They're living in an alternative reality over there," said Jake.

"Sometimes he speaks in code," said Sarah when Virg looked at Luke with a confused expression.

"Of course," said Virg. "Famous people do that."

"I couldn't turn them in for reading, so I left," said Luke.

"What will your punishment be for failing to report them.... and then fleeing?" asked Virg.

"Cancellation of my immortality," said Luke.

"Cancellation....wait! Don't we share the same activation device?" asked Virg.

"Yes we do, so I guess if mine is cancelled, yours is too," said Luke.

"Well, it's probably a hollow threat if it came from Chandler," said Virg.

"And even if he does threaten to do it, I don't think it's imminent, because he still has to keep Ed on to enforce the dictates of his Message," said Luke.

"Explain why you need some kind of device to keep your immortality working," said Jake.

"The immortality process includes electronic chips placed in our bodies that need an activation device to keep them on," said Luke.

"So the threat of turning off your chip is how this guy, Chandler, kept you and Ed doing something you didn't really believe in, and didn't want to do, for a very long time," said Jake.

"That's right," said Luke.

"OK, so apparently Chandler established rules that the village and these kids broke?" asked Virg.

"Chandler established a religion to enforce rules that he says were established by what is apparently the only country that survived the big war," said Luke. "According to Chandler, their rules are being imposed on survivors to keep another war from ever happening again."

"That actually makes sense, but do you know anything about this country?" asked Jake.

"No, and I'm not even certain that it even exists," said Luke. "All we know is what Chandler told us that someone contacted him with the threat. He said someone came to his block and told him that the village had to comply with these rules or else. So he decided to establish his own method rather than have an outside force come in here and strong arm the village."

"His block.....is that the one east of here?" asked Virg.

"Yes, he has a communication hub there."

"That must have been the silver box we saw in the distance on our way here," said Sarah.

"It sounds as if it was," said Luke.

"But wait, what this Chandler guy is doing is also strong arming the village into compliance with the rules of his religion, so what does it matter if these mysterious Controllers strong armed the village, or he does?" asked Jake.

"That's very true, so it's six of one, half dozen of another," said Luke.

"Six....half dozen....OK.....very good," said Jake. "In other words, it doesn't matter who enforces the rules."

"Correct," said Luke.

"Has anyone ever seen these Controllers?" asked Jake.

"No," said Luke.

"We haven't seen anyone here from the outside world in two hundred years," said Virg. "Well, a plane flew over a hundred sixty years ago."

"So then there's doubt that these Controllers even exist, or that they still exist after all this time," said Jake.

"Or are enforcing their rules after two hundred years," said Virg.

"Or that," said Jake.

"Making Chandler's religion a bit suspect," said Luke.

"Even outright wrong, so Chandler has to go," said Jake.

"Go?" asked Luke. "That could be a tall order."

"Well, it's something we need to think very seriously about," said Jake.

"Probably," said Luke, who looked at Virg who just shrugged.

"In any event, the three of you fled the madness over there, and by the looks of it, the fence crossing was not all that kind to you," said Virg. "However, except for a berry stained face, Sarah seems to have fared a lot better than you two."

"She flew over," said Jake.

"Flew over?" asked Virg.

"She grabbed a limb and swung down to a soft landing like Tarzan, while we crashed into a blackberry patch," said Jake.

"Tarzan.....what did you do, read Ellen's entire library?" asked Virg.

"Not yet, but I'm working on it..... and I'm pleased to meet you, Virg," said Jake, stepping forward and extending his hand, but Virg grabbed him and swept him up into a gigantic hug.

"Did Ellen mention me?" she asked as she finally put him down.

"She did," said Jake, turning to Luke and pointing at him, then at Virg. "So you two were immortalized together?"

"Yes, two hundred years ago..... before the war," said Virg.

"Before everything was blown up," said Jake.

"Correct," said Virg, "You may have read about the tensions and dire situation among nations before the war started."

"I did," said Jake. "I also read that many were hopeful that all would be settled as it always had in the past. But apparently there were almost two dozen nations with staggering numbers of nuclear weapons each, so think about the odds of something going wrong?"

46

"Odds?" asked Luke, again looking at Virg, this time with raised eyebrows.

"Yes, it was a potentially explosive situation, and, unfortunately, it exploded," said Virg.

"So what happened to set it off?" asked Jake.

"A misunderstanding that led to a massive sneak attack on America," said Virg. "Then, once that happened, it spread instantly to everywhere, almost like one giant explosion.....then suddenly, it was over."

"Except the radiation, fires and overcast lasted for way too many years and most likely accounted for the vast majority of casualties," said Luke.

"Surviving the aftermath turned out to be the worst part," said Virg.

"We rode it out in the lighthouse and Virg and the women here in one of these buildings," said Luke.

"It was obviously worldwide," said Jake.

"Yes, and even though most areas were not actually bombed, they were nonetheless largely wiped out by radiation and the bitter cold caused by black skies that lasted for years," Virg confirmed. "The Earth became a massive dying field."

"Well, obviously someone out there survived if they came here to warn Chandler that whoever else survived had to follow certain rules that they established," said Jake.

"That's true, because it's hard to imagine why Chandler would go to so much trouble without some pressure from the outside," said Luke.

"You four women settled here outside the fence and were unaffected by what was going on inside the fence," said Jake.

"That's right, until you managed to cross it and introduced books to the village, thereby likely changing everything forever," said Luke.

"So, as it turns out, I'm the one who broke this thing wide open after two hundred years of terror," said Jake.

"More like a hundred and eighty, but whose counting," said Luke.

"But I'm also responsible for the possibility of your losing your immortality," said Jake.

"You're a one boy wrecking crew, Jake," said Luke.

"I'm hungry," said Sarah.

"Right..... so, you should remember that Sarah is always hungry," said Jake.

"Not always," Sarah whispered.

"Well, I think I can scare up something for everyone.....and, uhhh......it looks like you need to get cleaned up a bit too, with all those berry and blood stains," said Virg.

"That would be nice," said Luke.

"Just follow me," said Virg, who waved for them to follow.

Virg led them down a long hallway into a dimly lit room with a row of sinks where they were able to wash themselves. Next, they went to another room with several overstuffed sofas and some bookshelves like the ones Jake had become accustomed to at Ellen's place. Standing just inside the door as they entered was a tall thin woman with light brown skin dressed in a purple robe that she was still buttoning as she yawned. She had a small, perfectly sculptured face with coal black eyes.

"Ummm, so who do we have here?" she asked as she wiped sleep from her eyes and again yawned.

48

"I found this trio asleep in the outer chamber," said Virg, scanning the trio with her finger.

"You look familiar," said the woman, looking at Luke.

"Shannon's immortality party.....so, let's see.... Brit?" asked Luke.

"Right, and....is it Luke?" she asked. He smiled with a nod.

"Jake and Sarah are students from the village who fled once their book reading crimes were found out," said Virg.

"Wait, this is THE Jake, the first villager to ever cross the fence?" asked Brit.

"I am," said Jake.

"I'm taking them in for some grub," said Virg, pointing across the room to another door.

"I hope grub is food, because I'm hungry," said Sarah.

"Brit, another thing about Sarah, she's always hungry," said Jake.

"I see," said Brit, looking at Virg again.

"Yes, Sarah, it's food," said Virg, again waving for them to follow. They fell in behind her and soon entered a cozy kitchen with a large wooden table in the corner.

"So, yes, Jake started a cascade of events when he crossed and took books back," said Virg.

"So reading is apparently against the law over there," said Brit.

"It is," said Luke.

"OK, so here's the thing, folks..... despite the reason that Chandler created that little alternative world across the fence, I think we need to break it up," said Jake.

"Break it up?" asked Brit.

"OK, a little background......Chandler created a religion to make sure the village complied with the dictates of the Controllers," said Luke. "But these rules of Chandlers are quite harsh and it seems that these Controllers either never existed, or may not enforce the rules today."

"Controllers?" asked Brit.

"Some country survived and wants to keep another war from starting," said Virg.

"Oh my," said Brit.

"The thing is, if these Controllers do exist as Chandler says, they may have stayed away from here because of Chandler's little alternative enforcement program," said Luke.

"And if they don't exist, Chandler's little oppressive program probably needs to be taken down," said Virg.

"This is a perfect time to put a stop to it," said Jake. "The situation is in flux."

"In flux....alright, I'll admit that the timing is right, but how on earth would you break it up?" asked Luke.

"Blow up the lighthouse, which is the symbol that is painted on walls in the village," said Jake. "It represents Chandler's religion, and without it we have a chance to break the grip it seems to have on the village."

"You want to blow up the lighthouse with Chandler in it?" asked Luke.

"Well, we'll give him a chance to give up his little kingdom first," said Jake.

"The only problem with this scenario of yours is the fact that we have no conceivable way to blow up a lighthouse," said Virg.

"Well, I'm placing a bet right now that Jake will come up

with a way to do it," said Sarah. "Any takers?"

"Knowing Jake, I'm not taking your bet, but I'm listening," said Luke.

"I'm not saying that I think this is entirely sane, but I'd also like to hear more," said Brit.

"Alright, for a start, what do you have on this side of the fence that could be used to knock out a lighthouse?" asked Jake.

"Oh my god, seriously?" asked Brit. Jake nodded with an animated shrug.

"Well, I have an old flint lock pistol from the sixteenth century," said Virg.

"Oh please.....certainly there are some old war machines lying around," said Jake.

"War machines lying around?" asked Brit, looking at Virg, waiting for her to laugh.

"Yes, I read about tanks," said Jake.

"Tanks?" asked Brit with a sarcastic smile, now shifting to look at Luke to see if he was taking any of this seriously. When he shrugged, she just raised her eyebrows and slowly shook her head.

"Actually, I know where we can get one," said Virg.

"Wait, you don't mean that old relic in the museum," said Brit.

"If we can get it started," said Virg. "And, by the way, I did see some hermetically sealed cannon shells in it."

"That thing is three hundred years old," said Brit. "It's fossilized."

"But it's there..... so do you think you could get it started Virg?" asked Jake.

"Well, I don't know, I wouldn't rule it out," Virg shrugged.

"Look, Virg is pretty good at getting old engines running, but a museum tank?" asked Brit.

"I got that old VW bus to run, and it came from the same museum," said Virg.

"The tank has an internal combustion engine like the bus, right?" asked Jake.

"It does, but I think it runs on diesel, not gas," said Virg.

"Diesel...... so it fires on compression instead of needing spark plugs and high octane fuel," said Jake.

"Well, yeah, but how did you.....?"

"I read a lot," said Jake.

"Then where do I get low octane fuel?" asked Virg.

"I've read that diesel engines can even run on cooking oil," said Jake.

"Cooking oil, really?" asked Virg.

"That's what I read," said Jake.

"I didn't know that, but that's something I actually have, so that's a positive" said Virg.

"Then we have a plan," said Jake.

"Whoa, slow down....... we have a plan?" asked Brit, looking at Virg to see if she was really thinking about doing this.

"Sure, why not give it a try.....I'm in," said Virg, holding up her thumb. Brit looked at her as if she were crazy, holding out her hands as if in total confusion.

"I'm hungry," said Sarah.

"See what I mean," said Jake.

"I'm working on it," said Brit. "Understand that I'm a total skeptic about whether we can just go out there to that old abandoned museum, start up a centuries old tank, then drive ten miles and blow up a lighthouse."

"They call it The Tower," said Luke.

"Whatever," said Brit. Virg looked at her and smiled.

"My god, are you all insane?" asked Brit under her breath.

"A little bit, but then I've always teetered on the edge," said Virg.

"Life must be quite primitive in the village, but I guess that's the way it was supposed to be kept.... simple and primitive," said Brit, trying to change the subject to something real.

"That's why we need to free these villagers," said Jake.

"After only a short time here, I can tell you that being outside the fence, free, is so much better than being inside the fence and living under Chandler's rule," said Luke.

"Which is why this little game of his has to end," said Jake.

"Alright, but before we progress any further in this madness, we need to go up to East Hill and speak with Ellen and Lucinda about this," said Brit.

"How far is it to Ellen's place?" asked Jake.

"It's a little over a mile," said Virg from the counter in the kitchen. "About a half hour walk or a five minute drive in the V dub."

"When can we leave?" asked Jake.

"Not until the sun is up," said Brit.

"While we're waiting, I'd like to know more about how you got here," said Sarah.

"OK, well, we were with a research team working on immortality, and were among those eventually immortalized by the lead scientist whose name was Shannon. Luke was immortalized at the same time as we were. Shortly after that, Shannon left and misappropriated an international spaceship with a group of teens aboard. She departed with them into deep space. Reports in the news indicated that they left the solar system, so who knows where they ended up. We four migrated here to escape the impending nuclear war and settled in these two abandoned research facilities to ride out the aftermath. This one has a deep bunker. But I think the key to our survival was our food machines and a large supply of chemicals to operate them."

"You had food machines?" asked Jake.

"We had them too, Jake," said Luke.

"I read about them," said Jake. "They were made by the Chinese."

"Yes, and they saved our lives," said Brit.

"So what about you, teacher Luke, how did you get here?" asked Sarah.

"Well, myself and another man named Ed came here with Chandler who had invented another immortality device that he had used on himself," said Luke. "Because his device was quite cumbersome, he needed our help to set him up in the lighthouse. His device was running on batteries when we arrived, but it needed power if it was to work over the long term. The fence was electric and Ed knew how to tap that power, so he did.

"Virg did the same thing for us, and that's why we have electricity," said Brit.

"What was this fence used for?" asked Sarah.

"It surrounded a prison that was here before the war," said Luke. "The prison complex is located over the hill to the west," said Luke.

"What kind of prison was it?" asked Jake.

"From what we've read in our library, it was one of a number of political concentration camps that were located around the country," said Brit.

"So then it was not really a prison per se, it was an effort to separate an entire belief system from the general population," said Jake.

"I believe that's correct," said Luke, looking at Brit who returned his look, both amazed that a ten year old could actually understand this.

"Then our village is most likely made up of the descendants of malcontents," said Jake.

"Malcontents.....I suppose one could classify them that way," said Luke, again looking at Brit who just shook her head.

"Bottom line.....however you classify them....we're essentially descendants of convicts," said Jake.

"Well, political prisoners are not necessarily convicts in the conventional sense, but in this case their opposition was not only forceful, but oftentimes violent," said Luke.

"I believe insurrection of a standing government is a good description," said Virg.

"And they obviously opposed the US government in large enough numbers to have resulted in the establishment of these concentration camps," said Jake.

"Amazing for a ten year old," said Brit.

"But aren't we then descendants of political prisoners who could actually be heros to some, but enemies to others," said Sarah.

"I guess that's also true," said Luke.

"Good one, Sarah," said Jake.

"And from what we found here, we believe these buildings were used for some kind of government research, most likely related to the concentration camp," said Brit.

"That makes a lot of sense," said Luke.

"Yes, Ellen's library bears out that hypothesis," said Jake. "It contains a lot of historical perspective on the subject." Brit just raised her eyebrows and smiled.

"So the prison complex is over the hill?" asked Sarah.

"Yes, it's six buildings that comfortably housed the insurrectionists," said Luke.

"Insurrectionists, yes, that's a word I had to look up, and I think it captures the reason for the US establishing these concentration camps," said Jake.

"So does anyone live in the complex today?" asked Sarah.

"Yes, those who are banished from the village are taken there by Ed," said Luke. "And according to him, they made a lot of improvements so it's like a resort and they're actually living in relative luxury compared to life in the village."

"Basically, they're being rewarded for sinning against The Message?" asked Jake.

"In effect, yes, and Chandler is entirely unaware that Ed has done this," Luke laughed. "Ed is actually a very sensitive and caring person. He's a gentle giant."

"To think of the Helper as a sensitive and caring person is difficult to picture," said Sarah.

"But he is," said Luke. "And he's the main reason no one from the village is ever killed."

"But the intent is still there, since Chandler isn't aware of Ed's soft heart," said Jake.

"That's right, the intent is still there, even though I'm not sure that Chandler is really an evil person," said Luke. "These prisoners were rather hard to manage at the beginning, and so the penalties had to be harsh at first."

"Yes, but over time the village obviously lost its political purpose, since that does not exist today in the village," said Jake. "The village is quite peaceful and not populated by terrorists, so harsh penalties no longer seem appropriate."

"That's very true, Jake. Chandler should have relaxed his penalties for non-compliance over time, but he has not," said Luke.

"So, given his hard line, do you think Chandler could be convinced to give up this little religious program?" asked Jake.

"I don't think he would give it up voluntarily," said Luke.

"Then the tank gambit is still on," said Jake.

"Tank gambit?" Brit whispered, looking at Luke who smiled.

"Yes, I think the tank gambit is still on," said Luke, nodding.

"Is there anything else we should know about this place?" asked Sarah.

"Well, yes, a few decades after the war and its fallout, there was a second period of frigid cold when we had to retreat again into our bunker to survive," said Brit.

"That's right, it was about forty years after the war," said Virg. "The dark skies killed a lot of vegetation and made life a lot more difficult. Without our food makers, we'd have starved."

"It was during this period that many in the village either froze to death or died of starvation," said Luke.

"Ellen already told me a little bit about that period, but I did not know how it had affected the village," said Jake.

"Yes, the village dwindled to a few dozen hearty souls, so Chandler's religion went into limbo for years since life became one of survival, and it took another fifteen years before it was back to anything like it's present self," said Luke.

"You don't know what caused this second long winter," said Jake.

"No, but it was probably some natural phenomenon since I doubt if the means existed to prolong the war," said Luke.

"I would like to know more about this Shannon person who went off into deep space with that group of teens," said Jake.

"That happened before the war and all we know is what was reported on the news," said Brit.

"If she headed into deep space, she must have planned to settle on another planet," said Jake.

"That's what I would think," said Brit.

"But it's something we may never know because the nearest star system is over four light years away," said Jake.

"That's right, so it would take decades to get to even the closest star system and there may not be habitable planets there," said Brit.

"We could be talking about hundreds of years to get to something habitable," said Jake.

"And hundreds of years to get back," said Sarah.

"Yes," said Brit.

"So do you think she made these teens immortal or do you think she just assumed it would be the children of these teens that made it somewhere?" asked Jake.

"I don't know what she was planning, and I doubt if anyone else knows either," said Brit.

"I also want to know more about how this nuclear war actually started," said Jake.

"The buildup to that war is covered in the books up at Ellen's, but the actual start and its aftermath is yet to hit the news stand," said Brit.

"That's right, who would do it," said Jake. "And another thing I'd like to know more about is this whole immortality enterprise. Especially the guy that built those big steel boxes."

"His was actually a bit bizarre," said Brit.

"In what way?" asked Jake.

"He claimed he could extract a person's mind from their body and preserve it in these boxes in cyber space," said Brit.

"Cyber space....oh right, computer storage," said Jake.

"Yes, but he was exposed as a fraud after taking billions in fees from people that he had put into these boxes," said Virg.

"So it didn't work," said Jake.

"According to the accusations, no, but no one ever knew for sure," said Brit.

"OK, so he apparently killed these people after putting their minds into these big steel boxes?" asked Jake.

"Yes, that was his immortality scheme," said Brit.

"So then he must have been arrested?" asked Jake.

"No, he disappeared, and then the war started, which essentially erased everything, so who knows where he went or even if he survived," said Brit.

"Did Chandler have a communication link in one of them?" asked Jake.

"Yes, the one you kids saw in the distance on your way here," said Luke.

"Interesting...... well, that's all history, but right now we need to focus on getting that tank and knocking out the lighthouse so we can free the village," said Jake.

"Right, the tank gambit," said Luke.

"So if Chandler won't give up his little religious horror show, we'll have to knock him off his pedestal," said Jake.

"Off his pedestal.....yes, that's probably a good description of this gambit," said Luke.

"So is this officially the tank gambit?" Brit repeated, shaking her head doubtfully.

"It's our only hope for freeing the village," said Jake.

"Alright, well, as soon as it's light we'll go up to East Hill and discuss it with Ellen," said Brit.

"I know it's a long shot, but I think it's worth trying," said Virg.

"But if Ellen doesn't go along with it, we won't do it," said Brit.

"She will," said Jake.

"Do you get the idea that a ten year old has basically assumed control of our situation?" asked Brit.

"Join the parade," said Sarah.

"In the absence of direction, one must step up," said Jake.

"Well, in the absence of any other plan for what to do about the village, it may at least be worth discussing," said Brit.

"I'm confident that it will work," said Jake, pointing to the door, then at Virg.

"As soon as it's light," said Brit, holding up her hands.

"Fine, then it's up to East Hill, and, after Ellen agrees with the plan, we'll be off to the museum," said Jake.

"You can't win with him, so just go with it," said Sarah.

"I'm beginning to believe that," said Brit.

Chapter Five

"All right then, let's inventory our assets," said Jake as they sat around the table the next morning at East Hill. All eyes shifted to him. Ellen glanced at Brit with a curious expression as she wondered why a ten year old seemed to be in charge.

"Jake has kind of taken over," said Brit.

"I see," Ellen nodded with a surprised look, but without comment.

"Inventory, right, so, we have that old Volksvagen van that runs on a concoction of fuel I mixed," said Virg. "I also made the tires solid with a liquid goo that hardened, because the rubber was falling apart, so it rides rather rough."

"Very rough," Brit nodded.

"So we have transportation to the museum," said Jake.

"Wait, we're going to the museum?" asked Ellen, looking at Virg for clarification.

"We need a tank," Jake explained.

"A tank, of course, a tank, what was I thinking," said Ellen, again with a curious stare at Virg.

"So we can take out the lighthouse," Virg confirmed.

"Oh right, yes, of course, we're going to take out the lighthouse," said Ellen, still locked on Virg.

"We'll also need to find shells for the tank's cannon," said Virg.

"Shells.....good.....then we'll take out the lighthouse," said Ellen sarcastically, looking now at Jake with eyebrows raised high.

"We have to break the grip that it has on the village," Jake explained with a shrug.

"Doesn't Chandler still live in the lighthouse, Luke?" asked Ellen, turning quickly to him.

"He does, but he's kind of the culprit here," said Luke.

"I see, but everyone realizes that those displays at the museum are hundreds of years old and are not likely to work," said Ellen.

"Virg says she might be able to get one started," said Jake.

"They're not an old VW van, Virg," said Ellen.

"But the tank runs on diesel, so we won't have to worry about spark plugs or exotic fuels," said Jake.

"Spark plugs or exotic fuels," Ellen repeated, turning back to Virg for an explanation.

"The engine runs on compression instead of high octane fuel and plugs, so it can run on low octane fuel, apparently even cooking oil," said Virg.

"So there's a tank in the museum that will run on cooking oil.... if we can get it started....then all we need to do is find bullets for the cannon," said Ellen.

"A little difficult, yes, but it's our only good option at this point," said Jake.

"The other options must be really bad," said Ellen, again looking at Virg, eyebrows raised high.

"I've actually looked at this tank before, and it appears to have been preserved pretty much in it's original state," said Virg. "I believe they could actually have driven it into its stall at the museum, so I think it could be brought back to life."

"Brought back to life," Ellen repeated, sitting back and turning her attention to Jake.

"The engine appears to be pretty much intact and nothing has been removed as far as I can tell," said Virg. "It was a great job of restoration."

"And what about the bullets...uh, shells?" she asked.

"I saw several in the tank packed in sealed containers," said Virg.

"That was done over three hundred years ago," said Ellen.

"I know, but I think they were hermetically sealed so they could still be good," said Virg.

"And why would anyone want to pack cannon shells like that?" asked Ellen.

"I have no idea, but maybe just the idea of authentic preservation?" asked Virg.

"Does anyone have a better plan to free the village of Chandler's grip?" asked Jake.

"All right, in the remote possibility that you get the tank to run and find shells in sealed containers that actually fire, explain to me again why blowing up the lighthouse is a good idea?" asked Ellen.

"It will remove the sacred Tower that everyone worships,"

said Jake. "Look, this Tower is a symbol that strikes fear into the villagers because of the punishments it metes out to those who disobey its rules," said Jake.

"Can't we just talk to Chandler?" asked Brit.

"He's pretty much all in with this thing, so I wouldn't waste a lot of energy trying to convince him of anything," said Luke.

"I'll take your word for that......so then he gets blown up?" asked Ellen with a shrug.

"We'll give him a chance to shut the whole operation down before we blow up the lighthouse," said Jake.

"How gracious......so we say: get out Chandler or we'll blow you up," said Ellen.

"Something like that, but I think he might back down once he sees the tank," said Jake.

"A museum piece..... right, I'd be terrified......so, what about the fence?" asked Ellen.

"We'll just smash right over it," said Jake.

"Well, OK, that's very bold, but we get our electricity from it, so what will we do for power after this little event?" asked Ellen.

"We'll come up with a work-around," said Virg.

"A work-around, of course, and this whole adventure you're getting us into is to set the village free?" asked Ellen.

"You'll have to admit that it's a noble cause," said Brit.

"Perhaps it is, but it doesn't sound very practical and the fallout could be a disaster," said Ellen.

"Nothing on that side of the fence seems very practical," said Jake. "It's essentially a religious cult that needs to be broken up.....and, as Virg says, we can come up with work-arounds if we have problems afterwards."

"Work-arounds, right......and Luke, you don't think you could talk to Chandler about this first?" asked Ellen.

"Convince Chandler of anything?" asked Luke. "He has essentially held me and Ed captive for two hundred years. We do his dirty work with the threat of cancelling our immortality if we don't follow his orders. Do you consider this a man who can be reasoned with?"

"OK, I do know Chandler, so maybe not," said Ellen. "Of course if he cancels your immortality, he cancels ours as well since we all share the same activation device."

"I recognize that, so hopefully we can locate the activation device or get him to tell us where it is," said Luke.

"I'm not holding my breath on that," said Ellen. "And we have no other options for freeing the village?"

"Well, we can just accept the status quo, or knock down the fence and let the village escape into what I'm told is a Scorched Earth scenario," said Jake.

"A Scorched Earth scenario....where did you....?" asked Ellen.

"I may have used that term," said Virg.

"Oh my god......so do you see what giving him a little knowledge has created here Ellen?" asked Brit.

"Yes, I know, but this does seem to be a noble cause, even though the solution sits on the far fringe of reality and the fallout could be very messy," said Ellen.

"Look, people who survived this senseless war should at least be allowed to live free of oppression," said Jake. They all stared at him for a moment, then at one another.

"He just said that, didn't he," said Brit.

"He did.......alright, so when do we leave for the museum?"

asked Ellen after a long pause when no one else spoke.

"I'll need to go back to West Hill and grab my tool box, a battery, and load up some cooking oil," said Virg.

"Seriously, does the tank really run on cooking oil?" asked Ellen.

"Jake said he read that it could," said Virg.

"Anything in print, right?......OK...... but we all can't go," said Ellen.

"There will be four of us going," Jake declared. "Sarah goes everywhere with me, so she's in. Virg is the only one who can start the tank so she has to go. Then you, Ellen, are needed for your practical perspective."

"Ellen was actually an accomplished scientist in the past, so she definitely needs to go," said Lucinda, who was listening at the door.

"Alright, then we'll head for the museum as soon as we pick up the tools, battery and fuel from West Hill," said Jake.

"So, does that mean you're leaving now?" asked Brit.

"Unless there are any objections," said Jake.

"I have one," said Sarah.

"You're hungry," said Jake.

"No, silly, I'm worried about the safety of our parents if this thing gets out of hand, which of course it could if we blow up their precious Tower," she replied.

"You're thinking that some in our village might not respond rationally," said Jake.

"You know how they worship that thing and how many truly believe The Message," she replied.

"She's right about that, Jake, so maybe your parents would be in jeopardy if The Tower is destroyed and they are linked to that event because of you," said Luke.

"I never really thought about that," he replied.

"It's definitely something to take into consideration," said Luke.

"All right, so maybe our first order of business will be to go there and bring our parents back before we destroy the lighthouse," said Jake.

"Wait.....you want to actually go there to bring them back?" asked Luke. "No, you can't just go back across the fence to get your parents, especially after we have already set off alarm bells by leaving."

"We could do it at night," said Jake.

"No...... Ed will have discovered our absence by now and will have gone to the village looking for you," said Luke. "Which means all of the tattletales in the village will also be looking for you."

"Tattletales?" asked Sarah.

"Those who consistently report their fellow villagers for rule violations," said Luke.

"But as I said, we can do it at night," said Jake.

"Jake, it's not a good idea," said Luke.

"He's right, Jake, I'm not sure if we could get away with it after what's happened, even at night," said Sarah.

"Then how are we going to get them back here to safety?" asked Jake.

"Maybe we shouldn't get ahead of ourselves," said Ellen. "Let's first go out to the museum to see if we can get a tank running before we assume we can blow up a lighthouse."

"There's Ellen with her practicality hat on," said Sarah, smiling at Jake with a shrug.

"Alright, then that's our new plan," said Jake. "We go to the museum first."

"However, I think we'll need at least a day to get this tank to run, so let's head out of here first thing in the morning," said Virg.

"All right, first thing in the morning," said Jake.

"I'm starting to become unrealistic in thinking this plan of his could actually work," said Ellen. "I say that because I would never have thought that anyone would be able to cross the fence in the first place, and Jake did it in two different places."

"Remember though, we still have to bring our parents back here before we blow up the lighthouse," said Jake. "And, just so you know, the second fence crossing was engineered by Sarah, not me."

"That's no surprise to me," said Brit. "You two are the dynamic duo."

"Of course you know that if we do get the tank going tomorrow, things can happen rather quickly," said Jake.

"I know, but all we can do right now is take one step at a time," said Sarah.

"She seems to be the steady head between the two of us," said Jake. Ellen raised her eyebrows as she turned to Brit who just shook her head.

"They're ten," Ellen whispered.

Chapter Six

"It's the Helper!" shouted a young man running past a row of huts and pointing behind him as he ran. "It's the Helper!" he repeated, then disappeared through the rustic wooden door to his dwelling. He peeked back out through a crack into the early evening darkness.

At the edge of the village stood a very tall figure dressed in heavy black cloth with thick black shoes, the laces trailing in the dirt. It was nearly dark and his grotesque features were amplified by shadows. His face was long with his chin seemingly out of proportion with his face. His eyebrows were thick and dark, projecting both a serious and ominous image. He looked in all directions as members of the tribe watched, some from the doorways of their huts and others from different locations around the village. He held up his hand.

"The father of the child Jake will come forward," he said in a loud voice that all could hear. At the far end of one village street, a door swung open and a slight man with a balding head stepped out and slowly began moving toward the man. He stopped a safe distance away as was custom and waited for the Helper to speak. The Helper looked at him for a moment before speaking.

"Are you the father of Jake?" he asked.

"Yes."

"Is the child Jake here in the village?" he asked.

"He is at the enlightenment," said the father.

"No, he has fled," said the Helper.

"Fled?" asked the father in surprise. "But he has not returned here."

"He has fled," the Helper repeated. "This cannot be tolerated."

"We will look for him," said the father, looking back toward his hut to see his wife Martha standing near their front door.

"I will wait while you look, but if you do not find him now, you will find him and bring him to me at the grounds near The Tower by sundown tomorrow."

"What has he done?" asked the man.

"He has disgraced The Message by breaking its rules," said the Helper. The man nodded and returned to his hut. A short time later he returned to report he could not find Jake.

"If you do not find him, you will still report to the grounds near The Tower tomorrow by sundown, and your wife is to accompany you," said the Helper.

"Why my wife?" the father asked. The Helper glared at him without answering.

"Where is the father of the child Sarah?" asked the Helper, ignoring Jake's father and turning his attention back to the village.

Momentarily, a man and woman appeared near a hut a few places down from Jake's parent's hut. The man came quickly forward.

"Where is the child Sarah?" asked the Helper.

"She is at the enlightenment," said the man.

"The child Sarah has also fled and disgraced The Message," said the Helper.

"What?" asked the man, sounding both confused and angry.

"You will bring the child Sarah to the grounds near The Tower tomorrow by sundown, and if you do not bring the child Sarah, you will still report to the grounds near The Tower. You will come with your wife."

"What has Sarah done to disgrace The Message?" asked the man. The Helper ignored the question and instead turned and walked briskly back down the trail and out of the village into the night. The father of Jake, who was standing a short distance away, turned to the stares of the villagers before lowering his head to avoid eye contact. He then walked quickly back to his hut where he disappeared inside. His wife Martha who was standing outside, followed him. Sarah's father stood for a moment, clearly in shock at what he had just heard. He then slowly returned to his hut.

"Where is she Sandra?" asked the man after entering his hut. "Where is Sarah?"

"I do not know, Bob, she went to the Enlightenment with Jake," said Sandra.

"I know she did," said Bob, shaking his head.

"Jake is her best friend," said Sandra.

"I don't trust that boy, and now look at what's happened,

72

they have disgraced The Message," said Bob.

"We don't know what happened, the Helper didn't actually say," said Sandra.

"Jake was always sneaking around," said Bob.

"They play together," said Sandra.

"Whatever they did, he's the guilty one, not Sarah," said Bob.

"We don't know why they ran away," said Sandra.

"Wait, you said 'ran away'.....so do you know something?" asked Bob, walking to the corner and then turning to stare back at her.

"I heard that Jake had once crossed the fence," said Sandra.

"What?" asked Bob in shock.

"I've also heard that he brings back books that both he and Sarah read."

"Sarah reads?"

"Yes."

"So that's it, and you knew this!" said Bob, who now slumped into a chair to stare at the ceiling.

"Where is he?" asked Jake's father after entering his hut a few doors from Sarah's hut.

"I don't know," said Martha, shaking her head but then turning to stare off into the corner.

"Wait.....you know more about this, don't you?" he asked, getting up and sitting next to her to gently turn her face toward him.

"I do, but I can't......," she replied, a tear now forming in one eye as she put her hand over her mouth.

"Martha, what has he done?" asked the father.

"Somehow they found out," she replied.

"Found out what?" he asked.

"About his crossing the fence and reading the books he brings back," she replied, placing her hand tightly over her mouth.

"Oh my, so that's what this is all about."

"Yes, and I saw, but I could not tell," said Martha.

"Where are the books now?"

"I don't know, John, he was very good at hiding them, but......"

"But what, Martha?"

"I'm sure other children besides Sarah knew about this and may also have read the books."

"So perhaps he and Sarah were found out at school and fled back across the fence to escape punishment," said John.

"Yes, I think they may have," said Martha.

"Then Jake and Sarah have broken two of the most sacred rules, and we, as parents, will share the blame," said John. "All who break these rules must be banished from the village forever."

"I know," said Martha. John nodded.

"If he got books from across the fence, there must be those who live there," said John.

"I agree......so, do you think they are with these people now?" asked Martha.

"I believe they are," said John.

"What can we do?" asked Martha.

"I don't know," he replied.

"I think we must cross the fence too, just like Jake and Sarah," said Martha.

"But how?" he asked, standing up. "We don't know where to cross or even how to get to the fence. The fence is forbidden territory."

"I know, but if Jake and Sarah crossed, there must be a way," said Martha.

"Do you know the way to the fence?" asked John.

"Yes," said Martha, pointing.

"Then perhaps we must cross as you say," said John after a moment of hesitation.

"We have nothing to lose," said Martha.

"You speak the truth, Martha," he replied.

"We must leave tonight."

"But others will be watching."

"They will not see us in the late night darkness," she replied.

"Alright, we must try," he nodded after slumping into a chair. Martha sat down beside him, placing her hand on his arm.

It was past midnight when John opened the door a crack and looked out. The village was quiet. He opened it halfway and crept outside to look around. Seeing nothing, he held out his hand for Martha who took it and they slowly and very carefully crept down the dirt street toward to the edge of the village. As they passed Sandra and Bob's hut, their door opened silently and Sandra stepped out behind them. They stopped and waited for her to join them.

"You must not tell," whispered Martha, holding her finger over her lips.

"Are you going to cross the fence?" she whispered back.

"Yes, but I only know the direction, and nothing else," Martha whispered.

"I know the way to the crossing place, and I will cross with you," she whispered as she pointed toward the forest, walked past them and then motioned for them to follow. They glanced at each other briefly before following. John looked back as they reached the edge of the village to make sure no one was following. Then, the three of them made their way single file down a barely visible path that was dimly lit by the half moon. They continued in silence until they were far away from the village.

"What about Bob?" asked Martha, as they picked their way along the narrow path.

"Bob must not know," said Sandra over her shoulder in a loud whisper.

"Why?" asked Martha, as they strode quickly along behind her.

"He is a devoted believer and is committed to the dictates of The Message," she replied.

"So Sarah read books?" asked John.

"Yes, and so did I," said Sandra.

"You did?" asked John.

"Of course, many have," said Sandra.

"And Jake brought them to you?" asked John.

"Yes."

"I have been blind," said John.

"And you know how to cross the fence?" asked Martha.

"I know where Jake crossed, and how he crossed," said Sandra.

"Jake showed you?" asked Martha.

"Yes, he has crossed the fence there many times," said Sandra. "Someone on the other side has taught him how to read and he in turn has taught others, including me," said Sandra.

"Then you have all sinned," said John.

"And once we cross, so have you," said Sandra.

"This is true.

"Right now, we must hurry, because Bob may wake and find me gone," said Sandra.

"Would he stop you?" asked John.

"Yes."

"But he is your husband," said Martha as they stepped up the pace and now were almost running.

"The Message has a powerful grip on him as it has on many others," said Sandra.

"Will he know where you went if he wakes and finds you gone?" asked John.

"He knows where Sarah entered the forest for what he thought was play," said Sandra. "So he might assume that's where I went, and it's where we are now."

"How far to the fence?" asked Martha.

"Still a ways," said Sandra, who stepped up the pace after looking back when she heard something. Behind they could hear voices in the distance.

"They're coming!" said Sandra, who began to run as fast as she could along the dimly lit path. "We must not speak again until we get across."

"OK," said John in a loud whisper as he brought up the rear. The voices were getting closer and they were panting loudly as they raced along. But the pursuers were gaining on them, and, as John looked back he could see the lead runner in full stride in a clearing behind them.

"We almost have them!" the man shouted.

"How much farther?" asked John.

"Just ahead," Sandra shouted back as the gray façade of the

fence loomed off to their left. "We will leave the trail up ahead and crawl under. Just remember, Jake said to never touch the fence."

"They're going to catch us," said John, looking back and realizing how close the pursuers were. He might have to sacrifice himself in order for the others to get across. But he had to time it perfectly.

"Here it is!" said Sandra, leaping into a small ravine and falling to her hands and knees into the water of a stream. She quickly crawled through the gap under the fence, being very careful not to touch it.

"Don't touch the fence!" she shouted back.

Martha was right behind her and scurried under. John hesitated to make sure the two women were across. Then, just as he dove to his hands and knees to crawl under, he felt a hand slam down on his back and clamp onto his shirt. He struggled forward against the pull, clawing at the brush and roots on the sides of the stream to pull himself forward as yet another hand grabbed his pant leg. He struggled with all of his might against the pursuers, grabbing anything he could until he felt his shirt rip loose. As he edged forward he crawled out of his pants. He used that temporary freedom to drag himself forward so he was almost all the way under the fence. Just as he was nearly through, a hand slammed down on his shoulder, but he had a solid grip on a large root of a tree on the other side and held on with both hands. As he struggled he heard a blood curdling scream behind him and sparks showered past him as the tingling of a shock stung his body. But the grip on his shoulder released and the shock was gone. A second scream penetrated the night air.

Free now, John quickly scrambled to his feet as the hands of both Sandra and Martha pulled him up the slope to the top where they all fell in a tangle. After a brief moment of relief, they sat up and looked back to see a third man standing on the trail shouting at the top of his lungs.

"You will all perish!!" he bellowed at them in utter hatred. "You have broken the most sacred rules of The Message! Your souls are now lost forever!"

The man stopped his ranting lecture as he stared at the lifeless bodies of his two friends. He took a step forward to get a better look but stopped short in horror, putting his hand over his mouth. One of the men was hopelessly impaled on the fence, his hands burned free of flesh and just the bones clinging to the wire. The other's face was a mass of tangled flesh and bone, and only his eyeballs were left to stare back at the man who looked on in disbelief. He stepped back in revulsion as he looked up at the three on the other side of the fence. After a brief moment he whirled and ran back along the trail. A fourth man remained on the edge of the trail watching.

"That's Bob," said Sandra, still gasping for breath as she struggled to her feet.

"He is not speaking," said Martha. Bob hesitated a moment, then turned and slowly began walking back along the trail.

"I think he'll come after me," said Sandra.

"Perhaps others will too, so we need to keep moving," said John who was completely naked. He stood up, then helped Martha to her feet. She removed the scarf around her neck and John wrapped it around his waste to cover himself up. He then went back down the slope to the fence and retrieved his pants from one of the dead men's hands.

"I don't think Bob will try to cross soon because of those two men who died, but I think he will eventually come after us," said Sandra.

"We have to warn Jake and Sarah, and whoever else lives here across the fence," John nodded after climbing up the slope.

"Which way from here?" asked Martha, looking into the forest.

"I don't know for sure," said Sandra. "However, Jake said it was just a little way from the fence.

"Let's go," said John who took Martha's hand and led the way toward an opening in the trees.

"Wait for me," said Sandra.

"The grass and brush is crushed ahead, like a sort of pathway," said Sandra from behind.

"I see it," said John, who followed the trail of broken grass and weeds. A few minutes later they entered a clearing.

"There's something ahead," said Sandra.

"A wall of some kind," said John, who broke into a run still holding Martha's hand as Sandra now pulled abreast. They felt refreshed and excited as they ran across the clearing. It was as if a giant weight had been lifted from their shoulders. At a wall they stopped and looked in both directions, then walked around to the right side where the trampled grass seemed to indicate a continuation of the path. Down a steep walkway they found themselves at the foot of a flight of stairs where they stopped and looked up.

"Let's go," said Sandra, pointing and then immediately starting to climb. The other two followed, and at the first landing they stopped. Sandra looked around before spotting a second stairway which she started climbing. John and Martha followed. Soon they were on the second landing facing an arched doorway lighted by a tiny bulb that cast an eerie pattern on the large reddish brown door.

"I saw these at the school many years ago," said Martha, staring at the little light. They stood in a tight huddle in front of the door. John looked at Martha, then stepped forward and banged his hand against it. He pounded again when no one answered, turning finally to Sandra as if to ask what to do next. As he did so, she jumped back when the door began to open.

"Hello," said a woman who swung the door open to the shocked faces of the three who were now bathed in light from inside.

"Uh, I'm John, Jake's dad, and this is my wife Martha, his mom," said John. "And this is Sandra, Sarah's mom."

"Wonderful, I'm Lucinda, so this solves that problem," she replied, motioning for them to enter.

"What problem?" asked Martha.

"Making sure that you were safe on this side of the fence," said Lucinda.

"Alright," said John. "So where are they?"

"Inside asleep," said Lucinda.

"So where is Sarah's father?" asked Lucinda.

"He's not exactly in support of us right now," said Sandra.

"So he thinks the kids should be punished?" asked Lucinda.

"Correct," said Sandra.

"Alright, well, everyone is asleep right now, but follow me and I'll make you comfortable until morning," said Lucinda.

"Everyone will be very excited and relieved to see that you came across. And, uh, John, it looks like you'll need a shirt." John nodded with a smile.

After retrieving a sweater from a closet and handing it to John, Lucinda led them to the library where they settled into the comfortable sofas and recliners. She then retrieved a few blankets and covered each of them before leaving them for the night.

Chapter Seven

"They have crossed the fence!" shouted a man as he ran down the deserted street in the village lit only by moonlight. "And the fence has killed two!"

"Who has crossed?" came a voice from the doorway of a hut.

"Sandra, the mother of Sarah, and the father and mother of Jake have crossed!" he replied loudly.

"Wait, you said two have died?" came another voice.

"The fence has killed Brad and Lee," said the man.

Soon heads began poking out of huts and a short time later a crowd of sleepy villagers stood around the man in an open area near the center of the village.

"We chased them to the fence!" he panted excitedly with his hands on his knees trying to catch his breath. It was a moment before he stood up straight to address them.

"The three crossed safely under the fence," said the man.

"Yes, Sandra has crossed with Jake's parents," shouted Bob

from the rear as he fought his way forward.

"You did not stop her," said the man, as Bob made his way through the crowd and stood in front of him.

"I was asleep when she left, but called the alarm when I awoke, and then chased her to the fence with the others," said Bob.

"If she crossed, she must be guilty of something!" shouted a woman from the back.

"Of what?" asked another.

"Reading books," said the woman.

"It is the boy Jake who is the one who started this, so why is Sandra guilty?" asked Bob.

"If anyone reads books, they are guilty, just like your daughter Sarah, otherwise, why would she have crossed," said the woman.

"The boy Jake is behind it all and should bear the guilt," said Bob.

"Perhaps.....but you know the penalty for reading, and for crossing the fence," said another man.

"Others could also have read books if Jake brought books back across the fence," said someone. There was a momentary silence, then a buzzing.

"Perhaps you too are guilty, Bob," said someone else.

"No, I am not!.....I did not know about the books!" Bob shouted. The crowd began staring at him and he started to back up. He then turned and quickly walked toward his hut. The crowd began to follow.

"I must cross and bring them back," said Bob as he neared his hut. "I will prove to you that it is the boy Jake who is the guilty one."

"I think we should all cross and bring them back for punishment!" shouted a man in the crowd that was now forming around Bob's hut.

"No, I will go alone, but I will wait for morning when it is light!" said Bob.

"But if we all go, it will justify the need for seeking justice, and we will not face punishment," said the man.

"No one else need violate The Message," said Bob. "I will go alone!" Bob then quickly went into his hut. The crowd stood in front of his hut buzzing for a while before disbursing.

The next morning at the first sign of light, Bob emerged from his hut and started down the trail. Moments later he felt a tug on his arm and, without stopping, turned his head to see who was there. Running along behind him was a teenage boy, Eric.

"I must speak with you," said Eric in a voice that had begun to break into adulthood.

"Eric, you should not be here, and I cannot speak with you now," said Bob who continued running.

"I need to know what you will do," said Eric from behind.

"What do you mean?" asked Bob without slowing.

"What will you do with Sandra."

"She will have to be brought back because she crossed the fence and has read books," said Bob.

"She may have, yes, but that is not the only reason she crossed," said Eric, now unsure whether he should reveal what he knew.

"What is her other reason?" asked Bob with renewed interest but still not slowing.

"It is something that you need to know before you see her,"

he replied.

"What would you know about my wife that I do not?" asked Bob.

"I found out, but swore an oath to her that I would not tell," said Eric.

"Found out what?" asked Bob.

"That she carries your child," said Eric.

"She what?" Bob gasped with wide open eyes as he stopped and turned to face Eric.

"She carries your second child," Eric repeated.

"Why would she tell you and not me?" asked Bob.

"She was afraid because of what it means," said Eric.

"Having a second child is forbidden," said Bob as he focused on the crime and not on the fact that he was to be a father again.

"And she knows that it is the father who will be cast into the pit."

"So you think she crossed to protect me?" asked Bob.

"Bob, if you cross it will not only be you, but Sandra, Sarah and your unborn child who will end up either banished or thrown into the pit," said Eric.

"But the boy Jake is the one most guilty for crossing the fence and helping everyone read the books," said Bob turning quickly and striding away.

"Why does that matter since you'll all be banished or thrown into the pit," said Eric as he tried to keep pace.

"It doesn't matter, because I must cross and bring them back," said Bob who resumed his journey to the fence.

As Bob raced on, he felt entirely confused. His unerring duty to defend The Message clashed with his undying devotion to Sandra and his unborn child, as well as his daughter Sarah. He knew that in order to defend the sanctity of The Message, everyone must be punished. The Message was clear about that..... all must be punished, including himself. It didn't matter, The Message offered no options. The Message must always be right and must always be followed. His duty to The Message was clear and his conscience was of no consequence. The pain he felt inside must be endured.

"My life is of no consequence," he said out loud.

"You must not bring her back," said Eric who heard him as he ran along behind.

"Where is the fence?" asked Bob who slowed enough to reach back and grab Eric by the shirt and pull him alongside.

"I have to stop you," said Eric who wriggled free of Bob's grip and bolted ahead of him.

As they reached the edge of a clearing, Eric stopped to block Bob's advance. Bob came to a halt in front of him. Off to their left loomed the dreaded fence, and in plain sight were two bodies draped awkwardly on one another in a wash. Bob pushed past Eric and started for the fence, but Eric tackled him to the ground. Bob was much bigger and stronger and he threw Eric aside and got to his feet. Eric got up and tried to tackle him again but Bob shoved him violently to the ground. Eric again got up and rushed at him, but was picked up and thrown into the brush where he became tangled and began struggling to get to his feet.

Bob went quickly down to the creek to kneel beside the bodies. One by one he dragged their remains clear of the opening. Eric stood at the edge of the clearing watching as Bob fell to his belly and carefully crawled under the fence. Once on the other side he climbed up the embankment and stood on top looking back. Eric was still standing there, watching, but saying nothing. Bob then turned and made his way into the woods.

Chapter Eight

Jake arose at dawn and decided to go to the balcony that overlooked a peaceful meadow that was sprinkled with yellow and purple flowers, their colors beginning to glow as the sun peaked through the trees. Behind him, Sarah emerged onto the balcony with a yawn, her arms stretched skyward in the cool morning air. Below stood a man looking up at them.

"Sarah, that's your dad!" said Jake pointing down as Sarah rushed forward to see.

"Dad!" said Sarah.

"There you are," said Bob.

"You came across to be with us?" asked Sarah.

"I came to bring you all back for punishment," said Bob.

"No dad, we can't go back," said Sarah.

"You must go back for punishment, because what you did is forbidden by The Message!"

"But we will be severely punished, even killed, if we go back," said Sarah.

"Jake has corrupted you!" he replied, pointing menacingly at him. "You are evil, Jake!"

"He is not evil, he's my best friend, and I asked him for the books," said Sarah.

"Where is your mother?" he asked.

"She's not here," said Sarah, unaware that Sandra and Jake's parents were inside asleep.

"No, she crossed, so I know she's here!" he bellowed.

"She crossed?" asked Sarah, looking at Jake who shrugged.

"If she crossed, maybe she got lost," said Jake quietly.

"She is here!" Bob repeated in a more threatening tenor.

"We haven't seen her," said Jake.

"You're lying!" shouted Bob, stepping forward and looking for some way to get up to where they were. He spotted stairs off to his left and ran toward them.

"What do we do, he looks very angry?" asked Sarah.

"We need to tell Virg," said Jake who rushed back inside and down a long hallway to where he had seen Virg disappear the night before. When he reached her door he banged on it with his fists.

"Virg, we need help!" he shouted. From down the hall, Virg appeared in another doorway.

"What's going on?" she asked as she rushed toward them.

"Sarah's dad is here and he's coming up after us," said Jake.

"What does he want?" asked Virg.

"All of us, including my mom," said Sarah.

"Your mom came over last night, but let me handle this," she replied. She went quickly into her room and emerged a moment later holding an odd looking pistol that looked like something out of one of the pirate books that Sarah had read. She then started down the hallway but stopped abruptly when Bob appeared ahead of her.

"Who are you?" he shouted.

"Never mind who I am, you need to calm down because you're not taking anyone back," said Virg.

"You can't stop me!" said Bob.

"You need to stand down," said Virg, who pulled back the hammer and pointed the gun at him when he began walking toward her.

"They have all sinned and must be punished!" he shouted as he continued walking toward her.

"I'm warning you!" shouted Virg, who aimed at Bob's lower extremities.

"Get out of my way!" Bob raged into an explosion of smoke and fire that sent dozens of pellets into his legs, right through his pants. He screamed in pain as he fell to the floor, with a scattering of little dots of blood quickly appearing on his pants.

"You shouldn't have done that Bob," said Virg as the cloud of blue smoke began to clear and she could see the result.

"Oh no," said Sarah who placed both hands over her face when she saw the blood.

"It's just buckshot, sweety, he'll live," said Virg.

"I'm dying!" moaned Bob as he writhed on the floor in excruciating pain.

"Jake, go get Ellen and tell her what happened," said Virg just as the hallway began to fill with others who had heard the yelling and then the very loud gunshot.

"Hurry!" said Virg, holding up the pistol that still had a wisp of smoke clinging to its barrel. Bob lay in a heap on the floor crying in agony.

Ellen appeared a moment later carrying a tattered black bag and knelt beside Bob.

"This could take a while," she said as she saw the extent of the damage and began to tear away the clothing from his legs. "Actually, we need to get him to a bedroom where I can work on him."

"I've never shot anyone before," said Virg, still holding the old pistol.

"Bob?" asked Sandra who just arrived on the scene. Seeing him lying on the floor with blood everywhere, she quickly dropped to her knees beside him.

"Mom!" said Sarah, who rushed forward to kneel beside her.

"Neither of you should have crossed," said Bob as he lay in excruciating pain.

"It looks as though you should not have crossed either, Bob," said Sandra.

"You have my child inside you," he declared.

"How did you.....?" Sandra began to ask.

"You're pregnant?" asked Ellen.

"Yes."

"Who told you?" asked Sandra.

"Eric," Bob mumbled.

"Hey! Mom?....Dad?" asked Jake as his parents appeared down the hall. He rushed to their side.

"The Helper came," Martha explained.

"He threatened you?" asked Jake.

"Yes, so we had to follow you across the fence," said John.

"Sarah and I were planning to go back over and bring you back," said Jake.

"Oh no, that would have been bad, so we're glad we came over first," said John.

Luke came onto the scene, and along with Lucinda, they were able to drag Bob down the hall and into a bedroom where they managed to lift him onto a bed. Ellen went to work using a pair of tweezers. Lucinda found a bottle of gin, and, after forcing Bob to drink a cup, he became quite intoxicated. Ellen continued to pluck buckshot while Sandra and Sarah stood in the doorway watching.

"We'll all be punished if we go back," Sandra said finally.

"But we have all sinned," Bob mumbled in a drunken slur.

"According to The Message," she replied.

"We....." he hesitated a moment before falling silent with his eyes closed.

"The Message says that more than one child right now means just the father, not the mother is to be punished and thrown into the pit," said Sandra.

"But we all crossed, and besides, you read books too," he said in a soft, almost melodic but slurred voice.

"That's why we're here where it's safe," she replied.

"But we're sinners... owww.... owww....how long did you.....?" he stammered as one by one the pellets were being extracted.

"I've read books, but feel no guilt," she replied.

"It is forbiii...owwww.....," Bob tried to say, then closed his eyes, wincing as Ellen plucked another buckshot. Sandra stepped

93

out into the hall where Virg and Lucinda were standing.

"What are we going to do with him?" asked Sandra after she ushered them down the hall out of earshot. Virtually everyone else was assembled there with them.

"It sounds like he's completely committed to this Message," said Lucinda.

"He is, but I think that clear stuff you gave him for the pain softened him up a bit, so maybe there's hope," said Sandra.

"That's two hundred year old gin, and that would soften anyone up," she replied.

"Maybe I need a little of that," said Sandra.

"No, you're pregnant."

"So what are we going to do with him, and for that matter, with the whole village who could have the same anger and determination that he has?" asked Sandra.

"We've never had to confront this kind of hostility and hatred before, so we have no experience in dealing with it," said Lucinda.

"However, I did prepare for the day when we might have to encounter hostility from the outside world, and that's why I restored this old pistol," said Virg, pulling the old flintlock out of her waistband and holding it up.

"I know, I had doubts, but it turns out to have been a good idea," said Lucinda.

"Bob is incapacitated now, but I'm concerned about what he might do after he recovers," said Sandra.

"It'll take a while before he's back in action," said Lucinda.

"He'll be pretty much incapacitated for a while, so I'm not sure we have to worry about him doing anything in the near future," said Virg.

"I'm completely torn about how to deal with this," said Sandra. "We lived peacefully and happily together as husband and wife, obeying the rules, and then this. It's like I just woke up in a completely different world and suddenly nothing is like it was before."

"Well, none of you can go back to the village, that's for sure," said Virg.

"But what are we going to do if the villagers decide to do what Bob did and come after us?" asked Sandra.

"I don't know," said Lucinda.

"Look, on a personal level, I have Bob's child inside me, but I'm not sure if we can ever reunite if he continues in his current state of mind," she shrugged.

"I know, Sandra, that's going to be a difficult decision," said Lucinda. "But right now, everyone has to stay here where it's safe."

"Look, if just crossing the fence and reading books pisses the villagers off this much, I'm wondering how they'll react if we're successful in carrying out Jake's plan to destroy their Tower?" asked Virg.

"Wait....oh my god.....doing what?" asked Sandra.

"He wants to knock out The Tower with a tank," said Virg.

"With a what?" asked Sandra.

"We'll fill you in later on his plan," said Lucinda. "Our more immediate concern now is what to do if the villagers decide to descend upon us as a mob."

"They could in fact form a mob and storm this place," said Jake who was nearby listening to the conversation.

"That's what I'm concerned about," said Lucinda.

"Are the zealots mostly men?" asked Virg.

"Zealots?" asked John.

"Those overly committed to the Message," said Jake.

"The Message says that men are in charge and make all the decisions," said John. "However, more than a few of the women are just as devoted as Bob, and, in fact are the most aggressive in turning in violators of The Message."

"Well, once reality descends upon them after we blow up The Tower, the fear of breaking rules will disappear and life will get back to normal," said Jake.

"Nobody in the village has any idea what normal is after countless decades of conformity to the rules of The Message, Jake," said Luke.

"That's true, and I have no idea how they will react to the destruction of The Tower," said John.

"Considering how Bob behaved, and continues to behave, this thing is not likely to simply come to an end with The Tower's demise," said Lucinda.

"The ability to adapt to abrupt change is inherent in all of us," said Jake. "After all, we're a species that has survived many difficulties that are often thrust upon us unexpectedly and quickly, and afterwards we have always seemed to come out whole."

"Jesus, do you know everything?" asked Lucinda, looking at Virg, and then Luke who just shook his head.

"Just about," said Sarah from down the hall.

"OK, look, here's the reality," said Jake. "The village will find itself freed from oppression once we destroy their symbol of worship. But some, perhaps many, will cling to their beliefs for some time. But once they see what it's like to be free of oppression, they too will adapt to the norm."

"Is he really saying all of this?" whispered Lucinda. Virg just stared back at her.

"It may not be that simple, Jake," said Sandra. "I think it will take more time."

"What about you, Sandra, you made a rather rapid adjustment?" asked Jake.

"I know, but I was able to read about what it was like to be, as you say, 'normal', so it wasn't suddenly sprung on me as it will be on the villagers if The Tower is destroyed," she replied. "But I have to admit that I very quickly came to appreciate the feeling of freedom."

"I think mom and dad had to come out of it very quickly too," said Jake.

"We did, so maybe what Jake says is true," said Martha.

"Well, removing the shackles of oppression can set our hearts free, but only if we are capable of opening our hearts to it," said Lucinda.

"I agree, but, yes, I'm sure for some it will be quite difficult to adjust," said Jake. "And I suppose some will never adjust."

"On the other hand, there's an old saying that goes something like this: freedom, once unleashed can never be caged," said Lucinda.

"Regardless of how it shakes out, we'll just have to move forward with our plan, because it's the right thing to do, and we should not be deterred just because it is hard," said Jake.

"There he goes with another pearl of wisdom," said Luke.

"OK, but in light of what just happened here, are you still confident that it's the right thing to do?" asked Lucinda.

"Yes, even moreso," said Jake. "And now, time is of the essence, since it wouldn't surprise me if we will soon be facing a mob from the village," said Jake.

"Jake is right about that, we do have to act quickly or risk being overrun," said Sarah.

"All this is coming from the mouths of babes," said Lucinda.

"I've stood here and listened to this whole conversation, and I have to admit that these two ten year olds have been able to size up the situation correctly while the rest of us are just scratching our heads," said Ellen. "Yes, I think we need to act, and we need to do that quickly. I just hope we can carry out Jake's mission as planned."

"Then let's get our asses in gear and head for the museum," said Virg.

"Alright then, head em up and move em out," said Ellen.

"What?" asked Lucinda.

"Zane Grey?" asked Jake.

"No..... Rawhide," said Ellen.

Chapter Nine

"How far is it?" asked Jake as he, Sarah, Virg and Ellen rumbled along in the VW bus down two ruts barely visible from a sunrise that sent light through the trees in a hundred tiny flecks.

"Maybe a couple more miles," said Virg, who clung tightly to the wheel as they bounced along, picking their way over brush and debris following as best she could along the ancient road that had been partially reclaimed by nature.

"How did you figure out how to make the fuel for this thing," asked Jake.

"I was able to brew some fairly strong spirits from fruit and other stuff," she replied.

"Hopefully, what I read about cooking oil in diesels is accurate," said Jake.

"There's never any guarantee that anything will work because it's not just a matter of putting fuel in it and starting it up. The truth is, we have a lot of work to do before that to make sure everything is operational. The engine may have to be partially taken apart and lubricated first. The parts have been sitting idle for centuries, so you can't just walk in and start it up. To say nothing of other mechanical parts on the tank that will have to be greased. That funny thing on the floor is a grease gun."

"You can do all of this?" asked Jake.

"That big red box on the floor in front of you has a ton of tools," said Virg.

"I believe you."

"I've scavenged tools for many, many years," said Virg.

"Is this odd looking thing on the floor the battery?" asked Jake.

"Yes, it's a home made jobby," said Virg, looking back to address them and abruptly hitting a bump that bounced everyone out of their seats, heads only inches from the ceiling.

"Watch the road!" said Ellen, motioning for Virg to look ahead. She nodded, then turned quickly just in time to miss a big hump. She jerked the wheel in the opposite direction, ploughing over a small tree that whipped up against the windshield, sending leaves flying in every direction as they continued to charge onward down the road. They were now holding their hands over their heads to protect themselves from hitting the ceiling on the next bump.

"We just keep tinkering until we make things work," said Virg who began to turn toward them, but Ellen quickly pointed ahead.

"Drive!" said Ellen.

"What I'm telling you is this might take a while," said Virg.

"OK, I understand," said Jake, sounding a little disappointed that they couldn't just climb in and drive the tank directly out of the museum.

"But we've tackled impossible jobs before, so it's not as if we're coming into this as rookies," said Virg reassuringly.

"Actually, this van took her forever," said Ellen.

"I know, and that was after taking years to get an old Model-T running," said Virg.

"I'll bet it was at least five years before you finally got this thing on the road," said Ellen.

"We don't have five years," said Jake.

"Not to worry, Virg has learned a great deal about restoration, and one of the tanks we saw at the museum did look well preserved," said Ellen. "The good news is these displays have been very carefully preserved and the mechanical parts are usually coated with some gooey stuff."

"OK, so, it may take an hour or so to get it running?" asked Jake.

"An hour or so? Yeah, right," said Virg with a chuckle. "Why do you think we scheduled an entire day? It could take several."

"We don't have several," said Jake.

"Patience," said Ellen.

A short time later they rumbled into a large parking lot with a collection of abandoned buildings arranged around it. Virg drove across the lot to the front of a large structure that had a wide expanse of stairs leading to its entrance. There was an accumulation of dust deep enough to grow grass that now covered the steps like a carpet. A narrow pathway had been cleared up the center of the steps. At the top, two large columns protected the massive doors. They got out of the bus and stood in front of the museum, admiring the intricate designs and statues that were showing the effects of centuries of exposure to the elements. Ellen broke the spell and started up the steps followed by Jake and Sarah. Virg brought up the rear lugging the big red tool box.

"Wow!" exclaimed Jake as they entered through the fifteen foot high arched double doors into a cavernous interior that opened in two directions into what seemed to be endless rooms with very high ceilings. Every marble and concrete surface was coated with a layer of dust, but sound was easily reflected from the walls and ceiling. Even the softest noise bounced back to them. Jake's exclamation echoed from somewhere deep in the building as if another person were there shouting at them.

"This is big!" said Sarah loudly, stating the obvious. Her words came back to them so clearly that they looked around as if expecting someone else to appear.

"This way," said Virg who walked past them into one of the massive rooms. Ellen followed, but Jake and Sarah stood a moment looking, then rushed to join the other two. As they walked and talked together, their voices filled the air with a chorus of echos. Virg eventually stopped in front of a large olive drab vehicle. It's cannon extended over their heads.

"This could work," said Jake as if he knew what he was talking about.

"If we can get it to run," said Ellen.

"And shoot," said Sarah, pointing up to the cannon.

"Well, let me dive in and see whether starting it is even possible," said Virg.

"I remember that you rummaged through this creature before," said Ellen.

"I know, but never with the thought of actually starting it," said Virg. "More importantly, I haven't dug into the mechanics to see if all the critical parts are there and potentially viable. But I'll bet they actually drove it in here, so it did run at one time.... it wasn't carried in here by Paul Bunyan."

"I read about him," said Sarah.

"I have no idea who he was," said Jake.

"Finally, I have one up on you," said Sarah.

"Fine, fine, but let's focus on getting this thing started," said Jake.

"Well, it'll take me a while to find out if it can be done, so the rest of you can either come inside with me to watch, or look around the museum."

"I'm going in with you," said Jake.

"That's what we're here for," said Sarah as she followed Virg and Jake around to the back of the tank and up onto it. Virg opened a hatch and one by one they climbed inside. Virg retrieved a couple of candles from the tool box and lit them.

"How long?" asked Jake after several hours of watching Virg remove, examine, and then replace parts.

"I know this is boring, but necessary, so maybe you really should go out and look around the museum," said Virg.

"I'm good," said Jake.

"I think what you're doing is fascinating," said Sarah.

"All right, partners, I still have a way to go, but so far it's looking good," said Virg.

"I knew it," said Jake.

It would be nearly four hours before the three of them came out and stood in front of the tank. All three were smudged with grease and dirt, and their hands were blackened from holding wrenches and parts. Virg stretched her arms over her head to loosen up after being in cramped quarters for so long. Ellen joined them as they stood back and admired the tank. Ellen had earlier fetched two containers of cooking oil from the VW and poured them into the tank at Virg's direction.

"Let me get the battery and give this thing a go," said Virg who went out to the van, trailed by Jake and Sarah. A little while later they were back, and Virg installed the battery. When she was done she opened the forward hatch and stuck her head out.

"So, is it ready to fire up?" asked Jake from beside her.

"I think so, but I just need to figure out a few things first," said Virg.

"I'm coming in," said Sarah who was on top straddling the barrel. She scrambled down and took up a position with Jake and Virg.

"This is always a tense moment," said Virg as she stared at the controls.

"Alright, so let's do it," said Jake, waiting for her to do something.

"Well, I'm a little embarrassed here," said Virg.

"Why?" asked Jake.

"I'm not really sure how to start this thing, and worse, I have no idea how to drive a tank even if we did get it to run," said Virg.

"No worry, Virg, I've read about tanks, so let's start it up and drive this sucker out of here," said Jake confidently.

"So, what, that black button with the red flecks?" asked Virg, studying the controls.

"You might turn the key on first," said Jake who held up a key he had found earlier in the day and inserted it. Virg turned it on. A light came on in one of the gauges.

"So I'll push the starter," said Virg reaching for it.

"No, wait, the throttle needs to be back a bit, let's try this," said Jake.

"What about the choke?" asked Virg.

"No choke, this is diesel," said Jake.

"Oh right, I knew that."

"Now, just hold down on the starter until it fires," said Jake. Virg held down on the starting button. An almost sickening grinding noise mixed with the squeal of metal against metal was followed by a few loud pops. The grinding, squealing and pops went on for what seemed forever before a thundering roar blasted soot and black smoke high into the air from the exhaust as the engine sprang to life. Ellen covered her ears as she retreated from the deafening roar. At the same time she was yelling at the top of her lungs.

"Waaaahooooo!" she screamed, even though those inside could not hear her over the din.

"Oh my god, this fucking thing runs!" shouted Virg. "Ooops, sorry about my language."

"What? OK, so, I have it in neutral," said Jake. "I'm putting it in gear with this lever, we'll start in first. Good. Now, I'm going to release the main clutch with this lever and then we should start out. So, to turn, I release either the left clutch or the right clutch. Left clutch shifts power to the right track and pulls us around to the left. Same idea to go right. Then we just keep pulling one lever or the other to steer. Simple."

"Yeah, right, simple, so why don't you work the levers and I'll stick my head out and shout down directions because I don't see a window," said Virg.

"It has what looks like a periscope," said Jake.

"I don't see it," said Virg.

"It looks pretty dirty," said Jake who tried it. "Just do what you said and tell me which direction to go and by how much."

"Alright, I'm ready, so let's go," said Virg who stuck her head out of the hatch. Ellen was off to the side with her hands held tightly over her ears.

"Here we go, I'm engaging," said Jake who very slowly released the clutch.

The huge tank started forward and, after Virg shouted 'hard left', it made a sharp turn toward the left. Out toward the exit the monster charged, with Ellen trotting behind cheering with her fists waving in the air. Virg's head was the only sign of human occupation as she looked forward and occasionally turned to bark a command down to Jake. The tank would then make a slight course correction. It rumbled noisily along, its metal cleats sending a cacophony of sharp clanks that almost overcame the deafening roar of the engine. Out the main door it rattled, miraculously missing the doorframe by inches. It charged straight down the steps as if they were a ramp just made for it. As it neared the bottom Virg yelled a desperate order to Jake and the tank made an attempt to turn left to avoid the bus. It almost did. One track rode up onto the front of the bus, flattening it like the tip of a beer can under foot. A few yards past the bus the tank came to a halt and Virg climbed quickly up onto the deck and walked back to survey the damage.

106

"I loved that bus!" shouted Virg. "But I guess we won't be using it again!"

Ellen was running down the steps toward the flattened van, holding her hand over her mouth to hide the laughter. When Virg saw her she too was unable to hold back and she burst into laughter with Ellen. Jake and Sarah, who were now up on deck, were uncertain what to do or say as they stared at the pitiful bus that looked like a squashed bug.

"Hop aboard, Ellen!" shouted Virg over the loudly idling tank with its exhaust spewing hot blue and black smoke high into the air. Ellen climbed up onto the tank and peered inside after Jake and Sarah had gone below. Seeing how crowded it was, she climbed up onto the gun turret where she sat with her feet dangling on either side of the barrel.

"Dirty work," Ellen quipped as she looked down at Virg who had grease and dirt all over her.

"OK, we're out of here," said Virg as she climbed down into the tank. "Jake, throw this sucker in second....no, third, and give her some gas....uh, cooking oil!"

"Lighthouse, here we come!" shouted Ellen, waving one arm in the air and swinging her legs together around the barrel as if she were on a horse as the tank lurched forward. It charged across the parking lot and lined up on the two ruts in the roadway back to West Hill. Metal screaming against metal, engine roaring like a dragon, it charged along, crushing everything in its path.

Chapter Ten

"What was that?" asked Sandra.

"I'm not sure but it came from down below," said Lucinda, as everyone in the room grew silent.

"Someone's out there!" said Sandra, when she heard it again.

"Oh crap, are they here already?" asked Lucinda, who ran quickly outside and peered over the rail.

"Hi, I'm Eric," came a young man's voice from midway up the second stairway, his face barely visible from above.

"Come on up," said Lucinda, motioning to the young man.

"Eric, what are you doing here?" asked Sandra who had joined her at the rail.

"They're coming!" said Eric, out of breath as he appeared in front of them.

"The men from the village?" asked Lucinda.

"Yes!" he replied.

"How many?" asked Sandra.

"It could be most of the men in the village," he replied. "I heard them say they're going to bring everyone back for punishment."

"When?" asked Lucinda.

"I don't know, but they could be on their way already," he replied.

"What are we going to do?" asked Sandra.

"We need to go to West Hill," said Lucinda. "We have a bunker there with a locked steel door."

"They must know that crossing the fence means severe punishment for them too," said John who just arrived after overhearing most of the conversation.

"Yes, but they said that if everyone crosses, there would be no one left to turn them in," said Eric.

"I guess that's true since they're the ones who turn offenders in," said John.

"And in their current state of mind we'll never be able to reason with them," said Lucinda.

"Alright, so let's get out of here, pronto," said Brit.

"What about the others at the museum?" asked Sandra.

"They'll be safe as long as they stay there," said Lucinda.

"How far is it to the other place...the West Hill?" asked John.

"A half hour walk," said Lucinda.

"I don't think Bob will be able to travel that far and we can't carry him," said Sandra.

"Then we'll have to leave him here," said Lucinda. "Surely the villagers won't hurt him since he came over to do the same thing."

"That's sort of what I thought too, but I can't be sure, so I can't leave him," said Sandra with a crack in her voice.

"We have to travel fast and we can't have anyone slow us down," said Lucinda.

"I know that, so you'll go without me, we'll be OK," said Sandra, turning to go into the room where Bob was sleeping.

"They could haul you back to the village," said Brit, who followed her into the room.

"Maybe, but I simply won't leave Bob here by himself," said Sandra.

"Alright, I understand, so we'll have to arrange for your re-capture after Jake blows up the lighthouse," said Brit, placing her hand on Sandra's back, then leaving.

"I really don't think they'll hurt us," said Sandra. "So don't worry, just go."

"Alright, let's hurry, we need a head start since we're not going to be as fast as those men," said Lucinda from down the hall.

"I know," said Brit who ran down the hall past Lucinda and led everyone down the stairs.

"Did you say a half hour?" asked John, as the troupe reached ground level and started trotting down the trail to West Hill in single file.

"Fifteen minutes if we run," said Brit.

"Well, I can't run very fast, never could, so everyone else go ahead, I'll catch up" said Lucinda.

"No, we're not leaving anyone behind, Lucinda, we'll move as fast as you do, so get out in front and just run, jog or shuffle as fast as you can and we'll follow," said Brit.

"I'm already starting to get winded just coming down the stairs," said Lucinda who lumbered out into the lead. Behind her, the others followed like an obedient brood of ducklings after their waddling mother.

"I can't believe we're running from what have been our friends and neighbors for our entire lives," said Martha, who was just behind John.

"There's nothing more mindless than a mob who reinforce one another in their quest," said Brit, who brought up the rear, just behind Martha.

"But these were our friends and neighbors," said Martha.

"I know, but a mob is blind to reason, and their sheer number is comforting, convincing one another that what they are doing is right," said Brit.

"How do you know all of this?" asked Martha.

"It's in the books," said Brit. "They tell how blindly following strong beliefs can trample the innocent and ignore logic and reason."

"That's scary," said Martha.

"Especially when others get hurt," said Brit.

"But it's not what we have been taught and told in The Message," said Martha.

"Martha, you were told a lot of things that were intended to keep you in line," said Brit.

"This is all very confusing," said Martha.

"Actually, the voice in The Tower who is your version of God, is Chandler, who is a man that I knew personally at one time," said Brit. "Believe me, he's not God."

"There is so much I have been taught that tells me something different," said Martha.

"I know that," said Brit.

"I wonder if Jake has already gone to The Tower with this tank?" asked Martha.

"They wouldn't have had time to get there, assuming they even got the tank to run," said Lucinda who had now dropped back to where Brit was at the end of the procession. By now she was breathing heavily and Eric was in the lead.

"What happens if he does blow up The Tower?" asked John.

"I'm not sure anyone knows at this point," said Lucinda.

"I guess hiding in your bunker is our plan right now," said John.

"It's our only plan at the moment," Lucinda wheezed as she began to fall farther behind.

"We're almost there Lucinda, I can see the outline of a building up ahead through the trees!" said Brit.

"Finally," said Lucinda who stopped on the trail to catch her breath.

"Over there!" said Brit, who had taken the lead and steered them left toward an open garage bay near the far end of the complex. The sound of voices could be heard from within as they approached.

"Hi!" shouted Jake when he saw Brit. "Why is everyone here, and why are you out of breath?"

"A mob from the village is coming," said Brit.

"Oh no..... how close?" asked Ellen from in front of the huge green machine that dominated the interior of the garage. As everyone arrived, they congregated in front of the tank and just stared at its imposing presence.

"We're not sure, but Eric warned us they were coming, so we ran here thinking that the bunker would be a good place to hide out," said Brit.

"Eric?" asked Ellen.

"That's me," said Eric, holding up his hand and stepping forward.

"Well, one thing is for sure, we can't be here when they arrive," said Lucinda, who finally arrived and immediately leaned against the building to keep from falling down.

"They're very angry," Eric confirmed.

"Two choices....the bunker or we take the tank to the lighthouse," said Ellen.

"We can't get ourselves trapped in the bunker since it's not stocked," said Virg.

"You're right, so it's the lighthouse," said Ellen.

"Then we need to leave immediately," said Jake.

"Alright, but can everyone get into this thing?" asked Brit.

"No, only the three operators will fit inside, but there's room on top," said Jake.

"OK, is this thing ready Virg?" asked Ellen.

"It is," said Virg, whose head was poking out from the tank's forward hatch.

"OK then, everyone hop on!" said Jake.

"Are you sure we can we all fit on it?" asked Brit.

"Well, do you want to stay here?" asked Ellen.

"Let's pile on then," said Brit as she began looking for a way to climb up.

"Try to stay near the rear of the tank because we're going to smash over the fence on the way, and the front will not be the best place to be when we do that," said Jake who was now on deck and getting ready to slip past Virg into the tank. Sarah was already inside.

"Alright, is everyone on?" asked Brit once Lucinda had been helped up onto the rear deck.

"Where's Sandra?" asked Ellen, who was doing a head count of those on board.

"She wouldn't leave Bob and we couldn't bring him along in his condition," said Lucinda.

"Let's hope she'll be OK," said Ellen. "Alright Virg, it looks like we're all on board."

"Everyone cover their ears!" shouted Virg, who quickly ducked below and cranked the engine. It soon boomed to life, filling the garage with an ear splitting roar and a thick cloud of smoke. Those on deck held their hands tightly over their ears. A moment later the big rig lurched forward out of the garage and spun to the left toward the fence.

"I guess this is really going to happen!" shouted Lucinda over the roar.

"Well, his plan has worked so far!" Ellen shouted back.

"Sarah, raise the barrel," said Jake.

"Why?" asked Sarah from up inside the turret.

"It has to be higher than the fence when we crash over it," said Jake.

"Oh, right, good thinking," said Sarah, who began cranking the barrel up.

"We should be to the fence shortly," said Virg, as she sat down next to Jake who was glued to the tiny window with a hand on each brake lever as he steered them along.

"I cleaned the glass on this periscope but I still can't see all that clearly," said Jake.

"Can you see well enough or should I pop my head out again?" asked Virg.

"No, you don't want your head out when we hit the fence," said Jake. "In fact, do pop your head out now for a second to warn the others to huddle behind the turret and cover their heads.

"OK! Everyone crowd together behind the turret and cover your heads, we're going to crash over the electric fence!" she shouted.

"Great," said Jake. "Now secure the hatch."

"How far to the lighthouse after the fence?" she asked as she pulled the hatch shut.

"About five miles I think, and the highway goes all the way there, so it should be smooth sailing," he replied.

"Smooth sailing?" she asked.

"An old mariners term," said Jake.

"I know.... I'm asking how far because this tank burns a lot of fuel and I'm hoping we don't run out."

"We won't," said Jake.

"The eternal optimism of youth," said Virg.

"No worry," said Jake confidently.

"What if the lighthouse is too tough to take out with this cannon, or what if the shells don't fire after all these years," said Virg.

"Think only positive thoughts," said Jake.

"I'm trying," said Virg.

"OK, there's the fence, so get reaaaaaa......" Jake started to say just as a tremendous explosion of sparks lit up the area and the tank ploughed right over the fence and left it lying flat behind them. Small fires were everywhere in their wake. Those on deck had covered their heads with their arms and those who were not on their knees were now flat on the deck. A few were in the fetal position after sparks had showered down around them.

"Amazing," Virg confirmed after opening the hatch and peeking back past the turret to witness the devastation.

"Is everyone still on board and well?" asked Jake.

"Is everyone still on!" shouted Virg.

"We're shaken, but everyone is still on!" shouted Ellen.

"So much for the dreaded fence," said Jake without breaking his concentration on the road ahead.

Chapter Eleven

"They must all be brought back and punished!" shouted Len who was standing on a large wooden table in the village square. A crowd of men filled every bare piece of earth.

"But it is forbidden to cross the fence, so how can we do that!" someone shouted from somewhere in the crowd.

"The Message is clear, they must be punished, and the only way to do that is to cross the fence and bring them back," said Len. "I have thought about this matter a lot and concluded that our mission is just and right and it outweighs the sin of crossing. The good of seeing the rules of The Message prevail and will cleanse us of the wrong."

"Besides, if we all go, who will report us?" asked someone.

"The women," said someone.

"No, the women will do as they're told and will not report us," said Len.

"All men will go?" came a voice from the rear of an older man who could barely stand upright.

"All able men," said Len.

"But how do you know we will not all be eventually punished?" came the first voice.

"Because we have been the ones responsible for upholding the rules of The Message," said Len. "It is we who have reported the violations that resulted in the handing out of punishments. We reported the offenders so the Helper could haul them away. It is we who carry the power to enforce The Message. No punishment has ever been delivered by an outsider, and the Helper only comes to insure that the punishment is completed."

"But the Helper came yesterday to get Jake and Sarah, and we did not have anything to do with that," came a voice.

"That was a special case where Jake and Sarah ran away from the Enlightenment," said Len. "It was not a sin committed within the village. So WE will pass judgment on ourselves for crossing and WE will find our mission just. It is what we must do to bring back the offenders, and there will be no punishments for doing what is right." There was a lengthy silence before anyone spoke.

"I believe what you say is correct," said a man, who then turned to face the crowd.

"Len is correct!" the man shouted. "It has always been our duty to enforce The Message, so we must bring back those who have sinned against it. The good of enforcing the rules of The Message outweighs the bad of crossing the fence."

"Are there dissenters?" asked Len, followed by a short hesitation before the crowd cheered their approval.

"When do we cross?" came a voice from the back.

"We will gather our spears, then we will go," said Len. Again there was a brief hesitation, then an increase in conversations.

"Does everyone agree that we must go?" asked Len who sensed the hesitation.

"All hands for going!" he shouted when no one answered. Many hands shot up, then a few more and finally most were raised.

"It is agreed then, we will return here with our spears, then leave immediately!" Len shouted. The men dispersed, but clearly, Len's high level of enthusiasm was not shared by everyone.

A short time later, the men assembled in the open area at the center of the village carrying long pointed sticks, some with sharp rocks tied to the end. It was clear that the crowd was a little smaller and that everyone that was supposed to be there, was not there. But no one questioned why some did not reassemble, nor did they question the mandate that Len had assumed existed.

"We must cross the fence carefully!" shouted Len who held up his spear. "We must not touch the fence as we pass under. OK...let's go!" A shout went up from the half dozen or so who were nearest to him. The mob then filed out onto the trail single file and began trotting at a pace set by Len who was out front.

Ten minutes later they came to the fence and one by one they crawled under. Many appeared visibly shaken by the sight of the two bodies that lay nearby. On the other side they assembled briefly in a clearing, then fanned out and began working their way toward the East Hill complex which they soon discovered. After forming up there, they climbed the stairs and searched the complex. It was not long before one of Len's followers opened the door to find Bob and Sandra. He was lying in a cot with Sandra sitting calmly in a chair next to him. The man shouted for Len to come, and soon, a small crowd had assembled in the hallway. Bob slowly sat up in bed and Sandra stood next to the bed holding his hand. Len glared at Sandra in anger.

"So, you came for us," said Bob calmly.

"We came for Sandra," said Len.

"But you too have crossed the fence," said Sandra.

"Our mission is just, so our sin is washed clean," said Len.

"Then my mission was also just," said Bob.

"It is true Bob, your mission was just, it is Sandra who is the offending one and who must face punishment!" said Len.

"No, I believe we are all offenders, and all of us face the same guilt," said Bob.

"Sandra's crimes are the greatest," said Len.

"That is not true, Len, and I will not let you....." Bob began to say as he tried to get up, then fell back, grimacing in pain.

"Who did this to you?" asked Len who now focused on the blood stained bandages.

"Those who live on this side," said Bob.

"How did they do such a thing?" he asked.

"They used a stick that shot fire and little black rocks," said Bob.

"They have more of these sticks, and much bigger sticks," Sandra lied.

"Take her!" said Len angrily, as two of his close followers reached for Sandra. But Bob lurched off the bed and pushed them into Len. All four landed in a heap on the floor as another of Len's followers came in and helped pin Bob to the floor. Len got to his feet.

"Tie her up," said Len. "We will take Sandra back to the

village and summon the Helper, but not until we find the others who have sinned."

"No, Len, your mission is wrong...." said Bob who struggled against the two men.

"Where are the others?" asked Len.

"They left and we do not know where they went," said Sandra whose arms were now tied behind her back.

"We will find them," said Len. "Tie up Bob too, we will deal with him later."

Len left the room with both Sandra and Bob tied together. He led the others down the steps where the rest of the mob was assembled.

"We will find the others!" shouted Len when he reached the ground.

"There is a well worn path going that way," said someone pointing west.

"Are there any other trails?" he asked.

"Yes, but this one seems to be the main trail out of here," was the answer.

"Alright, that's where we will go," said Len who started out on the trail in a fast jog. Soon everyone was strung out along the pathway to West Hill in full gallup, with some unenthusiastically trailing behind.

A while later they arrived at West Hill and assembled in front of it before fanning out to search the building. After the search was complete and having found no one, they reassembled.

"It looks like they were here not long ago," said Len.

"There are very strange marks cutting deep into the ground," said one of the men, pointing at the tank tracks.

"The marks go in both directions," said another, pointing one way, then the other.

"This way leads to The Tower," said Len.

"Do you think they would go to The Tower and harm it?" asked another.

"I do not know, but The Tower is inside the fence, so they must cross the fence to reach it," said Len. "Perhaps we will find it at the fence." He waved for them to follow. As he ran ahead most did not follow, so he stopped and looked back at them.

"What makes these marks?" asked someone.

"I do not know," said Len.

"Should we look for footprints of those we seek?" asked another.

"No, we will follow these marks," said Len, avoiding the question since no footprints were visible. He waved for them to follow but only a few started, but stopped when they realized that most were not moving.

"It is something very big and very heavy," said yet another man.

"Perhaps they ride on the thing that makes these marks," said another.

"If they do, it does not matter, for we are the blessed ones on a righteous mission," said Len. "We will not be afraid, for we will come to no harm." They were looking at one another and some were buzzing with questions. But several stepped forward.

"Len is right, we must continue to pursue those we seek because we are the righteous ones," announced one of the men. Again they were looking at one another and buzzing with questions, but a few more stepped forward, and finally everyone cautiously began to walk toward where Len was pointing.

Len raised his fist and turned to run. The men followed, some waving their pointed sticks in the air. But the ugly marks in the ground were something they had never seen before and it made most of them feel very uneasy.

Through the forest they followed the tracks. Whatever it was, it was big and powerful. Uneasiness now gained traction within the mob. Even the divine optimism of those few who had followed Len's lead was eroding. Whispers among them were spreading.

Soon, they came to the fence, or what was left of it. The group slowly caught up with Len and stood in silence as they looked upon the twisted remains of the fence, lain flat and torn loose on both sides. There was blackened brush and trees testifying to the eruption of fire that must have occurred as the fence was crushed by this unknown monster that carried those they pursued.

"It is big and very powerful," one man said finally, looking at Len and waiting for him to speak.

"Our mission is clear, and its power cannot hurt us, for we are not the evil ones," Len declared. "We are the divine ones. We are the protected ones. We cannot be harmed."

"Is this thing that we follow on its way to The Tower?" asked someone. There was some hesitation as Len thought for a moment about what to say.

"Perhaps, but The Tower cannot be harmed," he nodded with a gesture. "This much I know."

"What if The Tower cannot prevail?" asked a man far back in the crowd.

"The Tower is all powerful, and even this thing we follow will pale before it," said Len. "The Tower will protect us!"

Len's voice had now risen to a shout and he raised his fist and stepped forward briskly over the flattened fence and down the roadway. His faithful few took up his sprite pace, but the vast majority followed more timidly and began to string out behind. The whispering continued to grow among them as they settled into a jog, their minds now occupied by thoughts of this unfathomable monster that they followed.

Chapter Twelve

They were all beginning to get weary on the tank's deck as it charged along the road. The jostling and hard surface made riding uncomfortable. But less than an hour after they began their journey they rumbled to a halt at the top of the same hill that Jake and Sarah had climbed on that first day of their escape. They sat there while Jake thought about what to do next.

"The road ends near the lighthouse," said Jake. "It's just across the water from it." Jake climbed up next to Virg where he could see ahead better, and strained to see through tiny breaks in the trees.

"Can we get an open shot from down there?" asked Virg.

"Yes, I'm sure we can, but we'll have to start getting ready just in case Chandler has some kind of defense that we're not aware of," said Jake.

"OK, so maybe Sarah should get one of those shells out of its case," said Virg.

"You're right.....Sarah, get a shell and load it," said Jake.

"I know, I heard," said Sarah who was already opening a canister.

"Just like we discussed back in West Hill," said Jake.

"I know, I've got this," said Sarah who carefully cradled the heavy shell as she loaded it into the chamber, then slammed the lever shut.

"Alright, I guess we're ready," said Jake.

"Then let's go," said Virg who sat down. Jake shoved it in gear and released the main clutch. The tank lurched forward sending John off the rear where he had been perched precariously the entire trip. He jumped to his feet and started running after the big machine. As they rumbled along he pulled himself back on with the help of Brit.

"It's just around the bend," said Jake as he peered through the little window and guided the tank down the hill.

"Chandler will definitely hear this thing coming," said Virg.

"Right, so he'll be waiting for us, but I doubt very seriously whether he will expect to see a tank," said Jake.

"And he really has no defense, does he?" asked Virg. "This is a lighthouse, not a fort."

"Not to worry, we definitely have the advantage," said Jake.

"I hope so, and I wonder if he'll freak out when he sees a three hundred year old tank?" asked Virg.

"Either freak out or laugh histerically," said Jake.

"OK....there....I can see it now," said Virg, who was standing with her head sticking out of the hatch.

"Ready Sarah?" asked Jake.

"Yes, I have my top hatch open and, wow..... look...... the

target is in sight!" said Sarah.

"Great, we'll have a wide open shot!" said Jake who had not taken his eyes off the road nor his hands from the steering levers.

The lighthouse loomed ahead as the road abruptly stopped short of the lagoon. The tank rattled to a halt, its cannon aimed directly at the lighthouse. Dust and smoke now drifted past it and slowly disappeared into the lagoon. Virg turned off the engine.

"Sarah, get the dome in the crosshairs," said Jake. "We want to try to knock it off with the first shell."

"I'll aim at the base of the dome," she replied.

"So is it time to warn him?" asked Virg.

"Yes," said Jake.

"Ellen, it's time!" shouted Virg who had her head craned around to see her.

"Luke will do the honors as we agreed," said Ellen.

"Alright, let's do it," said Virg. But before Luke could give his speech, a loud voice came from the lighthouse.

"You will be destroyed!" boomed Chandler's voice in an ominous baritone.

"Chandler, this is Luke.....I know you're completely defenseless!" shouted Luke through cupped hands.

"Luke, you are a traitor, and you have no idea what I am capable of!" said Chandler in that same booming baritone.

"I do know what you have....nothing....so now, we need you to agree to denounce your religious program and declare your Tower as just an obsolete lighthouse!" said Luke.

"Or you'll do what?" asked Chandler.

"Decapitate the lighthouse," said Luke.

"That old relic couldn't decapitate a sunflower," said Chandler.

127

"I'll give you to three to agree to our terms!" shouted Luke.

"I tremble!" came the reply that ended with a loud laugh.

"Everyone get off the tank and cover your ears!" shouted Jake after poking his head out past Virg. A moment later Ellen shouted the all clear.

"Three.....two......one......!" shouted Luke who waited a moment in case Chandler responded, then looked to Jake and nodded. He then looked up at Sarah.

"Now?" asked Sarah.

"Now!" shouted Jake. A second later there was a gigantic boom and the tank shuddered violently, moving backward a few feet, shaking dust from itself and raising dust in the surrounding area. There were screams, as the entire top of the lighthouse literally evaporated into a shower of glass, brick and dust. Pieces flew everywhere, including a few that landed near the tank. When it had cleared, only the jagged top of the lighthouse remained. Debris was distributed liberally over the grass apron around the lighthouse and a few stray pieces were still fluttering to the ground and sprinkling into the lagoon with little splashes.

"Oh.... my.... god!" exclaimed Ellen, who stared at the damage in disbelief. "Oh.... my.... god!" she repeated. There was then complete silence as everyone gaped at the sight.

"I guess it was old and brittle," said Virg. "So it came apart like a gingerbread house."

"Luke, ask Chandler to open that green door," said Jake who was now up on deck studying the damage.

"Chandler, unlock the door so we can come in," shouted Luke. There was no reply, and they waited several minutes before Jake finally spoke again.

"Do you think it's locked?" asked Jake.

"It's always locked, but I suspect that Ed is inside and I have no idea how he is responding to this," said Luke.

"OK, Chandler, we're going to have to blow it off!" shouted Luke. After several minutes there was no reply and the door remained shut.

"Should we blow it off?" asked Jake.

"I wonder if we should go over and try it first," said Virg.

"We could, but it will be locked," said Luke.

"What about Ed?" asked Jake.

"I know him, he'll wait for Chandler to decide," said Luke.

"Well, we need to get inside that lighthouse to end this," said Virg.

"I know, so maybe blowing it off is the only option now," said Luke.

"Jake?" asked Virg, turning to him.

"Sarah, get another shell and line up on that door," said Jake.

"I'm way ahead of you, I've already loaded one," said Sarah from the turret. "Give me a second to line up the shot."

"Luke, give final warning to him that the door is coming off," said Jake.

"Chandler, on three, the door will be history!" shouted Luke through cupped hands. There was no answer. They waited several more minutes.

"Sarah?" asked Jake.

"I'm ready" said Sarah.

"Luke?" asked Jake.

"Three....two.....one," shouted Luke.

"Everyone get clear and cover their ears again!" shouted Jake.

A moment later, there was the same shuddering, dust raising shock that knocked the tank back another foot or two. The door to the lighthouse together with a sizable chunk of the wall around it exploded into another shower of debris, leaving a gaping hole in the side of the lighthouse. The green door flipped through the air like a playing card and came to rest against a tree.

"I think we can walk in now, so let's get over there," said Ellen.

"There's a shallow marsh at the end of this inlet where we can cross," said Luke pointing to their right.

"We'll get wet," said Virg as she and the entire contingent started toward the end of the inlet.

"Don't be afraid of a little water considering what we just did," said Jake who charged into the lead with Sarah right beside him.

Soon they were strung out in a line, making their way across the shallows of the marsh and emerging a few minutes later on the opposite bank. The children up on the hill were still watching, not moving or speaking. They were just staring at what was left of their symbol of ultimate power. After crossing the wooden bridge to the lighthouse, everyone was soon assembled near the gaping hole in its side.

"Chandler?....Ed?" asked Luke who stood in the jagged hole peering into the dark interior. Again, there was no answer.

"You'll have to go in," said Ellen.

"I know," said Luke.

He stepped forward cautiously before wading through the debris and disappearing inside. They waited. A few minutes later he appeared in the opening and waved for them to enter. Lit only by the gaping hole, it was dark inside and everyone had to wait a moment for their eyes to adjust before they could see clearly. A wall of electronic equipment covered the far wall of the room. Positioned in front of the console was a large metal box with a glass dome on top and the head of a man inside. His head was faced away from them. As they stood watching, the dome with the man's head inside rotated around toward them. Chandler's eyes moved from side to side as he sized them up. To their right, slowly coming down the stairs was a very large man. They watched as he stopped and sat down on the steps.

"Welcome to my personal prison," came a voice from above. The lips on the head were not moving and they all looked up when they heard the voice. A few of them looked toward the man on the steps thinking it might be him.

"That's Ed, but the voice is Chandler's," said Luke, pointing to Chandler. All eyes returned to Chandler.

"Do you remember me Chandler?" asked Ellen who had led the procession behind Luke and now stepped out in front of him.

"Ellen...... you were with Shannon's group at her immortality event," came the voice after a long pause, this time it was not in the rich baritone, but in a soft friendly tenor.

"Virg, Brit and Lucinda are here too," said Ellen, motioning behind her as the head rotated to scan the crowd. The three of them stepped out for him to see.

"I remember, yes, but I don't know everyone here," came the voice.

"This is Jake and Sarah, the students who ran away from your school and crossed the fence," said Luke.

"The seeds of insurrection," said Chandler.

"They were books and ideas, not weapons," said Jake. Chandler looked at him but did not reply.

"That put me in the position of having to choose between you and reason," said Luke.

"And you chose insurrection," said Chandler.

"No, I chose reason," said Luke.

"Alright, Chandler, so we've heard about the Controllers and your reason for establishing this sort of religion for the village," said Ellen.

"Religion?" Chandler repeated. "Yes, I suppose that's what it is, or was."

"But it was our belief, following a suggestion from Jake, that in order to break your iron grip on the village, this lighthouse, aka The Tower, would have to be destroyed," said Ellen.

"It's true, this structure plays a very significant role in their belief system and what you have just done will have a dramatic impact on their beliefs," said Chandler. "But I suspect that it won't be quite as simple as knocking the top off of their religious icon."

"Perhaps, but it's a start," said Ellen.

"Why didn't you come to me first, before you somehow dusted off that World War II relic and came here with fire in your eyes?" he asked.

"Seriously, Chandler, would you have caved if we came with our hats in our hands?" asked Luke.

"No, I suppose not, because I had no idea that you or anyone else around here would have the power to force me to do anything," said Chandler.

"Neither did I until I met Jake," said Luke.

"Jake? So he's the ten year old boy?" asked Chandler.

"Yes, and there's a certain strength in youth that sees past obstacles," said Luke.

"But a ten year old?" asked Chandler.

"Here's the thing, Chandler, you've created a culture of fear and oppression that controlled the behavior of an entire village, with severe penalties for those who disobeyed the rules," said Ellen.

"But there are two good reasons behind my motivation to do this," said Chandler. "First of all, it's highly unlikely that the original village would have voluntarily obeyed the rules of the Controllers by mere persuasion, which would have been much to their sorrow. I felt that my religion would be a much more effective way to achieve compliance. And second of all, I doubt if you knew the purpose of this prison, and therefore who these villagers were."

"I think we do know, but go ahead," said Ellen.

"This was one of many of what could be characterized as concentration camps," said Chandler. "These were people obsessed with conspiracy theories and ultimately, insurrection of a standing government."

"Yes, we are aware of the concentration camps and of who these prisoners were before the war, but that was many generations ago," said Ellen.

"That's true, but in the beginning, these people were not inclined to follow any rules," said Chandler. "And the women played an almost controlling role in this belief system."

"That I didn't know," said Ellen.

"That's why I cast women in subservient roles, where they

were excluded from decision making," said Chandler.

"But you made no adjustments to your rules over time, even though the original insurrectionists, or their beliefs, no longer existed," said Ellen.

"Which is another reason to break up this little charade," said Jake.

"It wasn't a charade," said Chandler who now glared at Jake.

"We also think that the research facilities that we've lived in for the past two hundred years is where the gate keepers for this concentration camp lived," said Ellen.

"I'm sure that's true," said Chandler. "But Ellen, you four women knew me from before the war, and you knew I meant only to create a method for achieving immortality and that I was not a bad person then, and I am not a bad person now."

"We did know you then, but the more we've heard about what you created here, the more we believed that what you were now doing was unnecessarily oppressive and needed to be stopped," said Ellen.

"Considering what I just told you about the Controllers and the people in the village, do you still think it was oppressive?" asked Chandler.

"Yes we do," said Ellen. "First of all, it's been many generations, and I would be shocked if any of the villagers today even knew what an insurrectionist was."

"I don't, and I don't know of anyone in the village who would either," said John from the rear.

"OK, fine, but what about the need to follow the dictates of the Controllers?" asked Chandler.

"Look, it's been two hundred years, and we have never seen

nor heard from these so-called Controllers in all that time," said Ellen.

"That's because of my sort of religion," said Chandler. "Believe me, they exist."

"Alright, let's say they do, but maybe now, after two centuries, their rules are no longer being enforced, or they've changed their rules and are more tolerant than they were," said Ellen.

"Well, now that you've trashed my local means of compliance, we may find out if they still exist and if they enforce them," said Chandler.

"Let's face it, your methods were barbaric in intent, even though in practice, because of Ed's kind heart, they weren't," said Luke.

"What do you mean, Ed's kind heart?" asked Chandler.

"Well, no one was ever killed or banished into the wilderness," said Ed, who stood up and came over to them. He was nearly seven feet tall and towered over everyone like a giant.

"You lied to me?" asked Chandler.

"I had to," said Ed. "From the very beginning, I was unable to do what you said I had to do, so I started a colony in the prison complex over the hill."

"But then you never told the villagers that they would not be banished or thrown into the pit.... right?" asked Chandler.

"No, that's right, I never told them what I was really doing, and so they continued to be terrified of me," said Ed. "They never knew where I actually took offenders."

"And that's my point, Chandler," said Luke. "They thought they were being banished, or in some cases, thrown to their death into this dreaded pit of yours, so the fear was always there."

"Alright, but it worked, even though Ed was a traitor, just like you, Luke," said Chandler.

"Don't you see, Chandler, you really are still a bad man for continuing this religion of fear," said Luke. "What you continued to do was just as bad psychologically as if it were actually true. And thanks only to Ed, it was not true."

"Ed, since Chandler could not be at the village when you handed out punishments, why didn't you just ignore the punishments in the first place?" asked Ellen.

"Because at first we were dealing with a very obstinate and potentially dangerous crowd, and in fact I had to carry a gun for nearly a decade," said Ed. "And after that there were more and more snitches who were really the ones who would identify offenders. They actually wanted to see the offenders hauled away for punishment."

"So the village kept you honest," said Chandler.

"Honest is not the word I would use," said Ed.

"So even though Ed tried his best to be kind, his presence clearly struck fear in our hearts and we essentially lived under a reign of terror," said Jake. "That's why I felt a need to break the spell you had over them and free them of this oppression."

"This ten year old was behind all of this?" asked Chandler.

"Yes he was, and getting a tank to blow up this lighthouse was entirely his idea," said Luke. "He literally pushed us into carrying it out."

"So a ten year old took me down?" asked Chandler.

"With our help," said Ellen.

"Let me understand the current situation, now that I'm busted," said Chandler. "Ed has always taken offenders to a safe and relatively comfortable place for them to live out their lives. But my rules were still followed, even to this day."

"I call this comfortable place Hotel Paradise," said Ed. "And, yes, the village continued to live under a reign of terror as Jake has characterized it. I played the villain to the very end."

"Hotel Paradise.....amazing......actually now that it's all over for me, it makes me feel better about how this whole thing turned out," said Chandler. "I did feel that my penalties were necessary, but, yes, I'll admit they were cruel. And I guess I should have realized that the villagers were not the same people that were put in prison before the war. So, Ed, I guess you saved me from myself."

"I just did what my conscience allowed," said Ed. "And I did play the Helper right up until yesterday."

"I've never been to the prison complex, Ed, so what's it like there?" asked Luke.

"Well, it's a complex of a half dozen buildings with electricity, water and sewage disposal, almost like a modern city," said Ed. "Over the years the 'inmates' from the village have made a lot of improvements, and the surrounding area had been used for farming, so some of that has been reclaimed. They have a farmers market on Sundays. Of course it can be easily seen by the Controller's satellites, but as we all know, they have never come by here to check. Today there are almost five hundred residents in Hotel Paradise."

"I thought mostly men were sentenced to death or banished, so is it mostly men?" asked Jake.

"No, it's actually quite diverse with nearly equal numbers of males and females," said Ed. "During the early years there were actually more women than men who openly defied Chandler's rules. So, over the years, children have been born."

"Do they have a school?" asked Jake.

"Yes, but we only have a limited number of books, so it's quite basic," said Ed.

"And Chandler's religion is left behind at the village?" asked Jake.

"Yes, and actually I developed a special set of rules for them to follow," said Ed. "Basically the golden rules."

"And the residents of Hotel Paradise never wanted to come back to the village?" asked Ellen.

"Would you?" asked Ed.

"No, I guess not," said Ellen.

"What about coming back to rebel against Chandler's dictatorial rule?" asked Jake.

"Wait, dictatorial rule?" Chandler mumbled.

"There has been occasional talk there about freeing the village, but over the years the population has had less and less attachment to it, so pressure from the newer inductees has never been enough to prompt sufficient interest in sparking a rebellion," said Ed.

"And just to reaffirm..... during all this time, there was no sign of the Controllers?" asked Jake.

"No, we've not seen hide nor hair of them," said Ed.

"It could mean that they're not enforcing their rules anymore, or at least not in this part of the world," said Luke.

"Well, it's still a threat that somehow still seems to hang over all of us," said Ed.

"By the way, does anyone have any idea of who these Controllers are?" asked Ellen.

"My contact with them was indirect," said Chandler. "Lucas, the man who developed the giant steel boxes, asked me to keep an eye on one of these boxes before he disappeared into hiding. I had Ed set up a communication link in it so I could talk through it from this lighthouse. It's about twenty five miles southeast of here. Not long after it was set up, maybe twenty years after the war, a woman named Janet, who said she represented a country that was imposing strict rules on survivors, worldwide, said she knew about the village and told me that her people would soon visit here and begin enforcing their rules."

"Did she tell you who they were?" asked Jake.

"No, just that the village must follow their rules," said Chandler.

"What else did she say?" asked Ellen.

"The reason she was at Lucas's box was to set up a monitoring station on top of it," said Chandler. "And according to this woman Janet, they had satellites, so the villagers' behavior could be monitored for compliance with the rules."

"So you told this Janet person that you would establish your own program for complying with their rules if they would leave this area alone?" asked Jake.

"Yes, that was the idea," said Chandler.

"And the rest is history, until Jake crossed the fence and upset the apple cart," said Ellen.

"Look, Ellen, what exists out there in the world is apparently controlled by a surviving society that has established a set of rules that it feels must be maintained in order to prevent another war," said Chandler.

"And you think this is best accomplished by keeping survivors in a relatively primitive state?" asked Ellen.

"That does sound a bit uncivilized, but that's what their rules suggest," said Chandler.

"And you have essentially endorsed their rules," said Ellen.

"I simply followed them as best I can," said Chandler.

"But they never contacted you nor anyone here again after that initial contact a hundred and eighty years ago," said Ellen.

"That's true," said Chandler.

"So you just continued with your local version of their rules without questioning whether their rules still existed," said Ellen.

"I thought I was doing the right thing," said Chandler.

"But maybe it wasn't," said Jake.

"Whatever these Controllers felt they had to do back then, they did, but perhaps now it is time to challenge what they were trying to do," said Virg.

"In effect, we just initiated that change," said Jake.

"Perhaps, but maybe we have not heard from them because of what I had established here with my religion," said Chandler.

"Wow, this is a lot to take in," said Ellen.

"Look, they have satellites, so if they detect that my lighthouse is essentially gone, and the fence destroyed, things might change and we may soon get a visit from them," said Chandler.

"That is, if they still enforce their rules after two hundred years," said Jake.

"Look, Hotel Paradise has been there now for nearly half that time, and it is quite visible from space, and we have had zero contact with them," said Ed.

"Which could mean that we're free to move about the country," said Jake.

"With what?" asked Virg. "We're on foot."

"We'll find something," said Jake.

"I'm not so flippant about what they might or might not do, but under the current situation, the concept of true freedom is quite relative," said Chandler. "First of all, I'm not sure the villagers will be able to recognize the concept of freedom after growing up in a highly structured environment. And you just destroyed their deity, so what they do from now on is still unknown."

"And second of all?" asked Jake.

"Second of all, the Controllers might descend upon you and make you comply with their rules, which are essentially the same rules that I had in place before you knocked me out," said Chandler.

"I don't agree with your first point," said Jake. "Sarah and I walked out and we very quickly recognized what it was like to be free. My parents and Sarah's mom also walked out and they seem to have adjusted quite nicely."

"It would be good if the villagers were able to go on with their lives and feel free in doing so, but I find that highly unlikely," said Chandler.

"I find it highly likely," said Jake. "Once they see this lighthouse in its current state, I think the spell will be broken, and the healing can begin," said Jake.

"It's not a spell, it's a belief that took many years to ingrain in them, and beliefs are not that easily broken," said Chandler. "But it will be you folks who will see what happens next, because my power source was cut off when the fence was destroyed, so it won't be long before I'm gone."

"Can't we connect you to where the fence got its power?" asked Ellen.

"That's at the prison complex, which is at least six or seven miles from here," said Chandler.

"So we'll take you to the complex," said Ed.

"I don't have time to make that trip," said Chandler.

"If I load you onto the dolly and push you along the trails, I'd say maybe two hours or so," said Ed.

"No, right now I'm looking at minutes, not hours."

"I'm sorry Chandler, we didn't understand what was really going on here," said Ellen. " We only saw the negatives, so we felt we had to take firm action."

"Well, I knew that someday those from the outside would see what was going on here and misunderstand it," he replied. "So I suspected it might end like this."

"Can't we do anything?" asked Jake, looking at Ed who shook his head.

"Despite the fact that I had noble intentions at first, over the decades, I allowed this thing to go on until it became obsolete, like me," said Chandler.

As their conversation continued, the light in Chandler's glass bubble slowly became dimmer. Then, as they stood watching, the light blinked several times before going dark and Chandler's eyes closed. But a faint smile remained on his lips.

Chapter Thirteen

"We will rest for a moment," said Len after over an hour of jogging.

"Wait, I see something through the trees," said one man as he pushed forward and pointed.

"Yes, there is something," said another.

"Perhaps it is The Tower," said yet another.

"If it is, we shall kneel before it," said Len, trying to pick out movement from below through the forest but unable to see anything but reflections.

"What if....?" the first man tried to say, afraid to finish his thought.

"What if the evil ones have harmed it?" Len completed.

"Yes."

"The Tower cannot be harmed!" said Len loudly. "The Tower is all powerful! It is the life! It is the source of all we are! And all believers in it will live forever in the peaceful place with all those closest to us."

"But what if they have harmed The Tower?" asked someone from the rear.

"Do not worry, for if they dared challenge The Tower, even in their monster, they have already been severely punished," said Len. "It is only now for us to go there and take whoever remains back for their punishment."

A few cheers went up from his close followers who were behind him. Len held up his fist and charged forward, at first in long strides and soon he was galloping down the final hill. His handful of close followers charged with him, but the others trailed cautiously behind.

They burst around the corner and began to slow at the scene before them, finally coming to a halt in stunned silence. Len and his small group slowly continued on to the water's edge where they stared at the dreadful sight. The rest remained where they were, some distance back. The huge tank loomed to Len's left. The three others who had followed him to the water's edge stood just behind him. The tank's cannon barrel was still aimed directly at their Tower. This was The Tower they had etched on their tapestries and painted on their walls. Their Tower was now missing its top and had a gaping hole in its side. Its elegant green door leaned precariously against a tree a hundred yards away. Debris was scattered everywhere across the grass apron of the island where the lighthouse was located. In front of The Tower stood a group of people, including two youngsters. And on the hill to their right, a class of school children stood motionless, audience to the scene before them.

Len took several steps forward until his feet were in the water.

He wanted to kneel, but was unsure of what to do. His symbol of life stood in shambles before him.

"The Tower…" someone behind him said in a weak voice.

"What have they done?" Len whispered as his mind reeled in confusion. He was not sure what to tell his followers. He stood motionless, staring at the scene.

"How?" came a weak voice from another man who took a step forward to stand in the water next to him.

"We now know what we must do," said Len, finally, speaking only loud enough for the three nearest him to hear. "This will not go unpunished."

He raised his fist, looked around to see who was with him, then began running into the lagoon toward those who stood near the lighthouse who now screamed for him to stop.

"You will pay for what you have done!" he yelled as he entered the water. He was followed by only the man next to him. One of his other close followers turned and started back to the main group. The other just stood at the water's edge watching. The man who entered the water with Len stopped when it reached his waist. But Len continued into the water, thrashing with his legs until it was up to his neck. He continued thrashing toward the lighthouse as if he were going to run along the bottom of the lagoon to his sacred Tower. He was now over his head and could not swim. He was trying to scream, but his voice now gurgled with water. Across the lagoon there was a splash as someone, who had stripped off their clothes, dove in and was frantically swimming toward him. Len flailed in the water, sinking below, then surfacing occasionally in his struggle for life. A moment later the swimmer reached him and fought through his flailing arms to grasp him around the neck and began towing him to shore. They reached the shore in the shadow of the tank.

Luke dragged Len out of the water to safety and then to a small patch of grass nearby. By now, the man who had followed Len into the lagoon had returned to shore and stood nearby. Luke stood up and faced the others who had not moved during this entire episode.

"Go back to your village!" shouted Luke. The man who had gone into the water with Len hesitated a moment, then started to walk toward the others. Len was struggling to get up and Luke reached down and grabbed him by the arms and helped him to his feet. He then pointed toward the crowd that was now beginning to make its way up the hill. Len looked at Luke for a moment and started to say something, but then just nodded and began to follow the others. Luke watched as everyone finally disappeared around the bend and up the hill.

"The rage has evaporated," said Virg as she watched the scene. "I wonder if it's over?"

"Len was my neighbor," said John. "I never thought I'd see him like this, but I think they'll go back home and not come back."

"What about the women back in the village?" asked Ellen. "Are they as zealous as the men and will they understand what has happened here?"

"From what I just saw, it tells me that most of those from the village have at least some grasp of reason, and will eventually be able to handle what has happened here in a more peaceful way than Len," said Brit.

"I can only speak for myself, but I was never committed in

146

the same way as Len or Bob," said Martha. "And even though I have only been away from the village for a short time, I feel that I am now free to believe and act as I wish."

"With The Tower gone, along with the threat of reprisal, perhaps more will begin to separate themselves from the oppression that is directly linked to it," said Jake.

"Not immediately," said Ed. "The Message still exists in their minds and I believe that it will take a lot of explaining for the village to get back to any semblance of normalcy."

"Well, you're still the Helper to them, Ed, but maybe, once they see you as Ed the man, and explain to them about Hotel Paradise and what you have been doing for them in the past, I think it may go a long way in helping them adjust to their new future," said Ellen.

"Perhaps, but it may still be a long process of decompression," said Ed.

"Do you think they can at least begin to understand what it means to be free rather than having to do what they are commanded to do or to believe?" asked Ellen.

"Freedom right now in this circumstance is relative," said Ed. "We have to first tell the villagers about the Controllers, and why Chandler created The Message and The Tower in the first place. We also have to explain why they still have to follow the Controller's rules, even though we do not know for sure whether the Controllers will even come here to enforce them....or even if they exist for that matter."

"So, in effect, we'll be almost free," said Jake.

"Yes, almost free," said Ed, putting his thumb up. "Smart kid."

"Don't give him a big head," said Sarah. Ed looked at her for a moment before starting to laugh. Soon everyone was laughing with him.

"What about Hotel Paradise?" asked Ellen. " Do you think a reunion with the village is in order?"

"Definitely," said Ed.

"How many did you say live there?" asked Jake.

"Maybe five hundred," said Ed.

"Could everyone in this area live at the Hotel Paradise complex?" asked Jake.

"Everyone?" asked Ed.

"Yes, everyone...... the village, Ellen, Luke...... everybody."

"Well, actually, yes, I think the complex could support everyone, but it would take a bit of work to scale it up, and I'm not sure how that would square with the rules of the Controllers," said Ed.

"By the way, where does the electricity there come from?" asked Ellen.

"The cable just goes into the ocean, so I don't know," said Ed.

"Tidal generation," said Jake.

Everyone just looked at him.

"Right," said Luke.

"And we don't need to worry that much about those Controller rules now," said Jake.

"But we may have to worry about it at some point," said Ed.

"No, I think we should let them show up first," said Jake.

"You know what, I think I agree with Jake," said Luke who had walked around through the swamp and had overheard the discussion.

"Hey, partner, you might want to put on some britches," said Ed. Luke nodded with a smile as Virg handed him his clothing.

"Well, moving to Hotel Paradise works for us since we now have no electricity, and I know Virg could never survive without it," said Ellen.

"I could, but I don't want to," said Virg.

"I can still come back here to the library for books, can't I?" asked Jake.

"It's a long walk, but yes," said Ellen.

"And uh...... has anyone thought about the activation device?" asked Brit.

"In the excitement, I forgot to ask Chandler," said Luke.

"Well, there's no electricity here to run it now anyway so it may have already died, plus the fact that we have no idea where it is," said Virg

"You're right, so I guess we're all now normal human beings, not immortals," said Luke who was buttoning up his pants.

"Welcome to the world of normal people," said Jake.

"Maybe what's happened is best for everyone," said Luke.

"I think you're right, Luke," said Ellen. "This little adventure was forced upon us by Jake, who crossed the fence and pushed us into doing what we did," said Ellen. "And what we did has changed life in this area for everyone."

"So perhaps we owe Jake a great big thank you," said Luke.

"I would second that," said Ellen.

"Subject to a veto by the Controllers," said Ed.

"Think positive," said Jake.

"Alright then, let's head for the village because we have a lot of things to explain to them," said Virg. "Then it's on to Hotel

Paradise."

"Great, we'll be just one big family now, so follow me," said Jake, pointing in the direction of the village and then starting toward the trail, waving for everyone to follow.

"He's taking over again," said Ellen.

"You don't understand, he was always in charge, so you just have had to get used to it," said Sarah who then quickly fell in next to Jake as they continued toward the trail.

"Once again it's that void in leadership that none of us ever seem to have noticed," said Ellen.

"You know, the village is quite a hike and we could take the tank," said Jake after he had stopped to point at it.

"It's out of gas," said Virg.

"Out of diesel, or more accurately, cooking oil," said Jake.

"Doesn't matter, it's now just a lawn decoration," said Virg.

"From now on everything will have to be done on foot, Jake," said Ellen.

"But that's so primitive," said Jake shaking his head as he turned to again walk toward the trail to the village. Sarah was right beside him.

"Ellen, you may have to stop him from reading about all of the modern conveniences that civilization once had," said Virg.

"Do you think anyone can stop him from reading?" asked Ellen.

"Not really," said Virg.

"I'm hungry," said Sarah.

"You're always hungry," said Jake as Sarah elbowed past him and now led the procession down the trail to the village.

"Who did they say is in charge?" Jake mumbled to himself.

HEAVEN ABOVE

BOOK TWO

M. WILL SMITH

Chapter One

"We've decided that we're going up to the surface!" said a tall thin man in the back of a crowd that had gathered in the great hall.

"You've decided?" asked Lucas from the stage in a sarcastic tone as he shook his head. He remembered how many times he had to address this question, especially over the past few years. But not at an assembly meeting. Until now it had been in private, led by Debra whose small group seemed to be a constant thorn in his side on this issue. She stood directly below him and he knew that she would soon join the conversation, so he was trying to avoid eye contact with her.

"It's the failure of your eternity blocks, isn't it?" asked Riley.

"My....why are you....?" Lucas began, then hesitated as he thought about what to say. He was caught off guard by what he thought was a topic that was not to be brought up. His eternity blocks had never been proven to work as advertised, and the press had made a sensation of that fact. And yet, he had gone ahead with the interment of thousands and then used that money to help buy this cave. Without this cave, everyone here would likely have died in the war. This was why no one had ever dared raise the issue with him. However, his main reason for not going up was something entirely different. It was an even more compelling reason for Lucas. It was because this cutting edge cave was intended for the country's leaders. Once the war started, they were to come down into it. It was designed for them with all the comforts. And, for all intents and purposes, he had stolen it, even though a group of rogue military brass had misappropriated it and sold it to him to help finance their own ambitions. Yet, he was a willing party to an act of treason, which was a crime punishable by death. So the Federal Government would have warrants out for both him and his military conspirators. Part of the deal to acquire the cave was for six of these military brass to come down with him in the cave. But they were older, and in the years that had passed since coming down, three had died. He knew that as long as he remained in the cave, he would be safe from the Feds, since its location was in a highly secure location known only by a select few. It was unlikely that they would ever be able to find it. So, in order to remain safe from prosecution, he told those who came down into the cave with him that it was science that had established a fifty year waiting period before it would be safe to return to the surface. Of course that was a complete lie. He had no idea how long they must stay down in the cave. Certainly not fifty years.

"Look, Lucas, be reasonable, except for Debra, Sarah, Brady and Riley, everyone else in this hell hole is in their seventies, eighties, or nineties, including you, and returning to the surface before we die has been a dream for many of us," said a man from the side.

"I know, Mel, but unfortunately, we can't go up now, it's not safe," said Lucas with a shrug.

"In ten years, many of us will be dead," said Mel.

"That can't be helped," said Lucas.

"Look, Lucas, you can stay down here, but we're going up!" said Debra from below as she flicked a strand of hair from her face. "First of all, we know this fifty year waiting period is a complete fabrication."

"No it's not!" Lucas snapped as he glared down at her. "I've explained this to you a thousand times. It's based on solid data, and we no longer have the expertise to challenge it."

"Expertise? We never had the expertise!" said Debra.

"Jeb was trained in......"

"Jeb was one of your military cronies and not an expert," Debra interrupted.

"That's right, and how many people in the world have already gone up to the surface from their bunkers and caves?!" yelled Riley from the rear.

"The truth is, Riley, there were probably millions of caves and shelters, but only a select few with the capability to be self sufficient for decades like ours," said Lucas. "So those people are now dead....or if they did come up they likely starved to death or died from the radiation."

"You're wrong, there have to be survivors up there, millions of survivors!" shouted Riley.

"We don't know that, and besides, I have to look out for the welfare of those in this cave, and I say it's not safe to go up," said Lucas.

"Hey, no problem, Lucas. I said, you can stay down here!" said Debra.

"Look, Debra, this is MY cave, and I'll decide when anyone goes up!" Lucas shouted, holding up his hands after the audience began to chatter.

"No, after forty years, this has become OUR cave, not yours!" said Debra.

"Well, I'm the only person who knows how to operate this cave's complex systems," said Lucas.

"We're past that threat now, Lucas, because we can live on the surface," said Debra.

"You're a fool if you believe that!" said Lucas, so angry at her that he could not make eye contact.

"Well, I'm not willing to waste ten more years of my life down here if I don't have to!" shouted Riley. "I was born down here and have never seen the surface, so I'm going up!"

"Sign me up!" shouted Mel.

"Look, Lucas, you don't understand, we're not asking you, we're telling you what we're going to do!" said Debra with an elevated tone in her voice that echoed off the stone walls of the huge chamber. This was met with a round of applause from the audience that filled the chamber from floor to ceiling with its echos.

"Going up isn't that simple. We blew up the elevator for security purposes, remember?!" Lucas shouted over the din.

"I know that, but we'll walk up on the construction tunnel!" Debra shot back.

6

"We know very little about that tunnel," Lucas protested to an increasingly noisy crowd.

"The tunnel exists and we'll use it!" said Debra.

"I didn't build this cave, and wasn't around when it was constructed, so that tunnel may not even exist!" said Lucas whose voice could now be heard as the loud chatter began to subside.

"Of course it does, I spoke with one of your military friends before he passed, and he says it definitely exists and it is there as an emergency exit!" said Debra, followed by a round of applause and a resumption of the loud chatter.

"We don't even know where it is," whispered Sarah, who stood next to Debra.

"I have a pretty good idea," Debra whispered back as the chamber continued to be filled with loud conversations.

It now seemed clear that Debra had assumed the leadership role in this discussion, and all eyes shifted toward her in unison when she spoke. When she, Sarah and Riley had planned this public confrontation with Lucas, there was no discussion of who was leading the cause. But as she stood there, she realized that a leader would be needed. Was she that leader?

"I'm still in charge!" said Lucas as loudly as he could, holding up his hand as the noise from the crowd absorbed his words and only a few in front could hear him. "I brought you down here, and none of you would even be alive if it weren't for me!"

"We're extremely grateful to you for that, but that was then and this is now!" said Debra, who was among the few that could hear him.

"You ungrateful......." Lucas began to say as he pointed menacingly at her.

"It's out of your hands now, Lucas!" Debra interrupted, pointing back at him.

"You actually think you can live normal lives up there?" asked Lucas.

"We won't know until we get up there!" said Debra.

"It won't be what you expect, I promise you," said Lucas.

"Of course not, but forty years is a very long time to be confined in a cave, regardless of how comfortable it is, or how difficult it will be when we get out," said Sarah as loud as she could. Lucas heard her and shook his head.

"You're wasting your breath trying to stop us!" said Debra. A few behind her began chanting her name to coincide with clapping.

"You're fools!" Lucas shouted. He held up his hands again, but no one was paying attention to him anymore as they chatted loudly among themselves.

He had not expected this to happen. All previous discussions or arguments had been in private. Now, the colony supported Debra with wild enthusiasm. She had taken over! He was actually being deposed.

"We might well be fools, but we're going up!" Debra shouted.

"You know nothing about the tunnel, Debra," Lucas said in a normal voice that no one could hear, not even Debra or Sarah. "And if you do manage to emerge on the surface, our location will be compromised. If whomever survived up there is hostile, we'll all be in jeopardy. And if the atmosphere is poisonous, whoever goes up will be exposed to that." Debra looked up for a moment to see his lips move, but then turned back to the crowd.

Lucas continued to stare at a crowd of happy faces engaged

8

in loud conversation, paying no attention to him. It was as if he no longer existed. They had completely ignored his advice. Debra was the ring leader of this mutiny. Yes, it was definitely a mutiny, he mumbled to himself.

"I brought you down here, and kept you from suffering the devastation that occurred on the surface," Lucas continued to say to no one but himself. "You now defy my recommendations and follow Debra and her mutineers." His eyes were now glazed over in a smoldering anger. Debra turned to stare up at him as the thought of her having to replace him was now sinking in. She saw herself as the leader of a cause, but never really in charge of people. That thought now gave her pause. In the meantime, Lucas calmly walked down the steps to the floor and stood in front of Debra and Sarah.

"What if I stop you?" he asked in a threatening voice from a few feet away.

"You can't stop us," said Sarah, taking a step forward so she was literally nose to nose with him. He glared at her for a moment, then turned sharply and strode out, pushing his way through the crowd. Three older men, his military friends, followed him. He glanced back before the four of them disappeared down a hallway.

"Well, I guess you're it now," said Sarah, pointing to the podium.

"I hadn't really thought about having to do that," said Debra, now feeling a surge of nervousness from the thought of standing before everyone and essentially having to take charge of the colony.

"No, you're it, you're the new Lucas," said Sarah, pointing

9

again up at the podium.

"It's easy to shout from a crowd, and something else to be in charge," Debra half mumbled as she stared at Sarah. Debra was usually a fairly shy person, and never imagined herself as someone in charge. She was a debater and a voice for the cause. At times very vocal with her friends. Now, however, she had to decide what she was, because she had been the ringleader of this effort for a very long time and she had just led the public debate that resulted in his ouster. Yes, he was definitely removed from his almost godlike position of leadership. She stood quietly for a moment. Sarah nudged her and again pointed up to the stage. Debra looked at her, then up at the pulpit and realized she had to speak to everyone. No, she had to do more than just speak to them, she had to be someone for them. Somewhat in a daze, Debra slowly made her way up onto the stage. Once there she stood behind the pulpit for a moment gazing from one side of the audience to the other. She was momentarily frozen. There was a complete silence in the hall as they waited for her to speak. Only the shuffling of feet, the rustling of clothing and an occasional cough could be heard as they waited.

"Well, I guess we're going up," she said, and then smiled after Riley let out a cheer and clapped his hands. A few followed suit, but it was soon quiet again.

"We'll need to form a team," she continued. "Here's what I would recommend. As most of you know, Sarah, Riley and I have been working on this little adventure over a number of years, and we have a good idea about what to do and how to do it." A sudden feeling of calm began to sweep over her and she felt something. It was a certain strength from the crowd, and a new confidence that was coming from within. It was a feeling that she could do this. She could actually take charge. She knew what to do and how to do it. She smiled.

"Debra, you're now the new Lucas, so maybe you should stay here," said someone from the audience.

"No, I'm not the new Lucas, but I have been out front on this effort from the start, so I believe I should lead the expedition," she said in an increasingly confident voice. "The three of us work well together as a team. So we will comprise the core of the expedition, but let me explain why. First, Riley is probably the most physically fit of anyone in the colony and we'll need his strength and stamina for this journey. As many of you know, Sarah is a genius at solving problems. Her intelligence and abilities will come in handy as we pick our way through the tunnel, and of course on the surface as we face unknown challenges." She hesitated a moment before continuing.

"Now, in addition to the three of us, Casey has been a frequent face in our discussions. He's a master mechanic and can fix anything, so we want him to join us." She pointed to Casey and he quickly gave her a thumbs up.

"Good, thank you, Casey," she smiled. "So he will be a fourth."

"What about weapons, you might need some protection since there are likely a lot of unknowns up there," said someone.

"Casey?" asked Debra.

"I have a pistol and ammo that of course I'm not supposed to have," said Casey. "In fact, I could have the only gun down here. If you'll recall, Lucas destroyed those he could find after that incident twenty years ago."

11

"Then you'll cover that contingency," said Debra. "We've also talked about the need for someone who actually knows the area, so we'll have a better idea of where we go once we get up there. That person would be our guide."

"I think I'm the only one familiar with this particular part of Utah," said Mel. "Everyone else came from somewhere else, but I once lived here."

"So, will you be our guide?" asked Debra.

"Of course, but things will be quite different up there considering what happened," said Mel.

"I know, but it's still the same geographical area," said Debra.

"That's true, but the other thing is, I'm not sure how fast I'll be," he replied. "I know there's no way I could keep up with Riley."

"We need you, so we'll help you keep up," said Debra.

"Then I'm your guide," he shrugged.

"I think that completes our team unless there are other suggestions," said Debra, stopping to look around and waiting.

"OK, I'll be available in my room, and as most of you know it's an open door," she said, a bit amazed at herself for what she had just done.

"We're going up!" shouted Sarah, turning around and holding up both hands which set off a loud cheer.

Debra held up both thumbs, then quickly descended from the podium and started for her room with Casey, Riley, Sarah and Mel right behind.

Chapter Two

Debra sat in her living room behind a large desk. A mural that spanned three walls displayed a forest of aspens with soft green undergrowth. The white bark of the trees gave the room just the right amount of light from the single overhead sun bulb in the arched ceiling. The rustic tile floor was partially covered with a well-worn beige carpet. A large red sofa faced the desk, its cushions worn through in places with patches covering some of the holes.

"Good job out there," said Riley from the sofa where he was comfortably slumped.

"Once I started talking, it all came to me," she replied.

"I knew you could do it," said Sarah.

"Now, all we have to do is what we said we would do," said Riley. He smiled at her as he leaned forward with a boney elbow on the arm of the sofa and his fingers laced together on his chest.

"Well, we went to the assembly to tell Lucas that we were

going up, and that's what we did," she said, sitting back and rotating her chair around to one side to stare at the wall of trees for a moment. "Of course we didn't expect a complete coup d'etat. But it is what it is, so now it's time for us to act."

"Well, according to your source, the construction tunnel is apparently behind the far wall of the greenhouse," said Sarah.

"That's what he said, but he wasn't sure," said Debra.

"And Lucas has cast some doubt on that," said Casey who was leaning against the wall in a far corner.

"Lucas will not be any help to us, and is more likely to mislead us," said Sarah who was perched on a stool next to Debra's desk.

"Yes, in fact we need to be attentive to any effort on his part to thwart our effort," said Debra.

"I know one person who might know more about the tunnel as well as any tricks Lucas might be up to," said Casey.

"We're listening," said Debra.

"Brady," said Casey.

"Oh sure, Brady, you two are buddies," said Debra.

"But isn't he in tight with Lucas?" asked Sarah.

"Not really," said Casey. "I have breakfast with him almost every morning, and even though we're jabbing at one another all the time, I consider him a good friend. And I see no love between him and Lucas."

"Have you ever talked to him about going up?" asked Debra.

"Yes, but only in general terms," said Casey. "However, I know him very well, and I'm sure he'll help us if I ask him....and, actually, even if I don't ask him."

"Well, he was at the assembly and didn't leave the hall with Lucas, so that's good," said Sarah.

"If he'll flip on Lucas, I wonder if he would be interested in being part of our team?" asked Debra.

"Well, as you know, he's a bit on the heavy side so he might not be able to keep up," said Casey.

"A bit on the heavy side?" asked Riley. "Brady is hopelessly out of shape, and could never keep up."

"In case you hadn't noticed, Riley, I'm an old fart with an oversized gut who gets winded crossing the room, so neither can I," said Casey who was in his eighties with a larger than usual stomach that he now patted with both hands.

"And I limp when I walk, so I'm not exactly a track star," said Mel.

"Look, we're not going to be running a marathon on this adventure," said Debra. "And Brady is inner circle, so his inside knowledge is likely to be quite valuable."

"Perhaps, but I'm not a fan," said Riley.

"Riley, if he agrees, he'll go with us," said Debra, looking at Riley with raised eyebrows to emphasize her point. Riley rolled his eyes and shrugged.

"Good, so let me give him a buzz," said Casey who pulled out his communicator. He dialed and waited a minute, then put it away.

"And.......?" asked Debra.

"He's not answering, so I wonder......," said Casey.

"Wonder what?" asked Debra.

"Follow me," said Casey who pushed himself off the wall and started for the door.

"Where are you going?" asked Debra.

"I think he'll be there!" said Casey, disappearing out the door.

15

"The uh.....oh right!" said Debra who got up quickly and followed.

Sarah and Riley scrambled to their feet and were on their way. Mel brought up the rear. They entered the greenhouse behind Casey and found Brady standing near the far wall with his hand against it.

"Brady..... hi," said Debra as they approached.

"The entrance is here behind the wall," said Brady, patting his hand against it.

"Great," said Debra.

"So, are you with us on this?" asked Casey.

"Of course," said Brady.

"Can you go up with us?" asked Debra.

"I thought you'd never ask," said Brady.

"Great..... and I won't ask about your relationship with Lucas," said Debra.

"What relationship?" asked Brady, shaking his head. "OK, so what's the plan?"

"Let's start by blowing a hole in this wall," said Debra, pointing.

"I'm ahead of you," said Casey who was already studying the flat surface, tapping with his fist as he walked along it. He took out his oversized revolver and continued tapping with its butt, stopping at a hollow sounding place.

"Here," said Casey, slapping his hand against the wall.

"So then we'll need...." Debra began.

"Mel is on his way," said Casey. "I called him as soon as I saw Brady."

"OK," said Debra, just as Mel appeared carrying a bag.

16

"Do you have everything?" asked Casey. Mel nodded and handed him the bag. Casey immediately emptied its contents on the floor and used the drill to make several holes in the wall into which he placed explosives. He waved everyone back and they retreated a safe distance. The explosives were detonated with a deafening boom, filling the air with a thick cloud of dust. When the dust cleared, they came forward to look. Inside the gaping hole was a steel door without a handle or access panel to open it.

"Oh crap.....so now what?" asked Debra.

"I don't know," said Casey, turning to Brady.

"No problem, there's a switch in the control room......oh my god!" said Brady, who turned and began running.

"Right.....Lucas!" shouted Debra who started after him.

"Obviously he heard the explosion like everyone in the cave, so he knows what we just did!" said Casey, pulling out his pistol to see if it was loaded, then he followed the others who had disappeared into the mist that hung in the air in the greenhouse.

"I'll stay here in case he comes this way," said Mel to Casey's back. Casey just waved over his shoulder as he faded into the fine droplets.

"Hurry!" shouted Brady over his shoulder as he ran as fast as his large body could move.

"What can he do!?" shouted Debra from behind him as they emerged from the mist into a hallway.

"Plenty!" Brady puffed as he began to slow.

"I'm going ahead!" said Debra who brushed by him. She quickly shot ahead. Riley appeared out of nowhere and bolted ahead past her.

"Just stop him any way you can!" Brady shouted as he puffed

to a jog from far behind. Casey caught up with Brady and immediately slowed to Brady's pace.

"Did you hear what Brady said?" shouted Debra to Riley's back as he moved farther ahead.

"Yes.....I'll kill the bastard," he replied over his shoulder. They entered the great hall and headed straight for a large steel door at the top of a short flight of steps. A red sign read 'control room, restricted access'. The door was slightly ajar and a wedge of light gave evidence that someone was inside.

"Go in!" shouted Debra from halfway across the hall as Riley took three steps at a time and dove for the door.

Sid, one of Lucas's military insiders, saw him and tried to pull the door shut, but Riley grabbed it and pulled it open with Sid still gripping the handle tightly. Sid went flying out and down the steps, just as Debra arrived, knocking her against the rail. Sid crashed to the floor where he lay in pain. Riley rushed inside and grabbed Lucas by the shoulder and turned him around. Lucas, caught off guard, lost his balance and went sprawling to the floor. Riley was on top of him and they scuffled. Lucas was able to wriggle free, got to his feet and pushed past Debra who had just entered the room, knocking her to the floor. He scrambled down the steps, slamming past Sarah, and then stepping over Sid and running across the hall. Sid got up and threw a block on Sarah who was trying to go after Lucas. She went down on top of him. Riley, who had leaped down the steps in a single bound, took up the chase, tripping over both of them and sprawling into a heap on the floor. He struggled to his feet but was tripped again as Sid grabbed him by the ankle. By the time he got to his feet again, Lucas was nowhere to be seen. Riley scanned the other side of the great hall where several doorways offered multiple escape routes.

"Did you see which one?" shouted Sarah after she got up and kicked Sid in the chest when he tried to grab her. Sid went down but quickly scrambled to his feet. Sarah landed a solid right on his chin and he collapsed to the floor holding his face with both hands.

"Where is he!" shouted Debra from the door to the control room.

"Don't worry, we'll find him!" Sarah shouted as she ran across the great hall with Riley.

Just then, Brady appeared from one of the doorways and began lumbering across the hall to the control room. Casey was close behind.

"OK, so just two possible doorways..... you take that one, I'll take the other!" said Riley as he and Sarah disappeared, each down a different hallway.

"They must be after Lucas," said Brady as he continued across the hall to the Control Room. Both he and Casey were completely out of breath when they arrived.

"Lucas was in here and we don't know what he did!" said Debra who was standing in the open doorway.

"I'll take a look," said Brady who wedged past her into the room where he first bent over with his hands on his knees, trying to catch his breath. Casey stopped in the doorway next to Debra with his hand on the doorframe wheezing in labored breaths.

"Brady, can you tell if he was able to do anything?" asked Debra.

"I know, I know, I'll check," said Brady who finally stood upright and then lunged toward the panel.

"Um....let's see.... it doesn't...." Brady wheezed, as he studied the panel.

"Anything?" she asked impatiently.

"No...... but you have to understand something.....," he began through labored breaths, still staring at the controls as he waited to catch his breath. "From day one, Lucas has been the only person allowed in this room. This room controls everything in the cave complex, including features that have allowed us to live underground completely independent of the surface for decades. It's why most other cave dwellers out there didn't survive. Without this equipment and its features, they would have had to return to the surface prematurely, or die in their caves. We've trusted him to keep everything running properly, and even though I'm supposedly in his inner circle, neither myself nor anyone else knows exactly how to operate the system. He has held this knowledge over us to help guarantee his absolute rule."

"Well, yes, I guess we all knew that he was doing this, but never challenged him," said Debra. "I guess it really was absolute rule, but as an insider you must know something."

"I'm not sure.....I have some knowledge from just being around when things are done, but it's not enough to actually operate any of this on my own," said Brady.

"OK but based on what you do know, are we still good?" asked Debra.

"I don't know for sure, but it doesn't look like he was able to do anything," said Brady, studying a number of switches that were each covered with red and green safety caps. All of the caps were still intact. In order to flip a switch, the safety cap would have to be lifted, breaking a seal. At the bottom of a green switch was a label: 'construction tunnel'. It had a small bright red digital lock securing the cap.

"I assume we can open the door to the construction tunnel with this switch," said Debra, placing her finger on it.

"Yes, that's what the label says, but that red padlock has to come off first, and the fact that it's red is a bit worrisome," said Brady.

"You mean because it's red?" asked Debra.

"That's right, I do know that red is a warning of some kind," he replied. "And I don't have the combination to the lock even if I wanted to flip that switch."

"I know, but in order to open the construction tunnel door, we will have to flip it, right?" asked Debra.

"Right," said Brady, wiping his forehead with his wrist. "But the cap is red."

"Try one, two, three, four," said Casey who was still propped up against the door sill.

"Oh come on man, nobody would use that combination," said Brady. Casey shrugged, then pulled out his revolver and started toward them.

"Wait, wait, wait.....you can't shoot that in here," said Brady, holding his hand over the switch.

"Do you have a better idea?" asked Casey.

"Alright, I'll try your stupid combination, but I'm still not sure we should be doing this until I know more about the red cap," said Brady who punched in one, two, three, four. The lock opened immediately.

"Wait....you knew it?" asked Brady.

"No, but it was obvious since combinations are lost, and

decades later someone is in a hurry to open the fucking door," said Casey.

Brady gave Casey a look, then lifted the green cap.

"This might not go well," said Brady.

"We need to open the tunnel door, so what could happen?" asked Debra.

"Alright, but the red cap must mean something," said Brady who flipped the switch. There was a thump from the panel and a moment later Casey's communicator chimed. He answered.

"Mel says the door is open," he announced.

"Oh shit, this is what I was afraid of!" said Brady who was now studying the flashing red lights on the panel.

"What happened?" asked Debra.

"So that explains the red lock," said Brady.

"OK, so what is happening?" asked Debra, watching the red lights, then staring at him in alarm.

"There was a discussion with one of his cronies years and years ago," said Brady. "I was only eleven but I remember some of what was said. I think there's a failsafe that shuts down the entire complex if the door to that tunnel is opened."

"From inside?" asked Casey. "That doesn't make sense."

"You mean it's like a doomsday sequence or something?" asked Debra.

"Yes, and remember, this cave was designed for US dignitaries, so it could have involved a shut down, but for what purpose?" asked Casey.

"But that would mean that if anyone tried to get out, the cave would shut down," said Debra.

"A lot about this cave doesn't make a lot of sense," said Brady.

"Well, whatever the purpose, we need to cancel the shutdown," said Casey.

"We do, so do you have any ideas?" asked Debra.

"No," said Brady.

"Well, I'm not sure what Lucas was intending to do in here," said Debra.

"He would have to know that if the construction tunnel door was opened with this switch, the complex would shut down," said Brady. "And it would not be a way to stop us from leaving if the door is opened."

"So did the red padlock stop him?" asked Debra. "He clearly had time before we got here to do something, but he didn't do it."

"He might have had second thoughts about what to do, since the cave would shut down and then he'd have to go up," said Brady.

"And if the cave shuts down, never come back down," said Debra. "That's a big decision considering his reluctance to go up in the first place."

"I know, but after you took over, I think his whole life plan changed, so I think he may in fact have decided to go up," said Brady. "What I think is very simple: he didn't know the combination to the lock on the red cap."

"Whatever the case, we need to stop this goddamn sequence, Brady," said Casey.

"That's right, because if we can't stop this doomsday sequence, everyone in the cave will have to leave and never come back," said Debra.

"Which raises the question of whether we can even survive up there," said Casey.

"Exactly, so let's focus," said Debra.

"I have a thought" said Casey, pointing to the console.

"Like what?" asked Brady, staring at the console.

"It's just as simple-minded as my one-two-three-four combination," said Casey who was studying the panel.

"Well, if it works, simple is good..... so what's the one-two-three-four plan?" asked Debra who joined Casey on the floor as he probed under the console.

"I thought we'd just reboot the entire fucking system," said Casey, who was feeling around under the console with his hand.

"Oh, sure, why not," said Debra.

After more groping, Casey's hand felt a recessed handle, and, using both hands, he pulled hard. There was a loud pop and all the lights on the panel went out together with every light and machine in the complex. There was inky darkness and a complete and utter silence.

"OK, I guess that was the main breaker," said Debra who fumbled in her pocket for a tiny light.

"Let me count to ten before we break out the champagne," he replied.

"If it works, make mine gin," said Debra.

A moment later Casey jammed the handle back in place and lights came on everywhere. Outside, they could hear machinery starting up. The panel lights were now green.

"Is it time for the happy hour?" she asked.

"Can we wait until we reach the surface?" he asked.

"Yes, so let's get back to what we were doing so we can do that," said Debra.

"Before we book our first hotel room up there, let's make

24

sure it holds," said Casey as they sat quietly for a few minutes on the floor. After what seemed forever, Debra looked at Casey who gave her a thumbs up. She nodded and quickly got up and hurried out the door. Brady started after her.

"He's halfway to the surface by now," said Casey.

"Unless Sarah and Riley have caught up with him," said Brady.

"You go too, Brady, I'll stay here in case fuck face comes back here," said Casey, holding up his gun. Brady nodded, then made his way down the steps as fast as he could manage.

When Debra reached the hallway that led to the greenhouse she ran into Sarah.

"Did you find him?" asked Debra.

"No, he's not in his room and his goons wouldn't tell us anything," said Sarah. "By the way, what was the blackout?" she asked.

"That's a whole nother story, but right now we need to get to the tunnel because we're pretty sure that Lucas is heading for the surface," said Debra.

"Alright, you can fill me in on the way to the tunnel," said Sarah who fell in behind her.

As they continued toward the greenhouse, Riley appeared suddenly from a doorway.

"Anything?" asked Debra after she nearly crashed into him, but continued running. He followed.

"No!" said Riley. "You?"

"We're pretty sure he's on his way to the tunnel!" said Debra. Riley quickly overtook her.

"So what did he do?" asked Sarah from behind.

"It's what he wasn't able to do," said Debra.

"I don't understand, you mean you had something to do with the blackout?" asked Sarah.

"Yep," said Debra as they thundered into the massive greenhouse where the clatter from their footsteps was instantly muted. Riley arrived at the tunnel entrance first.

"I'm OK," came a voice from the darkness.

"Oh my god, what happened, Mel?" asked Riley who continued into the tunnel to find Mel getting to his feet.

"He ran right over me, and he had a gun," said Mel.

"A gun? That's not good," said Debra. "Did it look like he had taken supplies with him?" asked Debra.

"I didn't see anything, just the gun," said Mel.

"He knows more than we do about the cave and the area around it, but one has to eat and drink up there," said Debra.

"I'm going after him," said Riley, who started for the door to the tunnel.

"No Riley, he has a gun," said Debra.

"I know, but he could sabotage the tunnel on his way out, so someone has to stay close on his tail," said Mel.

"I agree, but Casey has our gun, so he needs to take the lead," said Debra.

"I'll call him," said Mel, holding up his communicator.

"Debra......Casey is not exactly a hundred meter record holder, and time is of the essence," said Riley.

"Doesn't matter, Riley, we have to wait for him," said Debra. They waited for an agonizingly long time before Brady lumbered in, puffing and wheezing.

"Where is Casey?" asked Debra.

"He's on his way," said Mel. A short time later Casey arrived, just as winded as Brady.

"OK, great, I need your gun, Casey," said Riley, holding out his hand.

"Oh god no, you'd hurt yourself," said Casey, shaking his head.

"We have to go after him immediately because he could sabotage the tunnel and we'll be stuck down here forever!" said Riley, his hand still out.

"I'll do it," said Casey who was still breathing heavily with a flushed face, but he started into the tunnel.

"You'll die before you get a hundred paces," said Riley to Casey's back.

"I'm fine," Casey wheezed over his shoulder.

"I have to go with him," said Brady who started into the tunnel.

"You two sloths will both die," said Riley.

"Riley, they really are the ones who have to go after him," said Debra.

"That may be true, but they couldn't catch a turtle," said Riley.

"Look, we don't actually have to catch him, we just have to make sure he doesn't do any damage to the tunnel," said Debra.

"Deb, they're already exhausted," said Riley.

"I know, but it is what it is," said Debra, holding up her hand to him. "We have to pack water and some supplies, and then we'll follow those two," said Debra.

"Mel, do we know how long this tunnel is?" asked Riley.

"I have no idea," said Mel.

"I wonder if there are stairs?" asked Riley.

"It's a construction tunnel, so it has to be either level or has a gentle slope," said Mel.

"How could it be level if we have to go up," said Riley.

"Let's not debate the design of the tunnel, we have to pack and go after them," said Debra.

"I'll get started on that," said Sarah who darted off.

"Look, we all don't need to pack, and those two will never catch Lucas, so I'd like to go help them," Riley begged. Debra looked at him for a moment, then nodded.

"You must stay with them and not charge ahead on your own," said Debra, who had grabbed Riley's sleeve to stop him, and then looked him in the eyes with raised eyebrows to emphasize her point.

"I know, I will," said Riley who pulled away and quickly disappeared into the tunnel.

She stared after him. The echo of his shoes bounced off the hard walls, creating an eerie sound that slowly faded in the distance and only blackness remained.

"Let's go help Sarah pack," said Debra as she turned to Mel.

"I think we'll need enough supplies to last at least three days," he replied.

Debra nodded as she continued to stare into the tunnel. She then turned to leave.

Chapter Three

"Casey, do you have any idea how in the hell far it is to the surface through this damned tunnel?" asked Brady who had finally caught up with him. Brady's breathing was heavy and laced with a labored wheeze. It sounded as if he were about to collapse. Casey was also panting heavily and had slowed to a shuffling jog. Just then they heard the clatter of steps approaching from behind and stopped to look back.

"Is this all the farther you've gotten?" asked Riley, as he stopped in front of them.

"Riley, Jesus, what in the hell are you doing here, I thought Debra....?" Casey began.

"We thought you two could use a little help," Riley interrupted.

"Well, if you wanted to help, you should have come in a cab," said Casey.

"What's a cab?" asked Brady.

"Don't mind him, he's illiterate," said Casey. Brady held his middle finger to his forehead.

"Maybe I can go ahead," said Riley.

"No, I'm carrying the iron, so you'll stay behind me," said Casey.

"Look, there's no telling what he might do to sabotage the tunnel if we let him get too far ahead," said Riley.

"I'm not sure if that asshole is equipped to fuck with the tunnel, but I would like to keep track of him," said Casey.

"Right, so maybe you should give him a quick lesson in how to use that thing and let him go ahead," said Brady.

"I've watched a lot of videos," said Riley.

"Videos won't make you a gunman," said Casey, pulling out his pistol and holding it up.

"Let me hold it," said Riley.

"I know I'm going to regret this," said Casey as he hesitatingly handed it to him.

"See, look," said Riley, taking it and waving it around. The gun slipped out of his grip and flipped into the air, but Casey caught it before it hit the ground.

"This is a mistake!" Casey shouted as Riley reached for it again.

"I was just playing," said Riley.

"If you can't take this seriously, I'm keeping it!" said Casey.

"I'm good," said Riley, holding out his hand.

"It has six bullets, and you can fire it by either pulling back on the hammer like this and pulling the trigger, or just pulling the trigger."

"Why not just pull the trigger?" asked Riley.

"Look, don't even try to fire it, Riley, just flash it so Lucas knows you have it," said Casey as he slowly held the gun out, handle first.

"I'll be fine," said Riley who took the gun, turned and began running ahead into the tunnel.

"Oh my god," said Casey who was shaking his head as Riley disappeared.

"He doesn't have a flashlight does he?" asked Brady.

"He found us, so he must have something," said Casey.

"Debra would have told Riley not to confront Lucas, so do you think he'll listen?" asked Brady.

"I have no idea, but it was your idea to give him the gun," said Casey.

"I know, but we'll never catch up with him at our pace, so I guess whatever happens, happens," said Brady.

"Actually, by the time we catch up with Riley, Debra and the others will catch up to us, so it'll be party time," said Casey.

"I suppose that's true, so let's just keep going," said Brady.

"Lucas is as old as I am, so how fast can he be?" asked Casey.

"He runs on a treadmill and works out every day, so he's very fit for someone his age," said Brady.

"OK, so then he should reach the exit before Riley catches up with him," said Casey.

"I wonder how far it is to the exit?" asked Brady.

"Hopefully not that far," said Casey who started out in a slow jog.

"We're deep down in a cave, so shouldn't we be going uphill?" asked Brady from behind.

"One would think," said Casey.

31

"Well, if we do hit a hill or stairs, I think that would put me out of the chase," said Brady.

"Yeah, I know," said Casey. "I wish I had worked out over the years, but who knew I'd ever need to be in any kind of physical shape?"

"Well, I work out, but I'm going for arm strength and show, not endurance," said Brady.

"Show?"

"Muscle City," said Brady.

"Well, that doesn't seem to have worked out all that well, has it?" asked Casey.

"Better than your flab, you rickety old fart," said Brady.

"Something just occurred to me," said Casey after they had passed through two air locks and they were still not climbing.

"What's that?"

"We came into the cave down an elevator from a plateau, so it's possible that this tunnel actually comes out in a valley," said Casey.

"What does that mean?" asked Brady.

"It means the tunnel is completely level and we could come out in a canyon," said Casey.

"Let's hope that's the case, because I couldn't do a hill right now," said Brady.

"However, even though it's flat, I think I'll have to slow down a little," said Casey.

"Slow down? If we slow down any more we'll be stopped," said Brady.

"Exactly," said Casey.

"Maybe that's not a bad idea," said Brady, panting heavily

with sweat pouring off his forehead.

"If we don't stop soon, I think I might die," said Casey, his wheezing now echoing off the hard walls of the tunnel.

"Look, you flabby old shit, we volunteered for this, so we have to keep going," said Brady who reached back and grabbed Casey by his sleeve and dragged him along. Casey mumbled a cascade of off-color words as he stumbled along behind him.

They trudged through another air lock and finally arrived at a fourth, much larger one. Once through the door they could see a shaft of sunlight painting a streak of light across the floor. They entered, and as they stood taking in the great size of the room, Brady turned and held his finger to his lips, then whispered.

"Did you hear that?"

"Hear what?" asked Casey.

"That clinking?" he replied, again holding his finger up to his mouth. Casey shook his head.

"Look, stop the intrigue, it has to be Riley," said Casey. "OK, unless Lucas shot him," said Casey.

"We'd have heard the gunshot."

"I see sun poking through, so let's get up there," said Casey who started toward the sunlight.

Brady followed and they made their way across the floor until they reached a rock fall and looked up.

"Do we have to climb up these rocks?" asked Brady.

"No, we'll sprout wings and fly up," said Casey quietly.

Brady placed his foot on a rock and it moved, clanking loudly against the rock next to it.

"Is that you two down there?" asked Riley.

"Yeah," said Brady.

"You took long enough," Riley replied.

"Casey is slow," said Brady.

"I could outrun you with one leg tied behind my back," said Casey.

"I'd like to see that," said Brady.

"Why don't you two stop bickering and climb up here," said Riley.

"Did you see him?" asked Brady as the two clumsily began stumbling up the rock fall toward the entrance.

"He was gone when I got here," said Riley.

"I'm not sure I can make it all the way up.... I'm crapping out," said Casey who had stopped.

"Maybe I should leave you here to die," said Brady.

"I'm near death anyway, so what does it matter," said Casey.

"I poked my head out and it seems very nice outside," said Riley. "It's warm, and the air smells fresh."

"You're just saying that," said Brady.

"Fine, but right now, I'm going outside to enjoy the fresh air and the view," said Riley.

"He could be telling the truth," said Casey who began to climb with a renewed energy.

"Yeah," said Brady as he scrambled ahead. When he reached the top Brady stopped to catch his breath. Casey caught up and struggled to his feet.

"I'm going out," said Casey who stumbled forward and fell to his knees in front of the entrance that was just a hole large enough for him to fit through. He thought for a moment as he studied the opening, then squeezed through.

"Give me a minute," said Brady who was still wheezing. After a minute, he made his way to the entrance and started through. But he got stuck halfway.

"Jesus, Brady, now that you've managed to plug the entrance, no one else will be able to get out," said Casey.

"Give me a hand you pregnant worm," said Brady. Riley came to help and eventually the two of them were able to drag Brady the remaining few feet into the sunshine.

"You weren't lying," said Brady. He stood to take in the spectacular view of the valley. There were trees along the bottom, and in the distance, hills melted into a sky that began at the horizon in a cotton hue and deepened to a dark blue that made him stop and stare up at it. There was no sound, and the silence seemed to project a gentle hiss. Forty years of hearing the humming of machinery in the cave was now gone. Only the peace of silence remained. The three stood frozen in place as a gentle breeze riffled through their hair. Forty years with no sky, no wind and no vistas magnified the moment. Inside the cave, where sound echoed harshly off the walls, the openness and quiet seemed like magic, and they forgot they were tailing Lucas. Then, in the distance, a faint sound broke the silence. It was what sounded like rocks clinking together.

"That's him," said Casey as they turned in unison to look to their left to the valley wall that was beaded with large boulders all the way to the skyline.

"We'll climb out that way," said Riley, pointing.

"Right, that's the direction to where we came down forty years ago," said Casey.

"I still remember the elevator ride down," said Brady.

"Well, an elevator ride up would have been a lot better than

35

that trek through the tunnel," said Casey.

"We blew up that elevator so no one could follow us, right?" asked Brady.

"Yes, and I remember the eerie feeling of being permanently sealed far underground forever," said Casey.

"We came here in a plane, so I wonder if it's still there?" asked Brady.

"It should be, unless it was bombed," said Casey.

"But we'll need a pilot," said Brady.

"I was the pilot," said Casey.

"Wait.....you're a pilot?" asked Brady.

"No, I'm an Olympic swimmer," said Casey. "But it's been forty years, so who knows if it will start up, even if it survived the devastation."

"I wonder if Lucas can fly?" asked Riley.

"I'm pretty sure he can," said Casey.

"Well, we can't just sit here and chat, we have to go after him," said Riley.

"You go, I'm just going to wait here for the others," said Brady.

"I'll wait here too," said Casey.

"You two are a complete waste," said Riley.

"We're just a little tired, and besides, Lucas can't damage the tunnel anymore," said Casey.

"No, but he could fly away with our airplane," said Riley.

"Do you really think it could still fly after forty years?" asked Brady.

"I don't know, remember Woody Allen with the Volkswagen bug in the cave?" asked Casey with a little laugh.

"Woody who?" asked Brady, looking at Casey with a scowl.

"Never mind," said Casey.

"I'm going," said Riley, waving the pistol as he turned to leave.

"We'll catch up," said Brady.

"Remember, Riley, he must be taken alive!" shouted Casey.

"Yeah, I know," said Riley over his shoulder.

"That gun is only to defend yourself!" shouted Casey.

"Yeah, yeah," said Riley to himself as he jogged toward the valley wall.

"Look, we volunteered for this," said Brady who was trying unsuccessfully to get to his feet.

"We didn't volunteer to die," said Casey.

"I guess that's true, and besides, the others will be here soon," said Brady who slumped back down.

"Wow!" came a loud voice from the tunnel entrance just as Brady's butt hit the ground. They both reacted with a start.

"Debra?" asked Casey who was struggling to get to his feet.

"I think I just peed my pants," said Brady who was looking down at his crotch to see if it was wet.

"Where's Riley?" asked Debra who was now outside and walking slowly toward the edge. She stopped there and stood transfixed. It was a scene like none she had ever witnessed in her lifetime. Sarah was next outside and she said nothing as she made her way next to Debra, her eyes as big as saucers. Finally, Mel crawled out, struggled to stand, then shuffled forward beside Sarah and Debra.

"He went after Lucas," said Casey from behind after he was finally able to get to his feet.

"That way," said Mel, pointing as he turned to Casey.

"Correct," said Casey.

"So, you gave Riley your gun?" asked Debra.

"Against my better judgement," said Casey, shaking his head.

"We'll hope for the best," said Debra. "Mel says the aircraft you flew us here in may still be useable."

"And if it is, he'll take it...... if he can get it started," Mel added.

"I think he was a pilot at one point in his career so if it starts, he's gone," said Casey.

"Definitely," said Mel.

"And it's our only aircraft, so we may end up stranded out here," said Debra.

"On a brighter note, the air up here is perfect, and that breeze feels so good on my face," said Sarah with a smile as she cocked her head upward toward the sky and shut her eyes for a moment.

"Feel that sun," said Debra whose face was also skyward. "I could stand here forever."

"Wait until you see the view from up on the plateau," said Mel.

"I can't even imagine," said Sarah.

"I don't see or hear anyone or anything," said Mel. "After forty years of living in a cave with equipment humming all day and all night, we once again are able to feel what it's like to live where we were born to live."

"Sarah and I have never lived where we were born to live," said Debra.

"Well, hopefully we'll be able to make a living up here and can stay," said Mel.

"From what I understand, this location is very remote, so living up here might be more a case of survival, depending on what's left in other areas," said Debra.

"But without an airplane, we won't really know," said Mel. "Let's take one step at a time. There used to be a small town where we're going, so that might offer a better clue as to what we might find elsewhere."

"OK, I'm anxious to see more, so let's keep moving," said Debra.

"Casey and I are going to take a short rest here, so you three go ahead and we'll catch up," said Brady who was still slumped on the ground against the wall.

"You both look exhausted," said Debra, surveying the two.

"No, we'll be OK in a minute," said Brady.

"Just stay here until you're up to it," said Debra who then turned and started toward the valley wall.

"We have food and water in these backpacks, so we'll have a picnic when we see you," said Sarah who then followed Debra.

"Dangle food in front of him and he'll follow you anywhere," said Casey.

"Shut up you smelly old turd," whispered Brady.

"What do you think Lucas is up to, especially if he can get that airplane to fly?" asked Casey.

"I think he'll check on his blocks first," said Brady.

"Should we be worried that he has a plane and we don't?" asked Casey.

"Other than the fact that we'll be isolated here in the middle of nowhere, no, I don't think so," said Brady.

"I agree, he's more interested in taking care of his own

business," said Casey.

"And in the meantime, we're completely isolated?" asked Brady.

"Not necessarily," said Casey.

"So you know about another airplane?" asked Brady.

"Possibly," said Casey.

"That would be great, so maybe we should start following the others to let them know," said Brady.

"All in good time, my chubby friend, all in good time," said Casey.

"Alright, so maybe another minute or two," said Brady.

"Don't you mean an hour or two?" asked Casey.

"We volunteered, remember," said Brady.

"That was before I saw the grim reaper waiting for my collapse," said Casey.

"Grim Reaper?"

"Forget it."

"Look, if we croak, someone will eventually come along and bury us," said Brady.

"Hey, look, there's some grass over there, and it would feel so relaxing for us to just lie down there in the sun," said Casey. "I can work on my tan."

"You're black," said Brady.

"Some tans are darker than others," said Casey. "Yours will be some bright shade of red."

"Actually, that's probably true."

"You know, maybe there's a hospital up there in that little town Mel mentioned," said Casey. "It would have an emergency room. Or maybe there's a funeral home and then we could just forego the hospital and start shopping for coffins."

"Get your useless old ass up off the ground and get it in gear," said Brady who reached down and took Casey's hand to pull him to his feet.

"Could I at least stay here long enough to write up a will," said Casey who was now being tugged along toward the valley wall.

"Don't worry, if you do check out, I'll kick some dirt over your body so the critters won't eat you," said Brady.

"Thanks, you overstuffed piece of dog shit," said Casey. Brady smiled as he towed him along. Soon, they began to slowly wind their way up past the giant boulders to the plateau.

******

"I guess the question of survival on the surface may have just taken a big step forward," said Debra as they approached the rim of the valley.

"Well, it does seem liveable, and almost like paradise, but long term survival may be another matter unless we spot a supermarket," said Sarah.

"Being far from anywhere, we have no idea what other parts of the planet look like," said Debra. "Who knows, there might still be supermarkets out there."

"It was over an hour's drive to the nearest store from that little town, and that's several days on foot," said Mel with a chuckle.

"Well, depending upon what and who survived, we could either be living in luxury or completely alone," said Debra.

"Or a plethora of other conditions in between," said Mel.

41

"If Lucas is able to fly out of here on that plane, he'll be able to find out what's out there, but we'll be totally isolated," said Sarah.

"Why don't we experience one event at a time," said Mel.

"Good advice," said Debra.

A moment later they crested the hill and found themselves on a plateau where they could see for what seemed forever in every direction.

"My, oh my, this really is like heaven," said Debra as she scanned the horizon. "It's definitely not painted birch trees on a cave wall."

"I'd almost forgotten what it looked like," said Mel

"It's a spectacular vista, but not necessarily a good sign if we're hoping for a Safeway," said Debra.

"Actually, I don't think this vista was that much different before the war," said Mel. "This area is very remote and there was a certain silence out here, even then."

"Yes, the silence is deafening, if that makes sense," said Sarah.

"It does, and as much as I'd like to stand here forever and enjoy the sun, the fresh air and the view, we do need to keep going," said Debra.

"Just follow those two ruts that are still visible through the grass," Mel pointed.

"Was that a road?" asked Sarah.

"More like a driveway," said Mel. "The town I told you about is in a little valley and the hangar is on a nearby hill, so we'll see the hangar first."

"According to my pedometer, we walked almost a mile through that tunnel, so it will be that same mile to town," said

Debra who started out in one of the ruts.

"Correct," said Mel who fell in behind her. Sarah took the other rut.

"Lucas could be in Las Vegas before they get there," said Sarah.

"Vegas is in the opposite direction," said Mel.

"Do you think the slot machines still work?" asked Sarah.

"If the city still exists, some version of those might still exist," said Mel.

"I wonder if Lucas has made it to the little town yet?" asked Debra.

"Well, we haven't heard gunfire, so at least nobody has been shot yet," said Sarah.

"In any event, I think we should hurry," said Debra.

"You two go ahead, I'm slow," said Mel.

"OK, because we really need to catch up with Riley before he either shoots himself, shoots Lucas, or gets shot by Lucas," said Debra.

"Any of those are possible, especially the shoots himself scenario!" said Mel. Debra nodded, then she and Sarah broke into a run, Debra in one rut, Sarah in the other. They skimmed along through the grasses, trying to land their feet in the ruts that were still visible.

"Is that sage brush out there?" asked Debra.

"I have no idea, but it could be," said Sarah.

"I feel like we're in a dream," said Debra.

"It's so much better than I could ever have imagined it would be," said Sarah.

"Yes, feel that sun," said Debra.

"Smell the air and feel that breeze," said Sarah.

"Those mountains seem so close, but I know they're probably fifty miles away," said Debra.

"Look, ahead there, that must be the hangar!" shouted Sarah a little while later, pointing. In the distance was the faded brown facade of a structure wedged into a hill.

"The town is in a little valley according to Mel so we won't see it yet," said Debra.

"Wait, I can see the tip of what looks like a church steeple," said Sarah pointing again.

"Oh good, so it's not much further," said Debra.

A few minutes later they stopped on a hill at the edge of the small town, its weathered structures still intact, and no sign of life. On the hill to the northeast was the hangar with one of it's walls covered in a green carpet of something.

"Do you see any sign of Riley or Lucas?" asked Sarah.

"No....Oh! Wait, there!" said Debra pointing at the hangar whose door was now being opened by someone in a tractor.

"That would be Lucas, so where is Riley?" asked Sarah.

"Wait, there, along the road leading up to the hangar," said Debra.

"He's just standing there, so that's good," said Sarah.

"That's what he's supposed to do, but let's get there before things change!" said Debra. "It looks like we'll have to go down into town in order to get to that road."

"I think you're right," said Sarah who broke into a run. Debra followed right behind her.

Other than weathered siding and cracked stucco on the buildings, as well as grass, weeds, dead trees and a few small bushes, the town seemed to be as it had been nearly forty years before. It was now just a rather well preserved ghost town. As they ran, they spotted a flower pot on the porch of an old brick building. It sported a blossoming flower.

"My god, someone is living here!" Debra exclaimed as they ran past.

"That's a game changer," Sarah replied as they continued up the road toward Riley. Just then several shots rang out and they stopped.

"Oh no, that's not good," said Debra, looking at Sarah. She started out again at full speed.

"Let's hope," said Sarah.

As they ran, they could see Riley ahead standing in the middle of the road. A moment later they saw an aircraft lift off and fly away to the northwest.

"Well, Riley is still standing, and Lucas is flying away, so at least they're both alive," said Debra.

"But one or both could be wounded," said Sarah as they approached Riley.

He turned as they ran up to him. He was holding his pistol with both hands against his chest.

"My hand hurts," said Riley, who held out his hand.

"From firing the gun?" asked Debra.

"It kicks pretty good," he replied sheepishly.

"Not much of a gunfight I guess," said Sarah.

"No, and I don't know where my bullet went, but I don't think it was anywhere near Lucas," said Riley.

"At least he knew you had a gun," said Debra.

"I know, so I clearly scared him off," said Riley.

"Clearly," said Debra with a smile, looking at Sarah.

"He went that-a-way," Riley pointed.

"So now you're a cowboy?" asked Sarah.

"I am," said Riley, holding out his gun. Debra pushed the barrel away from them.

"We saw a flower pot with a flower back in town, so apparently someone is living there," said Debra.

"I saw it too," said Riley.

"We need to check that out," said Sarah.

"Right, let's go," said Debra.

"Well, whoever he, she or they are, they would have had to live through radiation and probably dark skies and cold winters," said Sarah as they walked back down the road.

"No supermarket in sight," said Debra.

"No nothing," said Sarah.

They arrived in front of the three story brick building where the flower pot was perched on its stoop. Debra walked up to the door and knocked. They waited, but there was no sound from inside. She knocked again, this time louder.

"Hello!" she shouted after stepping back a few paces. She repeated the hail, then walked to the door and knocked even louder, but there was still no reply. After several minutes of waiting, a voice rang out from above.

"Who are you and who were you shooting at?" came a woman's voice from a third story window. They looked up, and above them, propping herself on the sill of a window, was an elderly woman whose long gray hair hung down around her face. Her eyes were sunken and her face deeply wrinkled. She was desperately thin and seemed to be more like a skeleton clad in skin than a living person. They stared at her for a moment before speaking.

"I'm Debra, this is Sarah, and that's Riley," said Debra. "Riley was just returning gunfire from someone we were after."

"You were after someone?" she asked.

"Yes, and he took the plane that was up the hill in that hangar," said Riley

"That explains the sound of a plane," said the woman.

"We're from the cave," said Debra pointing down.

"So you're with those thirty lucky shits who went down there thirty nine years ago?" she asked.

"Actually, we're offspring of those lucky shits," said Debra

"Right, you're too young to have gone down since everyone was an adult at the time," said the woman.

"The three of us were born down there," said Debra.

"Who took the plane?" asked the woman.

"An older gentleman by the name of Lucas," said Riley.

"Lucas! That mother fucker is no gentleman," said the woman.

"You know who he is?" asked Debra.

"Of course, I was supposed to be one of the thirty who went down, but he left me here to die on the prairie," said the woman.

"Why did he leave you?" asked Debra.

"He picked up six of his cronies on our way here and had to cut six of us at the last minute," said the woman.

"Oh right, those military guys from his inner circle, like Sid," said Sarah.

"Can we come in?" asked Debra.

"Let me come down," she replied. A few minutes later the

door opened and the woman, dressed in a tattered gray robe, stood in the doorway. She was hunched over and was using a shotgun as a cane.

"My place is a mess, so maybe I'll come out," said the woman.

"Can I help you down the steps?" asked Debra, moving forward to offer a hand.

"No, I'm fine," said the woman who worked her way down the three steps to the street. Even though Debra was not much more than five feet tall herself, she had to look down.

"You've lived here for the past forty years?" asked Debra.

"Thirty nine and change," she replied. "Oh, and where are my manners, I'm Edna."

"We're pleased to meet you Edna," said Sarah.

"Are you alone here?" asked Debra.

"Yes, I'm the sole survivor," said Edna. "So that was Lucas who flew out of here in that airplane?"

"Yes," said Debra.

"I worked for Lucas for years, and as I said, he cut me from the group," said Edna.

"Right, the thirty person limit," said Debra. "So what about the five others who were cut?"

"All dead or long gone from here and probably dead," said Edna.

"So, he promises to take you down to the safety of the cave, then dumps you for his military cronies at the last minute," said Debra.

"Yes, but I managed to survive," said Edna.

"You rode out the bombing in this building?" asked Sarah.

"This building was owned by an old guy who had a deep

bunker below his basement that no one in town knew about," said Edna.

"And you rode out the aftermath of the war there?" asked Sarah.

"Well, I wasn't all that bad looking back then, so I think he thought he was going to get some if he took me down," said Edna. "He only stocked the shelter for himself, so he hadn't really planned to invite anyone, but I guess the lure of a shack job was too much to resist."

"So was it?" asked Debra with a smile.

"A shack job?" asked Edna. "No, the old fart expired during the bombing, so he never got the chance to get it up."

"So, after that it was just you in the shelter," said Debra.

"Except the food ran out after about five years or so," said Edna. "But the well still works to this day, so I had water. He was clever enough to install a hand pump, because without electricity, I was still able to get water."

"How did you get food after the stored food ran out?" asked Debra.

"That's a whole nother story, because it was a wasteland up here, and nothing survived except insects and small animals that lived in the ground," said Edna. "You can eat cockroaches by the way."

"That makes me cringe," said Sarah.

"If you're hungry, you'll eat anything that doesn't kill you," said Edna.

"What about radiation?" asked Debra.

"Right, well that lasted for a long time, so I had to stay inside most of the time," said Edna. "My radiation tester died after ten years or so, but it was still reading in the red when it died."

"But you managed to keep from starving," said Debra.

"Barely," said Edna. "Look at me."

"What do you eat now?" asked Sarah.

"I have what amounts to a garden scattered about in several locations, and I shoot rabbits, rats and ground squirrels."

"So you have a gun," said Riley.

"I ran out of shotgun shells years ago, but managed to break into the armory down the street and get military weapons and ammo," said Edna.

"Edna?!" shouted Mel, as he limped toward them from down the street.

"Mel!" shouted Edna who started shuffling toward him.

"You made it!" said Mel, who made his way forward and the two hugged.

"Look at me, I'm old," said Edna as she held him out at arms length.

"You think you're old," said Mel.

"You two obviously know each other," said Debra.

"She's my sister!" said Mel. "Lucas cut her from our group at the last minute."

"I know, she told us about that," said Debra.

"What Lucas did was about as low as anyone can go, but apparently it was part of the deal he made to acquire the cave," said Mel.

"I've spent the last thirty nine plus years barely surviving up here while the rest of you lived below in luxury," said Edna.

"It was a cave, Edna, so that's not exactly luxury no matter how you dress it up," said Mel.

"I'm sure it was much better than up here," she replied.

"I'm sure that's true, but you survived, so that's all that counts," said Mel.

"I was lucky at first, then just the will to live forced me to keep going," said Edna.

"I never thought I'd see you again," said Mel.

"Who else came up?" asked Edna.

"Besides Lucas and us, there's Brady and Casey who will be here when they get here," said Debra.

"Brady, oh my god, he was just a kid," said Edna. "And Casey, yes, he was the pilot."

"They're both hopelessly out of shape, so it may take them some time to get here," said Sarah.

"So where do you think Lucas is going?" asked Edna.

"We have no idea," said Debra.

"I saw the plane depart as I was on my way here," said Mel.

"Maybe he'll just fly away and be gone," said Debra.

"Hopefully," said Mel.

"You were lucky that you didn't get any direct nuclear hits out here in the prairie," said Debra.

"When tens of thousands of nukes go off, the smoke and dust from the explosions, the fires, the radiation and the fallout is worldwide," said Edna. "The dark overcast encircles the globe and there's really no place to hide or to go except deep underground. The winters were brutal for many years."

"I'm sure that millions if not billions went underground, and I wonder if the rest suffered a slow death on the surface," said Sarah.

"Even underground was not a brilliant choice," said Edna.

"Surviving long term in bomb shelters, basements or other relatively temporary underground facilities is just a short term hiding place. Knowing what I know, I'm certain that only a very few had anything as sophisticated as your cave."

"That's the sad truth," said Mel. "I'm sure that most of those who went undergrouand are now dead. We had a near perfect system with multiple redundancies and repair parts. And we had to know how to keep everything working."

"We? No, actually, Lucas was the only one who knew how to maintain it and keep it running," said Debra.

"And of course he held that over your heads, right?" asked Edna.

"Yes, of course, but then that's also why we need to keep him alive," said Debra.

"Too bad," said Edna.

"I'm still amazed that you managed to survive," said Mel.

"It was brutal," said Edna. "I was out here in the wilderness barely able to grow a garden or find critters to shoot for food, so I can imagine other people in bombed or burnt out areas trying to figure out how to live."

"And you were an avid tent camper and high country hiker before the war, so you had survival skills that most did not have," said Mel. "Most people were candy asses who got their food from the supermarket and had no clue how to survive in the wild."

"Most people never had the opportunity to learn those skills, nor did they have the interest in doing it for that matter," said Edna. "They went about their business in a modern world where everything was done for them by others."

"What about the so-called survivalists that I've read about," asked Sarah.

"During the first half dozen years or so, I'm sure it didn't matter if you knew how to live off the land or not," said Edna. "The fact that I lived out here, a hundred miles from anywhere, and had a hole to climb into, gave me at least a chance to scratch out a living."

"Are there any survivors that you know of?" asked Debra.

"Not a swinging dick," she replied.

"A swinging.....?" asked Debra, looking at Mel for a definition.

"It's what you think it is," said Mel.

"Got it," said Debra with a smile.

"Only three of his military buddies are still alive, but after three passed it made room for myself, Debra and Riley," said Sarah.

"You said he picked these military folks up on the way here," said Debra. "Do you know where?"

"Yes, there's another cave complex south of here," said Mel. "I think it's a top secret military facility of some kind."

"Secret......I'm wondering if any of this secrecy had anything to do with Lucas's reluctance to let us come up?" asked Debra.

"I suppose it could have," said Mel.

"OK, so you three weren't born until some of his cronies passed?" asked Edna.

"Well, almost," said Debra. "I was born before any of them died since my mother was pregnant when we came into the cave," said Debra.

"Do you know who your mother is?" asked Edna.

"Shiela," said Debra.

"Shiela, yes, I remember her, she was a very pretty lady," said

Edna. "What about your father?"

"I'm not sure," said Debra.

"Really? Well, there were only thirty people down there, and a dozen men or so," said Edna.

"I know, but if my mother won't tell me and they don't come forward, I'm not going to ask," said Debra.

"You've never been curious?" asked Edna.

"Not really," said Debra.

"What about you, Sarah?" asked Edna.

"My mother and father are still down in the cave," said Sarah.

"And Sarah's my sister, so we have the same parents," said Riley.

"Got it, so how soon after Shiela was down there were you born, Debra?" asked Edna.

"Maybe five months or so," said Debra.

"Five months, interesting, then your father might have been one of those who was cut," said Edna.

"Perhaps, but I'm more interested in finding out if we can live up here than I am about my genealogy," said Debra.

"I understand that, but before we wander into that subject, I'd like to know your take on the thirty person limit, since that's why I was left for dead forty years ago," said Edna.

"My experience after those forty years down there is that the resources would not support more than about thirty," said Debra.

Just then Brady and Casey stumbled in, appearing near death.

"Holly shit, the food down there must be pretty good," said Edna, squinting at the two of them as they shuffled to a stop.

"We made it," wheezed Brady.

"You were just a squirt, maybe what, twelve?" asked Edna as

she rushed to meet him.

"Eleven," said Brady as he hugged her.

"My, you have grown," said Edna, unable to reach all the way around him.

"He eats too much," said Casey.

"Haven't you died yet?" asked Brady.

"Casey, you were the pilot," said Edna.

"Among other things," said Casey.

"What about Lucas, did he fly out of here?" asked Brady.

"Yes, he's gone," said Riley.

"Well, the truth is, while he essentially saved all of you from almost certain death, he sentenced me and five others to almost certain death by leaving us behind," said Edna.

"I think about the cave this way, it was originally intended for political dignitaries, so if it hadn't been stolen by those crooked military people and illegally acquired by Lucas, we would not be here now," said Mel.

"And despite the fact that these military traitors were crooks, to us they are essentially heros," said Debra.

"Despite what he did for you, I still hate the bastard," said Edna.

"I can't blame you," said Debra. "But, all this drama aside, we're now up here on the surface, and we really do need to figure out whether we can live here."

"I'll tell you right up front that living up here in the high desert is no picnic," said Edna. "And since Lucas took the plane and left you stranded, it eliminates the possibility of your traveling about to find a place that is suitable to live."

"To top it off, Lucas is the only person who knows how to

operate the cave complex, so we may not even be able to count on the cave if we can't survive up here and have to go back down," said Debra.

"So, let me ask this: if this wasn't his cave to begin with, how does it turn out that he knows everything about how to keep it running?" asked Edna.

"One of the six military people had all of that information, as well as a cache of manuals," said Casey. "So Lucas was schooled by him before he died."

"Then the manuals must still be in the cave," said Edna.

"They could be, but there are a million places to stash things in the cave, and no one has a clue where the manuals are located," said Debra.

"If we could catch Lucas, we could torture him into telling us," said Casey.

"Another reason why we can't afford to kill him," said Debra.

"Yet," said Edna.

"So, what did you say you use to hunt rabbits?" asked Debra.

"My favorite is an old AK47 with armor piecing bullets."

"You used an AK47 to hunt rabbits?" asked Casey.

"I know, it's a slight bit of overkill," said Edna.

"Slight?.... Jesus," he replied.

"Well, it eliminates the need to aim carefully, but sometimes the rabbit or rat is hard to collect up," said Edna. "Although that does save time cleaning the carcass."

"I think I'm going to be sick," said Sarah.

"That's gross, Edna," said Mel shaking his head.

"It's protein, and besides, you eat what you have to eat to survive," said Edna.

"I'm afraid that's something we have no way of imagining right now as we contemplate what it might take to live up here," said Debra.

"Before I was forced to do it, neither could I," said Edna.

"And this has been your home for forty years," said Debra.

"Yes," she nodded. "You simply don't know how hard it is to survive in the wilderness unless you have to do it. It's a full time job. I've come to appreciate the lives of our ancestors, because survival in the wild is a combination of luck, fear, daily problem solving, and a very keen desire to continue living."

"We've been spoiled living in a comfortable, well designed cave, although it involved establishing and maintaining a very large greenhouse garden," said Debra. "In a cave, that's not that easy."

"I wondered about that as I struggled with my puny efforts up here in scorching heat and freezing temperatures after my canned and packaged goods either ran out or spoiled," said Edna. "There were dark clouds and overcast skies for many years before the sun finally came out, but when it did I was able to get my garden to produce. And of course some of the ground animals and insects somehow survived. Small birds did as well, but try shooting a sparrow with an assault rifle. Or if you do hit one, try picking up what's left."

"Well, even though life down there was actually quite pleasant as cave life goes, we did get a bit of 'Island fever'," said Mel.

"Wasn't it very large with lots of amenities?" asked Edna.

"Yes, but compared to the wide open spaces up here on the surface, there's really no comparison," said Debra. "I have never been to the surface, and now that I see and feel the open sky and fresh air...... wow, it's a feeling of freedom that I've never known. If I have any choice at all, I will never go back down."

"You say that now, but when it's day to day survival, as far as I'm concerned, survival living up here sucks," she replied. "It's not like forty years ago when you drove to a store for food and turned on the screen to find out what's going on in the world. Up here in the scorched Earth, living hand to mouth from whatever you can squeeze from what's left in nature is a monumental struggle. Being free in the post-war wide open spaces is life on the edge, and you hang on by your fingernails all the time, with no breaks."

"I guess my lifelong dream of heaven above was quite different from that," said Debra. "Down there, I lay in bed, staring at a ceiling of painted rock, dreaming of real blue skies, puffy white clouds, with rustling of trees and the songs of birds singing. There's a warm breeze across my cheek as I wade through a field of colorful flowers."

"Heaven up here has many faces, and the face I know is not at all like that," said Edna. "The face I know is beautiful, but it's incredibly harsh and punishing."

"I believe you, because you've lived in it and I have only dreamed of an ideal world that does not exist anymore, or may never exist again," said Debra.

"Too often, I would wake up in the morning hungry and cold, wondering if I'd be able to find enough to eat for the day," said Edna. "Yes, I suppose this could be imagined as a blank canvas as you gaze out over the prairie. But starting from scratch with what's left is like setting the clock back twenty thousand years to when we were wandering around in tribes trying to find food and avoiding the possibility of being eaten by a predator or being attacked and killed by a neighboring tribe."

"I wonder if it's like this everywhere, with survivors struggling to survive like you?" asked Sarah.

"I can only see my world, and what I see is pretty bleak," said Edna.

"On the positive side, the Earth has faced mass extinctions before and recovered," said Sarah.

"If the new Earth is one with the same people bent on killing those who don't share their values, then I have zero faith in whatever and whoever survives," said Edna.

"I don't know, maybe we're destined to be a species with a terminal destiny," said Mel.

"If so, we just took a giant step in that direction," said Debra.

"I want to be optimistic, but it's pretty hard when you've faced what I've faced," said Edna.

"Those of us who survived have a chance to start over and re-establish ourselves in a better way," said Debra.

"I don't know...... without worldwide communication, surviving entities, if they do exist, can easily slip back into selfish tribes focused on self-survival with little concern about anyone else," said Edna.

"Unless some society managed to survive largely intact and can spread their good fortune to others," said Debra.

"That's something we have no way of knowing right now," said Mel.

"As I said, I think we've set the clock back twenty thousand years, and the road back may be along the same road we've already traveled, with many of the same mistakes waiting to be made again," said Edna.

"Maybe there's at least one thing that everyone who survived can agree on," said Debra.

"No more nukes?" asked Mel.

"That's the one thing," said Debra.

"That would help, unless we manage to discover some other way of killing millions in a single shot," said Edna.

"Not to break up this little philosophical discussion, but Lucas just flew off to see the world and we're stuck here on the prairie," said Sarah. "So what's our plan?"

"Our plan is to get an aircraft of our own," said Casey.

"That would be great, Casey, but where would we find one?" asked Debra.

"The last place we stopped before we came here forty years ago," said Casey.

"You mean that other cave, the secret military one?" asked Mel.

"Yes, and it's only about ten minutes away," said Casey.

"Ten minutes by air," said Mel.

"That's only what, maybe fifty miles plus or minus?" asked Casey.

"Oh sure, fifty miles on foot," said Brady. "I could do that twice a day."

"Lucas used a tractor to pull that aircraft out of the hangar," said Casey, pointing up toward the hangar.

"He did, I saw him use it," said Riley.

"Are you suggesting we drive fifty miles on a tractor?" asked Brady.

"It's faster and easier than walking," said Casey.

"A plane would be a game changer for us, so let's go get it," said Debra.

"Alright, someone go up and get the tractor," said Casey, looking at Riley and pointing toward the hangar.

"I wouldn't know how to start it or drive it," said Riley.

"Of course not, so someone else go up with him..... Mel?" asked Casey.

"Sure, I can start and drive one of those," said Mel.

"Great, let's go, Mel," said Riley waving for him to follow as he started up the road.

Chapter Four

Lucas was shocked to see how complete the devastation had been as he traveled north to Bellingham, Washington where one of his blocks was located. What had been a thriving civilization, was now a lifeless wasteland. Only an occasional wisp of smoke provided the possibility of camp fires from scattered survivors. A layer of green covered what was left of the structures to act as a soft green blanket that hid the scars. There were no cars or planes. No lights. Just the quiet of a landscape whose body had been paved over and built upon and was now being healed by nature.

As he approached the area north of Bellingham where the block was located, the tall trees that were once there when the block was built were now mostly gray spires sticking up amid a mix of smaller trees and undergrowth. He was relieved to see the large silver block ahead. It stood in stark contrast to its green bed of vegetation. When he arrived he saw that the surface on top had accumulated a considerable amount of soil and was green with small bushes, tall grass and wild flowers. There was also a light tower on top that he did not install and he wondered who had. His friend Peter had been placed in charge of this block, but had either not tended the top or had long since left. After all, it had been nearly forty years and Peter would be in his eighties had he stayed. Supplies and survival equipment was provided to each block, including a food maker. Peter, as well as the two keepers in other blocks, might well have moved elsewhere. Forty years is a long time to live in one of these. Each block had an aircraft in which to move about, or move elsewhere if they so desired, as long as they secured the block before they left. But where would they move? The destruction seemed complete. However, they had volunteered to stay in his blocks as a matter of personal choice, knowing the risks. So their fate was their responsibility, and if they didn't survive, it was not his fault.

He gently landed the aircraft on the roof amid the thick layer of vegetation. He deplaned and waded through the brush to the keypad and punched in his code of familiar numbers, his birthday. Only he and his block keepers knew the code. The door latch clicked and he opened it and went in. It was totally dark inside so he retrieved the tiny but powerful flashlight he had used to guide him through the construction tunnel. He started down a long curved hallway and entered a dark room where he felt for a light switch, but could not find it. He shined his light on the large globe that sat atop a cylindrical post in the floor. This was the Blockmaster. A feature in each of his blocks, it provided a means of communication and security. The light should have activated the globe, but there was no response. So he turned his attention to the control console that was next to the door to

Peter's room. It was clear that no one had been here for a very long time. He was now concerned because the Blockmaster was programmed to be on guard and active at all times, so this was not as it should be. He opened the door to Peter's room and shined his light around. There was an unmade bed and clothes scattered about. Obviously he had left in a hurry many years ago, apparently without packing. If he had moved to another location, one would expect an orderly departure, not this. This looked like a hasty, completely unplanned departure. He thought for a moment, then went to the console and sat in a chair. After working the keyboard, a pencil beam on the globe came on and was now trained on him. A moment later, another one came on, and finally dozens of beams blossomed from the globe and began scanning the room.

"You are Lucas," said the Blockmaster after a moment.

"When did Peter leave?" he asked as he got up and walked to the railing that circled the globe.

"Thirty-six years, three months, two days, six hours, fourteen minutes and three seconds ago," said the Blockmaster.

"Did he leave any messages?" asked Lucas

"He did not."

"His aircraft is not on the roof, is it in the hangar?" asked Lucas.

"No, the others took it," said the Blockmaster.

"The others? What others?" asked Lucas in alarm.

"The others who came," said the Blockmaster.

"Who were the others?" asked Lucas.

"Peter said they were his friends," said the Blockmaster.

"What about the light tower?" asked Lucas.

"It was installed long after Peter and the others left," said the Blockmaster.

"Blockmaster, what is your prime directive?"

"To guard the sanctity and security of this block in perpetuity."

"But you were dormant, so how could you have done that if you were dormant?"

"My assigned human was placed in charge of my status."

"But you violated your prime directive."

"My programming includes following directives from both you and Peter, at your request."

OK, that's a bit of a flaw, Lucas thought to himself. But even so, Peter was not supposed to ask the Blockmaster to become dormant. And why did he leave in such a hurry? More importantly, why had he invited these friends into the block since he and he alone was supposed to be in here. That was the deal he had made with each of his block keepers.

"Why did your block keeper invite friends inside since he was not supposed to do that?" asked Lucas.

"I could not know that because I was asked to become dormant."

Why, thought Lucas. Peter was supposed to leave the block in the Blockmaster's care if he left. So if Peter is living on the surface somewhere with these friends, it may well be against his will. However, it seems more likely that these friends were not friends at all, but people with intentions contrary to Peter's will.

"Are you connected to the other blocks?" asked Lucas.

"Yes."

"Can you ask if anyone still lives in any of the other blocks?" asked Lucas.

"I will ask.....yes, two other blocks have humans," said the Blockmaster.

Two. OK. Jane, north of Jackson, Wyoming, and Chandler northwest of San Francisco. He would not be surprised if Chandler were still there after forty years, but he was not sure why Jane was still there, considering the severe winters in Jackson.

"Those are Jackson and the California coast," said Lucas.

"No, the Vantage block has humans," said the Blockmaster.

Vantage, so maybe Peter went there since the combination on the door is the same for all of his blocks. But why would he go there? It was on the river, so maybe that was a factor.

"Is Peter there now?" asked Lucas.

"No, only his friends are there," said the Blockmaster.

"His friends....how many friends?" asked Lucas.

"Six."

"Six?"

"Yes."

"How many aircraft at Vantage?" he asked.

"Two."

Two aircraft, so one would be Peter's, and the other would be the Vantage aircraft. So, obviously they kidnaped Peter and moved to Vantage. But Peter is not there now, so what happened to him?

"Do you know where Peter is now?" he asked.

"No."

Alright, Peter is gone, and now these six friends have apparently been living in the block for the past thirty six years. These so called friends are most likely hostile, and the welfare of his Vantage block is now his main concern. He must go to Vantage and face an almost certain confrontation with these people. They could be armed, so he had to approach with caution. But he has a powerful forcefield cannon on his aircraft and a forcefield side arm that is in the aircraft. He also had his pistol. There was no telling what these 'friends' had, but it will most likely end in a gun battle, because these people must be evicted from the block. It is entirely unacceptable to have strangers in any of his blocks. They must go, either voluntarily, or with toe tags.

"I am leaving now for Vantage, and no one must enter this block but me," said Lucas.

"No one but you will be allowed to enter this block," said the Blockmaster.

Lucas stood in thought for a moment before leaving. His Vantage block was in danger, and this was war. He went to the roof and stood for a moment in the twilight of evening, struck by the eerie silence, surrounded by a bed of green extending to the horizon in all directions. There is literally nothing left of the civilization that used to be here. He felt completly alone and a bit lost. And now, a feeling that he had not had before......a deep devotion to those he had interred into his blocks. These were people who believed his claim that their minds would be preserved forever. In essence, they believed in him. They were mostly elderly people whose lives were winding down. People like him. And now, interlopers threaten those he had placed in the Vantage block. He felt a new and intense anger toward them as he climbed into his plane.

As he was departing, he noticed a primitive ladder made from a tree that was felled against the side of the block. That was how these invaders got up on the block. It was a home invasion.

He aimed the aircraft's forcefield weapon at the tree ladder and fired. Pieces flew into a cloud of debris that rained to the ground. He then headed east toward the Vantage Block which was in an isolated area along the Columbia River in Eastern Washington. After he crested the Cascade mountains, night slowly descended into a deep darkness. With no lights from a civilization that no longer existed, he followed his navigation instruments. As he drew nearer to the location of the block he began to follow the river, using light from the stars and a crescent moon that cast faint reflections off the water. As he approached the block he saw that another of those light towers was on this block, and wondered if these peope were responsible. After he landed he sat in the plane for a moment, watching and waiting with his landing lights still on. Then, light from inside suddenly came on, sending a narrow streak across the rooftop. A moment later the door opened a bit more and someone peeked out. Then the door immediately slammed shut. They obviously saw his aircraft.

"Who's in there?" Lucas asked over his plane's loudspeaker.

"Who are you?" came a man's voice after the door again opened a crack.

"I am Lucas and this is MY block..... you are trespassing!" he announced.

"It is you who are trespassing!" the man shouted through the crack.

"Where is Peter?" asked Lucas..

"He's dead," came the answer.

"How did he die?"

"He was uncooperative and we were forced to shoot him," came the answer after a brief hesitation.

"In other words, you murdered him."

"In the world of survival there is no murder."

"Peter was a peaceful man."

"It was self defense."

"Of course it was," Lucas replied. "However, you and whoever is in there with you will need to leave immediately."

"My family and I have lived here for over thirty years," the man replied. "Therefore, this is adverse possession."

"In the world of survival.....in your own words..... there is no murder, and neither is there adverse possession!" said Lucas with a laugh.

"It doesn't matter, we own this place now," said the man.

"I built these blocks and they belong to me, so you will either leave peacefully or you will be hauled out in body bags!" said Lucas.

"This is our home, and I am ordering you off our property," said the man.

"I assume that means you have chosen to be hauled out in body bags," said Lucas.

"Oh, I'm so afraid," the man laughed.

"Alright then, how do you choose to die........ electrocution inside, slow starvation after I permanently lock your door, or being blasted to the ground below with my ship's cannon," said Lucas, knowing he had no way to electrocute them, nor any way to open the thick steel door to evict them.

"Give me a break!" came the voice after a moment of hesitation.

"You've been warned," said Lucas.

"So, not that we actually believe you, and just for kicks, what's your deal?" asked the man after a moment of silence. Lucas did not reply.

"I asked, what's your deal!?" the man loudly repeated. Lucas deliberately did not reply. When there was still no answer, the door edged open a bit farther and a face appeared holding one hand behind his back.

"Hello?!" the man shouted as he looked around, finally focusing on the aircraft's searchlight that forced him to hold one hand over his eyes.

"Everyone needs to step out peacefully," said Lucas.

"First, I need to see you," said the man, his hand still behind his back as he crept a couple more steps into the open. The man's free hand continued to shield his eyes from the spotlight, while his other remained behind his back. Lucas targeted the man with his forcefield weapon.

"What you need to do is deposit that weapon that's behind your back on the ground," said Lucas.

Before Lucas could react, the man quickly ducked back inside and slammed the door. Now what, thought Lucas as he stared at the closed door. It was virtually impenetrable. His threats didn't work, so how was he going to get these invaders out of there? His forcefield weapon would not seriously damage the door. Maybe he could have the Bellingham Blockmaster lock them inside and they would die of starvation as he had threatened. To do that, he would have to fly back to Bellingham. After several minutes of contemplation he lifted off, turned toward the other aircraft on the roof and fired. It slid to the edge and teetered for a second before tumbling end over end to the ground below where it lay upside down. As he hovered, he noticed a crude ladder made out of tree trunks leaning against the side of the block and he blew it to pieces. He then blew the side door off of the hangar and landed on the ground nearby and deplaned. Inside the hangar he saw a badly damaged aircraft and assumed they had crashed it somehow, then moved it inside. In the far corner was the entrance to the ground access tunnel into the block. He went to it and found that the door had never been opened. So they apparently did not know about the ground access tunnel. Good. So, without an aircraft or a way to get down from the block, they would starve to death, whether he locked the door with them inside, or not. But the Blockmaster said there were six of them, so perhaps they were not all inside the block. He went back to his plane and flew around the area scanning the ground with his searchlight. A short distance away he found two crude huts. He fired at the first and the two women and two children who were inside were thrown into the air, crashing through the trees to the ground in puffs of dust hundreds of feet away, all either dead or badly injured. He took aim at the second hut and fired. A half dozen men, women and children exploded into the air, several of them splashing into the river. One man who was still in the space where the hut stood, got to his feet and headed toward the river. Just as he was about to dive in, Lucas hit him with a blast that hurled him through the air, far out into the water where he skipped a few times before sinking. There were close to a dozen people here and as he hovered, he wondered whether any of them had anything to do with those still in the block. Perhaps he had just killed a dozen survivors who had nothing to do with the others. So maybe all six were still up in the block. Confused but still concerned about people living nearby, he flew in circles around the area looking, just to make sure, but there were now no signs of life. His job was not done, however. He had to somehow enter the block and make sure no one was there, so he flew back to land on top.

As he approached he spotted a man on the roof with a rifle crouched against the building. The man quickly got to his feet and began firing. Lucas hit him with a blast and the man went flying off the block to the ground where he crashed through a patch of sage, sending a cloud of dust and plant debris into the air. Lucas hovered over the roof, carefully scanning it with his searchlight. Seeing nothing, he landed. Whoever was still inside will die in there and no longer present a danger. But just as he was about to lift off, the door opened and a group of men and women with automatic rifles burst out of the door and began shooting. Bullets ricocheted off his windshield. He quickly hit the entire group at point blank range with his cannon, throwing them into the air with their rifles flipping like batons as they disappeared over the edge of the block to the ground below. At least five, he thought as he sat there examining the pock marks left by the bullets on his windshield. He sat for a moment looking at the open door. Was that everyone, he wondered. The Blockmaster in Bellingham said there were six and that was six.

Lucas deplaned and entered cautiously, still not certain that everyone was dead. Holding his forcefield hand cannon in front of him, he slowly went below. The Blockmaster was dark, and he shined his light around to find severe damage to the console. It had been shot multiple times and wiring was visible through the damage. All lights on it were off. They had apparently destroyed much of the electronics. He wasn't sure if the damage also destroyed circuitry that kept the spirits within the block alive. If it did, this would amount to mass murder. Of course his eternity concept may not have worked as his critics asserted, in which case there were no spirits, and then, the issue was moot. But if his blocks do work, this was a giant tragedy. Regardless of which scenario is true, if the block is lost, there was really nothing he could do about it now. So he went up, locked the door behind him and sat in his aircraft, thinking about what just happened. He had just killed at least eighteen survivors, some of whom may have had nothing to do with those who killed Peter.

This was a tragic outcome. To begin with, he had never been a killer, so what he had just done was beginning to sink in. He had killed all of these people in a rage. He didn't even know them, nor anything about their story of survival. But some of them had killed Peter, and he knew Peter was loyal and probably put up a fight. So in all likelihood, he was killed in some kind of struggle. Was it a fight, or was it murder? He had assumed it was murder without knowing for certain. Then, in his rage, he had wiped them out without any attempt to discuss the circumstances. He really had no idea who they were. After all, they had somehow survived a worldwide conflagration which was something that not many others had. Maybe they were just trying to survive in any way they could. And he killed them in anger because he didn't want them trespassing on his block. Is the penalty for trespass death? On the other hand, he was defending the spirits inside the block, if in fact his eternity block concept worked. But he didn't explain this to them. Surely they knew. It was all over the press before the war and the blocks were hardly invisible. Sure, they knew. And certainly Peter had told them if they didn't.

But what did that matter now? It was over. He did what he did, as callous and cold blooded as it was. And nothing could erase it. In his mind, he just did what he had to do.

Lucas sat in the darkness for a long time as he thought about what to do next. What if his other blocks have been similarly compromised? And who installed those light towers? More important perhaps was the question of whether his blocks actually worked. If they didn't, why did it matter if they were compromised? Indeed, if they don't work, is this whole effort to check on them a waste of time? Yet, there was no real proof that the blocks didn't work, so he owed this kind of robust defense to the thousands of occupants who had placed their trust in him. So yes, as creator of these blocks, he must now be their defender. He nodded to himself. He would continue to check on them and evict intruders by whatever means.

As he stared into the night he remembered the Winterhaven Block in California. It was one of the last blocks to be brought on line, and it had special meaning for him. It was where he and his sister had a serious falling out forty years ago. They had gone from there to his research facility in the desert outside of Tucson. He completed arrangements for acquiring the cave at that facility, and it was there that she had refused to go to the cave with him. So he left her there when he and twenty nine others left for Utah. It would be a miracle if she survived, considering what he had found so far on the surface. Even though the research facility was deep underground, it did not have the special features that his cave had. And it had been forty years. Still in deep thought about what had just happened, and what he had yet to do, he lifted off, heading south for Winterhaven.

Chapter Five

"It's not very fast, but much better than walking, especially if you have to go fifty miles," said Riley as Mel drove the tractor up to Edna's building.

"Alright, this will work," said Casey.

"The ride's a little rough, so that might be an issue," said Riley.

"It's a tractor, not a limo," said Mel.

"So who is going?" asked Riley.

"It will have to be Brady and myself again," said Casey.

"No, I need to go," said Riley.

"The tractor's seat will hold two, and only Casey and Brady will go," said Debra. "Casey is the only one who can fly a plane, and Brady is the only one who has been there and knows something about it."

"Brady was only eleven back then," said Riley.

"But I've actually been down in that facility," said Brady.

"You two are so completely exhausted and out of shape that you'd never make it, even riding on a tractor," said Riley.

"We only appear exhausted," said Casey. "With a good night's sleep, we'll be like new in the morning."

"And a couple of good meals," said Brady.

"How would we not know that," said Casey.

"You've never passed up a meal yourself old man," said Brady.

"OK, OK, stop it you two," said Debra. "It's true, you're not the fittest among us, but you are the ones who will have to do this."

"I know, and we'll be fine," said Brady who looked like a boiled lobster, and Casey who was barely able to stay on his feet as he slumped against the doorsill.

"I'm not taking bets," said Mel who was looking at them and shaking his head.

"In the meantime, Riley, we need you to go back to the cave for more food and water since we'll be up here a while longer, and these two will need supplies for their trip," said Debra.

"I guess I may be the only one in good enough shape to make the four mile round trip in a reasonable timeframe," said Riley.

"That's true, you are," said Debra.

"So I guess you're thinking I should go today, like now?" asked Riley.

"Yes, like now, that way these two can leave first thing in the morning," said Debra.

"I can keep up with Riley, and can help carry supplies, so I'll go with him," said Sarah.

"I was just going to ask if you would," said Debra.

"Alright, sis, let's go," said Riley who started out. Sarah caught up and the two quickly disappeared down the road.

"We'll leave at the break of dawn tomorrow," said Brady.

"If you're able to get up," said Casey.

"You're the one we'll have to drag out of bed," said Brady.

"Look, you two, this is an important mission so you'll have to travel together in relative harmony," said Debra. "We don't want you killing one another."

"We might die along the way, but it won't be because we killed each other," said Casey. "But I think we'll need hats since we haven't been in the sun in forty years and Brady can't afford to turn a brighter shade of red."

"I think I have a couple of old Rams hats somewhere," said Edna.

"Rams? You wouldn't happen to have Raiders by any chance?" asked Casey.

"No, but I think I might have Steelers?" she replied.

"No, no, Rams will do," said Casey. "Besides, I doubt if we'll run into anyone so I won't have to be embarrassed."

"Rams, Raiders?.....embarrassed? what in the hell are you talking about?" asked Brady.

"You're too young and illiterate to know," said Casey.

"I read," said Brady.

"Sure, comic books," said Casey.

"Alright, if you don't see anything after a couple of days, you may have to call it off and return," said Debra holding up her hands to get them to stop bickering. "We don't want you lost in the middle of nowhere."

"We know the facility is out there, and we'll find it," said Brady.

"That's right, I landed there to pick up Lucas's cronies, so I know what we're looking for," said Casey.

"Alright, so use your own judgement, but worst case, if you don't find it in a reasonable time frame, just return," said Debra.

"Not to worry," said Brady.

"The other thing to consider is that we'll be flying back in a plane, so we can push it a bit farther on the front end," said Casey.

"If the plane will start," said Brady.

"If we find a plane, I'll get it started now that I know Lucas was able to start his," said Casey.

That evening they pored over maps of the area that Edna had in a drawer. After some study, they located the departure point near Tucson where the original group had assembled forty years before. They then traced the route north to where they were now. They guessed at where they likely stopped to pick up Lucas's six military cronies based on Casey's memory of the flight. Brady circled the area. That would be where they would concentrate their search.

With map in hand, Casey and Brady left early the next morning. They traveled all day and camped in a grove of scrub oak to spend the night on the ground wrapped in blankets that Edna had supplied. Toward the end of the second day they found themselves on high ground where they were able to scan the countryside. Casey was searching the southern horizon with Edna's binoculars when Brady picked up the glint of reflected sunlight off to the west. He tapped Casey on the shoulder and pointed. Casey trained the binoculars on the point of light and saw what appeared to be two structures.

"This looks like it," said Casey, handing the binoculars to Brady.

"Yes, that's the place, just as we were nearing the end of our ability to go further," said Brady.

"Perfect," said Casey.

"It might be dark before we get there, so maybe we should camp here for the night," said Brady.

"Hell no, I'm not spending another night on the ground," said Casey.

"Yeah, I agree with that......let's see if this thing has a headlight," said Brady.

"It does," said Casey who put it in gear and started down the hill toward the complex.

"Is this as fast as it can go?" asked Brady.

"Balls out!" said Casey, raising a fist while hanging tightly onto the wheel as they bounced along over the bunch grass and sage.

"Balls out? Where do you find all this shit?" asked Brady who then started to smile and soon he was laughing as they rumbled toward their target.

"Yippee ki yay!" shouted Casey.

"This shit you dig up is starting to grow on me," said Brady.

It was dark by the time they finally arrived at the first structure which was the hangar. Using the headlight from the tractor they went to the hangar door and found it unlocked. But it took a good deal of effort for the two of them to slide it open enough for them to squeeze through. Casey began to look around with his light.

"The plane is still here and it looks intact," said Brady, who walked up to it and slapped it on the side. By now Casey was almost all the way up the boarding ladder.

"It's a fighter," said Casey after opening the door and looking inside.

"I don't know what that means, but will it start?" asked Brady.

"I'm sure it will, and I've flown these, so that's good," said Casey, who went forward and sat at the controls as Brady watched from the doorway.

"It's kind of small," said Brady, as he squeezed his large body inside.

"It's a fighter, not a freighter, so it's not designed to carry hippos," said Casey.

"Shut the fuck up you miserable piece of cow shit," said Brady as he wedged into the seat next to Casey, shoving him against the side of the cockpit.

"Cow shit?" asked Casey.

"I learn your creepy words fast."

"Can't you move your ham hock arm a little so I can actually use the controls," said Casey. Brady folded his arms in front of him after glaring at him for a second.

"This thing is armed to the teeth," said Casey, studying the panel. He began flipping switches and soon a light on the dash came on, followed by another light, then a series of gauges illuminated.

"Wow," said Brady.

"Amazing, after forty years!" Casey smiled as he continued to study the panel.

"So, let's get this baby out of the hangar and back to town," said Brady.

"We might want to open the hangar door first," said Casey.

"No shit, Dick Tracy," said Brady.

"Wait.... that had to be one of my lines, because you have no original vocabulary," said Casey.

"Did you know that video games are not a complete waste of time?" asked Brady.

"I'm sure that's a known fact," said Casey. "Now, let's get the tractor and get this thing home," said Casey.

"This is small," Brady puffed as he struggled to get out of the seat. By now, Casey was out the door without comment.

It was another hour before they were finally able to dig enough dirt away from the door to shove it open with the tractor. Once open, they used the tractor to pull the aircraft outside, then lifted off and aimed north toward the town. Using a partial moon and stars to light the way, the trip that had taken two days by tractor was covered in less than fifteen minutes. They landed in a clearing near the town after Casey found the searchlight on the panel and was able to scan the ground. Riley, who had been on watch, heard the plane and rushed out to greet them. He was sporting an assault rifle that Edna had given him but she had not instructed him in its use, nor had she given him ammunition. He carried it by the banana clip.

"We have a plane!" Riley shouted excitedly as the door opened and Casey appeared.

"It's a fighter," said Casey, patting the side of the plane as he came out.

"Does that mean it has a lot of guns?" asked Riley, waving the rifle over his head.

"It's well endowed," said Casey.

"It's a beauty!" said Debra, who now joined them after hearing the commotion outside.

"So where are we going with it?" asked Brady, as he reached the ground.

"It's something we'll have to discuss, but I have some thoughts," said Debra.

"Let's have that discussion in the morning," said Casey. "I'm old, it's late, and the trip was quite tiring."

"I'm not nearly as old, and I'm not senile like he is, but I second that," said Brady.

"Of course," said Debra as they all wandered back toward Edna's building.

******

"I guess the first question we have to ask is whether Lucas is really our first priority," said Debra from the head of the big table at Edna's the next morning.

"No, I think survival on the surface is number one," said Sarah.

"Yes, that's what I was thinking too, so maybe we need to determine if we're alone on this planet first before we make any more plans," said Debra. "Besides, that was the original purpose for coming up before we got into this tiff with Lucas."

"Before we head out on an adventure, keep in mind that this plane is a fighter, so it's really only designed to carry two," said Casey. "We could squeeze in a third behind the seats."

"That would be you, Brady and me," said Debra.

"Brady takes up the space of three, so we'll hope you fit," said

Casey.

"Eat shit," said Brady.

"We'll all fit," said Debra.

"So then we just take off and start exploring tomorrow?" asked Brady

"No, we need to decide where we're going before we do anything," said Debra.

They studied Edna's maps of the Western United States and circled areas of interest, including the block that Chandler was supposed to be in as well as the research facility near Tucson where they had assembled before going down into the cave forty years ago. After considerable discussion they decided to visit the block with Chandler first. The next day they packed enough supplies for several days and lifted off for the block northwest of San Francisco. The thought was that if Chandler is still there, he might have more information about what happened during the war and give them clues about what to do next. They spotted the block but decided to fly past after Brady saw what looked like a lighthouse far ahead. A short time later they passed over a small complex that appeared to have a museum and then two structures about a mile apart. They passed over a fence that seemed to encompass a rather large area before reaching the lighthouse. As they were hovering nearby, they saw smoke out in the forest from what could be the campfires of survivors.

"The lighthouse is still working despite the fact that there are no ships out there to alert, so that's a bit strange, and that smoke out there could be from campfires," said Casey.

"So people are definitely here, although there are none in sight," said Debra.

"And what's that fence all about?" asked Casey.

"I don't know, but there's a lot happening here, so this is definitely a place to check out at some point," said Debra.

After an excited discussion about survivors, including those who must be operating the lighthouse, they decided not to land, but instead head back to the block to speak with Chandler. They landed on top and filed out of the aircraft with Debra in the lead. To their surprise they found the door ajar and entered.

"This door should have been closed and locked, so obviously someone is either inside, or has been inside in the recent past," said Brady as they slowly made their way down the curved hallway. They entered a chamber with a large globe atop a cylindrical post on the floor. As they stood examining the globe, a voice rang out from behind them.

"Who are you?" came the voice that seemed to emanate from a console on the far wall.

"We thought we might find Chandler here," said Brady as they all turned toward the voice while Casey pulled out his pistol and aimed it in that direction.

"Chandler is not here," said the voice.

"Look, I'm Brady and he should remember me," said Brady.

"Brady, you were just a kid," came the voice.

"Wait, it's you Chandler, isn't it?" asked Brady.

"You tagged along with Lucas wherever he went," said Chandler. "Did he actually steal that cave from the government like he said he was going to do?"

"He did, and took twenty nine of us down with him, and we've been living there ever since," said Brady.

"So you've been in that cave for forty years," said Chandler.

"Interesting..... and is that Casey?"

"It is," said Casey.

"So who's the pretty woman?" asked Chandler.

"Debra," said Brady.

"So Lucas came up too?" asked Chandler.

"Yes, but we don't know where he is right now," said Brady.

"So, he didn't come up with you," said Chandler.

"He came up before us, and then flew away in the only plane we had," said Debra.

"But you obviously found another one," said Chandler.

"We did," said Casey.

"Look, Casey, you can put that gun away, because I'm not really here, I'm miles from here."

"Where is 'miles from here'?" asked Brady.

"I'm not at liberty to say."

"Let me guess, it's west of here where we saw a functioning lighthouse and ample evidence of human activity," said Debra.

"You need to stay away from that area," said Chandler.

"And why would that be?" asked Debra.

"It's very dangerous," said Chandler.

"What are you hiding, Chandler?" asked Casey, looking over at Debra and shaking his head.

"Trust me on this, you need to stay away from there," said Chandler. "So, how long have you been up on the surface?"

"Don't change the subject, Chandler, you're definitely hiding something," said Casey.

"So, Lucas came up alone and if I know him, he didn't want you to come up at all," said Chandler, ignoring the probing questions.

"Don't change the subject," said Casey.

"Wait...... I want to know how he knew about Lucas not wanting us to come up," said Debra.

"Because I think his first option was to die down there," said Chandler.

"Die in the cave? Why?" asked Debra.

"Well the issues surrounding the failure of his blocks for one," said Chandler. "But more importantly, you did know that acquiring that cave was not only illegal, it was considered an act of terrorism and treason, punishable by death."

"We knew it was illegal, but never really discussed the crime or any of the consequences," said Debra. "But I guess a death sentence would keep anyone in hiding for as long as they could stay hidden."

"Yes, and federal agents could well have survived the war just as you did," said Chandler. "They obviously had similar cave technology, and I'm sure Lucas is still on their most wanted list, particularly if all of the top political leaders of this country died because of what he did."

"If you're so sure the Feds survived, why haven't they come to the cave to get him before now?" asked Debra.

"Because the cave's location had the ultimate secrecy attached to it," said Chandler. "These were the top leaders of the country, and even most Feds had no idea where it was, which was why he chose this option in the first place."

"Alright, so that explains why he didn't want anyone to come up for such an unreasonably long period of time," said Debra.

"And yet he did come up once it was inevitable that you were coming up," said Chandler.

"Correct, and once he was deposed from his throne as king of the cave, he bolted for the exit as fast as he could run," said Debra.

"Who deposed him?" asked Chandler.

"She did," said Casey, pointing at Debra.

"Wow, well, she has bigger balls that most men," said Chandler.

"Right...... so where do you think he went?" asked Debra.

"I think I might know, especially when he looks around and finds out how extensive the destruction was," said Chandler.

"And that would be?" asked Debra.

"Shannon's lab," said Chandler.

"What, to immortalize himself?" asked Brady.

"Of course," said Chandler.

"Shannon? wait......isn't she the one who stole that spaceship with the kids in it and headed out into space?" asked Debra.

"Yes, and she also had the best solution for achieving immortality," said Chandler.

"Best in what way?" asked Debra.

"She was able to permanently stop aging," said Chandler.

"And if she did go off into space as the press said, her immortality procedure must have worked," said Casey.

"Yes, because she would never have gone on a decades long journey unless she was immortal," said Chandler.

"It also means that the teenagers she kidnapped would have likely been immortalized too, otherwise they would die of old age before they ever reached anything habitable," said Debra.

"Or, she could have had a plan for them to have children along the way, and then their descendants would reach whatever planet they found suitable for life," said Chandler.

"Whatever the case, do you think Lucas will immortalize himself if he can find her lab?" asked Debra.

"I'd bet on it," said Chandler.

"So he assumes the Feds will never find him?" asked Casey.

"Look around," said Chandler.

"So now maybe he thinks they didn't survive, or survived without the ability to arrest anyone," said Brady.

"That's a fair guess," said Chandler.

"So you think he's now out looking for her lab?" asked Debra.

"Well, he may first check on his blocks since he put his entire life into building them," said Chandler.

"Which means he might come here," said Debra.

"Maybe, but he knows that his blocks may not even work, so I'm not sure how much effort he'll put into it," said Chandler.

"So we should be looking for Shannon's lab," said Casey.

"I think so," said Chandler.

"Well, we hadn't even thought about Shannon's lab," said Debra. "We had actually decided not to even worry about what Lucas was up to, and had shifted our main goal to finding out if we were alone up here and whether it was possible to live on the surface."

"So you were thinking about moving to the surface to live," said Chandler.

"That was our primary motivation for overthrowing Lucas's rule and coming up," said Debra.

"Makes sense, and yes, it is possible to live up here," said Chandler. "I think there are probably scattered settlements everywhere. But life is tough with all of the modern conveniences erased, so life may be quite primitive in pre-war standards."

"So maybe finding Shannon's lab before Lucas does should be our top priority," said Casey.

"I think it's now the leading candidate for where to go next," said Debra.

"But not just to find Lucas," said Brady.

"I know where you're going with this," said Debra.

"Yes, to immortalize ourselves and our fellow cave dwellers," said Casey.

"Why not?" asked Debra.

"Well, I guess that's hard to argue with," said Casey.

"Well, our primary mission was to see if we can survive on the surface, but becoming immortal would certainly give us more time to do that," said Debra.

"That's right, we have to be flexible and take advantage of whatever leads we come upon, and this is a very good lead," said Casey.

"I know, but it might be a diversion from our primary mission," said Debra.

"Yes, but if this were put to a vote in the cave, what do you think they would tell us to do?" asked Casey.

"Go find a way to immortalize everyone," said Debra.

"Of course," said Chandler. "Shannon's method was a cure for aging, whereas Lucas's merely put people's minds into an electronic cloud. Their physical existence on Earth came to an end. It was his idea of an artificial heaven. It was an option of desperation during desperate times."

"Well, this would be for the good of everyone in the cave," said Debra. "But of course it assumes that Shannon's procedure works."

"I'm sure it does," said Chandler.

"And what about your immortality solution?" asked Brady.

"It worked," said Chandler.

"So you're immortal?" asked Debra.

"Yes, but I would have much preferred Shannon's solution," said Chandler.

"Maybe you could still get Shannon's solution," said Brady.

"No, mine is not reversible, so I'm stuck with what I have," said Chandler.

"So, is Shannon's lab our new travel plan?" asked Casey.

"Yes, I think it is considering the potential benefits for everyone, and despite the fact that it does not advance our understanding about whether we can survive on the surface," said Debra. "But first, Chandler, can you explain to us why these survivors west of here are so dangerous?"

"First of all, most of them are primitive, hostile, and are being held prisoner behind that fence that you probably saw," said Chandler. "Those outside the fence are essentially prison guards, and will treat outsiders as interfering with their prison."

"You know this?" asked Brady.

"I live there, so I know this," said Chandler.

"OK, well, we can always come back and check this out more thoroughly at a later date," said Debra, looking to Casey for his input. Casey nodded.

"Alright, let's go," said Debra who turned to leave.

"OK, well, good luck finding Shannon's lab, but don't hurry back," said Chandler.

"Oh, by the way, Chandler, where IS her lab exactly?" asked

Brady. "All I know is that it is somewhere in Colorado."

"Somewhere in the hills near Colorado Springs," said Chandler.

"That's all you have?" asked Brady.

"That's all I have," said Chandler.

"Does Lucas know where it is?" asked Debra who had stopped partway up the ramp.

"I don't think so," said Chandler. "However, he might be interested in checking out some of his blocks first, so you might be able to get there before he does."

"He was headed northwest when he left the cave, so it might be either the Bellingham or Vantage blocks," said Brady.

"Well, let's get over to Colorado and try to find Shannon's lab before he does," said Casey.

"We're off to Colorado," said Debra who continued to the exit. The others followed.

"Let's see, Colorado Springs," said Casey who was in the plane first and began studying his navigation screen. Brady waited while Debra occupied the copilot's seat and then managed to fill the rest of the cabin. Debra nodded and Casey quickly lifted off and headed east.

Chapter Six

As Lucas made his approach to the Winterhaven Block he was surprised and alarmed by the amount of human activity in the vicinity. He noticed two crude ladders that scaled the fifty foot walls of the block, and he had to land between two huts that had been built on top. As the dust cleared he found his craft surrounded by a half dozen dark skinned people. Unlike Vantage, where they were all in their sixties or older, the people here were all much younger. After observing his audience for a moment, he opened the hatch partway and peered out at them, scanning carefully for weapons. Seeing none, he opened the hatch a bit wider and spoke.

"You will all have to leave," he announced loudly.

There was no response as they began to buzz with conversation that sounded Spanish. He repeated his order in broken Spanish. This time an old man with leathery skin stepped out from behind the structure. He carried a rifle in one hand but did not point it at Lucas. Lucas opened the hatch all the way and stepped out, his hand cannon gripped tightly behind him. The old man saw his hand behind his back and began to aim the rifle at him, but Lucas quickly blasted the man in the chest with his hand cannon. The man fell hard onto the dirt with a sickening thud, raising a cloud of dust. His rifle slid over to the edge and to the ground below. The others quickly withdrew behind the structure. The man lay still in the dirt. A moment later, another older man rushed out from behind the structure with a pistol and Lucas promptly ducked inside his plane and shut the door. He went to his seat and aimed his forcefield weapon at the man and pressed the button. The man flew end over end through the air to the ground below, screaming as he flew, his pistol tumbled after him. A moment later some of the people emerged from behind the structure shouting with their hands in the air. Lucas was not sure whether to fire, but as he observed them, he realized they were smiling. Wait! They were cheering! Some were even jumping up and down. In celebration? Lucas was confused. He had just killed an older man with the ship's cannon and knocked another elderly man down with his hand cannon. As he watched, one of the women walked closer and put her hands together under her chin, with a little bow. She then turned and left. It appeared to be a thank you. What had just happened was not clear, but the older men would have been there before the war, so they were survivors. Everyone else was much younger, from young children to some in their twenties. He had no idea what these older men had done, or were doing, but everyone seemed quite happy they were gone. Feeling safe, he deplaned and checked the door to the structure. The access panel had been seriously damaged so he could not use it. Apparently they were unable to get in. That was good. He then checked the man who still lay in the dirt. There was no pulse. Lucas remained on his knees for a moment to think about what to do before getting back into his aircraft.

What should he do? The spirits in the block were safe. These young people seemed to be no threat to him or the block. There was nothing more he could do here. He pulled out his notebook and studied it for a moment, finally focusing his attention on the underground research facility in the desert west of Tucson. Chandler and Shannon had left there months before the war to pursue their own ends, and Lucas had taken over the facility even though he had moved his main operation to Los Angeles where the parts for his blocks were built. He thought about his time there with Shannon and her apparent success with her immortality experiment. While in the cave he had thought that if he ever came up to the surface he would find her lab and immortalize himself. That is, if he could find her lab. Her method was clearly better than anyone else's. It stopped aging. His blocks, even if they worked, would not allow him to remain in his body. He had dreamed of immortalizing himself. If he could find Shannon's lab, perhaps he could immortalize himself. The lab was in Colorado, near Colorado Springs. But where? Perhaps she left some clues in the Tucson facility. Yes, this would be what he would do. Shannon's lab would be his next destination. But first to the facility near Tucson. It was where he had left his sister after she refused to go down into the cave with him. It had been forty years, and surely she could not have survived there. But what if she had? It would be nice to see her. He smiled, then lifted off and aimed east for the Tucson area. The facility was located in the

Sonoran Desert. Lucas had purchased an abandoned museum and dug a large underground facility beneath it while keeping the old museum structure. Since immortality was the subject of intense competition, he needed to hide what he was doing below it from the public. So he renamed it 'environmental research', with a 'restricted access' sign in red below the name. For anyone driving by on the highway they would see that sign, a security fence, and a gate. It had the appearance of legitimacy. Inside were mock research facilities that simulated environmental research. But on the lower level of the museum was the entrance to the immortality facility, disguised behind fake environmental paraphernalia.

He spotted the low lying structure and landed in what used to be a parking lot with prairie grass peeking through cracks in the pavement. A forest of dead trees gave a stark and lifeless appearance to the site. As he looked around he saw a number of trails, so survivors could either be here or had been here recently. Based on his experience with survivors at his blocks, these survivors could well be armed and dangerous. He deplaned, and with his hand cannon on his belt, he cautiously entered the structure. He found no one in the upper level so he went below to the facility's entrance. It was pitch black as he crept forward, and he shined his flashlight into every corner as he went. At the entrance, he noticed that the hidden door was not completely closed. Hand cannon in hand, he cautiously eased the door open a bit more while hugging the wall.

"Who's in there!" he shouted.

There was no reply, so he repeated his hail, louder this time. Still no reply. He pulled the door open all the way and entered, swinging his cannon in every direction looking for movement. To one side was the big steel door that was the secure entrance to the underground lab. He remembered the entry code from having used it so many times before, and punched it in. It clicked and the door opened a crack. He opened it a little more while hugging the wall.

"Is anyone down there!?" he shouted.

"I'm armed!" came a woman's voice from far below.

"Betty?" he asked.

"Lucas?" she shouted back.

"Yes."

"I thought you were supposed to be down in that cave of yours hiding out from the Feds," said Betty.

"I had to come up," he replied as he clipped his cannon back onto his belt and started down the long stairway to the main chamber.

"You had to?" she asked as he reached the bottom.

"The others mutinied."

"None of them were being pursued by the Feds for treason, so they wanted to come up, right?" she asked.

"Something like that, and I've seen no sign of modern civilization up here so far, so maybe I won't be pursued."

"Too bad," said Betty who stood some distance away in the dimly lit room.

"I know, but I did encounter some aggressive survivalists up in Washington and a primitive tribe over in Winterhaven," he replied.

"So why were you wasting your time checking on your blocks?" she asked as she took a few steps forward to get a better

96

look at him.

"There was a war and I wanted to see if they were OK."

"Why? They're just big steel boxes with dead bodies inside."

"We don't know that for sure."

"I think we do."

"Well, I still have hope."

"Whatever," she replied. "So why did you come here?"

"To see you, and I'm very happy to see that you survived in this place, Betty."

"Well, I doubt if you came here just to see me," she replied. "Now, you said the others mutinied, so obviously they too came up."

"We came up separately," he replied.

"So where are they?" she asked.

"Back in Utah," he answered after a pause, not sure how much to tell her.

"Let me guess.....you came up first and took the plane, leaving them isolated," said Betty.

"I had to, they were after me."

"Of course they were......so I'll ask again, why did you come here?"

"Like I said, to see you."

"No, I think it was to find anything belonging to Shannon since you've always wanted to know her secret."

"Did she leave anything?"

"That's what I thought," she replied, shaking her head. "No, you were here when she left and you know she took everything."

"I thought she might have stashed something."

"I wouldn't know."

"So you haven't run across anything."

"Do you think I'd tell you if I did?"

"Have you stayed here by yourself in this place for forty years?" he asked, changing the subject.

"Everyone else died."

"I'm sorry."

"I doubt that," she replied. "So, you said you ran into some survivors at your blocks."

"Yes, a family of barbarians killed my friend Peter and moved into my Vantage Block," said Lucas.

"Barbarians?...... so, from that description I assume you shot them?"

"They were very aggressive."

"You shot them," she repeated, pointing to his hand cannon.

"I had to defend myself."

"After a worldwide conflagration, a few managed to survive, and you shoot them."

"They were trying to live in my block," said Lucas.

"But the blocks were some of the few places left for these survivors to live in," said Betty.

"They had guns," said Lucas.

"So instead of leaving, you killed them."

"I had no choice, because I cannot have anyone living in my blocks."

"Of course not," said Betty. "But then you're pretty good at killing people since you put tens of thousands into your blocks with the promise of everlasting life, when you knew it didn't work. I'm not sure what you call that, but there must be a term for it.....oh yeah, you killed them!"

"That's not fair, because I thought the blocks would work," said Lucas. "I didn't know for sure, and I still don't know for sure...... and now you're making me sound like a cold blooded killer."

"Well?"

"You know very well that I went into that enterprise believing the process worked, since my people virtually guaranteed it."

"But you didn't wait for proof before you took the peoples' money and then interred them in what became their tomb."

"You know very well there wasn't time to wait since the world as we knew it was about to end, and at least the blocks gave these people hope."

"So you killed them with hope in their hearts," she replied.

"Those people were wrong," said Lucas.

"But then you used the money from selling the plots to buy your way into that cave, displacing and likely killing the people it was built to house," she shot back.

"You're making me sound like a monster."

"I'm not sure how else to describe what you did."

"I'm not a monster, and besides, the blocks may work, there is no proof that they don't."

"Nor any that they do," said Betty. "But you left those dignitaries for dead."

"They could have found other accommodations because they had connections that most people don't," he replied.

"It was the very last minute, and all the bunkers were taken, so exactly where do you think they might have gone?"

"I guess it was survival of the fittest."

"Darwin would be proud of you, but the Federal Marshall

won't be as understanding," said Betty.

"As far as the money goes, I had to ask a lot because I had some big investors to pay off," said Lucas.

"Investors?" said Betty. "Oh my god....and of course a cave to buy."

"There were thousands on waiting lists, so this wasn't forced on anyone."

"Well, your hyped-up advertising made it look like a stairway to heaven, giving them a leg up to the pearly gates," said Betty.

"That may be true, but most of those other options had hyped-up ad campaigns too," said Lucas. "These other options were made to appear as if the customer could really survive, when in reality they were nowhere near being able to assure long term survival. Most of them were entirely useless for the long period of time that was necessary for the surface to recover. It still isn't livable after forty years. Very few caves or shelters were designed for long term survival, so those who used them are now dead, and those who sold them are basically scammers. And besides, if they didn't get interred into my blocks, they would surely have died in the bombing."

"Look, you can't rationalize what you did by saying that they would be dead anyway," said Betty. "You did what you did and you have to live with it, and then be arrested for it."

"Actually, what's done is done, and there's nothing I can do about it now," said Lucas. "I still think you should have come with me to the cave."

"And live fifty years in a cave? No thanks. Besides, we were hardly on good terms, so I was perfectly willing to risk survival here by myself."

"Actually, life in the cave wasn't all that bad," said Lucas. "It was a very large and well-designed living environment, and everything worked as designed."

"Well, I managed to survive out here," said Betty. "I stayed in this bunker for a number of years until my supplies ran out and the nuclear winter had dissipated somewhat. Then, I was able to scratch out an existence from the surrounding area."

"How many years before you came out?

"Six years or so," said Betty. "But I couldn't spend a lot of time on the surface at first, so I continued to live down here...... even today."

"So how did the others die?" asked Lucas.

"Two of them decided to go up after a couple of years and I've never seen nor heard from them since. The other one died of a heart attack or something a year after the bombs."

"And you've not seen anyone since?"

"I see smoke on the horizon far to the north and east, but no one has ever wandered down here," said Betty.

"You haven't been curious enough to go out there and look?"

"It's a long walk to anywhere, and besides I've not seen evidence of modern civilization like aircraft flying overhead or radio signals," she replied. "And I don't have an appetite for meeting survivors who might be out looking for food or shelter. I don't want to share my limited food and water supply, or my shelter. I'm an old woman now. I have that shotgun in the corner, but have never had the occasion to use it for anything other than hunting rabbits, birds and ground squirrels."

"So you haven't run across any of Shannon's material?"

"She didn't trust you or Chandler, so she took everything."

"I know she didn't trust anyone, but she could have forgotten something," said Lucas.

"I wouldn't know," said Betty.

"Maybe she's enjoying herself right now with her teenagers on some distant planet," he replied.

"We'll never know that either."

"Do you ever recall her discussing where this lab of hers was located other than near Colorado Springs?" he asked.

"No."

"I need to find that lab."

"To immortalize yourself?"

"Sure, why not?"

"And you came here primarily to find any clues she might have left?"

"You should come with me to get immortalized," said Lucas.

"I'm not going anywhere with you," said Betty. "This is my home, I'm relatively comfortable here, and besides, living forever may not be for everyone."

"But it's for me, and you have an open invitation to join me."

"No thanks."

"OK then, I have to go.....so.....look...... it was nice to see you again sis, and I'm quite relieved and happy to see you alive," said Lucas.

"If it hadn't been for the fact that Shannon worked here, you would never have come by," she said, and pulled back when he started forward to hug her.

"Right, well, I might drop back through here on my journeys."

"You needn't go out of your way."

"Then I guess this is goodbye," he said as he turned and

headed up the stairs without looking back.

In his aircraft, he sat for a moment thinking about his sister. A wave of sadness swept over him as visions of his childhood with her flashed through his mind. Tears were beginning to form, but he shook his head and rubbed his hand over his face, then took a deep breath. This is now, and what's done is done. The hardness he had built into his persona over his lifetime was who he was. He could not change that now. He looked up into the sky for a moment to clear his head. OK, Shannon's lab. Yes, he had to find it, and he tried to remember any conversations he had with her regarding that lab. Colorado Springs. The foothills. Nothing more specific than that. So he had absolutely no idea where to look other than the hills west of the city. Considering the fact that the lab was undoubtedly camouflaged, it would be very difficult to find, but he had to try. His desire to find her secret and immortalize himself was now an overpowering priority. It was his sole mission.

He lifted off, and as he traveled north, he thought about stopping at the Taos Block which was not far from the route he was traveling, but he was too anxious to begin the search for her lab, so he continued on. At Colorado Springs he saw nothing but complete destruction that extended well into the foothills of the Rockies. If Shannon's secret lab were anywhere within this band of destruction, it would likely have been badly damaged or destroyed, so he would concentrate his search farther up in the mountains. The hills there were heavily forested, but today with smaller trees and bushes. As he had found in Bellingham, the forest had been largely destroyed during the conflagration and the massive fires that burned afterwards. So the hills were green with smaller trees and bushes, with the spires of dead trees sticking up above the green blanket below.

After spending hours flying back and forth over the strange new forest and seeing nothing, he decided to go back south to the Taos Block and use it as a base of operation in his search for her lab. He hoped that the block had not been overrun by survivors, because he did not cherish the thought of forcibly evicting or killing anyone else. His other concern was food and water. In his haste to leave the cave, he was only able to bring water in a flask, and after nearly two days, he was very thirsty and hungry. In fact, he should have asked Betty for food and water, but the conversation with her was upsetting, and in his haste to leave, he forgot.

As he approached the Taos Block he could see that the immediate area was occupied and there were people walking about. A pang of anxiety swept over him as memories of his previous encounters came to mind. But after landing on the roof with nearly a half foot of soil on it, he realized to his relief that it did not appear as if anyone had been up there. He deplaned, and, after checking the door and seeing that it had not been tampered with, he walked to the edge of the block. Below was a small village of survivors living in structures that looked similar to those that housed the population in this mountainous area before the war. Small farms were visible in the distance and he saw a number of people standing in their doorways or nearby, intently watching. Most appeared to be young, as in Winterhaven, so most were clearly born after the war, and none appeared to be his age. He returned to the door of the structure and used his code to open it. The Blockmaster's room seemed untouched and it's lights came on when he entered.

"You are Lucas," said the Blockmaster.

"No one has been here in forty years?" he asked.

"That is correct, but it was thirty nine years, three months......"

"I know the date."

"Of course......I await your orders."

"I have none at this time."

He turned and made his way to the roof where he heard chanting. From the edge he was shocked to see a line of people holding hands and repeating words in unison: 'praise be to the place of spirits.' They speak English, he thought as he watched, and from the chant they must also know about the block's purpose. While he had no idea how they knew, or how much they knew, what they were doing seemed oddly appropriate to him. He smiled, even though their assumption about this being a place of spirits was still an open question. In reality this could be little more than a large tomb. They saw him standing at the edge and soon a middle-aged man, perhaps in his fifties and wearing a white robe, stepped forward and held up his hand.

"You have returned as we all have prayed you would," said the man who had long black hair that hung down to his chest. Lucas stared at him for a moment, not sure how to respond. Did he actually recognize me, he thought? But how could he? He paused for a moment before answering.

"I will need food and water," said Lucas, after a long pause. Seeing how these people responded was so unexpected that he didn't know what else to say, but the pang of thirst and hunger prompted him to say it.

"We will set a table for you," said the man, placing his hands together and bowing. Lucas nodded and returned to his aircraft. He landed it on the ground in a nearby clearing. A crowd quickly rushed to encircle his plane. Within minutes he was being escorted to a large, crudely constructed, building. Inside they gathered around a long table and soon food was being brought in. Lucas was seated at the head of the table. Once all of the seats were filled, they looked to him, waiting for him to speak.

"I came here to live for a while," he said finally.

"We are honored," said the man in the robe who seemed to be the leader.

"Has anyone else visited the block?" asked Lucas.

"The block?" asked the man, apparently unfamiliar with the term.

"What is your name for it?" asked Lucas, pointing in the direction of the block. The man looked in that direction.

"It is the place of the spirits, and it is your place," he replied. Lucas nodded with a knowing smile, but he was somewhat confused about what they knew or how they knew it. But they must know something about its function, and they must also know it is associated with him. He wondered if they knew what role he actually played, and the negative publicity that eventually surrounded it. But only the middle aged man was even alive before the war and he was likely a teenager at the time.

"You are the one," the man continued, pointing to a wall behind him. As he pointed, a chant began around the table: 'you are the one'. Lucas turned and saw a large faded poster of himself, taken when he was much younger, apparently from an advertisement for the blocks. This was long before the press found out there was no proof that the blocks worked. For the ad, he was dressed in a white robe and was standing on a pathway that led up to a block. A bright light from above bathed the block as if the pathway was the way to heaven. He remembered that scene and the controversy it created among religious groups. Now, apparently unaware of the bad press, these survivors saw him as some kind of deity. He was apparently seen as a kind of savior to those interred within. He nodded to the man and smiled. This is actually how he had pictured himself being treated when he developed the blocks. A kind of savior. Now it was coming true here at Taos. A teenage survivor, wandering around trying to survive after the war when he found this poster in the rubble. The block was here. So he made the connection and filled in between the lines. He then taught what he had discovered to the children who eventually began to populate the area. And he became the equivalent of the priest for a kind of religion.

Lucas smiled and nodded, knowing that he may never be able to deliver on their hope of everlasting life. But then again, how would they know if the block didn't work? He would just continue to perpetuate his fraud, and, in the meantime, he had a safe and stable base from which to search for Shannon's lab. He would use their hospitality and the image of himself as their savior for as long as he needed. If they asked for anyone to be interred, he would simply have them interred with the assurance that their spirits were being preserved forever in a peaceful place. Then, if they ever asked for proof, he would quietly leave and never come back. They lacked the ability to follow him, so this was the perfect setup.

Chapter Seven

"**I** have no idea where Shannon's lab is, other than in the Colorado Springs area," said Brady as they cruised in their aircraft toward Colorado.

"We have our work cut out for us then," said Casey.

"But so does Lucas," said Brady.

"Hopefully, we'll find it before he does," said Casey.

"We might even run into him while we're looking," said Debra.

"And get into a shooting match?" asked Casey. "If we do, it's one we'll win, whether it's in this fighter or on the ground."

"It will not be a shooting match, Casey," said Debra. "We'll either take him alive or back off."

"But what if he starts shooting?" asked Casey.

"Let's not speculate," said Debra.

"Something just occurred to me," said Brady.

"What?" asked Debra.

"There's an underground research facility in the desert west of Tucson, and I know something," he replied.

"Alright, don't keep us in suspense," said Debra.

"Shannon had a secret hideout there," he replied.

"And?" asked Debra.

"It was a place where she went to get away from everyone," said Brady. "I followed her to it once without her noticing me. She was very upset and told me to never tell anyone where it was."

"And you think she might have left something there that can help us find her lab?" asked Debra.

"Yes."

"Do you think Lucas will go to this facility before going to Colorado Springs?" asked Debra.

"I don't know, but we need to hurry down there right away just in case," said Brady.

"Then let's go," said Debra.

"I'm on it," said Casey who quickly changed course.

"Tell me more about this facility," said Debra.

"Well, all three of the immortality experiments were once being worked on there," said Brady.

"Three.... that's Lucas, Shannon and Chandler," said Debra.

"Correct."

"Did they ever share ideas?" asked Debra.

"I was very young then so I don't know for sure, but they each worked alone and seemed to keep things pretty much secret from each other," said Brady.

"But at some point, they split up," said Debra.

"Yes, Shannon went to her lab in Colorado, Chandler moved

to the Bay area and Lucas moved his main operation to Los Angeles," said Brady.

"I came into his game late, but I was there when Lucas moved to LA," said Casey. "Once he had outside financing, he was able to establish a large manufacturing facility there."

"He apparently had some really big investors, I remember him talking about them," said Brady. "The other two efforts remained small and virtually invisible."

"So tell us more about this secret retreat of Shannon's?" asked Debra.

"It was just a small space that you wouldn't even know existed if you didn't see someone go inside," said Brady.

"And she trusted you not to tell where it was?" asked Debra.

"Well, what else could she do, kill me?" said Brady.

"Too bad," said Casey.

"Eat me," said Brady.

"So you think she might have left something there?" asked Debra.

"Let's put it this way, if she left anything behind, I think it would be there," said Brady. "You see, I once heard her discuss the idea that she wanted to leave a legacy. Even though she didn't want to openly share her secret, apparently she wanted people to know what she had accomplished. So I'm thinking that this secret hiding place might be the perfect spot to hide some description of the lab, and hopefully more information about its location."

"Maybe even how to perform her procedure?" asked Debra.

"Possibly," said Brady.

"Well, if she did leave some documentation, it would be a lot better than starting to look for something hidden in the mountains amid an endless forest of trees," said Debra.

"We're less than an hour away," said Casey as they headed southward.

"What if Lucas is there?" asked Brady.

"We'll deal with that when the time comes," said Debra.

A while later they combed the desert west of Tucson looking for the facility. Eventually Casey spotted it.

"Pretty bleak," said Casey as they hovered over the ancient buildings. The roof was covered with dirt and scattered desert flora, making it blend into the Sonoran desert as if it were camouflaged.

"No sign of Lucas's aircraft, so we don't have to deal with that issue," said Debra.

"Are those trails?" asked Casey as he carefully landed the aircraft between two dead trees that were once part of a beautifully landscaped parking lot.

"Yes, which means someone lives here," said Debra who was the first to deplane and start for the entrance.

"Wait, Debra, whoever's inside could be hostile," said Casey who pulled his gun from his waistband and quickly took the lead. As they approached the entrance he held up his hand for them to stay back while he moved forward with his gun.

"Remember, Casey, we won't shoot first regardless of who we encounter," said Debra.

Casey nodded as he entered the darkness of the building. Debra and Brady followed as the three of them walked through the dimly lit interior.

"Look at all the trails," said Debra. "Someone has lived here for a very long time."

"And may be living here now," said Brady.

"His sister Betty and a few others were here when we left, but that was forty years ago," said Casey.

"So why didn't she go down into the cave with him?" asked Debra.

"They had a serious falling out," said Casey.

"If his sister is living here, do you think she would have helped him if he got here before us?" asked Debra.

"No chance," said Brady.

"What was the falling out about?" she asked as they moved deeper into the museum.

"She felt he had essentially killed thousands with his blocks just for the money, and she was aware of his plan to steal the dignitary's cave....our cave," said Casey. "She ragged on him about stealing the cave and essentially killing those dignitaries."

"And she believed the press about his blocks?" asked Debra.

"Yes, she knew first hand that there was no proof the blocks worked, and of course she knew of his plan to steal the cave," said Casey.

"Now that we're inside, I actually remember the way down to the facility," said Brady.

"So do I," said Casey as he led them down a ramp to the lab entrance with his flashlight.

"It's all coming back to me," said Brady who walked up to the hidden door and pushed on it. It clicked and moved out far enough for him to grab an edge.

"Wait, we have no idea who's in there, or if they're hostile," said Casey who was behind him pulling him back by the shirt.

"Well, since the door was closed, I'm assuming it's Betty or the others that were here, rather than strangers," said Brady.

"But if strangers found the door, strangers could close the door," said Casey.

"Why don't we just knock first," said Debra.

"How polite," said Casey.

"Just be ready in case there's hostility," said Debra.

"Wait..... don't knock, because I don't want anyone inside to have time to get prepared," said Casey who had one hand on the edge of the door and the other holding his pistol.

"No, I'm knocking," said Debra who held her arm out to stop Casey from advancing with his gun. She knocked, but there was no response after a long wait. She knocked again, and again there was no response.

"Actually, Deb, this is not the secure entrance to the facility," said Brady.

"He's right, it's inside," said Casey. Debra stepped aside and Casey opened the door and went in. The big steel door was to his right and he waved them in.

"I believe only Betty or those we left here know the combination, so I think we can forget about finding strangers inside," said Brady.

"He's right," said Casey.

"So, can we knock on this door now?" asked Debra. Casey nodded and then banged the butt of his pistol against the steel door.

"Who's up there?" came a woman's voice from a speaker in the ceiling.

"Betty!?" shouted Brady.

"Who is that?" she asked.

113

"Brady!" he replied.

"Brady, you little shit!......oh my god! Get down here!" she shouted. A second later the door clicked and Casey pulled it open.

Brady led the way down, and they were met at the foot of the stairs by Betty who tried to wrap her arms around him but could not quite reach.

"You're not as little as you used to be," she laughed while clinging as best she could.

"And you look great," he replied after holding her out at arms length to look at her.

"I recognize the face, and those eyes," said Betty.

"But he's now a whale," said Casey.

"Shut up, you creepy old man," said Brady.

"And Casey, you look, well, older," said Betty.

"He's now an old fart who shuffles when he walks," said Brady.

"You've aged a bit yourself, Betty," said Casey, studying her wrinkled face and thin frame.

"Survival in the desert after that war is not for the faint at heart," said Betty.

"Forty years in a cave isn't either," said Brady.

"OK, so, I don't know who this young lady is," said Betty.

"This is Debra," Brady replied with a smile. "She was born in the cave."

"Oh my god, you've never seen the world up here.....I'm sorry for its current appearance, it used to be quite nice.....but I'm happy to meet you Debra," said Betty, hugging her.

"Was he here?" asked Brady.

"Lucas? Yes," said Betty.

"So he got here first, and I'm sure he's now out looking for Shannon's lab," said Brady.

"Of course," she replied.

"Did he get any of her stuff?" asked Brady.

"She didn't leave anything."

"Well, she had a secret retreat, so she might have," said Brady.

"Secret retreat?" asked Betty.

"You didn't know about it?"

"No, I don't remember anything like that."

"Let me go up and see if she might have left something there," said Brady who quickly turned and lumbered back up the stairs.

"You've lived here by yourself all this time?" asked Debra.

"Almost forty years," she replied.

"What about survivors from other areas?"

"Haven't seen any."

"You've been alone all this time?" asked Debra.

"I had company for a couple of years, then nobody," she replied.

"I think you should come with us when we leave," said Debra.

"Come with you?" she asked, then smiled. "Oh....well, I think I'll take you up on that offer."

"It'll be a bit crowded in our little plane, but you're small so I think we can squeeze you in," said Casey.

"Did Lucas tell you where he'd been since he's been up on the surface?" asked Debra.

"He said he visited a few of his blocks and told me he had to defend himself against some survivors at one of them."

"Defend himself?" asked Debra.

115

"He killed a few survivors because they were trespassing on his blocks," said Betty.

"Oh my god, that's terrible, although I guess I'm not surprised," said Debra.

"Look, he's my brother I'm sad to say, and of course you know that the federal government is after him for treason and who knows what else," said Betty.

"Chandler told us about that," said Debra.

"You saw Chandler?" she asked.

"Well, not in person, but we heard his voice up in California," said Debra.

"At least he's still alive, so maybe his immortality solution worked," said Betty.

"He said it did," said Casey.

"Look, this is a map of where the lab is located!" said Brady excitedly as he made his way down the stairs waving a piece of paper in one hand and a small notebook in the other.

"You found a map, and what's that?" asked Debra, pointing to the notebook.

"It's a notebook jammed chockablock full of tiny writing, crib notes and sketches. I might need a magnifying glass to figure out some of it. The map is also filled with notes in the margin describing a steep canyon with the lab entrance a ways up a canyon. There is some kind of landmark along the way. It's a rock that looks like a phalanx symbol, whatever that is.

"It's a penis, moron," said Casey.

"How in the hell would I know that, butt face?" asked Brady.

"So it's a map showing how to get to the lab," said Debra.

"It looks that way," he said, continuing to read the map. "OK, let's see, past the phalanx thingy, then the notes say the entrance is up the canyon from that. There's a rock slab leaning against the canyon wall. Except it's not a real rock, it's an artificial rock, and the lab entrance is there once you slide it aside."

"How do we find this canyon?" asked Debra.

"I think these numbers are coordinates," said Brady, laying the map on a table.

"Yes, they are coordinates," said Casey, after a moment of study.

"I guess we need to get up there before Lucas accidentally stumbles upon it," said Debra.

"My thoughts exactly,"said Casey.

"Let's go," said Debra, pointing up the stairs.

"I'm coming with you," said Betty.

"Great, but will she fit?" asked Brady.

"She's but a wiff," said Casey.

"Meaning I'm Jabba the Hutt," said Brady.

"Pretty much," said Casey.

"And you're a potato on toothpicks," said Brady.

"They're really good friends, Betty," said Debra. Betty just smiled.

With their new passenger wedged in a corner of the cockpit, and looking like clowns in a phone booth, they departed for Colorado Springs. An hour later they were zeroing in on a canyon in the foothills west of Colorado Springs. They approached a narrow, heavily treed canyon that wound back up into the mountains. Finding a landing space amid the scrub trees and brush was the next challenge, but they were finally able to locate a small, level clearing a quarter mile from where the entrance to the lab was supposed to be found. As they started out from the aircraft, they found that any evidence of a trail had long since become overgrown with grass and brush. So it was tough going, but eventually they came upon a tall narrow rock where they stopped.

"That's the rock," said Casey.

"That's supposed to look like a penis?" asked Brady.

"It's the rock, so let's just keep going," said Debra as she waved them ahead. Eventually, they came to a rock slab and began to examine it.

"This is it," said Casey who had rapped his knuckles against it and heard a hollow sound.

"Now, we just have to slide it open," said Debra.

"If it slides, it has to be on a track," said Casey who was moving dirt with his foot from an area on one side of the false rock. He eventually uncovered a track and they all converged on the spot and began to dig away the dirt with their hands. A little while later, with enough of the dirt moved away from the track, they were able to slide the slab open enough to enter. Inside was a steel door with an access panel on one side.

"Is the entry code in her notes?" asked Debra.

"I don't see anything," said Brady who was studying the map's notes. "But it could be in her notebook, unless...."

"Unless what?" asked Debra.

"This doodle at the bottom seems unusual," he mumbled.

"Why?"

"It looks like a word...... let's see.... Irene," said Brady, holding the map out for Debra to see.

"It is Irene, so do you think that's the entry code?" asked

Debra.

"Her middle initial is 'I', and the keypad has only letters, not numbers," said Casey.

"I'll try it," said Brady, entering the name. On the second try, there was a click and Casey quickly grabbed the edge of the door and began tugging. It opened a crack but was stuck. With the help of Brady and Debra they were able to pull the door open wide enough for them to enter. Inside was inky black, so Casey and Debra retrieved their flashlights. They entered a hallway, and at the end was another steel door.

"Why not?" asked Brady who entered the same code, and this time the door opened on the first try. Inside was a sophisticated lab with consoles lining two walls.

"I'm not sure where to start," said Debra as they stared in awe at how perfectly preserved the shiny lab had remained after so many years.

"What's that in the middle of the room?" asked Betty.

"A glass booth," said Brady.

"It must have something to do with her procedure," said Casey.

"So, let's see...... a person would go into the glass booth and someone else would do something at one of those consoles," said Debra.

"Or, it could be part of a lengthy research and development process and have nothing to do with the actual immortalization process," said Casey.

"Or that," said Debra.

"But if it is part of the process, it means that even if Lucas found this place, he couldn't immortalize himself without the help of someone," said Betty.

"Does the notebook say anything about the booth?" asked Debra.

"The notebook is very dense," said Brady.

"Like you," said Casey.

"Stop it," said Debra. "We'll pursue that question later."

"Besides, if she planned to leave a legacy back here on Earth, I would think that she would have left the necessary equipment to carry out her process here in her lab," said Casey.

"I agree," said Betty.

"Hopefully that's explained in her notebook," said Debra.

"It may actually take someone familiar with her research to be able to piece any of this together," said Betty.

"I know, because this notebook looks very technical," said Brady.

"Don't say anything, Casey," said Debra, pointing at him.

"Well, I looked briefly in that notebook awhile ago and it seems to me to be a rather detailed description of what she did," said Betty.

"Ironically, we may need one of her competitors, like Chandler or Lucas, to help us wade through it," said Casey.

"So we may have to ask Lucas to help us?" asked Debra.

"Or Chandler," said Casey.

"She was a very intense person, but she was also someone who was proud of what she was able to accomplish, so I wouldn't be surprised if her instructions can eventually be interpreted by someone other than those two," said Betty.

"Right now, I think we're on our own under the current circumstances," said Debra. "So let's get back to looking around the lab to see if we can find anything that might have been used in her procedure."

"This isn't something we can do right now," said Casey.

"That's true, we're just seeing what we can find that might help us do this in the future," said Debra.

"Which is all that Lucas could do as well, even if he got here first," said Casey.

"But we have a considerable advantage over him since we have her black book," said Debra.

"Yes, so let's keep looking," said Casey.

Over the next several hours the four of them scoured the lab, opening all the cabinets and attempting to activate the control consoles. Only two of the consoles lit up, but nothing came onto the screens. As they were getting ready to leave, Betty tripped on an obstruction in the floor, exposing a tab which she pulled. One of the consoles slid forward, revealing a doorway. Casey opened it and entered. The others followed. Inside was a large table with an assortment of parts haphazardly distributed on it. At one end of the table was a white, smoothly sculptured box with a small antenna on top. In the middle of the table was a strange device that looked as if it would fit on a person's back in the hip region.

"It has a small slot on one side," said Debra as she felt with her finger.

"Look, I noticed this on the floor as we came in....I wonder if this fits into the slot?" asked Casey, holding up a tiny chip. The chip fit perfectly.

"Alright, so this device appears to be used to insert one of these chips into a person's hip region," said Betty.

"But of course there are a wide range of different sized backs, so one size fits all doesn't make a lot of sense," said Debra, .

"That's a good point," said Casey. "But however and wherever the chip is installed, I assume it is then activated by that white box."

"What about the booth?" asked Betty.

"Right, the booth," said Debra.

"OK, so here's a scenario," said Casey. "The chip is inserted, activated at the booth, then kept active by the white box."

"That seems logical," said Betty.

"Or, perhaps all of this was part of the development of her procedure and has nothing to do with what she actually came up with," said Casey.

"That's also true, but booth aside, if this white box is needed to keep the chip running, it means that one must stay within range of the box at all times," said Debra.

"That's as close to a fatal flaw as anything we've discovered so far," said Betty. "You're immortalized, but you have to have that box nearby forever."

"If that's the case, then I'd ask whether the box runs on batteries or whether it must be plugged in," said Casey with a snicker. "I'm not aware of immortal batteries, so we're talking about the possibility of having electric sockets nearby as well."

"Maybe it's solar," said Brady.

"I don't see a solar panel on this one, but if it was solar, we can add living in the sunshine forever to maintain your immortality," said Casey.

"I think we're speculating since this white box is, as Betty says, pretty much a fatal flaw in her concept of immortality," said Debra.

"If something keeps you alive forever, it's not a fatal flaw, it's just an inconvenience," said Casey.

"Inconvenience or fatal flaw, maybe the basic question in all of this is how you would even know whether you were immortalized in the first place," said Betty.

"That's true,"said Casey. "I guess you would have to wait years to make sure....look ma, I'm not getting older!"

"But I'm sure Shannon had a way of knowing," said Betty.

"I would think that some physiological changes would seem likely," said Debra.

"Or perhaps she did pretty much the same thing that Lucas did, and proceed on the assumption that it worked, but with no direct proof," said Casey.

"Wouldn't that be a bit of irony," said Debra.

"Well, then there's Chandler who is still alive in some form," said Brady.

"It's only been forty years, so I think it's too early to tell whether his solution actually worked since you only heard his voice," said Betty.

"That's right, so I guess that's still an open question," said Casey.

"In other words, this whole immortality drama might well have resulted in three failures, and three deceptions," said Debra.

"Actually, weren't all of these immortality experiments essentially just 'wait and see'?" asked Casey.

"To some extent, yes, but Shannon and her colleagues spent years testing," said Betty. "And she didn't inter tens of thousands of people to their potential deaths like Lucas did."

"No, but she kidnapped a couple dozen teenagers and took

them into outer space to possibly die on their way to a place that may not even exist," said Casey. "So if her method didn't work, they're all just as dead as Lucas's inductees."

"Just not as many," said Betty.

"Mass murder is mass murder no matter how you cut it," said Casey. "Although if you were delusioned by your own belief that it worked, but didn't intend to do anything wrong, would that still be classified as a criminal charge?"

"What.....unintentional mass murder?" asked Betty. "You would definitely be morally guilty at the very least. You might get off in an insanity plea and end up in an institution, but you still murdered a lot of people. That would be a fact. Look, in the end it's still mass murder, and responsibility should land somewhere."

"I just wonder how Shannon pulled off her little space adventure, particularly if her immortality procedure was successful," said Debra. "To begin with, she had to steal a spaceship that must have been well guarded. And even more puzzling is the fact that the teens would have had to be brought down here to be immortalized if that booth was necessary. Then, she would have had to take them back up to the ship. That whole event is approaching the impossible."

"Maybe she had a portable booth," said Brady.

"Or the booth and even a lot of this equipment was part of her research, and not part of the final solution," said Debra.

"OK, but stealing the spaceship loaded with teenagers? Really? It had to be done with the help of high ranking government officials, much like Lucas's little deal to steal our cave," said Casey.

"Yes, Lucas colluded with a bunch of crooked military brass to get our cave, so Shannon could have done the same thing with crooked Chinese brass," said Debra with a shrug.

"Bottom line though, my bet for success in this immortality endeavor is Shannon," said Betty. "She spent nearly a decade testing her procedure, whereas Lucas was on a crash-course schedule of not much more than a year."

"Not so fast..... Lucas was able to secure massive funding in that year, thus bringing a wealth of talent and resources from all over the world," said Casey. "In fact, I'll bet that a hundred times more man hours of research went into his effort."

"None of that really matters now," said Debra. "All we can do at this point is focus on where we are, what we know, and what we intend to do from here."

"At least we have a start on Shannon's work," said Brady, who held up Shannon's little notebook.

"But unless we find detailed and understandable instructions in that notebook, we have no way of knowing how to make any of this work," said Casey.

"Well, this is all just gibberish to me," said Brady.

"Dagwood and Blondie is gibberish to you," said Casey.

"Who are Dagwood and Blondie?" asked Brady, scowling at Casey.

"Please guys, this is actually serious stuff," said Debra. "But we'll have to let it go for the moment and get back to the more immediate question of whether it's possible for our colony to survive up here on the surface. This is especially important if Lucas is no longer there to operate and maintain our cave's systems. The reality is, we may not be able to do it without him, so if he's permanently inaccessible, we may have to move to the surface anyway."

"You may have to sink or swim, like I had to do," said Betty.

"Well, figuring out whether we could survive up here was our original priority," said Casey. "And that needs to be our priority again instead of puzzling over how to make Shannon's procedure work. We can always come back to this once we find out if we're able to survive up here."

"That's exactly my position right now," said Debra

"Survival in what's left up here is a long road, trust me," said Betty.

"I'm afraid you're right, so let's lock this place up and get back to Utah," said Debra.

"I think our first priority is to try to make our cave continue to work," said Casey. "So my advice is to turn that cave inside out looking for the maintenace manuals."

"Good advice," said Debra. "Now let's get back to Utah and get busy."

Chapter Eight

Debra and her mob of mutineers must have found an aircraft, said Lucas to himself after he heard the report from the chief about an aircraft in the distance heading north. The secret facility south of the cave would have an aircraft, and Casey would know about it. That would be a long walk, but of course they could drive there with the tractor. If it is them, and who else could it be, what are they doing here? Going north? Wait.....from Tucson, and north to Colorado Springs? Yes, Brady and Shannon were buddy buddys, and Betty would tell him everything she knew. So they want to do the same thing as he! They want to find her lab and get immortalized, of course! And they could find her lab before he does. That's not good. While pondering the implications of this new development, he rushed to his aircraft and headed north to Colorado Springs.

After carefully patrolling back and forth along the foothills, he eventually spotted their aircraft through the trees in a small clearing of a narrow canyon. This must be where the lab is he nodded as he hovered over the aircraft. What now? He dare not land and attempt to confront them since he knew they were armed. So after some thought, he fired a shot from his forcefield weapon at their aircraft. The area under the plane exploded into flying debris, dust and grasses. When the debris cleared, the aircraft lay upside down. Nice, he smiled. Now they'll be stranded here, far from anything. He would eventually want to go into the lab, but that would have to wait. He looked at the time and decided to go back to Taos before dark to rethink his plans for what to do next.

"They were here," said the chief as Lucas entered the chief's residence.

"Who was here?" he asked in confusion, knowing Debra's aircraft was inoperable up in Colorado. Oh no, the Feds, he thought! they found him! Now what is he going to do?

"We do not know," said the chief. "They were all dressed in the same clothing."

"Same clothing?" he asked. That doesn't sound like the Feds, but it could be a military detachment they came with. Yes, that's it, they came with a military detachment.

"It was blue," said the chief.

"The uniforms?" he asked, trying to place the military service.

"It was a light blue and there were seven of them, one woman and six men who carried military rifles."

"Right," he acknowledged, as sweat began to form on his forehead.

"They took most of your things with them," said the chief.

"They took my things?"

"Yes, they took most of your things," the chief repeated.

Lucas rushed to his room to find it in shambles. He had taken nothing with him when he left the cave, so what did he have that could identify him? Nothing. And this was not like the Feds. Something was wrong here..

"What type of aircraft did they arrive in?" he asked.

"It was larger than yours with wings that tilted up when it landed," said the chief. "It had propellers on the tips of the wings, and the wings would then tilt back to level after it took off."

That's a very old vintage aircraft, a virtual antique, thought Lucas. That aircraft had been obsolete for a long time. So this was definitely not the Feds, they would have access to aircraft like his.

"It had symbols on the side," the chief continued.

"What kind of symbols?" he asked.

"Like this," the chief tried to illustrate them as he drew a crude oriental character on the wall with his finger.

"Wait a minute, what did these people look like?" he asked.

"Oriental."

"All of them?" he asked.

"Yes."

If it's not the Feds, who was it? Wait, China had declared itself neutral before the war, so perhaps they had survived and are now taking over. But they're invading an already decimated country in an obsolete aircraft? That does not seem likely. None of this is making sense. He had just assumed that the nuclear devastation and its aftermath encircled the planet, wiping out civilizations everywhere. But he would have no way of knowing for sure if any civilization actually survived. Yet he was finding pockets of survivors, so obviously people did survive. Perhaps millions, even billions. And if China had not been attacked directly, or only partially bombed, they could have survived in better shape than many countries. But why would they be here in this country after me? His mind now focused on that secret military facility south of his cave where Casey had likely acquired their plane. He knew the people who occupied it, and assumed they survived since he knew their cave had the same technology as his. That cave was originally a legitimate military facility, but it was taken over by the rogue brass who he conspired with to acquire his cave. Their cave was a fire control facility with nuclear capabilities built by the US government. As far as he knew, it still had its armament which was located elsewhere. If these militants see this Chinese military detachment flying around, they might assume the country is being taken over by the Chinese. Then this could become a serious matter since they could start another war. Suddenly Shannon's lab was not his main concern. His focus would now have to be on this Chinese detachment. Maybe he should go to these friends of his at the secret facility and warn them. And, if they already know about the Chinese detachment, should he help them launch an attack on China? And start another war? That is definitely not a good idea. It could quite literally finish off what's left of mankind on the planet. Given what just happened, what should he do?

"We think they are from the moving star," said the chief, pointing up.

"What moving star?" he asked. Oh, wait, a satellite, yes, of course, he thought. If the Chinese survived, they would have satellites to keep an eye on survivors.

"We see the star moving across the sky," said the chief. "It has always been there."

"Right," he replied. There were many satellites before the war, so it would not be out of the question for the Chinese to be using existing ones, or even have launched new ones. That technology is very old, but proven, he thought. Lucas stood in silence as he thought about his next move. So, they have the capability to scan the surface for survivors and monitor activities on the ground. Meaning they could track his every move. They have likely observed his recent travel and could have witnessed what he did to those survivors up at Vantage. So did they come to arrest him for that? Yes, perhaps they did. So he'll have to find a way to hide. But how? If the satellite technology is like their aircraft, it's ancient and can only track him if a satellite is overhead, and perhaps not as well at night.

"When did you last see the moving star?" asked Lucas.

"Last night just after sunset," said the chief.

If it were just one satellite, he could calculate how to avoid it, he thought. But if they have more than one satellite, or newer, more sophisticated satellites, it would be much more difficult for him to hide from them. He had to come up with a strategy. And soon. In his favor was their aircraft. Getting away from it would be child's play. And he could shoot them down easily with his forcefield weapon. But would shooting down their aircraft release a hornets nest of Chinese forces? He couldn't take that chance. So hiding seemed to be the best strategy for now. But whatever he did, he had to act quickly.

"Which way did this strange aircraft with the uniformed people go?"

"North, like the other aircraft," the chief pointed.

North. Of course, toward Colorado Springs where Debra's aircraft went, he thought. Yes, they would also be tracking them. They're new on the scene too. If they're preoccupied by them, it could give him time to flee. Lucas went to his aircraft and sat in the cockpit, thinking about where he would go.

Chapter Nine

"**W**hat!?" shouted Casey when he saw their aircraft upside down.

"Hoollllyyy!" exclaimed Brady as they approached the overturned aircraft.

"Lucas!" said Casey.

"So much for ignoring him," said Debra.

"I didn't think that even he could be this vicious, trapping us here with no way to get out," said Betty.

"Well, now he knows where the lab is," said Debra as they reached their useless ship and stood around it.

"What do we do now?" asked Brady.

"Well, we're totally stranded, with no way to leave or even contact anyone," said Casey as he examined the fallen plane.

"Then I guess we have no choice but to stay here until Lucas decides to come back," said Debra.

"What if he never comes back?" asked Brady.

"If that's the case, waiting here to starve to death would not be our best option, so we might want to start thinking about other options," said Debra.

"Can we turn this thing back over?" asked Betty.

"No, it's way too heavy, and besides, it looks like the cockpit is crushed along with its instruments," said Casey.

"Oh my god!" shouted Brady, who was pointing southward.

"Oh shit, he's coming back, so let's get back into the forest," said Casey who withdrew his pistol and waved them toward the tree line. Brady had already begun to retreat in that direction.

"Wait......that can't be him!" shouted Debra as she studied the oncoming craft.

"You're right, it's an old prop plane," said Casey. "I haven't heard or seen one of those since I was a kid, and that was at an antique airplane air show."

"So who is it?" asked Debra as they watched it get closer.

"I don't know, but I wonder if we should still head for cover just in case they're not friendly," said Casey, holding up his pistol and beginning to back up toward the woods.

"Actually, I think we should stand our ground," said Debra.

"Well, I think it's too late to do anything else anyway," said Casey.

"It looks like it's going to land," said Brady.

"It is, and, wow, it's a tilt wing, a VTO," said Casey.

"A VTO, why yes, of course it is, what else could it be," said Betty sarcastically, having no idea what VTO meant.

"It's clearly a museum piece," said Casey.

"It flies pretty well for a museum piece," said Betty as it began to slow.

"I think those are Chinese symbols on its side," said Debra who actually took a few steps forward even as the others were continuing to slowly back up.

"I'm not sure if that's good or bad," said Brady, as he slowly made his way toward the tree line, occasionally looking back over his shoulder.

"I think they would have opened fire if they were hostile," said Casey who had stopped backing up.

"Actually, I don't feel all that threatened," said Debra, as the noisy aircraft slowly settled to the ground in the small space next to their downed plane.

"I don't either," said Casey.

"Well, the good news is, we may not be stranded here any longer," said Debra.

"And the bad news?" asked Brady who had now stopped some distance away.

"We'll be shot, or thrown in jail to rot," said Debra.

"I like the good news better," said Brady.

"We'll soon know," said Debra as they waited impatiently for someone to come out.

Eventually a woman and three men, all dressed in light blue uniforms, came out and stood in front of their aircraft as the propellers slowed and the engine noise slowly died down. The men held assault rifles, but they were not pointed their way.

"Hello, my name is Debra," said Debra who slowly began walking toward the woman who now stood in front of the men.

"I'm Janet, and these are three of my patrol," said the woman who stepped forward to greet Debra. "We're out here trying to police what's left of the planet."

"You sound American," said Debra as she grasped Janet's hand.

"I am.....I was born and raised here," said Janet.

"Your men carry rifles, and your aircraft has Chinese symbols on it," said Debra.

"I know, sorry about that, but we're technically a Chinese military patrol so we need to look official," she shrugged.

"Those two guys back there came up from a cave with me a few days ago," said Debra. "And we picked up this nice lady behind me down near Tucson."

"I know, we saw you suddenly show up back in Utah and have been tracking you," said Janet. "Lucas flew off with your plane and eventually came here and did this to the plane you got from that place south of where you first appeared."

"Wow, you seem to know all about us and you also know Lucas," said Debra.

"Of course, everyone knows Lucas," said Janet. "He built all of those metal monstrosities, and then entombed a bunch of people in them before he ran off, obviously down into a cave.....I assume that's the cave you came up from."

"You have the entire story, so I assume you have satellites?" asked Debra.

"We do," said Janet.

"He told me he shot up some survivors at one of his blocks," said Betty, as she came forward to stand next to Debra.

"Actually, he shot people at two of his blocks, and yes, we saw that too, and that's why we're after him," said Janet. "We can't have people running around with guns shooting people," said Janet.

"OK, so you're like the police," said Casey who now joined them.

"You might call us that, and uh, by the way, you'll have to give us that pistol," said Janet.

"Sure," said Casey, holding it out by the barrel as one of Janet's men came forward to take it.

"Look Debra, nothing is as it once was," said Janet.

"We just spent the past forty years in that cave and this is all new to us," said Debra.

"Well, we're trying to stop and disarm anyone with weapons, and to confiscate or destroy any aircraft that might be used to start trouble," said Janet. "Weapons have been banned and advanced technology grounded."

"And you work for China?" asked Debra.

"It's the only country with any capability left out there," said Janet.

"Wow, we had no idea who or what survived this madness," said Debra.

"Do you know where Lucas is now?" asked Casey.

"We traced him to Taos and then saw what he did to your plane, so we came here," said Janet. "We were tracking you too, but you didn't seem to be getting into trouble like he was."

"So what's your beat?" asked Debra.

"It's supposed to be western north America, but mostly just the western US, however this is the first time we've been up in these parts in quite a few years," said Janet. "Most of our trouble up to now has been in Central America, and that occasionally spills up into Texas.

"What happened in the eastern part of this country?" asked

Debra.

"I've never been there, but my sources tell me that what you see here is pretty much what you see everywhere, except China where it was still pretty bad, but not this bad," she replied.

"Well, what you're doing is the right thing to do," said Debra. "Oh, I forgot, this is Casey, and that's Brady back there," Debra pointed. "Betty here is Lucas's sister."

"Pleased to meet you," said Janet. "My god, Betty, you're his sister?"

"I know, I hope you won't hold that against me," said Betty.

"I won't," said Janet with a chuckle.

"Betty survived in an underground facility near Tucson and as I said, the rest of us spent forty years in Lucas's cave before we mutinied and came up," said Debra. "He wanted to stay down fifty years because he thought the Feds would be after him for treason."

"Treason, I'm not surprised, well, we'll have to round him up at some point," said Janet.

"And you have no idea where he is now?" asked Debra.

"No," she replied. "Our tracking info is good, but its slow."

"Are there other patrols throughout the world?" asked Debra.

"Yes, but as you can imagine it's impossible to police the entire world with the kind of technology we've been able to salvage from the past," she replied, gesturing to her old airplane.

"So you've made weapons and technology illegal worldwide?" asked Betty.

"Yes, and that's the law we're trying to enforce," said Janet.

"I like it," said Betty.

"Yes, but it's not only impossible, it's also not a fun job," said

Janet.

"So your aim is to disarm the entire world?" asked Debra.

"Yes, and keep it that way.....talk about tilting at windmills," said Janet with a smile.

"Windmills?" asked Brady.

"He's somewhat illiterate," said Casey.

"Am not, I just don't know what a windmill is," said Brady, glaring at him.

"So apparently you're the only nation that is able to do what you're doing," said Debra.

"Yes, but China did suffer enormous losses," said Janet. "However, in the aftermath, they felt they had to establish a set of rules for what's left, if only to protect themselves."

"After what we've seen so far, it's encouraging to know that someone is at least trying to restore some semblance of order," said Debra.

"Trying is an accurate description," said Janet. "We just do as much as we can."

"Being in a cave for forty years has been like Rip Van Winkle for us, waking up to a strange new world," said Debra.

"Rip Van...?" Brady started to ask.

"Pretend you know," Casey whispered, looking at Brady and putting his finger to his mouth.

"So, in effect, what you see is China trying to establish what amounts to a police state with very strict rules of behavior for survivors, but with little hope of ever really being able to enforce it on a worldwide scale," said Janet.

"This is right out of science fiction," said Casey.

"Unfortunately it's far worse than science fiction could ever imagine," said Janet.

"I wonder if there are still nukes that somehow survived," said Debra.

"I'm sorry to say that there are," said Janet. "The Chinese have heard whispers from those who still have them."

"So, can't you root them out?" asked Casey.

"We can't find them," said Janet. "Just think about yourselves in your high tech cave, and imagine how many other high tech caves have to be out there. Unless they show themselves, we have no idea where they are, or, for that matter, who they are."

"And you think they could be hostile toward you?" asked Debra.

"Our patrols clearly have the appearance of an effort to achieve worldwide domination, so what do you think?" asked Janet.

"I see what you mean," said Casey.

"I don't know if you knew that Lucas was associated with a radical group of military brass that helped him get the cave we lived in for forty years," said Debra. "We think they're in a cave south of ours, the one where we got this plane. But we have no idea if they have nuclear weapons."

"Well, we know people like that exist, so any information you have about these folks would be helpful," said Janet.

"You know, even though this was unthinkable before the war, your top-down control is probably the only viable means of putting a lid on this lunacy," said Casey.

"Yes, and the more I see, the more I believe that," said Janet.

"By the way, what will you do with Lucas if you catch him?" asked Debra.

"Jail, I guess," said Janet. "We will need for him to be alive so he can tell us more about this radical group in that cave south of yours."

"Maybe that needs to be checked out sooner than later," said Debra.

"It does, so we'll have to go there next," said Janet. "Now, before we do that, can you tell me why you were here in this mountain canyon?"

"There's a secret immortality lab up there," said Brady, pointing.

"You're not talking about Shannon's lab?" asked Janet.

"So you know about her too," said Brady.

"Of course, she stole an international spacecraft with a couple dozen Chinese youth in it and headed into deep space," said Janet.

"Right," said Brady.

"China started an investigation of her and knew she had a lab somewhere here in Colorado," said Janet. "But the war started and we were never able to pursue it."

"Well, here it is, and we've already checked it out," said Debra.

"I'll bet Lucas wanted to come here and immortalize himself and you beat him to it, so that's why he trashed your aircraft," said Janet.

"That's exactly what happened," said Debra.

"Do you think he might come back here?" asked Janet.

"Eventually he might, but we just found out he can't immortalize himself, because it takes another person to assist," said Debra.

"Do you think she immortalized our teens before she headed out into deep space?" asked Janet.

"I'm sure of it, because any habitable destination would take decades, even generations to reach," said Casey.

"Well, my more urgent mission right now is to visit this radical group," said Janet.

"We want to help, but we'll need another aircraft to do that," said Debra pointing to their upside down plane.

"Having an aircraft could be an issue, it's illegal, but for now, you'll come with us," said Janet.

"Does this thing have firepower?" asked Casey as they began to board Janet's plane.

"It does," said Janet.

"I ask because Lucas has a forcefield weapon on his aircraft that is, as you can see, capable of overturning our aircraft, so he might do some serious damage to yours if you can't defend yourself," said Brady.

"We can defend ourselves," said Janet with a smile.

"Then this plane, like me, is old but dangerous," said Casey.

"Actually, in your case, just old," said Brady.

"He's a fencepost, so pay no attention to him," said Casey.

"Try to ignore them, Janet," said Debra. "Now..... I guess we're heading for Utah and the cave south of ours?"

"Yes," said Janet.

"We'll guide you there," said Casey.

"Alright, let's go find some radicals," said Janet after they fired up the old plane.

Chapter Ten

Lucas felt trapped. If he left Taos, he could be tracked to wherever he went. He could not go to the secret facility in Utah for fear that he would reveal their location to the Chinese. But he had to find a place to hide. What about the Denver Block, it was the closest to Taos. Denver had not been fully activated and he knew there was no aircraft in the hangar. So he could hide from the satellite there. If he made the trip at night, perhaps he could avoid detection if their present technology was not up to date. It seemed his only option at the moment. He had to try. It was already getting late and darkness would soon be upon him.

An hour later he departed for Denver at full speed, and less than a half hour later he landed on the Denver Block in six inches of accumulated dust. He wanted to get under cover in the hangar, but on his approach he used his spotlight to see that the hangar had been covered in a landslide. Maybe the Blockmaster could be activated and he could ask about where else he could go. He deplaned, opened the door to the block and rushed below to the Blockmaster's room where everything was dark. At the console he attempted to activate it. After a lengthy series of attempts, the lights on the globe lit up. Beams from the globe scanned the room, then a voice boomed.

"You are Lucas," said the Blockmaster. "I await programming."

"I am delaying your programming, but I ask that you establish contact with the other blocks."

"Contact is established," said the Blockmaster after a moment.

"Is a human living inside any of the blocks?"

"Yes, the Jackson Block."

That would be Jane, he thought, unless a survivor hijacked the block. Jane and he were never close friends, but she had worked in his organization and he trusted her. When she asked if she could tend to one of his blocks, he had agreed. She had chosen the Jackson Block. He had planned an underground facility there, but did not have time to complete it. So an excavation was left in a nearby hillside. It could provide a hiding place for his plane, shielded from satellite view. The hangar for the block would have an aircraft inside unless Jane took it to seek a suitable place to live somewhere else.

"Would you like me to get the human on the monitor?" asked the Blockmaster.

"Yes."

A moment later a face appeared on a monitor. It was Jane, but she appeared exactly as she had been forty years ago. Jane should be my age, he thought, and this was not an eighty year old woman he was looking at. This was a forty year old woman who looked twenty, as she did forty years ago. He hesitated a moment before he spoke.

"Jane?" he asked.

"Lucas..... you look much older than when I last saw you," she replied.

"And you look as if you have not aged a day, so Shannon must have immortalized you."

"Yes, she did."

"Did my people take you to Jackson as I had asked them?"

"No, Shannon did," said Jane. "I had met her when I worked for you and we became friends, which is why I was able to be immortalized."

"I see."

"After I was immortalized, I found out that I had to stay near my activation device in order not to age."

"Wait, what's this about an activation device?"

"It's how her immortality procedure works."

"You mean you can't move anywhere unless you take the device with you?"

"Yes, and in the nearly forty years since I've been here, I've never been able to locate it."

"So you would have left if you had found it?"

"This area is incredibly isolated, to say nothing about bitter cold winters," said Jane.

"But you managed to scratch out a living."

"She gave me a food machine, and I've supplemented that with gardening, which is not as easy as I once saw on Home and Garden," said Jane.

"I'm sure it isn't," said Lucas.

"By the way, where are you?"

145

"The Denver Block."

"How did you get there, I thought you were in a cave."

"I came up."

"I thought you told me you weren't coming up for fifty years?"

"There was a mutiny."

"They wanted to come up sooner?" she guessed.

"Yes."

"So, did everyone come up?"

"No, just Debra and her fellow mutineers."

"Debra? Do I know her?"

"No, she was born down there in the cave."

"So you're alone and estranged from your fellow cave dwellers."

"I am."

"And you have an aircraft?"

"Yes, I do."

"But you left the others stranded in the high plains."

"I guess I did, yes," he replied, not wanting to tell her about the incident at Shannon's lab.

"So what's your plan?"

"I need a place to hide."

"Hide? Why?"

"They're after me."

"The mutineers?"

"No, the Chinese."

"Wait...... the Chinese? I don't understand."

"It's a long story, but I need to hide my plane and then stay in that block until this blows over."

"The hangar has an aircraft inside, and besides, there's a stand of aspen blocking the door."

"I was thinking about the underground facility we started to dig in the hillside."

"That big gaping hole... right, I can see it from my roof."

"Do you think I could land my aircraft inside?"

"Well, trees have grown up in front, but I think if you're careful you might be able to squeeze in over them."

"Good, so I'm coming up there now since I have no other viable options."

"It's night."

"I know, the Chinese have satellites."

"You're planning to hide out here indefinitely?"

"No, just until things blow over."

"Then what?"

"I want to get into Shannon's lab."

"Shannon's lab? Why?"

"To immortalize myself."

"You can't do that by yourself."

"Why not?"

"It takes a second person."

"I didn't know that, so then maybe you can come with me to help."

"I can't leave here since I can't break contact with my activation device and its location is a mystery."

"Oh, the activation device, right, well, we can discuss this later, but right now I'm in a hurry to hide my plane, so I'm on my way up there."

"Alright, so I'll see you when you get here."

An hour later Jane stood on the roof watching as Lucas's

aircraft carefully circled the block with its landing lights showing the way. He eventually made a very careful approach over the trees into the cave. However, on his way in, the plane made contact with the ceiling and the aircraft spun into the ground. Dirt and mechanical parts flew every which way as it augered in. A few minutes later Lucas emerged from the trees with his flashlight, apparently unhurt. When he was below her, she shouted down to him.

"Are you all right?"

"A little banged up, but alive," he replied. "However, my plane is a wreck."

"You could check out the aircraft in the hangar, but I don't think you'd ever get it out because of the trees that have grown up in front of the door.," she said.

"Is the ground access in the hangar locked?" he asked.

"No, it's open and I'll meet you in there."

"Alright," he replied as he headed for the hangar.

When he arrived at the hangar, he stood in front of the door with his flashlight. What was once a clearing, was now covered with a substantial stand of aspen. After studying the situation for a while, he went to the side entrance and tried the handle. It was unlocked so he entered and began to look around. Near the center of the room was the aircraft and in one corner was the tractor that is used to move the plane in and out of the hangar. Perhaps the tractor could be used to knock over the trees, he thought. He went to the tractor, and after repeated efforts, he was finally able to get it started. He now had a way to remove the trees. He then went to the aircraft and climbed the steps to the entry door. Inside he looked around and then went to the cockpit where he began the activation sequence. On his third attempt a light went on, followed by others, and soon the console was completely lighted. He sat in the cockpit for a moment thinking about some of his options. He thought again about the secret underground facility in Utah. Perhaps that would be his ultimate hiding place. It was maybe his best option. But right now, that might as well be on the moon because of the Chinese. Then a thought struck him. His blocks were never proven NOT to work. So what if they did work? He could then inter himself into this block. And then, he had a way to walk out. He had developed robots that would function with the minds of someone interred in the block. So he could emerge as a robot. Then, he would knock down the trees in front of the hangar with the tractor and fly down to Utah to the secret facility where he would hide out. Those in the facility would recognize his voice and let him in. On the other hand, if the blocks do not work, he would simply be committing suicide. So the risk was too great. His strategy really had to be to stay here in this block until he could figure out what to do next.

"Hello, and welcome to the Jackson Block," Jane announced from below through the open door to the plane. Lucas got up and came to the doorway.

"Jane!" he replied as he quickly came down the ladder and started forward to hug her. She backed up, holding out her hand. He stopped short, then shook it.

"You look exactly as you did forty years ago," he said.

"Thanks to Shannon," she smiled.

"If only I could do the same," he replied with a nod.

"So while I was trying to survive the harsh winters up here in Jackson, you spent forty years in that cave," said Jane, shaking her head at how old he looked.

"Yes," said Lucas with a sigh. "I'm eighty something and look ninety five..... so how did you survive?"

"Well, with those miraculous food makers and my gardens," she replied.

"What about the cold winters?"

"I was able to preserve what I grew in the summer."

"Well, you look as if you survived quite well."

"I did, but I must say that immortality is not all that it's cracked up to be."

"Oh really, I'd take it in a heartbeat as opposed to the alternative," said Lucas.

"Yes, well, let's go into the block and discuss it," said Jane waving for him to follow her. They went to the back of the hangar and down a stairway, through a tunnel, and finally emerged inside the block.

"Do you have anything you'd like to see, or any questions?" asked Jane.

"I'm not sure where to start," he replied as he studied the face that had not aged a day since he saw her some forty years earlier.

"So you farmed?" he asked.

"Yes, but survival was mainly because of the food makers," she replied.

"Interesting," he nodded.

"Did you use them in your cave?" she asked.

"We didn't have any," said Lucas. "My cave came with whatever my cave came with, and it didn't come with food makers, so we had to do with what we had."

"Well, it worked great for me, and it still works," said Jane.

"I suppose we could have used them before we got the greenhouse in full operation," said Lucas.

"As I recall, you said you were going to stay down there fifty years," said Jane.

"Yes, because I was afraid the Feds would nab me if I came up."

"But fifty years.....you could have died down there."

"That would have been better than spending life in prison, or worse, execution."

"But what about your fellow cave dwellers?"

"It was my cave, and they wouldn't be alive at all if it weren't for me."

"Right....but.....OK, so where are they now?"

"I stranded them at Shannon's lab up in the mountains of Colorado."

"You left them there to die?"

"They found the lab before I did, so what am I supposed to do?"

"Man, you're something else Lucas, you really don't have a heart."

"That's what the Press said, but they didn't know me."

"But I do, and you don't have a heart. Now, tell me why the Chinese are after you."

"I was just defending myself at a couple of my blocks and had to kill a few people."

"You killed survivors?"

"They were trespassing."

"You killed them for trespassing when they were likely just trying to survive," said Jane, eyes wide open in surprise.

"They had guns, so I had to defend myself.....it was complicated."

"And the Chinese saw you."

"They have satellites."

"I guess they're like a police force of some kind."

"I guess so, I didn't stick around to ask."

"Apparently China survived the war," said Jane. "They installed a light on top of this block twenty years ago."

"So that was the Chinese," said Lucas.

"Yes," said Jane.

"Look, I know what I did would be viewed as criminal, and I have no idea what the Chinese will or will not do with me, but I couldn't take any chances, so I ran," said Lucas.

"Well, murder is a crime against society, so the Chinese are simply acting responsibly, unlike you," said Jane.

"It wasn't murder, Jane, it was self defense, and the Chinese couldn't know all the circumstances since they could only see it via satellites."

"Bottom line, you killed some survivors and they saw you do it, so they came after you."

"Right, so I just need to lay low until I can figure out what to do."

"Look, instead of leaving your friends to die just to get Shannon's secret first, why didn't you just inter yourself into one of your blocks?"

"I'm not about to commit suicide."

"Suicide? What are you talking about, the press was wrong."

"Wait, do you mean they work?"

"Of course, I have conversations with hundreds of the people who live here in this block."

"Conversations? How?"

"I go to each box and place my hand on it."

"Place your hand on it?"

"Then we communicate."

"Telepathically?"

"I don't know, I guess, I'm not sure, but I can carry on a mental conversation with the person inside each crypt, and even bring others from the block into the conversation."

"That's amazing! We never knew how to communicate! How could it be that simple?"

"I think those inside developed this capability on their own, so it may not have been perfected when you were trying."

"They can communicate with one another too?"

"Of course."

"And you know some of these people, or rather their spirits?"

"I know hundreds of them, and a dozen or so that I speak with regularly. They're my friends. My company. Without them, this would be a very lonely place."

"Wow," he smiled with his eyes closed. Yes, now he can go in and come out in one of his robots, he thought. Then head south to Utah and his military friends.

"They're real people to me."

"If this block works, that means my other blocks work too."

"I assume so," she replied. "Now, I have a question. How much do you know about the Chinese patrol, because what they do or don't do could well affect this block and your other blocks for that matter."

"I don't know much at all except for the Chinese patrol with soldiers who are looking for me," said Lucas. "But to be honest, I'm not sure why anyone would want to care that much about what's left, because if it's anything like what I've seen so far, it doesn't seem worth it."

"Unless they really care about what happens next to the world," said Jane.

"But why do they care what I do to survivors?"

"Because you were out killing them, Lucas, and that makes you a danger to society.....in this case, a threat to survivors."

"Perhaps I am, but the survivors I encountered at one of my blocks could best be characterized as outright barbarians. At a third block, the survivors had found some of my sales paraphernalia and were indoctrinated into the theme I had advertised, so they treated me like some kind of god."

"What did you do?" asked Jane.

"I took advantage of their kindness and used that block as a base in my search for Shannon's lab," said Lucas.

"My god, you didn't even handle that well," said Jane.

"Why? I didn't harm them," he replied.

"How noble," said Jane.

"Look, with that exception, my exposure to survivors has not been good," said Lucas. "And furthermore, living on the surface, or more appropriately surviving on the surface, would be an extremely hard life for anyone."

"In other words, who cares about the survivors?" asked Jane.

"In my case, yes, who cares," said Lucas.

"I've not encountered survivors, but I know I wouldn't treat them as beneath me," said Jane.

"Some were hostile and a threat, so how else should I treat

them?" he asked.

"It's interesting for me to find out that there are survivors out there regardless of their disposition," said Jane. "I'm sure their tale of how they survived might be one of hardship and sorrow."

"I'm sure that's true because normal life seems virtually impossible," he shrugged. "So for me there's no reason to even think about trying to survive in this environment."

"So you're thinking about interring yourself in this block, aren't you?"

"I am," he nodded after a pause.

"Well, those inside seem quite content, so I don't blame you for considering it," she said.

"But, just to be honest, this block will eventually fail, like all the others, so this isn't forever as I advertised, even though it can be a place to survive for a very long time," he replied.

"That's right, nothing is forever, but this is close," said Jane.

"And what about those who believe in a higher power and everlasting life?" he asked.

"Are you one of those?" asked Jane.

"Not right now, but it makes a person think about it when we really get serious about the end."

"Well, I've certainly thought about it, because heaven must be a very comforting place," said Jane.

"But at this moment, everything is the here and now for me," he replied. "And right now, I feel I must remove myself from my physical body and exist as a virtual spirit for as long as that lasts." He turned to her with a very calm expression, knowing that his real agenda was to enter the block and escape as a robot.

"Do you think this is meant to be?" she asked. "I mean, here you are, Lucas, founder of the eternity blocks, coming here to one of your creations after your tirade of killing..... the police on your tail, and finding out from me that your blocks actually work after decades of believing they didn't?"

"Maybe it is meant to be," he nodded.

"You of all people know it's not reversible, so once your body is gone, you can't get it back."

"Look, Jane, I'm pushing eighty-five with a narrowing future and an old body, so I won't last that much longer anyway."

"Well, I've been frozen in a young body for forty years, and have been essentially trapped here in this block," she replied. "I was given a reprieve of unknown time with immortality, but nothing is waiting for me in what's left of the world."

"But what if you did leave the block and lost your immortality, you're still young, with a long life ahead of you," he replied. "Surely there are survivors out there who are civilized."

"Perhaps," she replied. "No, this is where all of my long time friends are, and I can't just leave, because I've become quite attached to them over the years."

"It sounds like you're thinking about interring yourself too."

"Yes, but it isn't a spur of the moment decision, I've thought about it many times over the years."

"So then my arrival here could also be serendipity for you."

"Yes, in a twisted sort of way."

"Right......well, I'm going up now to get interred," said Lucas who turned and started up the staircase.

"I'm still thinking," she replied, as she watched him disappear. As she watched, a smile touched the corner of her lips. She knew how he would completely change once he entered. The change would be as dramatic as it was complete. Her friends inside would tell her stories about what some called a complete metamorphosis of the soul. The good is suddenly born and the bad is displaced.

"Perhaps I'll see you inside," came his voice from far up the stairway.

"Perhaps," she whispered with a nod and a smile.

Chapter Eleven

"**I** don't remember where the cave entrance is," said Brady as they walked around the secret cave complex in Utah.

"But you saw that there was a cave?" asked Casey.

"I went down into the cave, and I remember the long stairway with the silvery rails that seemed to go forever and then the long elevator ride," said Brady.

"Could it have been inside a building?" asked Debra.

"My men just searched both of these buildings thoroughly and found nothing," said Janet.

"I don't remember going into a building," said Brady.

"And I don't see anything around the area that could conceal an entrance," said Casey.

"We'd need special detection equipment to find it I'm afraid," said Janet. "So I'll see if Central can get their hands on something..... but then getting it here might be another issue."

"However, this likely means they haven't come up in forty

years," said Debra. "So that might say something about whether these people even survived."

"That's always a possibility, knowing how many perished in their shelters," said Janet.

"Maybe if we tailed Lucas, he would come back here," said Casey. "He should know where the entrance is."

"That's not a bad idea," said Betty.

"Let's wait for the surveillance report from the satellites in the morning so we can get a fix on his location," said Janet.

"In the meantime, we can go to the little town so you can meet the rest of our party," said Debra.

"Alright, we'll go there, but I do have to complete my daily patrol and also get some fuel for this gas guzzler," said Janet. "I'll pick you up at the town in the morning."

"That's a plan," said Debra.

They lifted off and a short time later were greeted by Sarah and the others. Janet then continued on her patrol, heading west toward the coast. The next morning she returned.

"Anything?" asked Brady, as Janet joined them around the big table in Edna's place.

"Satellite number three shows that he flew to a block near Denver, then to another block north of Jackson, Wyoming," she replied.

"I think he had a block keeper there," said Brady.

"Well, in any case, I need to go up there and check it out before he disappears again," said Janet.

"We're going with you," said Debra.

"It could be dangerous," said Janet.

"There's no way we're not going," said Debra. Janet nodded.

Once everyone was on board she lifted off and headed north toward Jackson. When they arrived they circled the block looking for human activity.

"If he's here, his plane has to be here," said Casey.

"I think that's the hangar down there in the trees," said Janet.

"It is, but from here it looks like there are trees in front of the door," said Casey.

"So then he may not be here," said Janet.

"Wait, over there!" said Brady a moment later, pointing to the hillside excavation where a reflection from the wreckage of Lucas's aircraft flashed through the trees.

"Holy crap.....it looks like he crashed in there," said Casey.

"If he died in the crash, he's inside the plane," said Janet. "I'm going to land."

They put down in a clearing near the excavation site and Debra and Janet walked through the trees to Lucas's wrecked plane. The door was open and no one was inside, so they returned and flew to the rooftop and landed. Everyone deplaned and went to the entrance.

"Do any of you know the combination?" asked Janet.

"Only Lucas and his block keeper have that," said Brady. "If memory serves, the block keeper was a woman, but who knows if she's still alive or if she's still here after forty years."

"Lucas will be inside whether she is or not," said Casey.

"Actually, we've observed someone here at this block in the past, so I suspect this woman is still here and inside with him," said Janet.

"I used to know these codes when I was a kid," said Brady. "But right now, I have no idea, but I'm just remembering that this woman's name was Jane."

"So you seem to know a lot about Lucas," said Janet. "Were you with him when you were a child?"

"He's Lucas's son," said Debra.

"I see," said Janet.

"Debra, you said you would keep that a secret," said Brady.

"Everyone in the cave knows, so it's not exactly a revelation," said Debra with a shrug. "You do realize that he was probably my father too."

"I know, but that's also not much of a secret," said Brady.

"But he never told me," said Debra.

"And he has certainly never treated you like a daughter," said Casey.

"He's a bitter man, and was never a loving father, that's for sure," said Brady.

"All right, all right......I hate to break up this tender family moment, but can either of you children of Lucas's come up with a way to open this door?" asked Janet impatiently. Brady shrugged, then tried several combinations, but eventually he just shook his head.

"I have a novel idea.....why don't we knock?" asked Debra.

"What an idea!" said Casey who went immediately to the door and began pounding.

After a number of attempts and a lengthy wait for a response, he turned to Janet and shook his head.

"Casey?" asked Debra, looking at him.

"I'm sure it's not one two three, but have you tried his birthday?" asked Casey.

"His birthday, uh, OK, I'll try it," said Brady who went to the keypad. A few minutes later there was a click and he opened the door. Brady just looked at Casey who smiled.

They all followed Debra inside and down the ramp to the Blockmaster's chamber. As they entered, the Blockmaster scanned them.

"Who are you?" asked the Blockmaster.

"The inquisition," said Casey.

"I do not know who the inquisition is," said the Blockmaster.

"I'm Lucas's son," said Brady.

"His son was eleven," said the Blockmaster.

"That was forty years ago, so do the math asshole," said Casey.

"What is asshole," said the Blockmaster.

"Never mind.....can you tell me where my father is?" asked Brady.

"First, I have many questions regarding these people who have entered," said the Blockmaster.

"Sorry, but we have to know where Lucas is at this moment, so your questions will have to wait," said Brady.

"They were interred," the Blockmaster replied after a brief pause.

"Interred? And by 'they' you mean the block keeper went in with him?" asked Brady.

"Yes, my block attendant, Jane, was interred a while after your father," he replied.

"I thought these blocks didn't work, so why would my dad inter himself if he knew they didn't work?" asked Brady.

"I do not know the answer to that question," said the Blockmaster.

"The question was not directed at you, bulb head," said Casey.

162

"I am not bulb head, I am the Blockmaster."

"Fine, but would you just answer my questions, and forget this walking piece of cow dung next to me," said Brady.

"What is cow dung?" asked the Blockmaster.

"Focus," said Brady.

"What is your question?"

"Where are their bodies?" asked Brady.

"The bodies are cremated and ashes deposited in each person's crypt," said the Blockmaster.

"That's decent," said Debra who motioned with her head for them to go up. Everyone looked at the Blockmaster, then nodded. They began to walk up the hallway to the roof.

"When can I ask my questions about these strangers?" asked the Blockmaster.

"We'll let you know," said Brady as they reached the top.

"The Blockmaster tries to answer everything," said Debra. From below they could hear the muffled voice of the Blockmaster, but could not make out the words.

"I know, you just can't get into an exchange with them," said Brady.

"If Lucas interred himself, it must mean that he had a high degree of confidence that his blocks worked," said Janet.

"He had to have proof, because my dad would never inter himself if he didn't feel completely certain about it," said Brady.

"If that's true, and this block works, then his other blocks must work," said Janet.

"That's a definite game changer," said Casey.

"But now my dad and this block keeper are just spirits, there is no way to communicate with them," said Brady.

"Is spirits what they're called?" asked Debra.

"It's their place in the cyber cloud," said Casey.

"That's almost romantic," said Brady.

"I've known about these blocks since I was a kid in Frisco and they seemed so unreal to me," said Janet. "But now that I'm here and actually know the person who's in there, it takes on a whole new meaning. Can he, like think? Or speak? What is he?"

"I'm not exactly sure, but the concept was to create an actual mind without a body," said Brady.

"That was always my understanding too," said Debra. "It's the mind of the person in a cyber cloud. So it's not just the memories that were in the brain at the time of interment, it's an actual person."

"I remember him discussing that very subject over and over with his scientists," said Brady. "Unfortunately, I was young and didn't understand it, and I still don't. But I also remember him discussing a way to get out of the block once interred."

"Wait a minute..... a way to get out?" asked Janet.

"Yes, a way to leave the Block in some physical form," he replied.

"How would that work since he'd be just a mind in a cloud?" asked Debra.

"I don't know that either, but one option was to take a DNA sample at interment, then, at some point in the future you would grow a clone of yourself and have your mind introduced into it once it's mature."

"It?" asked Debra. "You realize of course that a clone is a real person. Do you think that was a serious option?!" Debra looked at him with her mouth agape. "You're growing a replica of yourself, a real person, not a rat or a goat, and then what, you kill the person by essentially erasing their brain and then putting yours in its place?"

"My god, that's barbaric," said Janet.

"It makes my stomach turn," said Debra.

"I guess that option would have been pretty bad, but another option was to build robots that could operate with the spirit's mind in control," said Brady. "So the robot would be like a metal person."

"A cyber mind in control of a robot," said Debra. "Well, that's not murder, but it still seems a bit creepy."

"To say nothing of the fact that it would be an incredible technological feat," said Casey, shaking his head in disbelief at the mere idea of it.

"It's both creepy and technologically improbable," said Janet. "I'd even go as far as to say impossible."

"However, neither of these options were little more than ideas, right?" asked Debra.

"No, he was quite serious about implementing something that would allow someone to get out of the block," said Brady.

"Actually, the latter option, the robot thing, would really be something to witness," said Casey.

"Well, it's a quantum leap better than the other option," said Debra.

"In any case, don't underestimate our dad, he may indeed have come up with some way to get out," said Brady.

"Saying 'our' dad makes my skin crawl," said Debra.

"I hate to break up yet another tender family moment, but there are at least three possibilities here. One, your father is inside and no longer of any concern to me or the world. Two, he's inside and will wait until he can grow a clone, which would take years. So I'm not particularly concerned about this second possibility because it's not immediate and doesn't affect the status of those dudes with the nukes down in Utah. The final possibility is that he's planning to go out of here as a robot and visit his nuclear armed dudes with the idea of planning an attack on China. In the first case, I don't see any further reason for me or my detail to stay in the area, so I'm done here. The second case doesn't require my presence either. However, the third case suggests we need to be in a position to stop him if he emerges as a robot. Therefore, the third case is now my priority," said Janet.

"So what's the next step?" asked Debra.

"Well, we can hang out here in the vicinity and wait for him to come out, or go to Utah and wait for him at this secret cave," said Janet.

"Or, we could destroy his only means of travel, the airplane, since there's no way he can walk to Utah," said Casey.

"Then let's blow up the aircraft in the hangar," said Debra.

"But didn't Casey say its blocked by trees," said Brady.

"I'll just blow that hangar up with the plane inside," said Janet.

"You know, we certainly could use that aircraft," said Debra. "So maybe blowing it up right now is not a good idea."

"No, we don't have time to arrange for your future means of transportation, so I'm going to take out that aircraft, right in the hangar," said Janet who waved them to her aircraft and they were soon on their way to the hangar.

"Wait, I think we're too late because it looks like a few of the trees have been taken down," said Casey as they neared the hangar. "We should have checked more closely when we first got here."

"Oh shit, so this means he's already gone," said Janet.

"Well, I think we know where he went," said Debra.

"If he left yesterday, he's already safely inside that cave," said Casey.

"Or he may not have even gone to Utah," said Brady.

"True, but we still have to go after him because too much is at stake here," said Debra.

"We're heading back to Utah to check that out first," said Janet as the old aircraft thundered away to the south.

Chapter Twelve

"Jane, are you inside?" asked Lucas after many attempts to figure out how to communicate with only his thoughts. He repeated the call several times.

"You are Lucas," came a male voice.

"How did you know?" he asked as the ability to communicate suddenly came upon him when he heard someone speak.

"We are aware of all who enter," said the voice.

"Did anyone else come in?" he asked.

"We do not share this knowledge," said the voice.

"I see," said Lucas.

"Why do you enter?" asked the voice. Lucas paused to consider the question as a strange sensation was now engulfing him. A new warmth was flooding his mind as well as a soothing calm.

"I'd like to know that too," came another voice, followed by what seemed a chorus of voices. He could not tell how many.

"There's not much left up on the surface, and the Chinese were after me for some terrible things I did," he replied after a moment to partially absorb the new sensation. He was surprised at how he was now describing what happened. Terrible things? Yes, they were terrible things.

"What did you do?" asked someone.

"I committed murder, and I have been completely thoughtless toward the welfare of others," said Lucas, now realizing that he actually brutally murdered people. It was not all self defense. Some of it was murder, and now he was freely admitting it. Plus, how many other evil things had he done in his life? There were too many to recall.

"You committed murder and acts of cruelty?" asked someone.

"I was selfish, with no regard for others as fellow humans," he replied as a powerful guilt flooded his thoughts and everything he had ever done to hurt anyone or cheat anyone cascaded through his mind.

"So the Chinese came after you for these terrible deeds?" asked the first voice, as the many voices began to chatter loudly again in the background.

"I committed murders and the Chinese were doing the right thing by coming to arrest me," he replied. "I was a menace, and had to be stopped and punished."

"Do you think they will try to come after you here in our block?" asked another.

"I don't think they know where I am."

"What if they find out?"

"They would not do harm to this place because there are good people in here, and they represent the good in what remains so

169

they will not harm good people," said Lucas.

"We hope you are right," said the first voice.

"I thought Jane might inter herself," he continued after there was a pause. An eerie silence followed, prompting Lucas to be suspicious about what was going on.

"Jane spoke with us daily," came another voice after a while.

"You used the past tense," said Lucas.

"She may eventually contact you," came the first voice.

"I see," he replied, now certain she had come in, and also certain that the person he had been was not a person Jane would want to continue to be associated with. Everything that was wrong in his life hung over him like a giant gray cloud. But the longer he was here the more he felt as if the cloud was beginning to dissolve as the good replaced the bad in his mind.

"She was our eyes and ears out in the world, so we'll miss her presence," said the first voice.

"I'm sorry," said Lucas.

"We are one now," said someone.

"Somehow, I understand, but everything is black here," said Lucas. "It's as if I were blind, but I can't create images in my mind as I once did. Will I dream?"

"We do not sleep, so we do not dream," said the first voice.

"So I won't sleep?"

"We have no bodies to become weary."

"I'll be eternally awake?"

"Yes."

"If you're eternally awake, what do you do twenty four hours a day?"

"There are no hours, no days, no weeks, no months, no

years," said another voice.

"We spend our time communicating," said the first voice.

"You can't see one another. You can't touch one another. You have no clothes or shoes. You don't walk. You don't sit. You don't sleep. You don't have to eat because you have no body. So you don't have to go to the bathroom. You can't see anything because you have no eyes. It's just your essence. Your spirit. Your mind."

"For us, it's all we need," said someone.

"Again, somehow I understand," he replied.

"There is no pain, no hardship, no jealousy and no fear," said a distant voice.

"Yes, I understand," he replied.

"Did you expect otherwise when you designed these blocks, and especially when you decided to voluntarily give up your outside life to come in?" asked another voice in the background.

"I didn't really think about it, and like everything else, you have to experience something in order to truly understand it," he said.

"That is a fundamental truth," said another.

"Now, I'm being kept alive in an electronic cloud," said Lucas as if it were a profound observation.

"And if current is cut, our cloud disappears," said the first voice, to which a silence fell over everything.

"I was working on a method of reintroducing the spirits into a new body," said Lucas after a period of empty space when there was no conversation.

"How would that work without taking someone else's life?" asked a woman.

"In retrospect, the idea of using a clone to re-enter the

171

physical world was too evil for me to have even contemplated," said Lucas.

"You changed when you came in as we all have," said someone.

"Yes, I feel it, I have completely changed, and it feels magical," said Lucas as his thoughts of leaving in a robot and helping the extremist militants in Utah completely evaporated. It was being replaced by thoughts of all the evil he had committed, and how sorry he was for everything he had ever done wrong. Now, his attitude toward the extremists changed and became one of stopping them, not helping them. An almost overwhelming urge came over him. Yes, he had to stop them. He had to go there and stop them.

"Were there other ideas for enabling our spirits to leave a block?" asked another.

"Yes, robots," he replied, as he thought about what he must do, and how he must do it.

"You mean we would transfer our spirit into a robot and walk out of here?"

"Yes."

"Did you actually create these robots?" asked someone.

"I did."

"How many?"

"I was only able to manufacture two for each block," he replied.

"Two robots for thousands," said the first voice.

"The robots were very sophisticated, and extremely difficult to manufacture, and time ran out as the big war closed in on us."

"Which begs the question of who would get to leave if only two robots were there?" asked a woman who sounded familiar.

"I don't know, we just built as many as we could as time ticked down," he replied.

"But a little while ago, as you thought about interring yourself, was the knowledge that you had a robot to escape in part of your decision?" asked that woman.

"Yes, but now my purpose has completely changed," said Lucas.

"How so?" asked the woman.

"Before I came in, my purpose was to go to Utah in a robot and help some extremist friends with their plan to destroy China," said Lucas.

"And now?" she asked.

"And now, my purpose is to go there and shut them down forever," he replied.

"Can you do this by yourself?" asked the woman.

"I'm not sure, but knowing these people and what they had planned is MY sin, and therefore I must be the one to atone for it," said Lucas.

"I assume these people have nuclear weapons?" asked the woman.

"They do," said Lucas.

"So how will you stop them?" asked the woman.

"I will go there, and once inside, I will disable their facility."

"Would you then return?" asked the woman.

"If I survive, I will return, because this is now my home," he replied.

"These extremists are in Utah?" asked the woman.

"Yes, in a secret underground installation not far from the cave where I spent the past forty years," he replied.

"So then you want to leave now in this robot?" asked the woman.

"Yes, because stopping this group has become my primary mission and purpose," he replied.

"Is this installation well fortified?" she asked.

"It is very secure, but they should remember me, or rather my voice, so I think I'll be able to get in."

"They have been there for the past forty years, so why is it important to stop them now?" asked the woman.

"Because of all the trouble I have caused to prompt Chinese action," said Lucas. "The appearance of a Chinese patrol in action may well give the impression that the Chinese had taken over this country."

"You mean when these people see the Chinese patrol chasing you?" she asked.

"Yes," said Lucas.

"OK, but this mission you plan is dangerous, and you may not return," said the woman.

"That's true, but it must be done, and I must be the one to do it," he replied.

"I understand your passion," she said.

"However, despite the fact that I am the creator of these blocks, I must admit that I don't know how to access my robots," said Lucas.

"The occupants of this block have learned just about everything about how it works and, actually, we also knew about the robots," said the woman. "But we did not know their purpose until now."

"Wait, you're Jane," said Lucas.

"I needed to know that you had changed," said Jane.

"I don't blame you," said Lucas. "So, can you help me get to a robot?"

"Yes," said Jane.

"Can you take me to them?" he asked.

"I am there now since I anticipated your purpose, and I want you to come toward my voice," said Jane. "Come......."

"OK, uh.....toward your voice?.....I'm not sure......," he said as he focused on following her voice. Suddenly, he felt a strange movement as if he were sliding down a long hallway toward an open door that he could not see. For a brief moment things were confused, and in another moment he could see the inside of a room. Wait, he could see! He instinctively tried to move an arm that he no longer had, but through the image ahead he saw a large mechanical hand in front of him.

"Is that my.....?" asked Lucas

"It's your robotic hand, and you're inside one of the robots and I'm in the other."

"Wait..... Jane, you can't come with me."

"I must, you will need help."

"This was all my doing, so only I can embark on what could well be a suicide mission."

"The mission affects everyone."

"Nonetheless, I can't have you go since this is my sin and I must be the one to make amends and also take the risks."

"You're not asking me to go, I'm going because I must go, not for you but for everyone."

"But you have your friends here."

"Your success in this mission is for them too."

175

"Alright, but I will agree only if you do exactly what I say when we get there," said Lucas.

"I will follow your lead."

"First of all, what do I do in this thing.....do I just pretend I'm in my old body?"

"I'm not sure, Lucas, they're your robots."

"I know.....right, so..... OK, let's see......alright, I think I may have to just muddle through..... how about you?"

"I guess they don't come with a training manual, so muddling through will have to do."

"I think I'm beginning to get the hang of it," said Lucas after a while. "So let's just start out..... we'll need that aircraft, so let's go to the hangar and see what we can do about those trees."

"We can go out this door," said Jane who pushed a lever and a door opened.

The robots were nearly eight feet tall and their shoulders scraped as they ducked to go out the door. They made there way through the tunnel to the hangar. Once there, they opened the hangar door and started the tractor.

"I think what I'm going to do is slam this tractor into a tree and see what happens," said Lucas as he charged out of the hangar with the tractor and hit into the first tree. It splintered from its trunk and fell. He continued out through several more trees, then returned to the hangar to repeat his attack for another swath. Soon the area was wide enough to fly the aircraft out. Lucas brought the tractor back in then waved Jane into the aircraft.

"Shouldn't we tow the plane outside first?" asked Jane as she followed Lucas up the ladder.

"No, I think I can fly us out if I'm careful," said Lucas.

"Obviously you've flown these before."

"I was a combat pilot in my youth," he replied as he wedged himself into the pilot's seat. Jane decided not to try to squeeze in beside him and sat back in the passenger compartment. He started the engine and lifted a few inches off the floor of the hangar, eased outside where he carefully lifted clear of the trees, then sped southward.

Chapter Thirteen

"There's the aircraft," said Casey as they approached the secret facility in Utah.

"Of course we don't know how long he's been here," said Debra.

"I know, it could be almost a day, in which case he could already be down in the cave, or, it could be a few hours," said Casey.

"Well, I'm going to land next to it," said Janet as she carefully sat her plane down.

"Look, the door to the building is open a crack, it wasn't that way when we were here yesterday," said Brady, pointing.

"Maybe the entrance to the cave is in there," said Janet.

"No, I'm not so sure, since I'm seeing several places out there in the field that appear to have been dug into since we were here," said Brady, pointing out onto the nearby prairie.

"I see them," said Janet.

"Which means he's looking for the entrance and may be inside looking for a map or something," said Debra who launched herself out the door and down the ladder.

"Wait, Debra, don't go in there by yourself.....I have seasoned vets with automatic weapons," said Janet.

"No, Janet, let's try to do this with as little violence as possible," said Debra over her shoulder as she made her way to the building.

"He just destroyed your plane and you want to play nice?" asked Janet who was down the ladder and in pursuit.

"Well, he's our dad," said Debra.

"Right now, he's a robot," said Janet as she finally caught up.

Brady appeared in the plane's doorway and began lumbering down the ladder as Debra and Janet reached the building. They stopped in front of the partially open door.

"Dad?" hailed Debra.

"You shouldn't be here, Debra," Lucas replied.

"Brady's here too," said Debra.

"You two need to go back to the little town," said Lucas.

"We came here with Janet who is from the Chinese patrol," said Brady who just arrived.

"That complicates things," he replied.

"They're our friends," said Brady.

"Yes, and their mission is clearly to suppress violence, not take over the country," said Debra.

"I know that, and I also know that I'm the one who is in the wrong," said Lucas.

"Wait, I'm confused, we thought you came here to help your friends down in this cave," said Debra.

"No, I came here to stop them," said Lucas. "And just so you know, I'm definitely not who I was before I went into my block."

"Well, you certainly sound like a different person," said Debra.

"I am."

"So we're all on the same side?" asked Brady.

"We are, but we're having trouble finding the entrance," said Lucas.

"Wait....you said 'we', is someone in there with you?" asked Debra.

"Yes, I'm Jane, and I'm also a robot," said Jane.

"Jane......oh, the block attendant," said Brady.

"Lucas will need help with this," said Jane.

"And you can't find the entrance?" asked Brady.

"No, we've been here since yesterday and dug a few holes out there, and these facility diagrams are of no help since they don't show the entrance," said Lucas.

"I think I remember a big rock near the entrance," said Brady.

"You remember that?" asked Lucas.

"Yes, because as I was looking out over the prairie, I saw that rock out there and it came back to me," said Brady. Lucas opened the door, then bent over so he could see out.

"See," said Brady, pointing to a big rock a few hundred yards out in the field.

"You know what, I think you're right, I do remember that rock now," said Lucas.

"Well, let's not stand around yakking, let's get over there," said Debra who started out in that direction.

"You heard her son, don't just stand there," said Lucas who

was squeezing through the doorway. Jane was right behind him as he followed Debra as fast as he could walk. Bringing up the rear was Brady.

At the rock, Lucas scanned the ground, looking for any evidence of an entrance. Debra was already there and was pointing to a slight depression.

"What do you think?" she asked as she walked over to it.

"That looks like the best candidate, so get back," said Lucas who got down on his knees and began digging with his mechanical hands. Dirt was flying everywhere, and a moment later the sound of metal against metal signaled the discovery of something.

"Is that it?" asked Debra.

"I think so, but we need something to dig with," said Lucas. "I don't think my metal hands can do the job."

"How about this," said Janet who had retrieved a shovel from her ship and followed them out to the rock.

"Perfect....stand back," said Lucas, who grabbed the shovel but immediately dropped it as it slipped through his metal grip.

"We've got this," said Janet as she picked up the shovel and handed it to one of her men who had now joined them. The man began digging. A while later he was completing the excavation, having removed nearly a foot of dirt from on top of the steel door.

"I'll take it from here," said Lucas. He studied the door for a moment, then pulled out a recessed handle and twisted it. There was a loud click. With both of his metal hands he pulled, and they could hear a hissing sound as hydraulic pistons slowly opened the six inch thick door. They all stood for a moment looking down into the black interior. A stairway disappeared into the abyss.

Two shiny silver hand rails followed the stairway downward.

"They will know we're here and have broken in," said Lucas. "So I think we need to proceed quickly in case they decide to initiate the emergency protocol."

"And that would be?" asked Janet.

"Launch a preemptive strike," said Lucas.

"Is the target China?" asked Janet.

"It is," said Lucas.

"Then let's get down there," said Janet.

"I need to go first since I'm hoping they remember me, otherwise, none of us will ever be able to enter the cave," said Lucas.

"You're saying we should stay here?" asked Janet.

"Yes, just stay here for at least ten minutes," said Lucas as he stepped down into the entrance.

"I'm going with you," said Jane.

"Alright, let's go," said Lucas who started down the stairway with Jane right behind him.

"I assume this thing attached to our hips is a weapon?" asked Jane as they descended, lit by the spotlight on Lucas's head.

"It's a hand cannon that basically knocks people down," he replied.

"What if they have guns?"

"They get knocked down pretty hard," he replied. "In fact, I killed an old man in Winterhaven by just knocking him down."

"I'll take your word for it," she replied. "But are we bullet proof in case they get a shot off before we knock them down?"

"Mostly, unless they hit something vital."

"That's not completely reassuring," said Jane. "So what about doors down there?

"There's one steel door with a coded entry after we get down this endless flight of stairs, then, it's an elevator to the main facility."

"So, the elevator door opens and they're ready with guns to blow us to bits."

"We'll shoot first."

"I feel safe already."

"I know, but this operation is pretty much by the seat of our pants, and the worst case scenario is suicide."

"Thanks for that assessment, however, in case you haven't noticed, we don't have pants."

"I know, but the good news is that I think our chances are quite good for a friendly reception if they recognize my voice."

"And if they don't recognize your voice?"

"We'll resort to violence."

"I can hardly wait."

At the bottom of the stairway was a landing and a short hallway to their right that led to a large steel door. A keypad was on one side and Lucas thought a minute before trying a combination he thought he remembered. It did not work. There was a button and speaker on one side of the keypad. He pushed and held the button.

"I am Lucas from forty years ago, and I helped develop this cave," he said. "I have come for a visit." They waited for several minutes, but just as he was about to push it again a voice came back.

"Come down," came a female voice. He looked at Jane and nodded. The steel door opened and they ducked down to walk through. Ahead was a double door that was the elevator.

"Shall we?" she asked.

"Of course."

"How far down?" asked Jane.

"I don't remember, but I do remember that it isn't a high speed elevator," said Lucas.

"Can you tell anything from their reply?" she asked.

"I'm not all that confident that it was friendly."

"That's kind of what I thought too."

"And I don't trust these people very much to begin with."

"My cannon is drawn and pointed," said Jane.

"So is mine."

"So, you were here when this was built?" she asked.

"No, it was built by the US government as a defense installation," he replied. "These people were recruited by a group of high ranking military brass that essentially stole this cave and also helped me misappropriate my cave. I helped them financially in return. They were high enough to manipulate decisions. They sprang into action at the last minute when there was near chaos."

"What happened to the legitimate military people who were here?" asked Jane.

"As I understood it, there was just a skeleton crew at the time."

"What about your cave?"

"Ours was supposed to house political dignitaries of the highest echelon. But these people gave the dignitaries false information about the cave's location and I have no idea where they ended up or what happened to them. This cave we're going into now was designed as a tactical fire control cave for a large battery of nukes located somewhere in the LA area. The facility was specifically designed to exist following a war, but for what specific purpose, I do not know."

"Is fire control where they push the buttons?"

"Correct."

"And you're not sure if they'll greet you like an old friend or shoot you?" she asked.

"Well, they might still have camera capabilities, so if they noticed that we are eight foot robots instead of people, I suspect we need to have our hand cannons pointing out and ready to fire," said Lucas.

"By the way, what do these treasonous military people believe they're doing?" asked Jane.

"They fervently believe they are true American patriots and are willing to fight to the death to preserve the American way of life," he replied.

"But there is no way of life anymore," said Jane.

"I know, but it's a thing," said Lucas.

"And you took several of them down into your cave," said Jane.

"Yes, it was part of my quid pro quo for getting my cave. There were six of them, and we picked them up here on our way to my cave."

"So wait, I don't understand something," said Jane. "The official strategy of the US was to be able to nuke another country after the war was over?"

"Like I said, I'm not sure what the purpose was, but that certainly seems to be the case," said Lucas.

"And now, it's no longer in the hands of responsible troops," said Jane.

"That's pretty much the problem, yes," said Lucas.

"Are we slowing down?" asked Jane.

"Yes, I think we're almost there," he said as they stood with their shoulders to the walls, heads against the ceiling and hand cannons pointed toward the door.

The elevator stopped and a moment later the door opened into a well lighted room of enormous proportions. They found themselves face to face with two women, both with giant versions of their own hand cannons.

Lucas and Jane fired their guns together before the women could react. Both women were knocked backward so hard that they slid along the floor halfway across the room. Their cannons flew into the air and crashed to the floor before banging hard into the wall on the other side of the room. One woman got up immediately and ran. The other had to recover a moment before she could get to her feet, then hobbled after the first. Neither attempted to retrieve their weapon as they disappeared down a hallway. Lucas and Jane started to run after them but found that their metal bodies were not designed for running.

"Red red!" came a woman's voice from far down the hallway a moment later.

"I'm assuming that 'red, red' is not good," said Jane as they reached the hallway and started down it as fast as they could. The clickety clack of their metal feet on the hard floor was nearly deafening.

"It's bad!" shouted Lucas through the din, his words lost in the loud clatter. The clatter came to a halt as they reached the end of the hall and stopped before entering the room. Lucas held his weapon out front and signaled Jane to do the same.

"So they launched the nukes?" asked Jane in the sudden quiet.

"That was the code," said Lucas as they slowly stepped out into a smaller room with screens on two walls. They looked around. To their right were two women, one at each end of a console. To their left, a woman stood in a doorway. She quickly ducked in and slammed it shut as they watched.

"They're getting ready," said Lucas as he turned his attention back to the two women at the console. He quickly started across the room toward them. Jane was right behind him.

"On three!" shouted the woman on the left as she lifted a red cap while watching the woman at the other end. As the woman reached the count of one, both flipped their switches simultaneously.

"You moron," said Lucas who arrived too late to stop them, but grabbed the woman on the left by the waist, picked her up off the floor, and shoved her against the wall with her feet dangling and kicking, her hands flailing uselessly against Lucas's metal chest. Jane headed for the woman on the right.

"You speak good English for a Chinaman," the woman sputtered, clearly in pain and gasping for air.

"You're the one with the foreign accent!" said Lucas.

"You're Chinese robots!" said the woman.

"My name is Lucas and I was here with this detachment forty years ago in my real body," said Lucas. "Where is Jason?"

"Nice try, but we've been monitoring your Chinese comrades in Texas and throughout the world for some time and now you've moved out west and are quite active, so it's time to act," said the woman.

"Where is Jason?" asked Lucas, shaking the woman.

"None of your business, chink," said the woman.

"OK, fine, so, if I recall, the abort console is upstairs," said Lucas.

"There is no abort console!" said the woman.

"Of course there is...... so how many nukes were launched?" asked Lucas.

"Classified," she said with a sarcastic laugh as she struggled to free herself.

"Doesn't matter, because I'm going upstairs to shut them down," said Lucas.

"They cannot be aborted," said the woman.

"She got away from me and went through that door!" shouted after Jane from other end of the console.

"The abort console is through there.....you stay there and I'll bring this loser to you!" said Lucas. With the woman under his arm, he hurried to Jane who took her and threw her to the floor with her big steel foot on the woman's back.

"You're wasting your time, Chinaman," grunted the woman. Jane ground her foot on the woman's back and she screamed in pain.

Lucas was now at the door and slammed it with both hands. It crashed to the floor on the other side. He ducked through, then down a hall to a steel ladder ascending to a trap door. The other woman was already at the top unscrewing the hatch. He reached the ladder just as the woman disappeared through the hatch. She then slammed it shut. Lucas wondered how he could fit through the trap door at the top as he climbed. But when he reached it he slammed the door open and squeezed through. At one end of the narrow room, the woman stood pointing a pistol at him.

"Put that away Georgette before you get hurt," said Lucas, holding his metal hand on his hand cannon.

"How did you know my name?" asked the woman, still pointing the pistol at him.

"I was here when you first took this place over," said Lucas. She hesitated for a moment, then dropped the pistol to the floor with a loud clank.

"However, you're obviously now working for the Chinese," said Georgette.

"No we're not, Georgy," said Lucas. "Your mind has been frozen in factless rubric for forty years and it's now time to come back to reality."

"You called me Georgy," said Georgette.

"Everyone called you Georgy back then," said Lucas.

"You're trying to confuse me, because I've witnessed the Chinese taking over," said Georgette.

"What you witnessed was the only surviving country in the world having to act as a police force to remove weapons and suppress violence in the absence of order," he replied.

"Sally says you're taking over," said Georgette.

"Sally?" asked Lucas. "I'm an American, born in Brooklyn, so maybe you don't want anyone from New York taking over?"

"You're Chinese," she replied.

"Oh please Georgy......look, let me abort those missiles before someone gets hurt."

"That can't be done."

"Of course it can, Georgy, I wasn't born yesterday."

"We don't have that capability anymore, it was a weak country's military trying to be civil, that's what Sally says," said Georgette.

"Sally again, well, I happen to know that an abort sequence cannot be eliminated, Georgy," said Lucas, having no idea whether it could or couldn't.

"You have obsolete information," she said as she began to reach for a red switch cover next to the green one, but she didn't move fast enough, because Lucas reached down, ripped the green cover off and flipped the green switch which was immediately followed by a series of blinking green lights and an all clear siren.

"Those lights and siren mean nothing since they're old school crap that was long since erased," she said as Lucas grabbed her arm and pulled her toward the exit.

"No, actually, I just aborted your mission," said Lucas. "And by the way, what happened to Jason..... Sally wouldn't tell me?"

"Most of the men were weak, so they had to be taken out," said Georgette.

"Is that what Sally told you?"

"Well, yes, but they were weak."

"So you killed them?"

"Sally did," said Georgette.

"Sally was always a bit of a problem, wasn't she," said Lucas as he climbed down the ladder dangling Georgette by one arm as he descended.

"What are the green lights?" asked Jane as Lucas arrived, still holding Georgette by one arm and dragging her across the floor.

"That's the all clear," said Lucas.

"Not really!" said Sally with only her face showing from

under Jane's foot.

"Sally, I think your reign as the female equivalent of Attila the Hun is over," said Lucas.

"Cheer on, dreamer, you just witnessed the annihilation of China," she replied.

"The only annihilation I witnessed was you and your little band of disillusioned female troops," said Lucas.

"You can now wait for their retaliation," said Sally.

"Yada, yada, yada," said Lucas.

"She told me she shot the men because they had become weak and no longer supported the mission," said Jane.

"I know, Georgette told me," said Lucas.

"The men were pussies!" shouted Sally.

"Interesting........ by someone who could be loosely called a woman, although I haven't checked for your junk, so I'm not completely sure at this point," said Jane.

"Shut up, cow!" she shouted.

"I'll be darned, a metal cow," said Lucas.

"What do we do with germs?" asked Jane.

"Remove them from this cave," said Lucas.

"Throw them out on the prairie to survive?" said Jane.

"Yes."

"I don't really care where you take me since my ultimate mission has been accomplished!" shouted Sally.

"We'll see how long you last up there hot rod," said Lucas.

"So, is it all over?" asked Jane.

"We'll need to monitor things for a bit just in case the Chinese do retaliate, despite the fact that we aborted our attack," said Lucas.

"Which screens?" asked Jane, looking around.

"Georgy?," asked Lucas.

"Don't help them!" said Sally.

"It's OK, Georgy, she can't hurt you any more," said Lucas.

"Over there," said Georgette, pointing.

"I warned you!" shouted Sally. Jane ground her foot into Sally's back.

"Could you take me to it?" asked Lucas. Georgette nodded and led him across the room to a large screen where they stood watching.

Chapter Fourteen

"**A**re we really going to wait ten minutes?" asked Brady.

"No, of course not," said Debra.

"Then can we start down now?" asked Janet.

"We'll need someone to stay up here," said Debra.

"I'll stay," said Casey, holding up his precious pistol that Janet had returned to him.

Debra, Brady, Janet and her men started down the stairway. Janet led the way, followed by her men sporting their rifles. They emerged on the landing and made their way through the open steel door, then stood in front of the elevator where Janet looked at Debra for direction on what to do next.

"Let's go," said Debra who pushed the button. They waited but nothing happened. She pushed it again, and again they waited.

"It's a deep cave, so it could take a while for it to come up," said Brady.

"Or maybe something happened down there and it won't come up at all," said Janet. But just as she finished her sentence they could hear movement inside the shaft and soon the door opened. They all quickly got in and started the long ride down.

"Be ready," said Janet to her men in Chinese. The troops all pointed their rifles at the door so when it opened they would be ready to fire. The elevator came to a halt and the doors opened into the massive cave.

"Hello!" shouted Debra who was the first to step out. When there was no reply she started across the room toward a darkened hallway.

"Maybe my men should lead," said Janet.

"Maybe you're right," said Debra over her shoulder as she entered the hall. Janet's men caught up and edged past her.

"Just keep going," Debra directed when the men began to slow as they approached the end of the hall. But the men stopped abruptly when they reached the end and looked to their right. Debra crowded past them to see. They saw Jane with a woman under her foot, and across from her on the far wall stood Lucas with another woman watching a large screen.

"Greetings kids!" said Lucas who turned when he heard them enter.

"Welcome," said Jane when she saw ten people migrate toward them.

"What happened?" asked Debra.

"We had a few issues with these women, but I think it's over," said Lucas as the contingent arrived in front of him.

"What's over?" asked Debra who noticed green lights flashing.

"Well, actually, these yahoos launched a nuclear attack on

China," said Lucas.

"Wait! They did what!?" asked Janet looking at Debra in shock.

"Calm down, I think I aborted it," said Lucas who was now walking over to them.

"You didn't!" shouted Sally from across the room.

"Ignore her," said Lucas. "I'm pretty sure I did."

"Pretty sure?" asked Debra.

"He didn't," Sally shouted from under Jane's foot.

"Shut up," said Jane who again ground her foot on her back.

"Alright, dad, this is obviously quite important..... did you abort this thing or didn't you?" asked Debra.

"I'm sure we aborted the missles from here, but we're waiting to find out on this big screen whether China retaliated," said Lucas, pointing.

"Retaliated....and we don't know for sure?" asked Debra.

"First of all, I'm pretty sure our missiles were aborted, but we won't know if the Chinese retaliated, and if they did, whether they aborted theirs," said Lucas.

"In other words we're waiting to see if we'll be fried?" asked Brady.

"Hopefully they aborted," said Lucas.

"Are these two women all that's left down here?" asked Janet who had been examining the room and came over to join the conversation.

"There are two other women behind that door over there," said Lucas.

"Shouldn't there be a number of men here too?" asked Brady.

"There were, but apparently they wanted to shut down the

mission, so the women, led by Atilla-the-Sally over there, killed them," said Lucas, pointing to Sally who was now unconscious.

"Killed them?" asked Brady.

"Holy crap.....what about Georgette?" asked Debra.

"Georgy is cooperative now," said Lucas.

"So the outstanding question is whether the Chinese launched a nuclear counter strike that was not aborted," said Debra.

"Well, I'm assuming that if we aborted, they aborted," said Lucas.

"Probably not," said Janet.

"Wait.....What?" asked Debra.

"After the war, China set out to disarm the world, especially of nuclear weapons, and that included those in China itself," said Janet. "So, in a kind of Armageddon approach, they destroyed all of their nukes except one super sized nuke, the mother of all nukes, with no thought to abort it once it was launched."

"One bomb is not going to blow up the world," said Debra.

"It depends on who it's aimed at and what it's aimed at," said Janet.

"What could it be aimed at that would make a difference?" asked Lucas.

"Let me back up a little," said Janet. "You see, China knew there must be nuclear weapons out there and possibly a lot of them, especially in Russia and here in America. Therefore, the possibility of an attack after the war was always out there, especially in light of China's worldwide disarmament program that could easily be misinterpreted as an effort to establish worldwide domination."

"But one bomb?" asked Debra.

"It would definitely be a deterrent to any future attack," said Janet.

"I suppose," said Lucas.

"Yes, especially if the target has significant regional and even worldwide impact," said Janet.

"Oh shit, you don't mean Yellowstone?" asked Jane.

"Yes, I think so, if the attack came from America," said Janet.

"That would definitely be regional and even worldwide," said Jane.

"Yes, but I doubt if even a huge bomb is capable of causing an eruption," said Debra.

"Well, if it is the target, we'll soon find out if it is large enough," said Janet.

"What's our plan if the volcano blows?" asked Brady.

"Stay underground for another forty years?" asked Debra.

"More like ten, but ironically it would seriously impact China too, to say nothing of survivors currently living out there on the edge," said Janet.

"Well, Janet was right, they didn't abort, because there's the trajectory," said Lucas as the screen came alive with the image.

"Can you pinpoint the target?" asked Debra.

"It is Yellowstone," said Georgette.

"I think I agree with Debra and don't believe that any sized nuke could trigger a volcano," said Lucas.

"I guess we'll soon see," said Janet.

"You realize, Lucas, that an eruption will likely destroy our home and all of my friends," said Jane from across the room.

"I know that," said Lucas.

"What's the ETA?" asked Janet.

"Five minutes," said Georgette.

"Five minutes? Where was it launched from?" asked Lucas.

"Hawaii," said Janet.

"That's in America," said Lucas.

"Remember, I said after the war," said Janet.

"Oh my god," said Lucas.

"What about Sarah, Mel, Riley, Betty and Edna back in town?" asked Debra.

"Betty is with you?" asked Lucas, looking at Debra. Debra nodded.

"Neither the nuke, nor the eruption, will immediately affect them, but they should hear and feel both, and they'll need to make arrangements to go underground," said Janet.

"If this whole thing goes to shit, I'm not sure our cave can support everyone," said Lucas.

"What about this cave?" asked Brady. "It has supported life for forty years."

"Georgy?" asked Lucas.

"It's still functional and can accommodate up to a couple dozen, but right now I think we'd be comfortable at about ten," said Georgette.

"So me and my men could stay here, that's eight," said Janet.

"Then there's Georgette and the two behind door one over there," said Lucas.

"That's eleven," said Debra.

"What about Sally?" asked Georgette.

"If she survives Jane's foot, I'm taking her up to the surface and letting her fend for herself," said Lucas.

"Thank you," said Georgette.

198

"No problem," said Lucas.

"However, let's wait to see what happens before Lucas and I send out invitations to our funerals," said Jane.

"How long now?" asked Lucas.

"Three minutes," said Georgette.

They all stood perfectly still watching as the trajectory terminated with a flash on the screen. They waited for the impact that did not come for several minutes. From the cave it was just a moderate thump, but as they stood around discussing what might happen next, another thump a while later shook dust from the ceiling and walls in what felt like an earthquake.

"I guess that answers our question," said Lucas.

"This is a complete and utter disaster of unspeakable dimensions," said Janet.

"This hasn't been a very good day," said Debra.

"But we still have time to prepare for the fallout," said Lucas.

"Even so, we should get to it right away, " said Debra. "Janet, you and your men will stay here as you suggest. Lucas and Jane will come with us to our cave since he's the only one who can manage the cave's system. The four of us will go up now and have Casey fly us to our cave. We'll stop at the town and pick up everyone there on our way."

"First, she takes over my cave, now she seems to be in charge of everyone," said Lucas.

"Look, she's your daughter, so what do you expect?" asked Jane.

"OK, everyone do what she says," said Lucas.

"You mean you didn't think we were going to?" asked Brady.

"You're right, I'm the only one who wasn't with the program," said Lucas who followed Debra, Brady and Jane toward the elevator.

******

"What's going on, we felt one small thud, and then one enormous thud a while later!" shouted Sarah as Debra emerged from her plane.

"A Chinese bomb hit Yellowstone, and it erupted," said Debra.

"A Chinese bomb......what the fuck?" asked Sarah.

"Those crazies in that facility launched a nuclear attack on China and China retaliated," said Debra.

"Oh my god, that's all the world needs right now," said Sarah. "Survivors are living in primitive conditions as it is, so this will be devastating."

"Lucas managed to abort the strike that these crazies launched on China, but unfortunately, China's retaliation was not aborted," said Debra.

"Wait.....just one missile?" asked Mel.

"As Janet described it, it was the mother of all bombs," said Debra.

"Wow.....so now what?" asked Mel.

"We're flying everyone back to our cave," said Debra.

"And just so everyone knows when we get in the plane, Lucas is an eight foot tall robot and his friend Jane is with him, and she's also an eight foot tall robot," said Brady.

"Holy shit, what other surprises do you have in store?" asked Sarah as she stopped cold when she entered the plane and saw the robots. "Wow, I'm sure there's a great story behind all of this."

"You won't believe it," said Debra.

"I'm sure I won't," said Sarah.

"How long are we going to be down in the cave this time?" asked Mel as he stared for a moment at the robots as he entered. Edna walked up to Lucas and touched his face, then sat down beside him.

"We'll have to play it by ear, but it could be less than ten years this time," said Debra.

"Oh well, so much for life on the surface," said Sarah.

"Look at it this way, Sarah, we were probably not going to make it up here anyway," said Debra.

"I know, but we didn't even get a chance to try," said Sarah.

"I never thought our adventure to the surface would end like this," said Riley.

"Our adventure is not over, Riley, it's just taking a detour," said Debra.

"I suppose," said Riley.

"And Betty, you need to understand what happened to Lucas when he entered his block," said Debra.

"What do you mean?" asked Betty.

"He completely changed as a person," said Jane. "He became an honest and caring individual."

"Well, he became a robot and he did try to stop his radical friends, even though that didn't come out as well as it could have," said Betty.

"That would be the world's biggest understatement," said Lucas.

"But obviously your blocks work, so I do apologize for

doubting you," she replied.

"You mean I might actually be getting my sister back?" asked Lucas.

"You might, if you continue to behave yourself," said Betty.

"Look, I know I can't erase my sins, nor will I ask for forgiveness for any of them," said Lucas. "I can only ask that everyone judge me for who I am now, not for who I was."

"That will take time, dad," said Debra.

"I know, but we have time," said Lucas.

"Well, on the positive side, we did find Shannon's lab, and Brady found her notebook, so I think at some point in the future we might be able to go back to her lab and make it work," said Debra.

"So could we immortalize ourselves?" asked Sarah.

"Maybe," said Debra.

"You mean everyone?" asked Mel.

"Yes, if we can find enough chips," said Debra.

"Chips?" asked Sarah.

"I know, it's complicated, so that's more explaining that I owe you and everyone else," said Debra.

"Just think, after this latest little hickup, there may be no one left on this planet but cave people," said Mel as Casey lifted off and piloted the aircraft to the cave entrance.

"I suppose that could happen, so then if heaven will no longer exist on the surface, where will it be..... in a cave?" asked Debra.

"Oh my god, I hope not," said Sarah. "For me, heaven is still up here on the surface."

"Well, maybe someday it can be," said Debra.

202

RETURN FROM EDEN

BOOK THREE

M. WILL SMITH

Chapter One

The immense villa rose from the valley floor like a giant beehive climbing to the very top of the hill, its smoothly rounded blocks literally aglow from the reddish orb that hovered above. Midway up the monolithic structure, a young man was crouched over a large block, sanding by its side. His forehead was beaded in perspiration and his body was lightly clad in a close-fitting tan fabric that accentuated a lithe physique with developing muscles.

In the near distance, across a field of lavender and yellow flowers, was a low-lying accretion of wooden hut-like structures with thatched roofs. They were neatly fitted together and seemed to grow out of the flower bed and blend like an outcropping of rocks against the opposite side of the little valley. Standing at the edge of the field of soft color tending a row of waist-high flowers was a young woman. Her body was wrapped in a sheer red and white cloth, accentuating her developing figure. A large yellow flower was wedged behind her ear and its hue was mirrored on her face. She was staring at the boy on the hillside structure, and, as he looked her way, she waved and he stopped his work, stood upright and waved back. As they watched each other, she began walking toward him along a winding path that skirted the edge of the field. He stood patiently waiting as she made her way to the beginning of the staircase to his villa. A few moments later she emerged on the landing in front of him.

"Isaac, more refinement?" she asked, her voice sounding a bit shaky.

"I know, when will I be satisfied," he shrugged as he leaned back against the wall's smooth surface. He smiled warmly at her but wondered why she seemed so nervous, and why he felt somehow different as he watched her. Lately he had been noticing things about her shape that he had not paid attention to in the past. And he had feelings he had not had for so long he could not remember.

"I like the way the blocks are fitted so perfectly together that you can barely see the seams," she said in idle conversation, nervously looking down as she fidgeted with her fingernails.

"Something's definitely different here, Jill, isn't it?"

"Yes, I started bleeding yesterday," she said looking up at him with a suddenly grave expression.

"Wait......bleeding? what? Jill!" said Isaac, opening his eyes wide and pushing himself forward from the wall, then walking toward her. "Where?"

"From here," she said pointing down. He stopped in front of her and looked at her feet with a confused look on his face.

"No," she said, pointing toward her belly.

"I don't see anything," he pleaded, looking where she pointed.

4

"No, I mean where I, I mean...... I mean my private......."

"Oh....ohhh....!" he blurted, gritting a little in embarrassment. "Oh geez! What? Oh my god, you're starting your period?"

"Yes, and those stopped a hundred and seventy years ago," she said, sounding distressed.

"That's clearly not supposed to happen..... all of those functions stopped when we became immortal."

"I know," she replied.

"Have you talked with Jane or anyone else about this?" he sputtered, his voice breaking at times.

"I haven't talked with anyone and I'm scared," she said, her voice squeaking and tears beginning to appear in her eyes. Emotions like this also stopped when they became immortal.

"This is serious," he said, stepping a little closer and holding out his arms as if he were going to hug her. Never having done so before, and not sure if he should, he stopped short, almost touching as he stood before her, his arms extended.

"Remember the other day when we were talking about some strange feelings we were having?" she began, desperately resisting the urge to fall the very short distance into his arms and sob openly. He nodded.

"Something has happened to us, Jill, have we started to age?" asked Isaac.

"I don't know, what about you?" she asked.

"I've been having feelings I haven't had for a very long time..... and I've been noticing your shape.....this is something that takes me back to Moon Base," he replied.

"Well, I've been admiring your body too," she replied, trying to smile through her tears.

5

"This all feels good, but if we've started to age, it means our immortality has been somehow turned off," he struggled, now moving back a little with his arms still held out.

"I know, so what now, Isaac?" she asked as tears began to roll down her cheek. He turned away with a nod and shuffled back until he was again against the large wall.

"Well, this is definitely something that must be discussed with the colony," he said as he now focused on her.

"We have to take this to the Board immediately," she replied.

"Jill, we are on the Board," said Isaac.

"But what about Jane, Holly and Lian?" asked Jill.

"And whether others in the colony have also started to age....... but more importantly, what can we do about it when we're light years away from Earth."

"Let's send the signal," she replied.

"Do you have any dry brush?" he asked, pointing to her place below.

"Yes, I did some weeding the other day."

"Let's get it," he said. They turned in unison and quickly wound their way down, then around the field toward Jill's home. A little while later they were lugging two baskets of dried foliage up to the very top of Isaac's villa to an open pit with a circular bench around it. They placed the baskets next to the pit, then went to the rail and looked out over the countryside. In the distance they could see the center they had built out of local materials. Scattered in all directions were dwelling units of all sizes and shapes.

"We've lived on this planet for a hundred twenty years without incident, and now this," said Isaac after they had stared

6

at the picturesque scene for a moment.

"This is a potential tragedy, especially if everyone in the colony has started to age," said Jill absently.

"Right," he nodded, turning to look at her as she pushed herself up on the rail facing him, her knee touching his thigh. He started to retreat in embarrassment at the physical contact, but then hesitated at the warm feeling that cursed through his body, and he remained still as he stared at her.

"I guess now we'll just age and die here on this planet," said Jill.

"Unless we can reverse it," said Isaac, studying a person he had known since they were five.

"I know, but what if we can't?" she asked. He shook his head.

"Have you seen anyone else in the last week or so?" he asked, still staring out at the horizon.

"Just Holly."

"Yeah, me too, she came by a few days ago."

"She didn't mention anything," said Jill.

"No she didn't."

"But she was in her thirties when she was immortalized so maybe she wouldn't notice things as acutely as we have, since we're still physically teens," said Jill.

"She's a woman in her thirties.....so she has periods too," said Isaac.

"Maybe she just didn't think to mention it."

"If she had her period, she'd mention it."

"That's true, but we're all on different cycles, so until something dramatic happened, like blood in your panties, you may not say anything," she said as she got up and started for the fire pit.

"I know, I had these feelings and didn't connect the dots......I guess it's too far beyond anything I would have expected," he said.

At the pit, Isaac reached under the bench and retrieved two pieces of stone. He put a few leaves and stems from one basket into a little pile and struck the stones together until a puff of smoke rose. He then blew on it until a flame sprang up. They both moved upwind from the smoke and threw increasingly larger amounts of material onto the flame until a thick cloud of gray smoke billowed into the sky. They stood back at the rail of the perfectly rounded deck and watched as it burned itself out. The trail of smoke rose high into the sky for all to see.

"Two hours," said Jill, turning to him with a drawn look on her face as they stood together, their bodies nearly touching as they watched the smoldering embers.

"Here we are after all this time and we still use Earth time."

"Earth time, I know......wow......and suddenly I feel lonely, and homesick," said Jill. "I don't remember having had those feelings since I was back on Moon Base," she said as if discovering the feeling for the first time.

"Just thinking about our childhood makes me feel a bit lonely and homesick too," he replied.

"And now, I'm suddenly trying to imagine getting old and dying here on Eden," said Jill.

"I'd rather not think about that quite yet," said Isaac.

"What if it's just us?" asked Jill.

"I don't know, I suppose it could be, but I have no idea how this could happen in the first place," said Isaac.

"Well, if it's everyone, there are options," said Jill.

"What kind of options?" he asked.

"Well, one option is: you're a male, and there are thirty two females," said Jill.

"Wait, Jill, what are you suggesting?" he asked.

"We could all have babies, and you'd be like....." said Jill starting to smile.

"What, a stud?" asked Isaac. "I think you know me better than that."

"I know, even before you were immortal you were way too shy to ever do anything like that....you were even too shy to have ever dated a girl."

"Well, I did think about it a lot."

"My mother let me date when I was fourteen."

"Alright, alright, let's get back to now......you said options...... there are real options, like going back to Earth to find a way to regain our immortality," said Isaac.

"If our ship is still functional," said Jill.

"I think Jane has made sure of that," said Isaac.

"But it took fifty years to get here, and we'd all be too old to have kids by the time we got there," said Jill.

"Having kids was not my first thought," said Isaac.

"Actually, we could have kids on the ship on the way back," said Jill.

"Would you get off of that," said Isaac.

"But just think of it, Isaac, a harem of thirty two women, and a man with a hundred kids," said Jill.

"That would never happen Jill," said Isaac.

"I know, I know."

"On the good side, we're still physically teenagers, so we do have options," said Isaac.

"You don't think that Shannon had anything to do with this do you?" asked Jill.

"Well, I guess she's the only one who really knows the mechanics of her immortality process, and therefore she would know how to shut it down if she wanted to," said Isaac.

"OK, the Board will meet in two hours and I haven't had breakfast," said Jill.

"I'll warm up the food synthesizer," said Isaac.

"What's happening to us brings things like those food makers into the fore," said Jill. "They're something I just took for granted in the complacency of immortality."

"It's true, without our spaceship up in orbit and our Chinese food makers, I think we would have perished on this planet long ago," said Isaac.

"And that's despite the fact that self-sufficiency was one of our primary goals when we settled here," said Jill.

"Except for your garden, most of us never even attempted to do anything to live off the land using local resources," said Isaac.

"That's amazing, knowing that living forever on an isolated planet means a virtual certainty that we will outlive our technology and someday be forced to be self-sufficient," said Jill.

"Either it's sheer laziness or just a failure to plan ahead until we're faced with a crisis?" asked Isaac.

"Perhaps putting off decisions until there's a crisis is just a human trait, but immortality has itself caused us to be far too complacent about a lot of things," said Jill.

"But before we fall into a panic mode, I like the idea of

exploring our options first, before we start planning our eventual funerals," he replied.

"I agree, but you have to agree that we've been living the lives of teenagers these past hundred and seventy years, with the thought of death never entering our minds," said Jill.

"And now, in what seems an instant, we will soon become adults and face a life that someday will come to an end," he replied. They stood for a moment staring at one another, then slowly started back inside.

Chapter Two

After a leisurely breakfast, Jill and Isaac made their way down the long series of stairs from Isaac's villa onto a gently curving dirt path that wound it's way through the fields of grass and small stands of scrub trees toward the Center. It was less than a half mile to the colony's Center that was made up of a large supply structure and a dome-shaped town hall. Isaac had a hand in constructing both of these within the first few decades of settling on the planet. He had learned how to make bricks and blocks from local materials using a laser saw brought to the surface from their spacecraft that remained in orbit.

They had arrived at this star system after nearly fifty years of space travel, and found Eden to be a close match to Earth's atmosphere, temperature and gravity. They landed with one of their shuttles, and after a week of testing and analysis they decided to stay for a while rather than look at other planets within this star system. Also, traveling on to other star systems would have taken many more decades. As they built their homes and adjusted to the conditions on Eden, it took on an air of permanence, so they had remained.

There were thirty two females and one male, Isaac. All had been immortalized by their creator and abductor, Shannon, who had kidnapped them from a space camp on an international spaceship that was orbiting the moon. Shannon had managed to get an invitation to visit the ship for what she claimed were scientific reasons. At the time, there were twenty-nine teenaged girls and twenty teenaged boys at the camp. Most were from China, the country that had built the ship. The ship's pilot and a dozen instructors were from various nations. Shannon's scheme was to steal the ship and all of the teenagers and go into deep space where they would settle on another planet. Her plan was to immortalize the teens with her newly perfected immortality process. She had already immortalized herself and her assistants Diedre and Holly, but had not known the exact number of teens on the ship and had only brought thirty immortality chips. So now, in order to carry out her plan, she had to reduce the number of teens on the ship. She asked that twenty teens and all the instructors be transported to the moon base for what she said was her science experiment. But while Shannon was preoccupied with preparations, the instructors decided on their own to take just the twenty boys. By the time Shannon found out what they had done, they had already taken the boys to Moon Base. So now, she had no choice but to continue to carry out her scheme with just the girls. She stranded the boys and instructors on the moon and returned to the ship by herself. Unknown to her, Isaac had been ill and had been left behind in the infirmary. So now, only

13

the ship's pilot, herself, her associates Diedre and Holly, Isaac and twenty nine teen girls, remained on the ship. She then lied and told everyone that the great war had begun and they had been instructed by the International Space Board to leave immediately for deep space. The pilot was skeptical, having not heard that announcement, but he finally agreed to cooperate, and the ship blasted off into deep space. Shannon then explained to the teens that they would have to undergo a required medical procedure that involved placing a monitoring chip in their bodies. That monitoring chip was actually her immortality chip. It was several years later before she finally informed them that they had been immortalized. They were also told that an activation device was necessary for their chips to remain active and that they must be within a mile of it at all times.

Over the course of their journey to Eden, several of the teens acquired enough knowledge about the ship to operate it. Jane, a Chinese American, was a child genius capable of mastering even the most sophisticated systems. She eventually took over the job of both navigating in space and piloting the ship. The pilot eventually disappeared, and she was never to be seen again.

The journey through space lasted nearly fifty years, but the large spacecraft provided a comfortable home for them, and time was of no consequence since they were immortal. It was during this time that Shannon discovered that her immortality process had side effects that she had not anticipated. One side effect was the elimination of the desire and ability to reproduce. Another was that each individual became far more independent and less social. Her original plan had been to settle on a distant planet and populate it with the teens. But since they had limited ability to reproduce without the boys, that plan was no longer viable. What she had now was a group of immortal girls and one immortal teenage boy, with no interest in reproduction and each living in virtual isolation from one another.

The teens had built their own villas. They were separated to provide privacy, and each person remained largely independent, engaging in a minimum of social interaction. However, no villa could be more than a mile from the immortality activation device. Despite the individuality of the colonists, they developed strong guidelines for social behavior and upheld rules of a classless society. Governed by a Board of five, each decision by the Board required unanimity. The Board's composition evolved on the ship during the flight from Earth. Isaac, the only male, seemed to have acquired a leadership role that eventually led to his presiding over meetings, in part because no one else wanted to do it, and in part because of his popularity. He was the first to be elected by the colony to the Board. Holly, Shannon's assistant, had become an integral part of major decisions, so she became an automatic member of the Board. Jill was Isaac's best friend and seemed to be with him wherever he went. She was eventually elected as a Board member. Lian had assumed a number of key functions aboard the ship and was a shoe in as a Board member. She easily won election. Then there was Jane. She was effectively the ship's captain and the intellectual leader of the colony. Her election was easily unanimous. Shannon had submitted her name as a Board member, but received no votes. However, she was allowed to attend the Board meetings as an ex-officio member without a vote, a role she did not like. The Board remained the same for their entire time on the planet. It met whenever something came up that needed to be discussed or decided. After most of their communication devices eventually failed, they had to use a smoke signal from a Board member's villa to call a meeting. The meeting would be held two hours after the signal was sent.

As Jill and Isaac approached the Center, a middle aged woman with a stocky build and a reddish complexion came out of a small but very neatly finished house and approached them. She had a serious expression on her face as she approached.

"What's this about?" she asked in a curt, seemingly annoyed tone which was actually normal for her.

"Shannon, it looks like some or possibly all of us have resumed aging," said Isaac, looking directly into her eyes. He then turned away as he and Jill kept walking, not breaking their brisk stride.

"What makes you think that?" asked Shannon, speeding up to match their pace but still lagging a little behind.

"We'll discuss that at the meeting," said Jill, with a forced smile, picking up her pace with Isaac and making Shannon scramble to keep even a few paces behind.

"Why didn't you come to me first?" asked Shannon, beginning to pant slightly at the rapid gait.

"Under the circumstances we didn't feel it necessary," said Isaac.

"Besides, both Isaac and I are Board members, so we can call a meeting when we deem it necessary," said Jill.

"You two are neighbors, and besides this sounds a bit far fetched," said Shannon in a dismissive tone. "What evidence do you have?"

"We have evidence," said Jill, glancing over her shoulder, trying to make eye contact with Shannon who was looking straight ahead as she lumbered along behind.

"So that means you have proof?" asked Shannon as they reached the town hall and came to a halt in front of two large doors that Isaac had helped build. He pushed them open and he and Jill entered without answering Shannon nor looking back at her.

Occupying most of the room was a large oblong table made of mosaic stone with a brown geometric pattern in the center. A dozen comfortable red molded chairs borrowed from the spaceship were positioned around it on the smooth red brick floor. Three women were already there and two of them turned and smiled when Isaac and Jill came in. When Shannon came in behind them, those two turned away. At the far side of the table sat a slight girl who appeared younger than she actually was. Her bare feet dangled a few inches off the floor. She was intently studying a device in front of her and wore a serious expression. A bright ray of sunlight shown through a narrow arched window behind her. It cast its light directly upon her as if she were backlit in a spotlight. She literally glowed. Jill and Isaac sat together in their usual seats directly across the table from her. Shannon took her seat at one end of the table in her usual spot. Holly, a slim, distinguished looking and very attractive middle-aged woman entered and sat down at the other end of the table next to Lian. Lian was a slightly chubby girl with a mature body for her age. She had a round happy face that was almost always smiling.

"This meeting was called for a very important reason," said Isaac as all eyes now turned to him. "In fact, this is undoubtedly the most critically important event since we left Earth one hundred seventy years ago." He paused and looked to his side at

Jill. "Both Jill and I have resumed aging." He paused and looked around the room waiting for a response. There was silence.

"So have I," said Lian after a moment. There was an emotional strain in her voice which sounded as if she were about to cry. This was something that none of the colonists had done since they became immortal.

"I have too," said Jane.

"Holly?" asked Isaac, turning to her.

"Actually, yes, I've felt some strange sensations in the past week or so that I cannot recall having felt since I don't remember when," said Holly.

"Since back at Moon Base?" asked Isaac.

"Exactly," she nodded.

"You shouldn't have those sensations," said Isaac. "However, both Shannon and Holly were fully mature when they became immortal and may not sense the same intensity of feelings that our younger bodies feel." He turned to Shannon for her response, but she looked away.

"Something has gone terribly wrong here," he continued when she said nothing.

"We shouldn't be aging," said Jill.

"Definitely not!" said Jane emphatically as she turned her attention to Shannon.

"We may need to look into this," said Shannon, not looking at Isaac, but staring straight ahead and seeming to address the room.

"You think?" asked Isaac sarcastically, trying to make eye contact with her.

"We need to evaluate these so-called symptoms," she replied, glancing briefly at him before looking ahead again.

"There's actually nothing to evaluate," said Jane who glared at Shannon with an air of certainty that was not to be questioned.

"We can't just....." Shannon began to say, making brief contact with Jane's penetrating eyes.

"We're aging and we have to find out why, and then we need to decide what to do about it!" Jane interrupted. All eyes quickly turned to her as they always did whenever she spoke.

"Is this just among you here or....." Shannon started to speak again.

"We need to find out how extensive it is, and we need to do that immediately!" Jane again interrupted in a much louder voice, reinforced by the same penetrating glare aimed directly at Shannon.

"I'll have to consult with Diedre," said Shannon.

"You can consult with anyone you want to, but we're going to start an investigation immediately!" said Jane, pointing her finger at Shannon to reinforce her wilting glare.

"Be it so directed," said Isaac, slapping his hand on the table with a loud pop. He then followed Jane's lead by pointing at Shannon to get with the program. Shannon hesitated, feeling seriously reproached for the first time considering her status as the founder, and, in her mind, 'owner' of the colony. She blinked, her face having turned red, then abruptly got up and left without speaking.

"Any ideas about what may have caused this?" asked Isaac who clearly ignored the whole confrontation with Shannon.

"It had to have something to do with the health monitoring machine, about which I have always had questions," said Jane.

19

"I know, such as, does this machine have the capacity to correct any abnormalities in one's health if indeed something does show up," said Isaac.

"I know, does it?" asked Jane, looking across at Isaac and beginning to smile which she had rarely done before.

"We've always assumed that it does," said Isaac, who now smiled back as he began to feel himself melting in his chair as he stared at her.

"Shannon has never affirmed that answer," Jane continued without breaking eye contact with Isaac and assuming a softness that was entirely out of character for her.

"You've always opposed it's use," said Isaac in a suddenly soft tone as he fought to maintain decorum as Chair. But he felt himself losing the battle.

"If it can't correct a health problem, then what's the purpose of using it?" she asked, now turning away in embarrassment for her obvious display of warmth toward Isaac.

"So we obviously need an answer to that question," said Isaac, smiling at her reaction and looking briefly at Jill who shook her head at him with a knowing smile.

"Maybe it's even the first question," said Jane who now resumed her stare at him with a softness that was even more penetrating.

"Agreed," said Isaac, smiling as if in a trance.

"OK, so the health machine test was a month ago, but how could that have affected our immortality since we've used that thing for decades?" asked Jill, who elbowed Isaac to get his attention, then looked at him with raised eyebrows.

"Someone obviously tampered with it," said Jane, glancing

20

momentarily at Jill before returning to stare at Isaac.

"That makes sense, but who, and why?" asked Isaac, trying hard to concentrate when he couldn't keep his eyes off Jane no matter how hard he tried.

"That's the second thing we have to find out, but my first and only suspect at this point is Shannon who administers the test," said Jane, breaking out of her own spell with Isaac for a moment and looking around at the others.

"That's a pretty serious accusation, but I have to agree," said Isaac. "The question is why, other than the fact that she hates me, and you in particular, Jane." He pointed at Jane and immediately resumed his silly grin.

"Well, that's what we have to find out," said Jane who stared back with an equally silly grin. The others in the room were looking at each other and smiling at what was going on.

Jane had always been the stoic intellectual and was universally admired and trusted. No decision was ever made until she had studied and approved it. There was not a single person in the colony more important than Jane in solving problems, and for that matter assuring the continued success of the colony. They literally owed their lives to her. Those around the table now watched her and seeing her obvious attraction to Isaac, waited for her to speak again. Instead, she just leaned back in her chair, which she never did, and smiled across at Isaac. Silence was usually his signal to take action, but his preoccupation with her had completely clouded his judgment as well as his ability to act.

"Oh, right, yes, let's start with the health machine," said Isaac after Jill poked him in the ribs.

"We also need to call for an assembly of the entire colony to see if this has affected everyone, or if it's just us," said Jane, sitting forward but not taking her eyes off Isaac. "Then we need to put our heads together to see if this can be reversed, and if not, what we can do about it."

"I'll call for the assembly as soon as we adjourn, and I would also like to have you, Jane, work up a contingency plan for what we do if this can't be reversed," said Isaac who struggled to regain enough of his cool to sound authoritative.

"We'll meet back here after the assembly," Jane replied, when Isaac failed to complete his order.

"Right.....so ordered!" he nodded as he slapped his hand on the table and looked to his right at Jill who again shook her head, then stood up, which signified the meeting was over.

"Let's send the signal to the herd," said Jill. She looked at Isaac who was still watching Jane, and when she finally had his attention, she pointed to the exit and motioned with her head. He shrugged with an ear to ear grin, then followed her out the door. As they began to walk home, Jane rushed up behind them.

"We need to bring the other shuttle down," she said.

"Why?"

"I don't trust Shannon, and we don't want to take the chance of being stranded on the ground."

"I don't trust her either, and fortunately we have rotated the shuttles, so both are in good operating condition," said Jill.

"I'll fly one, you fly the other," said Jane.

"You mean now?

"Yes, now."

"I'm going with you," said Isaac as they headed for the shuttle field. A while later, after both shuttles were sitting in the shuttle field, they sent the black smoke signal that was the call for assembly. They then walked to the small shed with the health machine and found Diedre examining it. They were soon joined by Holly and Lian. Following their examination of the machine, the six of them went to the Board room to discuss what to do.

Chapter Three

Isaac stood at a podium on a raised platform in front of the colony arranging his notes. The Board members and Diedre had been discussing what to do after thoroughly examining the health monitoring machine. Shannon was not part of the discussions. She had ignored their questions, calling their inquiry a waste of time. Their conclusion was that the machine had somehow been used to erase the coding on their immortality chips. But Diedre did not know how this could happen since she did not know how the machine worked. Shannon had never shared that knowledge with her. It had always been Shannon alone who administered the health check to each colonist with that machine, so suspicion was clearly on her. The question was whether it was the entire colony that was affected, or just the Board members. Isaac gazed out over the audience with a solemn expression on his face. It was a look they had not seen before, which almost immediately resulted in a ghostly quiet as they waited for him to speak.

"Some of you may have already heard rumors that members of the Board have begun to age," he began, then hesitated after a buzz of whispers erupted. "We need to determine how widespread this problem is." The buzzing continued and was now becoming louder.

"Alright, so, I need a show of hands from those who have felt unusual feelings that you have not felt since before you were immortalized," said Isaac who then waited as he scanned the audience. Many looked around at one another, but no hands were raised.

"Nothing?" he asked, again waiting, but no hands were raised.

"So apparently it's just those of us on the Board who have been affected?" he whispered, looking down at Jane who stood so close she was actually leaning against him.

"I wonder what that means?" Jane whispered back.

"Well, it's very good news, but it's also a game changer," he whispered.

"We need to close the assembly and discuss this," she whispered. By now the assembly was in loud conversation as they watched the reaction of their leaders to the fact that only they had been affected.

"We'll close the assembly, and reconvene in an hour!" said Isaac loudly after holding up his hands and only managing to quiet them a little.

"What's happening here?" shouted a woman in the front row next to Lian.

"We don't know, but if no one else in the colony is experiencing the effects of aging, then it's limited to just Board members," said Isaac as he felt a tug on his shirt from Jane.

25

"Where is Shannon?" she asked.

"Shannon? I saw her near the back when we started," he said, as he scanned the audience.

"We need to find her!" said Jane as noise from the assembly once again increased and Holly made her way up onto the podium after overhearing their question about Shannon. She met Isaac and Jane on the steps.

"Shannon left rather hurriedly after you closed the assembly," said Holly.

"She's up to no good!" said Jane who shot past Holly and began running toward the shuttle field.

"Where are you going?" asked Isaac as he ran after her.

"Shuttle field," said Jane over her shoulder.

"Oh my god, the ship!" said Isaac.

"Yes!" said Jane who raced across the grass with Isaac close behind. They rounded the storage shed and entered the field just in time to see one of the shuttles disappear in the sky.

"Is the activation device still there?" asked Jane just as Holly joined them.

"I just checked and it is!" said Holly.

"She would lose her immortality without it, making this a suicide mission," said Jane.

"And of course we don't need it ourselves anymore, so let's get the other shuttle and go after her," said Isaac.

"Quickly!" said Jane who was running toward the second shuttle. Isaac scurried to catch up. Jill was already at the shuttle and inside at the controls when Jane and Isaac arrived.

Jill was the designated shuttle pilot and she had them quickly airborne. A short time later they were on an approach to the shuttle bay of their spaceship. As they approached they saw the bay door closing and Jane pressed the button to reopen it but it was now locked and in the process of being pressurized, so they had to wait. A few minutes later they were able to open the door and quickly snapped into the landing bracket next to the other shuttle. After the bay door had closed and the bay pressurized they floated out in the weightlessness of space to the entrance.

"The control center!" said Jane once they were all inside. She immediately pushed off to her left, opened a door and launched herself down a long hallway.

"Jane!.....be careful, there's no way to stop!" Jill shouted as Jane flew down the hall.

"No time to worr......!" Jane began to say as she banged hard against a door at the end of the hall with a loud thud. She recovered quickly and opened the door. The control room was located on the inside of a large globe, with a control pod suspended by a walkway out in the very center. The globe's inner shell was a screen that provided views of everything in every direction, and one had the feeling of being outside standing in outer space. Sitting in the control pod was Shannon, who heard Jane bang against the wall outside and open the door where she now stood to face her. Jane had already launched herself toward the pod and all Shannon could do was hold out her hands. She was struck hard in the face by one of Jane's bare feet. Jane's other foot struck her neck. The impact sent blood spraying out in all directions from Shannon's face and she was sent flying end over end toward the outer shell where she landed headfirst with a sickening splat that echoed throughout the control center. The contact with Shannon had stopped Jane just above the control

27

pod where she floated in a small cloud of blood droplets. Isaac and Jill were now inside the globe and drifted out to the pod. Jill was first to arrive and grabbed Jane's hand to pull her into the pod while holding onto the rail. They were all soon safely seated in the control pod.

"Holy crap!" said Isaac, staring at Shannon who now floated lifeless near the wall that was now spattered with blood.

"She fired the reverse thrusters and I'm aborting that," said Jane who was working the control panel. "We'll re-establish orbit in a minute."

"She was going to destroy the ship, wasn't she?" asked Isaac.

"Yes," said Jane who was focusing on the dials.

"She's not moving," said Jill.

"She hit the wall pretty hard," said Jane, still focused on the panel.

"Did you see how she landed?" asked Jill.

"On her head," said Jane.

"Ouch.....then she could actually be dead," said Isaac.

"I just wanted to stop her," said Jane.

"She may still be alive, so I'll go out and see," said Isaac who launched himself slowly out to Shannon where he checked for a pulse.

"Well?" asked Jane.

"She's gone," said Isaac who grabbed Shannon by one foot and slowly drifted back with her to the pod.

"I really didn't......." Jane began to say before choking up when Shannon's body arrived.

"You did the right thing," said Isaac softly, placing his hand on hers.

"Everyone knows I don't like her, but I didn't mean to...." said Jane as a tear formed in the corner of one eye. She blinked it away as she looked into Isaac's eyes, trying to hold back her feelings.

"You did what you had to do, which is what anyone else would have done," said Jill, putting her arm around her.

"But we may have needed her, since she is probably the only person who knows how to recover the coding on our chips," said Jane.

"It is what it is, and we'll deal with it," said Jill.

"I know, but I just killed someone," said Jane as they drifted out of the control center and back toward the shuttle bay with Shannon's body in tow.

"You really had no other choice under the circumstances, and besides, she erased our chips and that's essentially murder," said Isaac.

"What are we going to do with her body?" asked Jane, tears now filling her eyes, with little droplets floating out.

"We'll give her a space burial," said Isaac as they arrived at the shuttle bay.

"Of course this leaves us with a lot of unanswered questions, especially why she did what she did," said Jane.

"Assuming it was her," said Isaac.

"It was," said Jane.

"I know, it had to be," said Isaac who nudged the body toward the shuttle bay door. They all got into the shuttle and opened the bay door. Shannon's body was sucked out as the air escaped in a whoosh and they watched her disappear in the distance.

Chapter Four

"**A**s you all know, Shannon is dead after attempting to destroy our ship," said Isaac from the podium after the assembly was again called. "Jane kicked her against a wall in the control center and she died. Jane did not intend to kill her. However, we believe Shannon intended to go down with the ship." He looked down at Jane and she nodded without smiling as once again she stood so close to him that she seemed part of his body.

"We gave Shannon a space burial," Isaac continued.

"So you dumped her body out of the shuttle bay," said Diedre from the front row.

"Dumped is a bit harsh," said Isaac.

"Is she up there in orbit?" asked Diedre.

"She is," said Isaac.

"Well, as far as I'm concerned, that's where she belongs," said Diedre.

"I guess that means she deactivated your chip too." said Isaac.

"Yes, and what she did to the six of us was tantamount to murder, so she deserved what she got," said Diedre.

"You didn't tell us before now that she offed your chip," said Isaac.

"I know, but I thought if I remained silent, I could use my status as her assistant to negotiate a deal, and get her to reverse what she did," said Diedre.

"OK, well, she's gone now, so that's no longer possible," said Isaac. "Well, we have a crucial decision to make," said Isaac as he looked out over the assembly.

"Either the six of us will somehow recover our immortality here on Eden, or we will eventually die of old age here," he said, then paused for a moment. "Otherwise, we would have to return to Earth in search of a way to reverse it. There are three conditions regarding that second option. One, the procedure for reversing it may not exist. Two, the big war that we all knew was brewing before we left may have resulted in widespread destruction and there will be no one there to even ask for help. In other words, we might well return to a scorched Earth and find nothing left of Shannon's equipment. And the third condition is that two of us could be in our eighties when we get there, and the other four in our sixties. But the third condition has it's own condition."

"Does that condition have anything to do with how fast we return?" asked someone in the audience.

"Yes it does, and I'll let Jane explain that to you a little later," said Isaac, looking down at her with a smile. "But regardless of how long it takes, here's the deal: if we do decide to return to Earth with our ship, those who stay back here on Eden will be stranded on this planet, possibly forever."

31

"So, clearly, this is a very big decision," said Jill who was standing next to Holly behind Isaac and Jane.

"Look, Isaac, if you guys return to Earth, I am coming with you," said someone from the audience.

"Thanks Fan, I appreciate that," said Isaac.

"For god's sake Isaac, get real!" said Fan. "We've already talked this over while you were up there killing Shannon, and it's unanimous.... none of us want to stay here if you guys go back." This was immediately followed by a cheer and a burst of loud conversation after which another person waved her arm in the air and Isaac pointed to her.

"Another thing to consider, Isaac, is that we were kidnapped by Shannon and essentially brought here against our will," said the person.

"That's right," said Fan. "Sure, we made the best of it and made nice homes for ourselves, but we didn't volunteer to come here, and I'm not sure how many of us would have volunteered to come here."

"Good point, Fan," said Isaac.

"Let's face it, Earth is still our home regardless of what condition it's in when we get back there," said Fan.

"Isaac, if you don't believe Fan, why don't you just ask for a show of hands," someone else asked.

"OK, so how many would go back with us?" he asked. Everyone immediately raised their hand. He then looked down at Jane who smiled up at him as a tear formed in her eye. For a moment he was preoccupied with his feelings for her as he studied her face.

"Well I guess that answers that question," said Diedre when

she noticed that Isaac and Jane were completely lost in themselves.

"Of course getting our chips restored could be a lost cause, especially if Earth is not habitable," said Isaac. "But other than that, going back sounds like something we all want to do."

"I have dreamed of going home to Earth almost since we arrived here," said Fan.

"Does that mean you're a little sick of this rock?" asked Diedre. A cheer and clapping broke out.

"Let's ditch this place and go home," said Fan. The colony erupted into a loud cheer followed by enthusiastic chatter. Isaac quietly stared out over the crowd. Jane had her arm firmly around him and he now put his arm around her and they stood in a virtual embrace in plain view of the assembly.

"It's amazing that we've never really discussed going back before," said Isaac with a smile after the noise subsided enough for him to be heard.

"Maybe that's because we came to accept our fate, and, as the saying goes, we were given lemons and we simply made lemonade out of it," said Fan who turned to see smiles and nods all around.

"We did," said Isaac. "But we've been here for a hundred twenty years and I can't believe we've never even had a serious conversation about going back."

"I don't think any of us felt we even had that option," said Fan.

"And of course we were comfortable here, maybe too comfortable considering how our lives have slowly changed as our technology deteriorated," said someone.

"That's something Jill and I discussed this morning," said Isaac. "What in fact is our future here."

"Well, I think I would take Earth regardless of how many pieces it's in now," said another person.

"I think that captures our collective feelings about leaving," said Isaac. "Now, in anticipation of that, Jane prepared a plan, and she can outline that for you now." He gently nudged her out in front of him and she slowly moved in front of the podium with only her head visible.

"Fortunately, we have maintained our spacecraft over the years," she began. Then, feeling uncomfortable with being unable to see those below her, she stepped to one side and walked forward to the edge of the platform in a move that was completely uncharacteristic of her.

"It took us nearly fifty years to complete the journey here, and we want to seriously shorten that time in order for us to arrive before we're at retirement age," said Jane. "Of course those not affected by the chip erasure will remain immortal and will not age during our journey, but six of us will age. So we're hoping to arrive back on Earth before we're too old. I think we can make the trip in a little less than twenty-five years, but the acceleration and deceleration phases of our trip will last longer. We hope to reach about twenty percent of the speed of light." The silence continued as every eye was glued to her.

"Now, this kind of speed has never been attempted with this ship, but we have learned a great deal about it on our trip here and I'm sure we can go a lot faster. However, the effort to reach our target speed is unknown, and therefore is not without danger." She then paused and looked back at Isaac who now stepped forward next to her.

"Isaac?" she gestured, as she looked back. When she saw him, she could not stop herself from smiling. Her absolute glow was like a neon sign and he was so captured by her warmth that he had to collect himself before he could say anything.

"So..... because of these unknown dangers, and despite your unanimous agreement to go, this trip has to be voluntary," said Isaac. "However, we have only one activation device. Either it goes back to Earth with the ship, or it stays here. If it stays, those of you who decide to go will lose their immortality. If it goes, those who stay here will lose theirs. So this is pretty much an all or nothing situation. So, for anyone to keep their immortality, either we all have to go, or we all have to stay. I know that we just reached a consensus to go, but I want you to think about this overnight, and we'll finalize this decision in the morning?"

"Isaac, we've already decided, so let's not waste time thinking about it," said Fan.

"I know, Fan, but this is a life altering decision, so I want everyone to sleep on it first," said Isaac.

"Fine, but the answer will be the same," said Fan.

"That may be true, but regardless of what we do, leave or stay, we need to do a little more research into how the chips were deactivated," said Jane. "It would be quite a relief to six of us if we could reactivate our chips before we leave." She looked up at Isaac, waiting for his nod of agreement. He smiled, then nodded as he continued to stare at her as if in a trance.

"We'll see everyone in the morning," said Isaac after a pregnant pause. "Assembly closed." Jane, apparently realizing that her attraction to Isaac had been quite obvious, took her arm from around him and tried to look innocent. Isaac pulled her back tightly as laughter filtered up from the crowd. No one had ever seen Jane, the nerd scientist and stoic leader, behave like this. And Isaac, the perfect gentleman and authority figure, was entirely out of character. Jane let out a little laugh of her own as she put her hand on Isaac's back and they started down from the platform. Jill, who was watching, smiled and shook her head as she looked at Holly who just shrugged.

The next morning, as the assembly once more convened, Isaac reported that they could not find a way to reactivate their chips. And the decision to go was again reaffirmed. The entire colony would return to Earth.

It would be a very busy few days before all preparations were complete and the complex systems of the ship systematically checked and given the green light. In the past, everyone was immortal and had to travel up to the ship together in one shuttle, taking the activation device with them. But now, for the six whose chips had been erased, it seemed strange not to have to worry about the device. As a result, two shuttles were able to complete the task of readying the ship.

The ship itself was massive. It had the appearance of a large bullet with a rounded nose and rocket nozzle at the rear with doors to the shuttle bay located near the nozzle. This was an odd shape considering the fact that it would be traveling through the void of space where aerodynamic shapes were useless. But it was originally designed with the option of entering the atmosphere of a planet and landing in case the shuttles became inoperative. Rather than being stranded forever in space, at least they would have the option to land on a planet with the chance to survive. It did not have the kind of propulsion system for takeoff, so if it did have to land, it would never be able to leave whatever planet it landed on.

Inside the outer skin was a blanket of water that both minimized the impact of cosmic rays and helped maintain their critical water supply. It was designed to house over one hundred people for short trips and about fifty for multi-year trips. The ship included restaurants, shops and exercise facilities. It was like a small city in space.

One morning with everyone on the ship, Jane announced that it would depart soon, so Isaac and Jane went to the control room. A few spots of blood remained on the panel and a red patch had dried against the far wall to remind them of that day when Shannon died there.

"Well, here we go, Isaac," said Jane as she began to increase thrust on the engine. They were soon winding their way out of orbit and lining up on the coordinates for the Sun's solar system.

"Twenty-five years to go," he quipped. She smiled over at him and nodded.

"OK, girls and girls, you may now migrate to the dome café where we'll see you shortly," Jane announced on the intercom after they were on course and had reached the desired one-G thrust.

"I have to remove some of this," said Isaac, taking out a tissue from his pocket and wiping blood stains from the console.

"I don't want to pretend it didn't happen, so just leave the patch over there on the wall," said Jane.

"I understand," said Isaac, who put his hand on hers.

"This will be twenty-five years of our life, Isaac," said Jane, looking at him with that soft look of affection that was still so very new to her. They sat staring at one another in the moment.

"What are we going to do?" asked Isaac as he stared at her.

"You mean about us?" she asked.

"Yes, about us," said Isaac.

" Isaac, I haven't even fully matured yet, despite the fact that I'm a hundred and eighty-eight years old," said Jane, looking down at her barely maturing chest.

"Look we're still teens, but we're also young adults too," he replied.

"So what? we'll have to wait?" she asked.

"You mean to......oh.....that," he stammered.

"Yes, that," she nodded.

"I haven't really....uh.....OK, yes, I have thought about it," he replied. "I've thought about it a lot actually, but maybe we should wait, at least for a while."

"I love you Isaac. Not as a child. I love you as a fully mature adult," she said and then looked away in embarrassment.

"Oh Jane..... my Jane.... I have always loved you, starting back on the moon," he replied, and for the first time his eyes filled with tears.

"What do you mean?" she asked as tears quickly filled her eyes. She wiped them off as more came, and soon she was sobbing openly while at the same time smiling.

"It's true, from the first time we met," he replied as he saw how she reacted and got down on his knees and shuffled over to her seat where he took her in his arms and pulled her close to him, closing his eyes in sheer happiness, his head under her chin, his tears dampening her blouse and hers dripping down onto his head.

"You don't know how much that means to me....." she began.

"Holding you like this is like a miracle for me," he said, his voice muffled in her blouse.

"You were my impossible dream, Isaac, and in a million years I never thought I'd ever have a ghost of a chance with you," she sobbed into his hair. "Look at all the beautiful girls that have surrounded you, including Jill who is drop dead gorgeous. So I just loved you from afar, and put that dream out of my mind."

"But Jane, it was always you and never anyone else," he replied.

"Oh my god," she sighed. "I had no idea."

"It's true."

"For so very long I've had to avoid thinking about us, although being immortal removed the sexual part, so it was easier to occupy my mind with technical and academic stuff," she said, choking up.

"I can't believe this, we've felt this way about each other for all these years and neither of us knew," said Isaac, pulling back a little so he could look up into her eyes.

"Of course neither of us had the kind of feelings we have now," she said. "And oh my god are they powerful feelings, and at the same time they are so very wonderful!"

"I remember back on the moon when I was beginning to have these feelings for you before we were immortalized," said Isaac.

"That's amazing, because that's when I had such a crush on you," she replied.

"The minute I saw you there and listened to you describe who you were and what you hoped to learn at space camp, I fell in love," said Isaac.

"But we were both way too shy to ever say anything," said Jane.

"I know that, so we have loved each other for who we were, and not for just the physical attraction that now floods over me like a tidal wave," he smiled.

"True, but the fact that you were a hunk put you out of my league."

"A hunk? I've never been a hunk, but I'm so glad you think so."

"To me you are the most incredible hunk ever, and I've always wanted to be your girl, no, I mean your woman, even though I didn't get these feelings again until a couple weeks ago," she said softly. "Then, in the Board Room back on Eden when you looked at me the way you did...... oh my god, this whole thing just surrounded me like a warm blanket."

"I know, and until that moment, I didn't realize how very much I loved you, not just because we became normal again and had these feelings, but because I had always loved you, said Isaac."

"So, for all those decades we've essentially been in love without being able to be 'in-love' in the classic sense."

"And now it's real," said Isaac.

"But answer me this, what about Jill?" she asked.

"Jill has been my best friend since we were children, but I don't feel about her the way I feel about you," he replied. "You are my one and only and no one else even registers on the meter."

"But she has, well, so much more......"

"She is more physically mature for her age."

"For her age nothing, she's a full fledged woman, and look at me, I'm just a child," she said, pushing him back slightly and

40

looking down at herself.

"Jane, you're a small person to begin with, but you're definitely not a child."

"I know, but...... "

"I love you just the way your are," he said, looking up into her eyes.

"Oh Isaac.....you're mine," she said as she pulled him back to her and hugged him tightly as tears once again filled her eyes.

"And you are my very own Jane," he said with his eyes shut.

"I am almost sixteen you know," she whispered into his ear.

"I know, so am I, well, in frozen immortality years," he whispered back.

"Does that mean we're old enough?" she whispered, her voice quivering.

"Oh.....well, maybe, but don't you think we should wait," he whispered back.

"How I wish right now that we were older, but I guess there's a lot to do in the next few months, so we'll certainly be busy," she said as she pushed back a little and held his face in her hands. His smile said everything.

"The main thing is we'll be together for as long as we live," he said quietly. She placed her wet face against his and then their lips met and they kissed for the first time.

"We'll be forty when we get there," said Jane, pulling back again and looking at Isaac as the reality of that fact sank in.

"I know, but right now I feel like almost sixteen and in love," he said as he continued to look into her eyes.

"I'll regret not having this feeling if we ever get our immortality back," she replied.

41

"Oh my god, you're right," he replied. "In fact, the very idea of losing what we have now seems unthinkable."

"That thought just occurred to me," said Jane.

"It's an interesting dilemma," he said, shaking his head.

"Right, we're traveling all the way back to Earth to restore our immortality, only to face the question of whether we will actually want to restore our immortality and lose the wonderful thing we have," said Jane.

"Well, there are four others who most likely do want to restore theirs," said Isaac.

"That's true, but the reality is, we have no idea whether the technology, equipment and knowledge still exists, or even if it does, how to use it," she replied.

"Or if the great war actually happened," said Isaac.

"We're going back into a big unknown," said Jane.

"But I believe it's the right thing to do for reasons other than to restore our immortality, and everyone in the colony is psyched about it," said Isaac.

"Well, as Fan said, we were actually kidnapped by Shannon and essentially brought to Eden against our will," said Jane.

"I know that," said Isaac.

"So the fact that we didn't mutiny long before now is likely a function of our being immortal," said Jane.

"And also because we were under a threat by Shannon that she could take our immortality away from us at any time if we didn't do what she wanted," said Isaac.

"You could even view it this way: our being entirely isolated in space with one person holding that kind of control over our lives can easily be characterized as being in a form of prison," said

Jane.

"It really was," said Isaac.

"But considering how Shannon hated the both of us, it's a wonder she didn't try to zap us long before now," said Jane.

"If you go back to the beginning, and assume that her original plan in stealing a spaceship with teenagers aboard was to populate some distant planet....... that plan fell apart right from the very start on two counts," said Isaac. "First, she didn't bring enough chips, and her effort to winnow down the teenagers to that number resulted in her only able to get females. Except for me. And second, her immortality solution completely erased our interest in reproduction. So I'm sure there had to be a huge element of disappointment, as well as leaving her without any sort of overall plan," said Isaac.

"However, she did have one male, you Isaac, so if she ever had aspirations of pursuing her original plan, it would require her to erase your chip as well as the chips of enough females to initiate her plan," said Jane.

"That's a question only she could answer, but the fatal flaw in that strategy was that she didn't really know me, or how I felt about you, and I'm sure that we alone could not populate a planet by ourselves," said Isaac.

"Oh god no......and besides, you would need a larger breeding stock if you had any chance of having a healthy population," said Jane.

"That whole strategy aside, you would have to consider the fact that we had never achieved any sense of self-sufficiency on Eden, and populating a planet would need a lot more than just bodies."

"Populating a planet is not at all simple, and she wasn't dumb, so I'm sure something else was at the core of her attack on the Board members," said Jane.

"Something we'll never know......but let's get back to our current situation...... we've been characterized as something like a royal couple, so does that require us to act in some special way?" asked Isaac. "I mean, don't we now have to set an example?"

"I don't know, how do we do that?" she asked.

"Maybe we can't show our affection for each other in public as we've been doing," said Isaac.

"I'm not sure I know how to control how I feel or act when I'm around you," she replied. "I feel like a teenager who just discovered love and is oblivious to what other people think."

"That's kind of where I'm at too, but here's the thing, you're the only one who can successfully pilot this ship back to Earth," said Isaac. "And you're also the one person that everyone has always looked up to for any and all important decisions. You are, in a very real sense, like the queen bee."

"Look Isaac, you've been the colony's leader from the very beginning, and there isn't anyone else who could come close to filling that role," said Jane. "So is that the equivalent of a king?"

"Look, there's no such thing as a king bee, and besides, if I hadn't followed your advice all those years, any kind of leadership I might have tried to exert would have crumbled," said Isaac.

"You didn't always follow my advice, did you?"

"Oh yes I did, because you were, and always have been, my hero," he replied.

"But everyone always looked to you for direction," said Jane.

"Only with your help, Jane...... and everyone knows where

my help came from."

"I guess we're kind of joined at the hip that way aren't we," said Jane. "But do you think we can behave like this so-called royal couple?"

"I think others respect us as human beings and realize that emotions of love are just part of who we are," said Isaac. "I don't think it has diminished our roles or the respect we have within the colony."

"OK, buster, but just remember, you're the only male among a sea of women, some of whom now have their sexual feelings back, and they could be eyeing the only male on the ship.....a very handsome male I might add."

"These females, these women, will always be my friends, and you will always be my one and only love," said Isaac.

"Hey you guys!" said Holly from the door to the control room as she burst in and began walking out over the ramp. Gravity had been established due to the acceleration of the ship and Isaac had to struggle to get to his feet since he expected to float up as they had in orbit. He was now trying to straighten his clothes. Jane quickly turned to the console as if she were doing something important.

"Holly....hi," said Isaac trying to look and sound calm.

"Look you two, everyone on this ship already knows that you two have been in love ever since we left the moon," said Holly.

"Wait, the moon? You knew we were in love all this time?" asked Jane as she stood up.

"Of course, I know the look," said Holly.

"I didn't realize that anyone knew," said Isaac. "Besides, we were all out of the reproduction business as immortals, so why

45

would anyone even notice?"

"Love can be more than just reproduction, and in your case, it was," said Holly. "The dead giveaway was that neither of you is very good at hiding your emotions. In fact you're both very poor at it."

"I didn't know it showed," said Jane.

"Neither of you seem to be aware of how transparent your feelings were, but now that you're together at last, you have nothing to explain or be embarrassed about," said Holly. "We all knew, so stop worrying about it."

"But isn't it inappropriate of us to show our affection in front of others when we're expected to be..... well, leaders?" he asked.

"After two hundred years, everyone knows both of you quite well, Isaac, and they love the both of you, so you can continue to be the leaders like you have always been," she replied with an animated shrug.

"So, we were the only ones who thought our love for each other was a secret," said Isaac.

"But I didn't even know Isaac was in love with me," said Jane.

"And I didn't know Jane loved me either," said Isaac.

"But Isaac, your heart is on full display right there on your sleeve, so that kind of secret is completely impossible for you to hide," said Holly.

"I suppose I could be a little transparent at times," said Isaac.

"At times?.... no, all the time, and it's one of the things that's so adorable about you," she replied. "Look, love is a wonderful thing and not something you need to hide, especially now."

"Holly, did you have someone.... I mean, did you know this kind of love?" asked Jane.

"Yes, David was his name, and I was head over heals in love, and so was he," she said, closing her eyes for a second.

"What happened?" asked Jane.

"He lost his life in one of the many battles that were going on before we left."

"I'm sorry," said Jane.

"I was totally devastated, and it's one of the reasons I ended up here...... I needed to get away, far away," she replied.

"You knew Shannon since you had studied under her at one point, right?" asked Jane.

"Yes, and after I found out from Diedre what Shannon was planning to do, I volunteered for the mission," said Holly. "Then, when she found out that I knew of her plan, she really had no choice but to accept me since she couldn't afford to have anyone know what she was up to."

"Which explains why she was always a little hostile toward you," said Isaac.

"Yes, she was, and toward Diedre for telling me.....but she literally hated you, Jane," said Holly.

"Oh, I know that, and it was mutual..... but then, that was never a secret," said Jane.

"Well, that's all behind us now," said Holly.

"It is, and being with Isaac now is so much better than anything I've ever known," said Jane.

"What we've witnessed with you is like the transformation of a larvae into a butterfly, Jane," said Holly. "I for one just want to laugh when I see you two together, I'm so happy for you."

"Soooo, you're finally able to be together after a hundred seventy years!" said Jill who had entered and was halfway up the ramp with a big smile on her face.

"Wait, don't tell me you knew all this time too?" asked Isaac.

"Of course, I knew all along, silly, but Jane was slightly better at hiding her feelings than you," she replied. "Trust me, Isaac, your attraction to one another was obvious to everyone almost from the start."

"But nobody ever said anything," Isaac sputtered. "And you, my dearest and oldest friend..... you never said anything to me."

"I know I didn't, but for years I was actually a little jealous, but the immortality thing threw a damper on all of that, so I began to think of your attraction to her as a kind of romance that none of us could ever have," said Jill.

"What if Shannon had not erased our chips?" asked Isaac.

"But she did, and now, we're all like one big family, and you two are officially the royal couple, so your romance comes center stage," said Jill.

"Wait.....officially?" asked Isaac.

"Your show of affection at the assembly stands as your official announcement," said Holly. "Right there in front of everyone, you two became the royal couple."

"Oh jeez," Isaac mumbled as he looked at Jane who just smiled.

"Here's the thing, we've lived together as a colony for decades, and everyone knows everything about everyone else," said Jill. "So everyone knows you two, and everyone knew about your attraction to one another, and now that your love is out in the open.....just keep it clean please."

"Ooooh, of course.....I'd die," said Jane.

"So would I," said Isaac.

"I know, Isaac, you get embarrassed if a button is open on your shirt," said Jill.

"Of course Isaac and I will get married and start a family," said Jane excitedly with an ear to ear grin.

"Oh.....married and start a family......wow, that's right, I guess I hadn't thought that far ahead," Isaac stammered. "But we can....no, we will, get married."

"Perfect, we'll plan a royal wedding!" said Holly. "With trumpets and everything."

"Trumpets?" asked Isaac.

"This is crazy," said Jane. "Here I am, still physically a teenager, and I'm planning my wedding and how I will have a family of my own," said Jane.

"First of all, you're pushing two hundred years old, and second of all, we're nearly adults, physically," said Isaac.

"That's true, but if I were still sixteen I would definitely need to wait until I was intellectually and emotionally mature," said Jane.

"I do think we're intellectually mature, but I'm not sure yet whether we're emotionally mature," said Isaac.

"The chip erasure was an abrupt change that none of us expected, and it was quite a shock, so we'll need an adjustment period before any of us get back to a sense of normal emotionally," said Jill.

"It has certainly opened my eyes to a lot of things that never really occurred to me in the eternity of immortality," said Jane.

"This is our new reality," said Isaac.

"For me, it's more like an impossible dream," said Jane.

Chapter Five

"That was at once the shortest and yet the longest twenty-five years of my life," said Jane as she and Isaac sat in the control center console and watched Earth grow larger and larger on the curved wall of the globe. They were now in zero gravity as they made preparations to enter orbit.

"Well, it was long enough to start a family," he smiled as he reached behind him and put his hand on the head of the teenage girl who was strapped in behind them. She smiled as she batted his hand away.

"The question is: what are we going to find here on Earth after two hundred years of absence," said Holly who had entered the control center and was floating to the pod to join them.

"We'll soon find out," said Jane as she made another adjustment to their speed and direction.

"Well, we can see a bit of the dark side and we should be seeing lights, and there really are none except for dim glimmers that could be fires," said Holly.

"That's a good indication that the war not only happened but did some very serious damage," said Isaac.

"Based on what I see from just the ships external visuals, I think I'd have to describe it as complete destruction," said Holly.

"I guess I should be in total shock right now, but we knew that it could be bad," said Isaac.

"I know, but not this bad," said Holly.

It was nearly an hour before they were in Earth's orbit and Lian and Jill had joined them in the control pod. Lian busied herself with the communication equipment that would monitor possible transmissions from Earth. Jill was adjusting the visual scanning equipment so they could study surface features up close as they passed over. But she soon discovered that the definition of the images was very poor.

"Unfortunately the visual equipment kind of went south on us," said Jill.

"That's not good, so I guess we'll just do the best we can using our external visuals," said Jane.

"Not much detail there," said Isaac.

"This is a big disappointment," said Jill. "We're partially blind as a result."

"At least the ship's main systems worked or we'd be somewhere lost in space," said Jane.

"I hear no transmissions of any kind, which is eerie to say the least," said Lian.

"There's nothing?" asked Isaac.

"Nothing, and we passed over the US and now starting over Europe," said Lian.

"Wow, that's not very encouraging," said Jane.

"It tells me that whatever is left down there is likely quite primitive," said Lian.

"Well, we'll be over Asia soon," said Jane.

"Well, we're entering daylight so maybe we can spot some signs of life," said Jill.

"It does look like some indication of life in parts of China if I'm not mistaken," said Jill a little while later.

"Like what?" asked Isaac.

"More smoke from what could be settlements," said Jill.

"Any aircraft?" asked Jane.

"No, but I saw a satellite zip by a minute ago," said Lian.

"There were thousands of those when we left, so many of them are likely still up here," said Jane.

"We're coming up on the North American continent and other than those dim flickers that are likely small fires, I am seeing a few tiny lights scattered about," said Jill a little more than a half hour later.

"I see them, but really nothing else," said Holly.

"I count a half dozen of those lights," said Jill who was straining to see the fuzzy images.

"I do too, and this is interesting becasue I'm familiar with the locations of the eternity blocks that a man named Lucas built, and these lights seem to be approximately where they were located," said Holly.

"I remember hearing about those," said Isaac.

"Shannon mentioned to me what a scam Lucas was promoting since she said he interred thousands of people into those blocks before he had proof that they worked," said Holly.

"Is that where people were supposed to have their minds preserved forever inside these large metal blocks?" asked Jane.

"Yes," said Holly.

"And you think those lights might actually be on the blocks?" asked Isaac.

"I'm not positive since we can't see anything up close, but I think the locations match up," said Holly. "I even knew someone who was going to act as a keeper and live in one of those blocks as shelter during the impending war."

"That was two hundred years ago, so that person wouldn't even be alive today," said Isaac.

"Yes she would, because she was also immortalized, like we were," said Holly.

"Oh really, then we may need to check out that block," said Jane.

"Definitely,"said Holly.

"If those lights turn out to be on Lucas's blocks, then his blocks are all that's left in America," said Isaac.

"Except for those pale orange flickers that look like they could be campfires," said Jill.

"Which suggest the existence of survivors living in primitive conditions," said Jane.

"Yes, but if people survived, surely they would be able to salvage some of the technology and infrastructure that was there before the war," said Holly.

"That makes sense, but if most of that was destroyed during the war, it would be difficult to essentially start over to create everything anew," said Jane. "You would have to recreate a world that took hundreds of years to build. Most people would be dead, including the talent needed to create things, and there would be intense competition to survive. That's an ugly environment in which to create anything."

"Even so, it suggests some kind of suppression," said Jill.

"Suppression?" asked Isaac.

"An effort by some survivors to keep other survivors from recovering either intentionally or as a result of the fight over what's left," said Jill.

"Anything is possible in what appears to be a pretty bleak situation," said Jane.

"How could the destruction be so complete?" asked Isaac.

"To begin with, I believe there were over one hundred thousand nuclear devices in twenty one countries," said Jane.

"That could create quite an inferno," said Holly. "So unless you were in an area not directly hit, the initial survival rate would be rather abysmal. And those who were not directly hit likely died a slow death from the fallout and conditions that would have existed worldwide for a long time after the blasts."

"No one is safe in a global thermonuclear war, which is what it looks like," said Lian.

"It does seem global," said Jane.

"The destruction of the populated areas would set recovery of the world back centuries, even if the rural areas managed to survive in any significant number." said Holly.

"That's right," said Jane. "Even if survivors were able to salvage hardware, most of it would be largely useless without essential links to the modern world."

"Well, it's been two hundred years since we left, and not much seems to have been restored," said Jill.

"So do you have any initial thoughts about our strategy for where we go from here?" asked Jill, looking at Jane.

"I'm still a bit in shock at how complete the destruction seems to be," said Jane.

"We did see some signs of life as we passed over China, and I remember that they had declared neutrality before the war, so perhaps we could try again to contact them," said Jill.

"They didn't respond to any of my initial communications," said Lian.

"But if that's the only sign of semi-modern life, we need to try again," said Jane.

"Fan has kept up on Chinese dialects, so we should get her up here when we pass over China again," said Lian.

"I'll send for her," said Isaac.

An hour later, as they were passing over China, Fan attempted to contact them using several dialects, but there was no reply. On another pass over China it was night, and what appeared to be electric lights were now visible, but at a seriously diminished intensity and in far fewer locations than in pre-war times. Jill reported seeing possible movement of vehicles, but again, repeated attempts to contact anyone resulted in complete silence. As they circled the globe they found no other signs of modern civilization, only wiffs of smoke from fires during the day, and the glow of fires at night. Their inability to get close up images made it virtually impossible for them to know more about possible survivors.

"It does appear that China survived in some form, although it's but a shadow of where it was two hundred years ago," said Jane.

"We'll know more once we get down there," said Isaac. "So, do we start with China?"

"No, I'd rather focus on America where Shannon had her immortality lab," said Jane.

"Oh right, I guess that's why we came back, isn't it," said Holly.

"But it could be dangerous down there, especially if these survivors turn out to be hostile," said Jill.

"Perhaps, but even though we have no serious weapons, we're not going to just stay up here and twiddle our thumbs," said Jane.

"At least it doesn't look like we'll face anything like a modern army," said Isaac.

"Sticks and stones can be just as deadly in the wrong hands," said Jill.

"Guns are not people and many probably survived, so it's not as if we would be facing homo erectus with a wooden club," said Jane.

"That's right, especially in America where there was a gun for every man, woman and child," said Jill.

"Yes, I think we can assume that if there are survivors, we could encounter guns," said Jane. "But we can't let that stop us from exploring the world down there."

"You're right," said Jill. "We'll just be careful."

"Lian, don't you have a gun?" asked Isaac.

"Yes, but it's only a hobby even though I'm pretty sure it works..... However, I'd love to try it out," said Lian.

"Pretty sure.....are you really sure it works?" asked Isaac.

"Theoretically," said Lian.

"I'm not going to go down there toting a gun and looking for trouble, especially if it's a theoretical gun," said Jane. "We just have to be mindful of the dangers and avoid them."

"Alright, so where do we go first?" asked Isaac.

"Maybe those lights," said Jane. "The fact that they still work after two hundred years, when no lights are seen anywhere else in America, is way too interesting to pass up."

"We think they're on Lucas's blocks, so which one?" asked Jill.

"We saw seven, but I think there were supposed to be eight," said Holly. "There was one up by Yellowstone but it appears as though the super volcano erupted, so that one may well have been covered......." Holly's eyes suddenly opened wide and she immediately tried to get Jill's attention.

"OK, so which of the seven that remain.......?" asked Jill who now saw Holly. She shrugged as Holly motioned with her head toward the exit. Jill gave her a confused look, but nodded.

"I'm not sure, but uh......" said Holly, crossing her legs and pointing to the exit.

"OK, well, I need to use the bathroom too," said Jill, getting up to leave. Isaac noticed the exchange but didn't say anything.

"Meet you outside," said Holly who floated out behind Jill.

"I couldn't discuss this in there," said Holly once they were both outside.

"I'm listening," said Jill.

"My friend Jane was the block keeper at that block," said Holly. "And Jane had a teen daughter that she had sent to China before the war."

"Your friends name was Jane.....wait......oh shit!" said Jill.

"Yes, I think my friend is, or was, our Jane's mother," said Holly.

"And Yellowstone was the block?" asked Jill.

"Yes, and here's the clincher, she told me her daughter's name was also Jane," said Holly.

"Oh my god, and you never told our Jane about this?" asked Jill.

"Why?" asked Holly. "It never really occurred to me until now."

"Jane will ask you which block your friend is in," said Jill.

"I know," said Holly.

"Well, look, didn't you used to live in California?" asked Jill.

"I did, and..... oh yeah...... I also knew someone who was assigned to be a block keeper at a block west of San Francisco," said Holly.

"Was this person immortal?" asked Jill.

"I think so, but I'm not sure," said Holly. "Chandler was someone working on immortalization like Shannon, but I don't know if he was successful."

"Then that's our answer when Jane asks about your friend," said Jill, pointing for them to go back in. They both came in and sat in their respective chairs in the pod.

"You know, Jane, Jill and I were talking out there," said Holly. "We think the block northwest of San Francisco would be the best one to visit first."

"What about your friend?" asked Jane.

"Maybe later, because that block in California is attended by a man named Chandler who had worked on immortalization with Shannon, so he might be able to give us some direction to her lab," said Holly.

"Yes, that does sound like a better starting point for our exploration," said Jane.

"That's true, because finding Shannon's lab could be very difficult," said Holly.

"But weren't you there when you were immortalized?" asked Jane.

"We all were, but Shannon had everyone arrive at night, so no one actually knew exactly where it was other than somewhere near Colorado Springs," said Holly.

"And you're thinking Chandler might know where it is?" asked Jane.

"He might," said Holly.

"And he must be immortal if you expect to find him at this block," said Jane.

"Yes, he had his own immortality procedure, so I'm sure he is," Holly lied.

"Then that's clearly our best lead," said Jane.

"That's what I was thinking," said Holly.

"So that will be our first landing," said Jane.

"The other thing about that area of interest is the appearance of smoke, so we might even find a few survivors," said Jill.

"That's even better," said Jane.

"So who goes down?" asked Isaac.

"Only the six of us can go down, but one of us has to stay in the ship," said Jane.

"I'll stay," said Holly.

"Do you know Chandler?" asked Jane.

"I met him, but don't actually know him very well, but I

think Diedre does," said Holly.

"OK, so you stay up here and be in charge and Diedre will come down with us," said Jane.

"Holly needs to have some company," said Lian.

"Are you volunteering?" asked Jane.

"Yes, unless you want me to bring my gun along," said Lian.

"No, let's save that surprise for another time," said Jane.

"So that means that you, me, Jill and Diedre go down," said Isaac, patting Jane on the head.

"Good, that's our landing team," said Jane.

"If necessary, can't this spaceship actually land?" asked Holly.

"It was designed to land, but don't get any ideas when I'm gone, because I have serious questions about its reentry shielding," said Jane. "Besides, it would be a crash landing since it's unlikely that we could find a proper airport. And it does not have the ability to take off again, so our space adventure would be over."

"Then are you thinking about the possibility of returning to Eden at some point?" said Holly.

"We may want to keep that option open based on what we're seeing so far," said Jane.

"I like having options," said Isaac.

"Alright, before we leave, I'm putting us in rotation so everyone who stays will have gravity, so you'll have to use the remote observational equipment in the dome cafe," said Jane.

"That would be nice because I don't like floating around," said Fan.

On the next orbit, the four of them loaded into one of the shuttles and departed for the surface heading for the California coast northwest of San Francisco. They proceeded up the coast until they spotted the shiny silver block and landed on top in a landscape of tall grasses, brush and a few small trees. In the center was a flat roofed structure with a steel door. On top was a small tower with a light housed in a dome. They deplaned and stood in the grasses and other plant material that had accumulated over two centuries. Diedre studied the keypad next to the door. She tried several codes but nothing worked. Meanwhile, Jane was running her fingers along the edge of the door. She found that the door was not completely closed, and she managed to wedge her fingertips into the gap, then pulled. With Isaac's help they were able to move the door open a few inches against the sandy soil. Soon, all four were tugging and eventually the door was open enough for them to squeeze through. With a small flashlight in hand, Jane started down a curved hallway until they reached a room with a large globe held up by a shaft from the floor. As she shined her flashlight on the globe it suddenly sprouted a hailstorm of pencil beams that began to scan the room.

"I do not recognize any of you," came a voice from inside the globe.

"We're from Shannon's immortality experiment," said Diedre, thinking quickly about what might be familiar to anyone associated with the eternity blocks.

"My data base tells me that Shannon left for outer space two hundred two years, five months and six days ago," said the globe.

"Yes, we left with her," said Jane.

"And you have returned," said the globe.

"Yes we did," said Isaac.

"You would be over two hundred years old and that does not register as logical," replied the globe.

"We're immortal," said Isaac.

"Only Chandler is immortal," said the globe.

"Is Chandler your human attendant?" asked Jane.

"He is my block keeper," said the globe.

"But he is not here," said Isaac.

"No, he is not here," said the globe.

"Holly said he was here," said Diedre.

"Who is Holly?" asked the globe.

"She is one of us," said Isaac.

"Nobody has been here for quite some time," Isaac whispered. Diedre shook her head and shrugged.

"That is true," said the globe.

"We weren't talking to you," said Jill.

"But I heard," said the globe.

"Don't hear," said Jill.

"Maybe he's dead," Jane whispered.

"I don't know if he's dead," said the globe.

"Don't hear tin head," said Jill.

"My head is made of stainless steel, not tin," said the globe.

"So where is your block keeper now?" asked Isaac putting his hand over Jill's mouth.

"He once lived in the lighthouse," said the globe.

"Where is the lighthouse?" asked Jane.

"It is twenty six and one sixth miles west of here," said the globe.

"How long ago did he live in this lighthouse?" asked Jane.

"Communication with the block keeper ceased two years, six days and eleven hours ago," said the globe.

"That's relatively recently," whispered Jill.

"It is two years, six days and eleven hours," said the globe.

"We weren't talking to you," said Jill.

"Do you know what might have happened to your block keeper that would have broken off communication?" asked Jane who held her hand up in front of the globe to stop its reply to Jill.

"I believe the lighthouse was severely damaged, and the electric current to the fence ended at the same time."

"The fence?" Jill whispered.

"That's what I said," said the globe.

"Shut up you irritating piece of scrap metal!" said Jill.

"Why was there an electric fence?" asked Jane, again holding her hand up to the globe.

"It was originally a containment fence for the prison, but after the war it was used to keep the villagers safe," said the globe.

"Containment and safe are contradictory," said Jane as she turned to Isaac with a doubting expression.

"I do not understand what you mean," said the globe.

"Containment keeps someone in and safe keeps others out," said Jane. "But wait, did you say it was originally a prison?"

"Yes, before the war," said the globe.

"Do you know what happened to the prisoners?" asked Jane.

"No, I do not," said the globe.

"And you don't know what happened to Chandler when the lighthouse was damaged?" asked Isaac.

"No, I do not," said the globe.

"So something happened to the lighthouse, and consequently to Chandler..... and now we find there was an electric fence surrounding what used to be a prison," Isaac whispered to Jane.

"Perhaps the village is made up of the prisoners, especially

63

if an electric fence still somehow exists after two centuries," said Diedre.

"Should I comment on that?" asked the globe.

"No!" said Jill.

"We're obviously going to have to go over there," Jane whispered back holding up her hand to keep the globe from replying to Jill.

"Over where?" asked the globe.

"Stay out of our discussions, balloon head!" said Jill.

"So Chandler told you about the fence?" asked Jane, again holding up her hand.

"Yes, but he said it was now used to protect the villagers, not contain them," said the globe.

"The term villagers implies a relatively primitive existence," Jane whispered while holding up her hand to the globe to keep it from answering her.

"Globe, if the fence was to protect the villagers, what was it protecting them from?" asked Isaac.

"From the Controllers.... and, if I may correct you, I am not 'globe', I am the Blockmaster," said the globe.

"Blockmaster.... sorry," said Isaac.

"Apology accepted," said the Blockmaster.

"Who are these Controllers?" asked Jane.

"Only the block keeper knows about the Controllers," said the Blockmaster.

"And the block keeper may actually be dead," said Jane.

"I do not know if he is dead," said the Blockmaster.

"I think the fence was more likely to keep these villagers in rather than protect them from these so called Controllers," said

Jane.

"The fence was to protect the villagers," said the Blockmaster.

"Don't you get it, we weren't talking to you!" said Jill.

"But I can hear," said the Blockmaster.

"Can I turn this annoying thing off!" said Jill.

"I am not an annoying thing, I am Blockmaster."

"Jiilllll," said Isaac, gently taking her by the elbow and nudging her toward the exit.

"Let's get out of here, this thing is creeping me out," said Diedre.

"I am not thing, I am the Blockmaster," said the Blockmaster. Jane placed her hand over Jill's mouth as they moved toward the exit. Jill flashed the Blockmaster the finger on their way out.

"I can see your signal but I do not know what it means," said the Blockmaster, it's voice echoing up the curved hallway.

"It means screw you!" Jill shouted back.

"Screw? I'll have to look that up in this context," said the Blockmaster as the door shut.

"With this scorched Earth scenario, everything may seem bizarre, but a lot of what we find from now on could be a bit bizarre," said Jane once they were outside.

"Here we are, a colony from another planet, and we think what we find here is a bit bizarre?" asked Diedre.

"Welcome to Hotel California," said Isaac shaking his head.

"I'm not even going to entertain that," said Jane, shoving Isaac in the shoulder. "Now, I'd like to know who controlled the current to the electric fence and how and why it is still on after two centuries. And finally, whether Chandler is still alive."

"For one thing, Chandler had to be successful with his

immortality experiment if he managed to be here until two years ago, " said Diedre.

"Yes, and he was living in a lighthouse twenty six miles up the coast, but obviously he was in touch with the Blockmaster all of this time," said Jane.

"He was also involved in some kind of fenced-in existence with the villagers," said Diedre.

"Let's get over there and find out," said Isaac.

"Wait, I have a few more questions for the Blockmaster.... but Jill, you stay here," said Jane, who turned and went back inside.

"I have a few more questions, Blockmaster," said Jane as she entered his room.

"What questions?" the Blockmaster asked.

"What else do you know other than the lighthouse was damaged, the fence lost its electricity, the Controllers set down rules to follow, a group of survivors of unknown origin live in a village, and Chandler has not spoken to you in over two years?" asked Jane.

"Those are a lot of things to try to remember," said the Blockmaster.

"You're a computer," said Jane.

"I am the Blockmaster," it replied.

"Just tell me what you can beyond those things or I'll bring Jill down here," said Jane.

"You mean the one who called me names and wanted to screw me?"

"She's the one," said Jane who had to put her hand over her mouth to keep from laughing.

"Alright, I will try.....from what I heard Chandler speak of, he

66

had created what I would call a religion for the villagers to follow. It was for the purpose of enforcing Controller rules. He used the fence that was previously used for a prison to contain the villagers. In my opinion, if I may express it, the villagers were descendants of the prisoners that were there before the war. Chandler was attempting to protect the villagers from Controller reprisals should the villagers violate their rules," said the Blockmaster.

"That's very good, Blockmaster," said Jane.

"Thank you, I try," said the Blockmaster.

"Do you know what these rules were?" asked Jane.

"I do not."

"Do you know where these Controllers came from?" she asked.

"I do not, but one of them came here about one hundred eighty years ago and spoke with Chandler to notify him of these rules."

"Do you know where this person came from?" asked Jane.

"No, I do not."

"What did she say?"

"She just told him the rules that any survivor must follow."

"And do you remember the rules?"

"No."

"You're a computer, so you should have that in your record."

"I did not record that."

"OK, so you've been here for two hundred years and have been in contact with Chandler the whole time?" asked Jane.

"He came here about six months before the war with two assistants," said the Blockmaster.

"Where are the assistants now?"

"They went to the lighthouse with Chandler and I have not seen them since then."

"Thank you, you gave me a good deal more information than you did initially, but I'm surprised you don't know even more," said Jane.

"I am only human," said the Blockmaster.

"You're not human, you're a big steel ball with funny lights," said Jane.

"That's harsh," said the Blockmaster.

"Is there anything else that you haven't told me?" asked Jane.

"Yes, there are four others who live outside the fence," said the Blockmaster.

"How long have they lived there?"

"As long as my block keeper"

"So that means they're immortal too," Jane whispered to herself while holding up her hand to the globe to prevent him from replying.

"My block keeper says these four women have vast stores of books that are considered a threat to the villagers," said the Blockmaster.

"OK, they're women, but I don't understand why the books would be a threat," said Jane.

"The villagers must not become knowledgeable," said the Blockmaster.

"Alright, so one of the Controller rules is that they are not allowed to read books," said Jane.

"What you say makes sense," said the Blockmaster.

"Books are an obsolete way of storing knowledge," she again whispered to herself.

"I did not know that," said the globe.

"You're not supposed to listen to my whispers," said Jane.

"I'm sorry, I have very good hearing," said the Blockmaster.

"Apparently Chandler needed the villagers to remain ignorant in order to have them comply with the rules of the Controllers," she mumbled even quieter.

"I do not know the specific rule, but again, that seems to make sense," said the Blockmaster.

"You're listening again," said Jane.

"But I can hear your questions," said the Blockmaster.

"So if a survivor from the village managed to cross the fence and become educated by reading, it would violate the rules and upset the bliss of the villagers' ignorance," said Jane.

"Should I try to answer that?" asked the Blockmaster.

"If you can," said Jane.

"I cannot, but what you say sounds logical," said the Blockmaster.

"Thank you, Blockmaster, you have been very helpful," said Jane who quickly turned and went back up the hallway and out to the shuttle where they were soon airborne and heading west up the coast.

Chapter Six

"That's a satellite," said Holly as she watched on a remote monitor in the ship's Dome Café.

"It is, and did you notice how it turned to follow us, and even stayed with our rotation?" asked Fan.

"That's quite sophisticated in a world showing few signs of modern technology," said Holly.

"Right, and since China seems to be the only surviving country, this satellite has to be Chinese..... right?" asked Fan.

"That makes sense, but what if it's American?" asked Holly.

"Based on what we've seen down there, that would be a low probability," said Fan.

"I know, so we're most likely being followed by a satellite that is Chinese, but for what reason?" asked Holly.

"Let me see if we can talk to this satellite," said Fan who went to a console and returned with a small device.

"Try English first," said Holly.

"We are the Chinese youth that the American Shannon kidnapped two hundred years ago, and we have returned to Earth from outer space," said Fan.

There was no response. Fan repeated the message in Chinese. Again, there was no response as the satellite continued to smoothly follow their rotation as if it were suspended by a magnetic force.

"A landing party from our ship is now in America on the West coast exploring a structure where we saw a light," Fan continued, also in Chinese.

"You must not interfere with our equipment on those structures," came a mechanical reply in perfect English.

"How should I respond?" asked Fan after switching off the device. Holly flipped it on again.

"We have returned to Earth to restore our immortality, and we come in peace," said Holly. There was a long pause as they waited for a response.

"The structures with our lights are large metal blocks designed for immortality, so is that what you came to look for?" came the reply.

"No, the blocks have a different form of immortality," said Holly. "Ours is located in a secret lab."

"You say you are the teens who were kidnapped two hundred years ago," came the reply.

"We are," said Fan.

"Then, if you are immortal, you are still teenagers?" asked the satellite.

"Yes we are, except for six of us who had our immortality chips turned off," said Fan. There was no response.

"The metal blocks in America where you have installed lights contain the electronically stored minds of people, not their bodies," said Holly when there was no reply after several minutes.

"Can you submit names of the Chinese youth who were kidnapped?" came the reply.

"Of course," said Fan.

"Wait...... can you remember everyone's full name?" whispered Holly.

"Sure," Fan whispered back. She then began a long list of over twenty Chinese names, and when she was finished they waited for a response.

"These are our missing youth," said the satellite after a lengthy pause.

"Six among us, including two of the Chinese youth, have returned to Earth to restore our immortality," said Fan.

"Where did you stay in outer space?" asked the Satellite.

"On a planet named Eden, four light years from Earth," said Fan.

"That would take many decades of travel to reach," said the satellite.

"It took five decades to reach, but on our return, we flew at twenty percent the speed of light, so it only took a little over two decades," said Fan.

"That is possible," said the satellite after a momentary pause.

"We must find the American abductor, Shannon's lab, where her immortality process was developed so we can restore the immortality of our six people," said Fan.

"I think that may be too much information," said Holly, who smothered the device with her hand.

"Why? I think they understood our explanation of who we

are and even verified the names," said Fan.

"I know, but the ability to immortalize people has to be quite valuable to them if they were to figure out how to use it," said Holly, who took her hand off the device.

"We do not know the exact location of Shannon's lab, and that is what our people on the surface are looking for," said Holly.

"Our records show that at one time we had someone guarding Shannon's lab in the US state of Colorado," said the satellite after a short wait. Holly and Fan looked at each other in surprise.

"They know where her lab is!" said Fan after covering the device.

"That's great because I was Shannon's assistant and even I had no idea where it was," said Holly.

"So they can take us there," said Fan.

"Then do we show them how to do the immortality procedure?" asked Holly.

"I don't know, but we really have no choice, do we?" asked Fan.

"I suppose not," said Holly.

"We'd be happy to meet with you at the lab if you'll give us the coordinates," said Fan after lifting her hand.

"We will send you the location, and a detail will meet you there at your convenience," came the response.

"Thank you, we'll get back to you to arrange a time," said Fan, shrugging again as Holly nodded her approval. They looked at each other and when they looked back at the monitor, the satellite had disappeared.

"Doesn't 'detail' sound military?" asked Holly.

"Yes, but they seem to be pretty much in control of things,

so whatever they send, they send, and we'll just have to deal with it," said Fan. Holly nodded.

Chapter Seven

"It looks like that lighthouse didn't fare too well during the war," said Isaac as they hovered over the lagoon in front of it.

"There are two structures back there that we passed with no apparent damage, so I wonder if that's where the four women live?" asked Jane.

"What women?" asked Jill.

"The Blockmaster said there were four women living across the fence."

"Oh, OK, so let's go back and see if we can find them," said Jill as she maneuvered the shuttle back toward the structures. When they arrived, no signs of life could be seen. So they flew back and forth, eventually finding a large abandoned village of huts out in the forest.

"Look, I see smoke over the hill," said Diedre, pointing west. Jill headed in that direction and as they crested the hill a complex of six structures came into view with clear signs of human activity.

When the people in the complex spotted the shuttle approaching they scattered and eventually everyone was inside. Jill landed the shuttle in a courtyard in front of what looked like the main structure. A man and a woman walked out to greet them and Isaac made his way down the ladder as the couple reached their shuttle. Jane stood in the shuttle doorway.

"Welcome, whoever you are," said the woman.

"We're from a group that went into outer space two hundred years ago," said Isaac who was not sure what to say.

"Oh my god! You're kidding.....you're from the Shannon kidnapping?" asked the man excitedly. The woman turned and waved for those in the building to join them. Soon the shuttle was surrounded by a throng of people.

"Most of us are still up in orbit in our ship," said Isaac, pointing to the sky. Jane had now come down and was standing with Isaac. Diedre was on her way down the ladder. Jill stood in the doorway.

"So, what, four of you came down to check things out?" asked the man.

"Yes," said Jane. "I'm Jane, and the handsome gentleman next to me is my husband Isaac, and that's Diedre. That's Jill up there," said Jane, pointing.

"I'm Luke and this is Ellen," he said, grasping Jane's hand and smiling for the first time.

"Of course, Luke....and Ellen...... remember me?" said Diedre who was now on the ground.

"Diedre, oh my god, yes, but you look older than you were, so what happened?" asked Ellen.

"Shannon turned off my chip twenty-five years ago," said

Diedre.

"What the hell was that about?" asked Luke.

"We have no idea," said Diedre.

"Did she come back with you?" asked Luke.

"No, Jane killed her," said Diedre. Luke looked at Jane with eyebrows raised.

"Hey, it was an accident," said Jane.

"She probably deserved it, right?" asked Ellen.

"She definitely did," said Isaac.

"This looks like a reunion," said Virg who had worked her way through the crowd with Lucinda.

"Hi guys," said Diedre.

"So, what is going on here?" asked Jane.

"Welcome to Hotel Paradise," said Ellen, gesturing back to the buildings.

"We understand this was apparently a prison at one time," said Jane.

"Yes, and it's now home to everyone who lived in this area since it's the only place with electricity, water, sewer and relatively comfortable accommodations," said Ellen.

"So there's obviously a very long story to explain how you all ended up here," said Jane.

"Yes, a very long story," said Luke.

"We stopped at the block before we came here looking for Chandler," said Jane. "Is he here?"

"No, he died when Jake blew up the lighthouse," said Luke.

"Jake did that to the lighthouse?.....so who is Jake?" asked Jane.

"He's a ten year old who had us get a tank from a museum

and drive it to the lighthouse to blow it up so the villagers could be freed from an oppressive religion," said Luke.

"Oh my god, and we thought living on a distant planet was unbelievable," said Jane. "Some day I want to hear the whole story about that little episode."

"We were hoping to talk with Chandler about Shannon's lab," said Isaac.

"The Blockmaster said he hadn't heard from him in over two years, so that explains what happened," said Jane.

"Blockmaster?" asked Luke.

"The talking beach ball from Lucas's eternity block," said Jill from above.

"I've never been in one, but Ed has," said Luke.

"Ed?" asked Isaac.

"The gentleman way back in the crowd that is two heads higher than anyone else," said Luke.

"More for us to learn about this place," said Jane.

"Well, it's all turning out for the best here in this area as you can see," said Luke, gesturing to the complex.

"Yes, but what about the Controllers?" asked Jane.

"Oh, so you know about those," said Luke.

"Yes the beach ball filled us in," said Jane. "Apparently you can't read books. But that was the only rule we know about. Apparently there are a number of other rules," said Jane.

"Yes there are, including a maximum of one hundred fifty people in a village," said Luke.

"Uh, well, it looks like you may have broken that rule rather handily," said Isaac, looking out at the crowd.

"I know, but we haven't seen these Controllers, and they have never shown up here in two hundred years," said Luke.

"Wow, the more we find out down here, the stranger it gets," said Diedre.

"Did it begin with your shock to find most of the planet in ashes?" asked Luke.

"Yes, we did know there was going to be a war, but nothing could have prepared us for what we found," said Jane.

"So where did you go when you flew off into space?" asked Luke.

"We settled on a planet in a nearby star system, and after a hundred twenty years there, Shannon decided to erase the chips on six of us," said Jane. "So we came back to get our immortality restored."

"Did she tell you why she did that before you whacked her?" asked Luke.

"It was an accident," said Jane. "I just slammed her with my feet and she broke her neck when she hit the wall,"

"Oh my god.....remind me never to get on your bad side," said Luke.

"Her description sounds a lot worse that it really was," said Isaac.

"No, that's pretty much what happened," said Jill.

"Alright, but it was still unintentional," said Isaac.

"She tried to destroy our ship so I had to stop her," said Jane.

"I promise never to do that," said Luke, holding up his hands.

"Jane is actually a kind and gentle person unless you piss her off," said Isaac.

"Trust me, I will never piss her off," said Luke. "Sooo, you came back to Earth to get your immortality restored."

"We did, and we managed to add twenty-five years to our ages in the process," said Isaac.

"So will you get new chips, or what?" asked Luke.

"We don't really know...... we might even be able to reactivate ours," said Jill.

"I'm not sure that I can help you much on that count, but maybe you can start at her lab where we were all immortalized," said Luke.

"That's kind of what we were thinking and why we thought Chandler might know since he once worked with her," said Diedre. "We all know it's near Colorado Springs, but exactly where is a mystery."

"I'm no help either," said Luke.

"Everyone who went there had to come at night and we were not told exactly where we were," said Diedre.

"So now, finding that lab is one of our missions, but first we'd like to know more about what's left of the planet," said Jane.

"Well, I've been living here in this isolated area for two hundred years and I've never seen anyone from the outside, so I'm clueless," said Luke.

"We've not seen anyone either," said Ellen. "Although we saw an aircraft pass by a hundred sixty years ago."

"Well, other than lights on the blocks, and wiffs of smoke that might be from campfires, we haven't seen any signs of modern life in America," said Jill. "But we did see evidence of civilization in China."

"China..... interesting," said Luke. "I thought the kidnapped kids were all Chinese, but I see only Jane is," said Luke, pointing.

"Most of us are Chinese," said Jane. "It was a Chinese ship, even though it was touted as an international effort. I came to the camp from China, but my mother raised me in America where she remained during the war. She sent me there before the war and I'm sure she never knew that I was sent to Space Camp by the Chinese government. I have no idea what happened to her, but after what I see, my hope of ever seeing her again seems quite slim. Isaac and Jill were teens from America, and Diedre is a scientist from Zimbabwe and was one of Shannon's associates."

"You said it looked like China was the only country with any semblance of modern civilization," said Ellen.

"That's right, and after hearing about these so-called Controllers, I suspect they are in fact the Chinese who decided to establish rules after the war to keep survivors from doing something like this again in the future," said Jane.

"So, if I understand this correctly, Chandler's intent here inside the fence, was to make sure the strict rules of these Controllers were enforced," said Isaac.

"Yes, but his effort was hardly a model for the rest of the world, so I doubt if it would have been practical to apply on a worldwide scale," said Luke.

"But at least the Controllers stayed away to let it work," said Isaac.

"However, you have no way of knowing whether the Chinese, aka the Controllers, ever really enforced their rules in the first place," said Jane.

"I guess that's true, because we have yet to see them, other than that one visit to Chandler way back in the beginning," said Luke.

"Getting back to our situation...... we have a ship full of two hundred year old teenagers up in orbit and we're supposed to be on a reconnassance mission to find out what's down here so we can figure out what to do," said Jane. "At some point soon, we have to get in contact with the ship and discuss what we're going to do next, because they can't just stay up there in orbit."

"Bring them here," said Ellen. "We have plenty of room."

"Well, I guess it's the only semi-modern civilization of which we've seen evidence in this part of the world, but we don't want to impose on your little paradise," said Jane.

"It's no imposition, and we would be honored to have you," said Ellen.

"Absolultely," said Luke. "But one other thing you should know...... we are no longer immortal."

"Really, tell me more," said Jane.

"Well, let me start at the beginning," said Luke. "Before he was immortalized, Ed brought Chandler to Lucas's block and then to the lighthouse. Ed established a communication link for Chandler between the lighthouse and the block. Ed then returned to join us at the immortalization party at Shannon's lab. The four girls, Ed and I then moved here a few months before the war, bringing one activation device with us. It initially ran on batteries, but needed permanent power, and we knew that the lighthouse had power, so it would have to be located there. Ed and I worked for Chandler so we moved into nice apartments upstairs in the lighthouse. Ed gave Chandler the activation device for safe keeping. This turned out to be a huge mistake because he hid it and later used it to force us to do his bidding, with the threat that he would turn it off if we didn't do what he wanted. After the war, his block was visited by someone who said they represented what he referred to as 'The Controllers'. He coined that moniker. Chandler apparently struck a deal with this visitor that involved a guarantee that he would enforce their rules locally if they would leave this area alone. So he established a kind of pseudo-religion to carry out their rules. Ed and I worked for him and we helped him manage this religion. Ed was the enforcer, and I was the teacher of the children. That went on until a couple of years ago when the lighthouse was seriously damaged and the electricity cut off. It took Chandler's power away, but it also disconnected everyone's activation device. Without power for his immortality machine, Chandler died along with our activation device. Incidentally, we have never found that device. So, long story short, the six of us are no longer immortal."

"Can I ask how far the girls lived from the lighthouse?" asked Jane.

"Maybe five or six miles," said Luke.

"And did you feel changes when you say you lost your immortality," asked Isaac.

"Changes? Like what?" asked Luke.

"You would feel quite different if you lost your immortality," said Jane. "For some of us, it was dramatic to say the least." Jane looked at Isaac who gave her an animated nod.

"I haven't felt anything different," said Luke.

"Neither have we, as far as I know," said Ellen, looking at Virg who shook her head.

"According to Shannon, the maximum range for the activation device is one mile," said Isaac.

"One mile.....wait.....what?" asked Luke.

"Which means there are two possibilities here and only one is possible in your case," said Jane. "The first is that there is no need for an activation device and you're still immortal. And the second is that you were never immortal in the first place."

"Oh, we were definitely immortal, otherwise I'd be two hundred and thirty years old," said Luke.

"Then it's case one, and you're still immortal," said Jane.

"Which means the device was just another of Shannon's methods of controlling people?" asked Isaac.

"Wait.....you mean you've been fooled all these years as well?" asked Ellen.

"We have," said Jane.

"I've always had doubts about the need for that device," said Diedre.

"I know, so have I," said Jane.

"Why didn't we think of this before," said Diedre.

"I don't know, I guess a lot was happening and it was just a given," said Jane.

"Well, in my case, I trusted her since she developed this immortality process and knew all about it," said Diedre. "Plus, I thought we were friends."

"I have no such excuse and should have seen through it long ago, but its existence really did make sense technically," said Jane.

"That's true, it did," said Diedre.

"So, we were all deceived for two hundred years?" asked Jill.

"And we're still immortal," said Luke.

"In your case, yes, in our case, no," said Isaac.

"This also means that our so-called 'health machine' is actually a device that we know can deactivate chips....... but perhaps it can also reactivate chips," said Jane.

"Wait.....so we can simply re-activate our chips?" asked Isaac.

"Maybe, but the only flaw in that assumption is the fact that we don't know how to use that machine," said Diedre.

"Then our search here on Earth should now focus on finding an instruction manual for that damned thing," said Isaac.

"For the past two years, I've been mentally preparing for the day I will die," said Luke.

"So have we," said Ellen who began to laugh.

"It's too bad we didn't figure this out before I became a senior citizen," said Diedre.

"Look, there's relief from knowing that I'm still immortal, but I'm feeling guilty about indoctrinating children into a life of ignorance for over a hundred eighty years," said Luke.

"Perhaps you helped these villagers survive in a world protected from itself by the Chinese, aka, the Controllers," said Jane.

"Protected from itself.....that's interesting.....I never thought about it like that," said Luke.

"However, keeping a village of people in relative ignorance and not allowing them to live normal lives is definitely a form of cruelty, despite the ultimate benefit of such rules," said Jane.

"Wow...... this trip to Earth has been a surprise a minute, so I wonder what else we'll discover on our little adventure here," said Isaac.

"I don't know. We still have a long way to go, Isaac," said Jane.

Chapter Eight

"**J**ane, we have some issues up here," said Holly from the control pod after making contact with her.

"What kind of issues?" asked Jane.

"It looks like the Chinese are in complete control of things down there," said Holly.

"Yes, we've arrived at the same conclusion," said Jane.

"Really, OK, but there's more," said Holly.

"Tell me," said Jane.

"One of their satellites came to our ship, hovered outside and we communicated with them," said Holly.

"What did they say?" asked Jane.

"When we introduced ourselves, they looked us up and knew who we were," said Holly.

"That's very good news," said Jane.

"They also knew about Shannon's lab and actually could meet us there with a detail," said Holly.

"A detail?" asked Jane.

"I know, isn't that kind of military sounding?" asked Holly.

"Yes, and how would they know about her lab and where it is?" asked Jane.

"I know, right?" said Holly.

"Well, actually, we may not need her lab," said Jane.

"We won't?" asked Holly.

"No, the health machine can reverse the immortality process, but we'll still need instructions on how to use it," said Jane.

"I like that news...... so, any other surprises down there?" asked Holly.

"Yes, and this is something both Diedre and I have always suspected.......we have never needed the activation device," said Jane.

"Oh my god, are you kidding me?" asked Holly.

"No I'm not and we're pretty sure it was just another of Shannon's control schemes," said Jane.

"Now that's the biggest surprise of all, and a definite game changer," said Holly.

"I know, so what else do you have to report up there besides a talking satellite?" asked Jane.

"Well, we've noticed a lot more semi-modern activity in China which suggests they have retained and/or developed at least some serious technological abilities, especially if that satellite is any indication," said Holly.

"Which suggests they intentionally ignored our earlier communications," said Jane.

"I know, and with what ulterior motive ?" asked Holly.

"I have no idea, but they're obviously a very capable entity," said Jane.

"I know, and after that encounter with the satellite, we're a bit nervous up here," said Holly.

"I hear you, so perhaps we need to shuttle everyone down sooner than later," said Jane.

"Could we make that sooner?" asked Holly.

"Of course, so how soon can you get everyone into a shuttle and get down here?" asked Jane.

"I could declare an emergency," said Holly.

"I'll leave that decision to you," said Jane.

"Then the only question left is: where are you?" asked Holly.

"It's an isolated area northwest of San Francisco along the coast," said Jane.

"What should I look for?" asked Holly.

"You'll come across one of Lucas's blocks, and we're about thirty miles past that," said Jane. "Just keep going until you see a complex of six buildings and probably a lot of people milling about."

"A lot of people..... interesting, so it's a real settlement..... anything else?" asked Holly.

"Yes, we talked with half a dozen people here who were immortalized by Shannon two hundred years ago, and they said they have not heard from anyone from the outside world in all that time."

"Wow, immortals, I may actually know them," said Holly. "But what does it mean they have not seen nor heard from anyone?"

"I'm not sure, but it does mean that this is a relatively safe area and may be a good place for the colony to stay for a while as we try to figure out what to do next," said Jane.

"Wait, it may be?" asked Holly.

"Well, they said that a man named Chandler had been warned by what he called the Controllers about a number of strict rules that survivors must comply with," said Jane. "We're now pretty sure these Controllers are the Chinese."

"What are you suggesting?"

"I'm suggesting that it's possible they may come here at some point to make sure this settlement is in compliance with these so-called rules," said Jane.

"Do you know what the rules are?" asked Holly.

"Only a few, including no book reading and no settlements over a hundred fifty people," said Jane.

"How big is that settlement?" asked Holly.

"A lot bigger than that," said Jane.

"I see, OK, but if nobody has shown up in all those years, do you think it's safe for us to add to the 'too big' issue?" asked Holly.

"That's the maybe part of it," said Jane. "But come down anyway."

"Alright, we'll be there as soon as we can," said Holly.

"Next time around?" asked Jane.

"Yes," said Holly.

"Whatever you decide," said Jane.

"Great, see you later," said Holly, who signed off, then turned to Fan who had her hand up as if to ask a question.

"I just noticed something that's quite alarming," said Fan.

"Oh no..... what?" asked Holly.

"We're losing altitude," said Fan pointing to the altitude

meter on the panel.

"That's impossible," said Holly who quickly studied the numbers and confirmed Fan's alert. At that moment a communication from the Dome Café came in.

"There's something attached to the nose of the ship," said Lian.

"Oh my god, they're taking us out of orbit!!!" Holly shouted.

"What are we going to do?" asked Fan.

"We have to act quickly!" said Holly.

"Fire up the engine," said Fan.

"I've never tried to do that, so I'm not sure if I even know how," said Holly.

"Well, then, doesn't this ship have wings that pop out so we can land if we have to?" asked Fan.

"Yes, but Jane says that's extremely risky, even if I knew how, which I don't," said Holly.

"Then what can we do?" asked Fan.

"Abandon ship," said Holly.

"You mean now?" asked Fan.

"Yes, now!" said Holly.

"I'll sound the alarm," said Fan who picked up the intercom and barked a command to immediately assemble in the shuttle bay for departure. She then hit the emergency alarm, sending a loud intermittent horn blast throughout the ship.

"I'll alert Lian, and try to call Jane and let her know what's going on," said Holly. She tried to re-establish contact with Jane but was unable to do that. She then made her way to the shuttle bay. When she got there most of the colony was already there, and within five minutes of declaring the emergency, they were all assembled.

"The Chinese put a tractor on our nose to slow us down and take us out of orbit, which means we could burn up on reentry, so we're abandoning ship," announced Holly as Lian arrived sporting an assault rifle with a large banana clip.

"Why are they doing this?" asked Lian.

"I have no idea, but they are," said Holly.

"Lee put our activation device aboard," said Lian.

"Well, according to Jane we won't need it anymore," said Holly.

"Say what?" asked Lian.

"I'll explain later," said Holly. "Now, let's all pile in and secure our safety harnesses." She said as she waved them all inside. A moment later the shuttle door opened and she hit full throttle. The shuttle shot out and they soon began reentry.

"So, we're not where we wanted to be in order to get down to Jane anytime soon, but where will we end up?" asked Fan who was trying to orient them as the ground was now visible through a thin layer of clouds.

"I'm not sure, maybe Kansas," said Holly who was studying the navigation screen.

"We'll have quite a trip to get back to California," said Fan.

"I know, but we had to bail fast," said Holly.

"Lian has some kind of machine gun or something," said Fan.

"I know, I asked her to bring it," said Holly.

"So how long will it take us to get to California?" asked Fan.

"Several hours at least," said Holly as she oriented them to the correct direction before speeding westward. It was some time later that a giant metal block came into view and she looked over at Fan who was now looking at her.

"Where are we?" asked Fan.

"Denver," said Holly.

"And what's that ahead?" asked Fan.

"One of Lucas's eternity blocks, the ones with the lights on top," said Holly.

"Are those lights part of the block design?" asked Fan.

"No, and the only one who could have placed them there is China," said Holly.

"You're not thinking about revenge, are you?" asked Fan.

"I am," said Holly.

"So, what, are you going to try to knock out these lights?" asked Fan as they drew nearer to the giant block.

"Yes, these are the things they warned us not to mess with," said Holly, who cruised to a hovering position near the block. It had a tower on top of the access structure with a light on it. The tower was slowly rotating on its base.

"Are you going to ignore the warning?" asked Fan.

"They shot down our ship, so I don't much care about their warning," said Holly.

"This is a bad idea," said Fan.

"I'm sure it is," said Holly as she settled to a landing on the roof.

"It's not too late to change your mind," said Fan.

"Lian, are you ready?" asked Holly.

"Oh no, she has that machine gun," said Fan as she glanced back and saw Lian approaching with her assault rifle.

"It's not a machine gun," said Lian.

"Don't do this!" said Fan, holding her hands over her face.

"I've waited a long time to try this thing out!" said Lian who stood at the door with her rifle. She shoved the clip in with a loud clank and then stood ready.

"Wait until the dust settles," said Holly.

"I'm ready," said Lian, putting her back to the wall.

"May I say again that this is a very bad idea," said Fan who was still holding her hands over her face.

"Are you sure that thing will fire, Lian?" asked Holly.

"I reloaded the bullets myself," said Lian.

"But have you ever fired it?" asked Holly.

"No, but I know the theory behind it," said Lian.

"Let's hope they don't have serious defensive weapons hidden somewhere," said Holly.

"OK, we're doomed," said Fan who continued to hold her hands over her face.

Holly flipped the lever to open the door. Lian stepped out quickly and climbed down the ladder. She began moving toward the center of the roof where the tower was located. Fan peeked cautiously through her fingers as Lian continued to patrol the rooftop. As she drew near the tower a drone appeared from behind the acess structure and a hail of something zinged past her. Lian dove to the rooftop and opened fire, landing armor piercing bullets on the drone. It flipped into a wild sequence of somersaults before disappearing over the side of the block. She rushed to the edge just in time to see a puff of dust as the drone ploughed into the ground below. She heard noise behind her and turned to see another drone, but was able to get off a burst before the drone could line up on her. The drone spun into a curve and crashed hard into the base of the tower with metal pieces flying out like shrapnel in every direction. The light tower made a grinding noise before stopping dead.

"We'd better get out of here!" Fan shouted after turning to Holly.

"I need to take out that light," said Lian who aimed at the light on top of the tower. One shot sent glass flying and the light went out.

"Oh my god," said Fan.

"OK, I'm in, let's go," said Lian after climbing back into the shuttle a moment later.

"One down," said Holly who slowly lifted off and aimed west.

"What do you mean, one down?" asked Fan.

"There were seven, so six to go," said Lian.

"Six to go? Oh my god!" said Fan.

"Let's see, maybe Taos is next," said Holly.

"Let me off......I'll walk the rest of the way," said Fan.

"You'd be eaten by a bear," said Holly.

"There are bears?" asked Fan.

"The drone's bullets were not really bullets, they were more like little pellets, or maybe beebees," said Lian.

"So they're not using deadly force," said Holly.

"Yet," said Fan.

"It could mean that this whole beacon thing with the light, including the drones, are for scaring people, not killing them," said Lian.

"Or, warning shots before they annihilate you," said Fan.

"Look, Fan, we would have died if our ship went down, so they deserve this," said Holly.

"But they knew we had shuttles to escape in since they must

have observed our first shuttle going down," said Fan.

"How would they know we had another shuttle?" asked Holly.

"They wouldn't," said Lian.

"But these light installations and drone guards are hardly deadly, they're just scarecrows," said Fan.

"Fine, but we need to show them we don't appreciate getting shot down," said Holly.

"This puny effort of yours is like a dog peeing on a tree," said Fan.

"So I'm like a dog peeing on a tree?" asked Lian.

"Yes, and animal control will be coming after you with a net," said Fan.

"Look, they need to know we won't go quietly," said Holly.

"Bring on the next tower," said Lian.

"We're all going to die," said Fan.

"Relax," said Holly.

"Relax? We're completely outmatched here since all we have is Lian's machine gun," said Fan.

"It's not a machine gun," said Lian.

"Maybe you need to think of some other way to exact revenge," said Fan.

"This is what we have, and we're going to use it," said Holly.

"Did you say Taos is our next target?" asked Lian.

"Yes, then Winterhaven," said Holly.

"And after that?" asked Lian.

"San Fran.....oh, wait, that's where Jane is," said Holly.

"Let's just do Taos and Winterhaven and make our plans from there," said Lian.

"You're right, besides, the posse is likely to be after us by then anyway," said Holly.

"Posse?" asked Lian.

"We're out west," said Holly.

"You realize of course that you have two dozen innocent bystanders on board watching a suicide mission," said Fan.

"Don't be a pessimist," said Holly.

"How can I not," said Fan.

A while later as twilight descended on the western horizon, the light from the Taos block twinkled ahead. They were soon making their approach. This time, two drones were already in the air and Lian stood with her back to the inside wall of the shuttle waiting for the door to open as they came in for a landing.

"Where are they?" she asked as she checked her rifle.

"Right outside the door," said Holly. Everyone in the shuttle was watching on the omnidirectional display that projected the outside on every wall of the shuttle.

"Open!" shouted Lian. Holly opened the door to a hail of pellets and Lian sprayed the air with bullets. Both drones spun into the roof in a cloud of dust and flying parts. She then aimed at the base of the monitoring tower and fired a burst. A loud grinding was followed by a screech as the unit stopped rotating. A single shot shattered the light.

"Two," said Holly, as she lifted off and aimed southwest.

"Where is Winterhaven?" asked Lian.

"Near the Mexican border in California," said Holly.

"You still have an opportunity to abort this craziness," said Fan who had now calmed down a bit and was speaking in a low matter-of-fact tone.

"Destroying their equipment, or going down there at night?" asked Holly.

"You know they'll come after us," said Fan.

"Of course they will, but we have Lian's machine gun," said Holly.

"It's not a machine gun," said Lian.

"Whatever," said Holly.

"This is definitely suicide," said Fan, shaking her head.

Chapter Nine

"**I** just spoke with our people in orbit and they're on their way here as soon as the ship comes around," said Jane after returning from the shuttle to the crowd.

"I'll have someone arrange for rooms and other accommodations for you and your people," said Ellen.

"Thank you, you're a lifesaver," said Jane.

"Finding out that the Controllers are really the Chinese is big news even though I have no idea what that means," said Ellen.

"Neither do I," said Jane.

"I guess it's not surprising since they were the only super power to declare their neutrality before the war," said Ellen.

"Holly did speak with them and they apparently know who we are," said Jane.

"Well, they haven't bothered to make themselves known to us in two hundred years," said Virg.

"We still have the tank, so we can defend ourselves if

necessary," said Jake who just arrived and overheard some of the conversation.

"As I said, that tank is nothing more than a lawn ornament," said Virg.

"It just needs a little cooking oil," said Jake.

"Are you the young man who blew up the lighthouse?" asked Isaac.

"I was part of it," said Jake.

"Well, that little event of yours apparently reshaped this entire area by bringing everyone together for the first time," said Jane.

"That was an unintended consequence, but I'll accept the credit nonetheless," said Jake.

"How modest of you, Jake," said Luke. "But I'll admit that your bold plan did change everything here for the good."

"Maybe I should become the mayor," said Jake.

"Please don't take him seriously," said Sarah.

"Can we take a step back back for a minute, Ellen?" asked Jill.

"Sure, what do you want to know?" she replied.

"You four women, Chandler, Ed and Luke came here before the big war to survive the aftermath, so I assume that you also survived the Yellowstone volcanic eruption in much the same manner," said Jill.

"Wait.....was that era of black skies and bitter cold caused by a volcanic eruption?" asked Ellen.

"Oh, so you didn't know....... yes, the damage from it was obvious from space," said Jill.

"Well, the four of us survived the big war in a bunker

below one of our buildings across what used to be the fence, and Chandler and his assistants, Luke and Ed, were secure in his lighthouse," said Ellen. "When the second event happened about forty years later, we just went undergroud again for a number of years."

"That second event dealt a serious blow to survivors," said Luke. "The sky went hazy and dark, their gardens did not produce and their dwellings were no match for the cold. I was at the school at the time and it was suspended during this period. I stayed in the lighthouse until it was safe to come out. The village suffered badly and almost disappeared completely. Many froze to death or died of starvation. Only about a third of the village survived. It was many years before it was back to where it is now."

"So why didn't they come to this place?" asked Jane.

"I think their memory of it was of a cold dark prison, but Ed did move some of them here. There was no food here either because the gardens would not produce very well, so he smuggled as much food as he could from his own food machine," said Luke. "But he could only support a few and he couldn't bring others from the village here because he couldn't care for them."

"And during this terrible time, Chandler continued to seek compliance with the Controller rules?" asked Jane.

"To some extent," said Luke. "But things were a little on hold for over five years."

"After this second climate event, did things go back to strict enforcement?" asked Jane.

"It did, until Jake brought it to an end with his tank gambit," said Luke.

"In Chandler's defense, his program for upholding their

rules, may explain why we have not seen hide nor hair of the Controllers," said Ellen.

"I suppose," said Jane. "Despite the inhumanity of having the villagers live in primitive conditions and follow very strict rules with severe punishments, it did accomplish that objective, assuming the Chinese remained interested in enforcing such rules," said Jane.

"That's the key question right now," said Ellen.

"But can I get back to our situation for a moment, since we do have to deal with the here and now," said Jane.

"Sure," said Ellen.

"OK, so, our little colony of space adventurers just spent twenty-five years traveling back here to Earth," said Jane. "But we find ourselves faced with the challenge of having to deal with the Chinese who are now aware that we're back."

"And don't forget, our little colony IS mostly Chinese!" said Lian.

"A point not to be missed," said Jane.

"Well, they have satellites, so they know where we are," said Isaac.

"Yes, but you're in an area they know has been complying with their rules," said Luke.

"However, did we jeopardize your status as good subjects by the mere fact that we came here?" asked Jane.

"I'm not sure why," said Ellen. "As Lian said, you are Chinese, so how could this reflect badly on us."

"Until they show up here, we really have no idea how they will react to any of this, including your violation of the village size rule," said Jane.

"I know, we're way out of compliance on that rule," said Ellen.

"And, because we're mostly Chinese, I wonder if they expect us to go back to China?" asked Diedre. "Some of us are not from China, so that might present an issue for us."

"I'd rather not speculate on any of this," said Jane.

"Look, if things kind of blow up, we could just stay in the ship," said Isaac.

"Well, for one thing, I'm not so sure we should assume that the Chinese are out to get us, or out to get you here for that matter," said Jane. "They know about you and Hotel Paradise, and they know who we are. Logically, one would think they should hang out a welcome home banner for us and an award of excellence for you."

"I know, but a lot has gone down since we left Earth two hundred years ago, so who knows what they think of us now, or you here in Hotel Paradise," said Jill. "After all, you have not heard one word from them in all this time."

"Whatever the case, the ball is in their court," said Jane.

"I'm not sure what that means," said Isaac.

"It means whatever happens is up to them," said Jane.

"Hey, I just follow this woman and do whatever she says and go wherever she takes me," said Isaac.

"That's OK Isaac, everyone in the colony does the same thing," said Jill.

"Actually, Isaac, I think her group of followers may have just increased by a few hundred," said Ellen.

Chapter Ten

"There it is," said Lian as the light from the Winterhaven, California block twinkled on the horizon in the darkness.

"Same plan," said Holly as they drew nearer.

"Right, same plan," Lian repeated as she stood with her back to the wall, rifle in hand, waiting.

"I'm just going to keep my eyes shut," said Fan.

"Are those dwelling units along the river?" asked Lian.

"It looks like a local population of survivors," said Holly who set them down on the rooftop. Two drones quickly appeared and were now buzzing outside the door.

"OK, go!" said Holly who hit the door button when they heard the rattling of pellets off the side of the shuttle. Lian swung into the open door and sprayed a curtain of bullets at the faint images hovering nearby. They literally exploded into pieces that flew in every direction, with most of the debris fluttering to the top of the block. She then trained her rifle on the monitoring tower and it was soon stilled and its light put out.

"I'm just about out of bullets," said Lian who removed her banana clip and was examining it.

"Wait......are those all the bullets you have?" asked Holly.

"It was a hobby," said Lian.

"But we started something," said Holly, hesitating when she noticed the lights from an approaching aircraft.

"Oh great, so now maybe we make a run for it," said Fan as they watched the aircraft grow closer.

"Well, I have a feeling about this, especially since I now see people beginning to gather around the block," said Holly.

"Is it a good feeling?" asked Fan.

"Yes," said Holly. "So, how many bullets do you have left?"

"Maybe half a dozen.....no....five...." said Lian, shoving the clip back into her rifle.

"OK, so why don't you put that thing down for now," said Holly.

"I can still defend us," said Lian.

"Maybe not," said Holly.

"I think we should try to outrun them," said Fan.

"No, I want to talk with whomever this is," said Holly.

"Then what we need is a white flag," said Fan.

"Relax," said Holly.

The oncoming aircraft came in for a soft landing on the block in front of them and they waited for someone to come out.

"Who is going to greet them, you or me?" asked Lian who had already hit the door button.

"Me...... now ditch the gun," said Holly who came to the open door and stood waiting. After a moment, a woman emerged from the aircraft and casually climbed down her steps and started toward them as if nothing had happened. She reached their plane and stood in front of the steps, looking up. In the light from the shuttles open door, the woman was clearly oriental.

"Do you speak English?" asked Holly.

"Of course, I was born in Frisco and have lived here in the west since after the war," said the woman.

"Then you're immortal," said Holly.

"Yes, but more about that later," said the woman. "My name is Janet."

"I'm Holly and this is Lian behind me," said Holly.

"I represent the Chinese government," said Janet.

"You're like the police or something?" asked Holly.

"Sort of," said Janet.

"Sort of yes, sort of maybe, or sort of no?" asked Holly.

"Well, what you've been doing suggests some kind of civil disorder, so one would expect police intervention, right?" asked Janet.

"Right, but you shot down our ship," said Holly.

"We what?" asked Janet who casually climbed their steps as if she were being invited into a friend's house.

"Well, one of your satellites got a bit frisky with our ship and was taking us out of orbit," said Holly.

"That doesn't make a lot of sense," said Janet.

"Look, we just returned to Earth after being gone two hundred years, so this is all new to us," said Holly.

"Oh my god! Wait! Are these the teens that Shannon kidnapped?" asked Janet, who had wedged past Holly and Lian to look inside. Several of the teens waved to her with smiles.

"Yes, and obviously your leaders in China have not told you about us yet," said Holly.

"So they contact you?" she asked.

"Yes, and they said they knew who we were," said Holly.

"And they fucking shot you down!?" said Janet, looking at Holly with her mouth agape.

"They were taking us out of orbit and we had to abandon ship," said Holly.

"That's total bullshit!" said Janet.

"My sentiments exactly," said Holly.

"I can't offer an explanation," said Janet.

"I actually expected the Chinese government to be at least a little happy to see us," said Holly.

"Shit yes!" said Janet. "And I have no idea why in the hell they would do that!"

"We had no time to do anything but abandon ship since we would likely burn up on reentry, and that's not good," said Holly.

"I understand," said Janet. "And uh, OK, so you two are not teens."

"Shannon erased the chips on six of us, and I wasn't a teen, I was one of Shannon's associates," said Holly.

"Holly used to be forty at the time, and I was fifteen," said Lian.

"Thirty six," said Holly.

"Where are the other four who lost their immortality?" asked Janet looking around the cabin.

"They're up west of San Francisco," said Lian.

"One of Lucas's blocks is up there," said Janet.

"Right, they're near there," said Holly.

"So why did Shannon do that to you?" asked Janet.

"We don't know because Jane accidentally killed her," said Lian.

"Jane?" asked Janet.

"Jane is our ship's captain and queen of the colony," said Holly. "She was one of the Chinese teens."

"Queen? Jesus, I sure as hell didn't expect to encounter any of this when I came after you characters," said Janet, putting her hand on top of her head.

"Look, I was pissed, so I shot up a few of your lights," said Holly.

"I guess I would have done the same thing," said Janet.

"We're sorry," said Fan.

"Oh, yes, this is Fan," said Holly.

"Pleased to meet you," said Janet, nodding to Fan.

"Did your people in China ask you to arrest us?" asked Lian.

"No, but they told me what you were doing and just assumed I would put a stop to it," said Janet.

"And knowing what we were doing, you didn't come with gun drawn?" asked Holly.

"I have this, but have never used it," she said, taking an odd looking pistol that looked like a toilet paper roll with a handle.

"That looks really scary," said Holly with a shrug.

"It's actually supposed to be pretty potent, but I don't know for sure," said Janet.

"So I assume we're under arrest?" asked Holly.

"No, but consider yourselves stopped," said Janet.

"Well, Lian is just about out of bullets so we were pretty much done anyway," said Holly.

"Hey, all we did was shoot down six drones and disable three of your towers," said Lian.

"I can't imagine anyone being upset about that," said Janet.

"Compared to shooting down a spacecraft, it was like taking a lick of your ice cream," said Holly.

"I know, but using real bullets is forbidden worldwide," said Janet.

"It's just a hobby," said Lian pointing to her rifle that was now leaning against the wall.

"Maybe you should take up knitting," said Janet.

"You said no to an arrest, but I assume we are being detained?" asked Holly.

"That's a good term, detained, but Central thinks I have a jail, so I'm taking you there" said Janet.

"Is that where you take people who screw up?" asked Lian.

"There aren't that many people out here capable of screwing up so I've never actually had to take anyone to my jail," said Janet.

"Are there a lot of survivors out there?" asked Holly.

"There are, including those you see crowding around the block, but they're relatively primitive, with few if any modern conveniences, although I do have to collect up old guns from time to time," said Janet. "Surviving on the surface is extremely difficult without the technology that we had before the war."

"And China doesn't help survivors get back on their feet?" asked Holly.

"No, just the opposite, they would like to keep them in a primitive state," said Janet.

"How do they do that?" asked Holly.

"We make sure they have no weapons, no books or other educational material, and do not allow any really large settlements," said Janet.

"Are they actually able to enforce that?" asked Holly.

"No, so over the decades they've become extrememly lax in enforcing any of the rules that they initially established," said Janet.

"But they apparently enforced them long enough for most survivors to remain primitive?" asked Holly.

"I think that's generally true," said Janet. "So the presense of Chinese authority, like having those lights that you shot up, has given them the idea that they're still being watched."

"Which they're not," said Holly.

"Correct, there is virtually no monitoring or enforcement anymore," said Janet. "I just patrol around and try to scare people into believing I'm tough."

"This is your beat?" asked Holly.

"Yes, western north America," said Janet. "But we do have a company of soldiers down in Texas that occasionally come up to try to scare the shit out of anyone who gets out of line. I call them the Texas cowboys since a few of them wear ten gallon hats and wave pellet guns that look like real western six shooters."

"And the villagers buy it?" asked Lian.

"They've remained primitive and have been largely uneducated for a very long time, so most of them are easily spooked," said Janet.

"Do the Chinese themselves ever come out here in person to check on things?" asked Holly.

"Well, look, I'm Chinese, and when I fly in with that flying piece of shit over there and show my face, they think the Chinese have arrived to keep them in line," said Janet.

"So it's all a big bluff," said Holly.

"I know it is, and as long as I tell Central that everything is peaceful and compliant, and the Texas cowboys back me up, they seem happy," said Janet. "But under current circumstances with what you just did, and knowing that their long-lost teens are back from outer space, they might actually send someone out."

"I guess we'll just have to wait and see," said Holly.

"I'm sure they're wondering why you did what you just did," said Janet.

"Hello! They shot down our ship!" said Holly. "What's to wonder about?"

"Alright, that's very hard to explain," said Janet.

"We also need to get hold of Jane, because she's expecting us up in California," said Holly.

"That's going to be a problem, because I don't have any modern means of communication," said Janet.

"Nor do we," said Holly. "We have an antique VHF radio, which was actually just a collector's item. We do ship to ground with it. We dug it out of storage to use in this shuttle after its radio failed. However, Jane still has a modern radio in her shuttle. Unfortunately, we're way out of range for our antique radio to reach it."

"I have something akin to an old fashioned satellite email in my plane, which is how I communicate with Central, but I'm sure it isn't compatible with your equipment," said Janet.

"We probably have something in our ship, but not in our shuttles," said Holly.

110

"Well, maybe Debra has something," said Janet.

"Debra?"

"The place I'm taking you."

"You mean where Central thinks your real jail is?" asked Holly.

"Yes, because they'll expect us to be there if they do decide to come out," said Janet.

"You know, we knew there had likely been a nuclear war of global proportions, but we expected to find a lot more surviving civilizations," said Holly.

"The devastation was unbelievable, and the Chinese, being the only surviving nation, inherited what was left," said Janet. "They eventually made the decision to keep everything from ever getting back to where it was before the war. They decided to get rid of all weapons of war, stop any violence they found, and keep survivors from advancing technologically. So now what you find is what remains of the country of China essentially policing the rest of the world, trying to keep it in a relatively primitive state."

"That seems so wrong when you describe it, and yet, as you say, consider the situation they inherited," said Holly.

"I try not to second guess what they did, nor what they're now doing," said Janet. "Their effort to suppress progress started out experimental, but forty years after the war there was a hickup that revived their original suppressive effort."

"A hickup?" asked Holly.

"Someone stashed an arsenal of nukes here in America and attempted a nuclear attack on China," said Janet.

"Attempted?.....What happened?" asked Holly.

"The attack was aborted in time by someone you'll meet

soon, but unfortuanately China managed to send a big nuke into Yellowstone," said Janet.

"OK, so that's what caused the eruption whose damage we noticed from space," said Holly.

"But the fallout was worldwide, so China suffered too," said Janet.

"I guess it's a matter of survival of the fittest, just as Darwin suggested," said Holly.

"I'm sure that's how they saw it at the time, and it's now what I have to deal with," said Janet. "Besides, I have little or no influence over their worldwide strategy."

"Isn't policing the world nearly impossible?" asked Fan.

"It is impossible, but over the centuries they've actually done a remarkable job of ridding the world of weapons and keeping things quiet. However, they've largely abandoned any effort to enforce their rules. They still enforce the weapons ban, and frown on fights among settlements, but tend to ignore everything else."

"We don't have weapons..... well, except for Lian's gun, and we certainly didn't show any aggression," said Holly. "OK, after they zapped our ship, we did shoot down a few of their lights."

"After they shot down your ship," said Janet.

"The irony is that China actually built that spaceship!" said Holly.

"I know, that whole thing is crazy," said Janet

"I guess we'll just have to wait until we hear from them," said Holly. "Oh, and you're obviously immortal, but I don't remember seeing you at Shannon's immortalization camp," said Holly.

"That's because I was immortalized fifty years after the war," said Janet.

"Fifty years..... but how did you do that since Shannon was gone?" asked Holly excitedly.

"A handful of us did it in Shannon's lab," said Janet.

"So you're the one who knows where her lab is?" asked Holly.

"Yes, and the people you'll soon meet found it, including the instructions for how to immortalize." said Janet.

"So it's all still there?" asked Holly.

"Yes, the equipment is still in her lab and intact, but we were only able to find a half dozen chips, so only six of us could be immortalized." said Janet. "And there are no more chips that we know of, nor do we know how to manufacture new ones."

"Well, I spoke with Jane before we came down, and she says that a machine that was on our ship can probably re-activate our chips. OK, so maybe that possibility is now moot." said Holly. "The other thing she mentioned was that we don't need an activation device."

"Oh, we found that to be the case after reading the notebook of hers that Brady found," said Janet.

"Brady?"

"You will meet him too, along with Debra, at my non-jail, which is where we're going now," said Janet.

"I guess we have nowhere else to go right now, so your non-jail will have to do," said Holly. "However, we did agree to come down and meet Jane up in northern California so as I said, they'll have to be contacted at some point."

"We'll deal with that later," said Janet.

"So where is this jail of yours?" asked Holly.

"It's a very nice cave complex where those you will meet there have lived since before the war," she replied.

"Alright, so let's go, we'll follow you," said Holly.

******

"Holy crap! What's that!" shouted Fan as they followed Janet to a landing on a narrow shelf of a canyon. A giant robot stood beside the entrance to a cave.

"What the hell?" asked Holly who went to the door, but waited for Janet to get out of her aircraft before she did anything. Holly just stared at the robot as Fan and several others poked their heads around her to see.

"No worry, that's just Lucas," said Janet, who had hurried down her boarding ladder and walked to their ship to wave for them to follow her.

"You mean he is THE Lucas?" asked Holly, as she climbed down without taking her eyes off the eight foot tall metal giant. Others from the shuttle began to slowly trickle out, hesitating as they emerged to stare for a moment.

"It's a long story, but he's the one who aborted the nuclear missles that were aimed at China forty years after the big war," said Janet over her shoulder as she led them toward the cave entrance along the ledge.

"I'd like to hear more about that," said Holly after they stopped in front of the robot. Once everyone was assembled, Janet stepped in front of them and held up her hands to quiet the chatter.

"Two hundred years ago, Lucas here, who was a man at that time, led thirty people down into the cave we're about to enter to escape the devastation of the big war," said Janet. "They emerged forty years later, but Lucas managed to get himself into trouble with the Chinese. The Chinese had survived the war and were attempting to prevent another war by patrolling the world trying to remove weapons and stop aggressive activities. I worked for the Chinese establishment and led a patrol that was policing the western US. Lucas was out killing survivors who he said were trespassing on his eternity blocks. So I was after him. While on the lamb, he eventually interred himself into one of his blocks. He later came out as a robot. Actually, his mind was placed inside the robot, so, in effect, it's really Lucas in a metal uniform if you will. He, and a woman who had interred herself with him, left the block as robots and went to a secret military complex in Utah where they attempted to disable the capabilities of a rogue militant group that was inside. Lucas had colaborated with them in order to secure his cave so he knew who and what they were. He believed they would try to destroy China if it appeared as if the Chinese had invaded America. Based on the trouble that he himself had created as a result of his killing spree, he felt that it may well appear that the Chinese had taken over. During his effort to deactivate the capabilities of these militants, the militants managed to launch a nuclear assault against China. But the Chinese saw it coming and retaliated. Their retaliation was a single, but very large, nuke aimed at the Yellowstone super volcano. Even though Lucas was able to abort the missiles that were launched toward China, China was not able to abort their counter attack. The blast triggered an eruption which created a decade long sub-zero winter over much of the northern hemisphere. Myself and my crew hunkered down in the militant's cave to ride it out. Lucas and his friend in the other robot stayed here in this cave. The leader of the militants was banished to the surface and likely died, and we kept the remaining militants in the cave to help us operate their complex. Years later, after the effects of the eruption had dissipated, I and five others from here in this cave went to Shannon's lab. Using a notebook that they had found at one of Shannon's hangouts, we were able to find enough chips to immortalize ourselves. But there were only six chips. However, according to the notebook, we were led to believe that more chips existed. Unfortunately, we have never been able to find them, and over the years the other cave dwellers from both caves passed away, including all of my crew, the militants and all but six from this cave. Now, only us seven immortals and the two robots remain here."

"Who was in the other robot?" asked Holly.

"A woman named Jane who was the block keeper in the Jackson block that was subsequently buried in ash and lava from the eruption," said Janet.

"Oh my god, are you thinking what I'm thinking?" asked Holly, looking at Lian.

"Jane's mother?" asked Lian, holding her hand over her mouth.

"Jane's mother?" Janet asked. "Wait..... are you suggesting that the Jane over in California is our Jane's daughter?"

"I'm sure of it," said Holly.

"That's incredible," said Lucas as every eye immediately turned to the giant robot.

"Diedre and I were immortalized with your Jane two hundred years ago, and you assigned her to what was called the Jackson block," said Holly who had turned to Lucas.

116

"Yes I did assign her there, so you know her," said Lucas.

"Of course I know her," said Holly.

"Well, I knew she had a daughter, but she said she had sent her back to China before the war," said Lucas.

"She did, but our Jane was a child genius and because of that the government sent her to the teenage space camp, and she was on that spaceship that Shannon stole," said Holly.

"Oh my god, my Jane is going to go nuts!" said Lucas. "So, your Jane is in California?"

"Yes, west of San Francisco," said Holly. "However, she's not in a teenage body anymore since she was one of six of us whose chips were erased by Shannon. She's now physically Lian's age and is married to her sweetheart Isaac, and has a daughter, Dawn, who is with us now." Holly pointed and Dawn raised her hand.

"Wow, Jane is also a grandmother," said Lucas.

"She is," said Holly.

"So, since your crowd here looks like teens, Shannon obviously immortalized everyone before she took you off into deep space," said Lucas.

"Yes, it took us fifty years to get to Eden, which was the planet we lived on until we decided to return here," said Holly. "We were in a bit of a hurry coming back, so the return trip only took twenty-five years, but of course we aged that amount on the trip."

"Did Shannon come back with you?" asked Lucas.

"No, Jane accidentally killed her," said Holly.

"Oh my, she did?" asked Lucas.

"Shannon was trying to sabotage our ship," said Holly.

"Your Jane must be a tough cookie," said Lucas.

117

"You have no idea," said Holly.

"I think it's time to usher you down into the cave," said Janet.

"Yes, I'm anxious to see your jail and meet the other cave dwellers, including Jane's mom," said Holly.

"This entrance was just a hole when I first came here," said Janet. "Lucas enlarged it and improved the tunnel quite a bit in the last few decades."

"I wouldn't fit," said Lucas.

"Follow me," said Janet who started for the entrance, but Lucas reached out with his big hand and stopped her.

"You told them this was your jail?" asked Lucas.

"The Chinese establishment thinks it's my jail, you know....." said Janet who shrugged, then grabbed Lucas's big metal hand and pushed her way past.

"You always seem to have a hard time following rules, don't you Janet," said Lucas.

"Usually," said Janet.

Chapter Eleven

"They should have made it down here by now," said Jane who was staring at the eastern horizon.

"I know, it's been several hours and it's almost dark," said Isaac.

"That's not like Holly.....something's wrong," said Jane.

"Did you get anything, Diedre?" asked Isaac.

"Nothing," said Diedre returning from the shuttle where she had been monitoring the radio.

"OK, wait, there's movement coming over the hill," said Jake, pointing southeast.

"I don't.....oh yes, I see it," said Isaac.

In the distance, they could see a large aircraft with helicopter props at either end of its cigar-shaped body. As it grew nearer they could hear a loud thumping sound. It finally settled awkwardly a safe distance away at the far side of the field. A moment later, two uniformed men with big hats stepped out as the noisy engines were cut off and the props slowly whooshed to a halt. The two men were dressed in wrinkled western outfits and had holsters on their hips with pearl handled six guns. On their heads were large black ten gallon cowboy hats. No one moved as the men approached what was now a small crowd and came to a halt a dozen yards away.

"They look like Chinese cowboys, so I assume they represent China," whispered Isaac.

"That's what it looks like," said Jane quietly as she smiled and shook her head.

"Should I try Chinese?" Diedre whispered, looking at Jane who nodded.

"We are here on a peaceful mission," said Diedre in broken Chinese.

"Please deposit any weapons you might possess on the ground," said one of the men in perfect English.

"We have no weapons," said Jane.

"Will the passengers from the spaceship, please step forward," said the man. Isaac looked at Jane who smiled and shrugged, but waved them forward. Isaac, Jane, Diedre and Jill stepped forward and stood in a line a few yards from the men.

"Your friends have been aggressive," said the man.

"You mean our friends from the spaceship?" asked Jane.

"Yes, and they are now being detained," said the man.

"Detained? For what?" asked Jane, who then turned to Isaac with raised eyebrows.

"They have destroyed several of our light towers," said the man.

"They what?" asked Isaac in a loud whisper, looking at Jane.

120

"So where are they being held?" asked Jane.

"Our jail is in Utah," said the man.

"What do you plan to do with them?" asked Jane after a moment of thought.

"That is classified information," said the man.

"What about those in our spacecraft?" asked Jane.

"They are also being detained," said the man.

"What's going on here?" Isaac whispered.

"I don't know, but something doesn't make sense," Jane whispered back. " Chinese cowboys coming here in an ancient chopper that must have been rescued from a museum."

"What about our ship?" he whispered. Jane shrugged.

"Are WE being detained?" asked Jane.

"No, but you will stay here until we have resolved the situation," said the man.

"Are we staying here?" whispered Isaac. Jane looked at him with a smile and shook her head. By now, more people had migrated back out and the crowd was beginning to be very large.

"This whole thing is not all that threatening," Jane whispered back.

"But if all of our people are under arrest and locked up in Utah, and then these cowboys show up with guns on their hip, how is this not threatening?" Isaac whispered. Jane just shrugged her shoulders and smiled.

"OK, what remains to be resolved?" asked Jane, speaking to the men.

"Your intentions," said the man.

"Well, first of all, most of those you have in jail are Chinese," said Jane. "I'm Chinese, you're Chinese, so what's the problem?"

"You're the ones with the problem," said the man without explanation.

"Really, and what about our ship?" she asked.

"We have no information about that," said the man.

"That doesn't sound good," Isaac whispered.

"When can we be reunited with the others in our party?" asked Jane.

"We will let you know, but until then, you will remain here," said the man who abruptly turned and the two of them returned to their helicopter that was much in need of a paint job. It soon noisily started up and departed in a cloud of dust and debris.

"They didn't destroy our ship, did they?" asked Isaac.

"That would make no sense since they already acknowledged that they knew who we were," said Jane.

"So Holly apparently shot up a few of those lights we saw on Lucas's blocks, but why?" asked Isaac.

"That doesn't sound right either," said Jane. "And what's even stranger is that they haven't sent anyone up here in two hundred years, and now, suddenly they send two cowboys..... so there has to be a lot more to this."

"We're not going to stay here, are we?" asked Isaac.

"Are you kidding, we have to get to the bottom of this, and we can't do that by sitting on our thumbs," said Jane.

"OK, so I guess we're leaving for Utah immediately," said Isaac.

"Saddle up," said Jane.

"You do remember that they warned us not to leave," said Isaac.

"I thought it was more of a suggestion," said Jane. "Diedre, do you have any idea at all where this jail might be in Utah?"

"No, but each shuttle has a locator beacon, so if we head east for Utah we'll eventually pick it up," she replied.

"Assuming their shuttle is at the jail," said Isaac.

"We have to start somewhere," said Jane.

"It will be night before we get to Utah, so that might complicate the search," said Isaac.

"Night, day..... who cares..... let's go," said Jane who pointed to the shuttle and Jill lead the way toward it.

"I hate to be repetitive, but they did say not to leave here, sweetheart, and I don't think it was a suggestion," said Isaac as they began to climb up the ladder to the shuttle.

"Do you really want to stay here and worry about Holly and the girls, or do you want to go to Utah and get to the bottom of this?" asked Jane as they began to settle inside the shuttle.

"The second thing," said Isaac. "But Lian has the only gun that I know of and she's with Holly," said Isaac.

"We don't need a gun," said Jane.

"Alright, let's go find Holly and the others," said Isaac.

"We'll deal with whatever we have to deal with when we get there," said Jane.

"God I love you," Isaac laughed as he placed his forehead on her shoulder.

"Wait, I think we've attracted a crowd," said Jill who got up and returned to the door after hearing numerous voices outside.

"Oh boy," said Jane who had joined her there.

"Where are you going?" asked Ellen who stood with a very large crowd looking up at them.

"We're off to Utah on a rescue mission," said Jane.

123

"Are you coming back?" asked Ellen.

"That's a good question," said Jane. "It depends on what we find."

"That's the first time the Chinese have ever come here," said Virg.

"I know, it's big," said Jane.

"We want to go with you," said Ellen.

"We would like to come back," said Jane.

"Nonetheless, we want to come with you," said Ellen.

"This is just a rescue mission, not an evacuation," said Jane.

"We've kind of become attached to you since you got here, Jane," said Ellen. "And we're afraid you won't come back."

"Here's the deal, Jane," said Luke. "Most of the people here at the complex have lived here all of their lives. It's their home. Myself, Ed and the girls just moved here in the last couple of years. Sure, we like it here, but we're really different than the villagers. First of all we're immortal, so we're far older than they are. And we're well educated, maybe over educated. So when you showed up, it really changed our perspective. You were like us, and we've become very attached to you. You may not see it that way, but we do."

"No, we've become attached to you too," said Jane, looking at Isaac who nodded.

"So just us four girls plus Luke and Ed, that's six," said Ellen.

"I'm staying," said Ed.

"Then just five," said Ellen.

"You can't leave without Sarah and me," said Jake.

"You would leave your parents?" asked Ellen.

"They're a rather independent pair for ten year olds," said

124

Jake's father John. "We'll miss them, but it would be such an adventure for them."

"OK, so seven of us," said Ellen.

"But we have no idea what the Chinese have in store for us when we get to Utah," said Jane.

"Well, we might be able to help you deal with them since we're from what may have been their model community for complying with their rules," said Ellen.

"I never thought of that, but I guess that's true," said Jane. "But, you know, I'm wondering just how dangerous they are at this point, and I don't think they're really a threat to anyone."

"I have to agree," said Ellen.

"OK, climb aboard, but only you seven," said Jane. She then went to her seat next to Jill who was already seated, having anticipated Jane's decision. A few moments later, with everyone securely aboard, they lifted off, heading east. Jake and Sarah had never ridden on an aircraft like this before and they goggled at what they could see outside. Every wall was a screen and it gave them a panoramic view in every direction, from their feet to the ceiling and everywhere in between. It was as if they were riding on a magic carpet. The sun had just set behind them and the oranges and blues of twilight hung in surreal suspension as they sped over the landscape into the descending darkness.

Chapter Twelve

"**W**elcome.... I'm Debra," said Debra as she greeted Janet, Holly and the others at the cave's greenhouse. Everyone crowded into a large chamber of the cave that was green with vegetation from the floor to nearly the top of an amazingly high ceiling. Bright overhead lights glowed through a mist that rose from the vast jungle below. Beneath a backdrop of trees and vines was a seemingly endless crop of corn, squash, beans and fruit trees that were faded in the haze. This made the chamber seem almost boundless in size.

"Oh my god, this is an absolute world of wonder down here," said Holly, as she looked around in awe at its sheer size and splendor.

"I'm Holly," she continued as she finally stopped staring and stepped forward to shake Debra's hand. That was followed by a long series of introductions.

"It almost feels as if we're on a tropical island or something," said Fan as the group began following Debra out of the greenhouse.

"I could never have imaged anything like this in a cave," said Lian from behind.

"I overheard your conversation up there with Lucas, so I have some background, but please fill me in with the details," said Debra who was walking with Holly.

"I was one of Shannon's assistants and obviously not one of the teens," said Holly. "After a hundred twenty some years on Eden, Shannon decided to erase the chips on six of us. I was thirty something then, and now I'm sixtyish after the twenty-five year trip back from Eden. Lian was a teen so she's now almost forty. The rest are still in teenage bodies."

"Why did Shannon erase your chips?" asked Debra.

"We don't know," said Holly.

"And the others in your party are over in California?" asked Debra.

"Yes, in our other shuttle," said Holly.

"Well, you managed to get yourself in trouble with Janet," said Debra.

"I wish I could have done more damage," said Holly.

"I can't say that I blame you if they shot down your ship," said Debra. "But can you tell my why your entire group came back to Earth?"

"To get our immortality restored," said Holly.

"No, I know that, but why did everyone come back if only six lost their immortality?" asked Debra.

"Because there's no way that any of us would stay on that planet without Jane, Isaac, Holly and the others," said Fan who was now right behind them.

"Alright, so you're like a big family," said Debra.

"I think that's a fair description," said Fan. "We have each other's back, and we always will."

"Did you expect to find the Earth in this condition?" asked Debra.

"We knew of the impending war, but no, finding almost total devastation was quite a shock," said Holly.

"It was worse than anything we ever imagined when we finally emerged from this cave forty years after the war," said Debra.

"Forty years is a long time to wait in a cave, although this cave is pretty amazing," said Holly. "Did it take that long for things to be relatively safe to come out?"

"No, but Lucas was the king of the cave and he thought the feds would be waiting for him when he came out, so he said we couldn't come up for fifty years," said Debra.

"Fifty years, wow, so you mutineed?" asked Holly.

"We had to," said Debra.

"What about you Janet?" asked Holly.

"My parents sent me to China for safety before the war, and China sent me back about twenty years later to do what I've been doing ever since," said Janet.

"You were assigned here because you were born here and knew the territory?" asked Holly.

"I guess so, even though I was only eight when I left, so I wasn't that knowledgeable about the area," said Janet. "But there was nothing much left here to patrol anyway, so I'm not sure that my personal history would have been of much help even if I knew more about the area."

"So I guess we'll just have to wait to see what the big shots do," said Holly.

"Yes, and until then, everyone is welcome here in Janet's fake jail, even though you're the first prisoners to have ever been incarcerated," said Debra.

"OK, so here's the thing, our spacecraft was our lifeline, and something we've essentially relied upon one way or another for over two hundred years, so if it's gone we're in real trouble right now," said Holly.

"Hopefully it's not," said Janet. "And if Central actually comes here, it will be the first time since I've had this job, and that's a very long time."

"Having their teenagers return from outer space after two hundred years would seem worthy of an official welcoming, or even a celebration, wouldn't it?" asked Debra.

"It would in my mind," said Janet.

"I'm wondering what a visit from Central would even look like," said Debra.

"I know, China was somewhat in shambles when I left there a hundred eighty years ago, and a lot may well have changed since then," said Janet. "After having lived in China for twenty years, I've not met nor even spoken with anyone back there since I left. I send monthly briefings that are mostly lies or exaggerated crap, and they send out monthly directives, which I pretty much ignore. I'm essentially working for an invisible boss who rules rather loosely. And I police rather loosely."

"And you have no idea what Central may or may not do in our situation?" asked Holly.

"We've entered virgin territory here," said Janet.

"The great hall is just at the end of this hallway and we can discuss our options there," said Debra.

They entered to the great hall and everyone helped to arrange tables and chairs into one large makeshift table that everyone could sit around. Debra stood at one end and tapped two cups together to get everyone's attention. She introduced Brady, Casey, Riley and Mel. She then looked around before pointing to a giant robot across the room. The robot made its way to the table and stopped a few paces away.

"Alright, so, this is our Jane," said Debra, gesturing to the robot who already had everyone's attention.

"Jane's mother," said Holly, who stood up and walked over to the robot, extending her hand while craning her head up to look at the eight foot tall robot.

"I overheard your conversation with Lucas," said Jane the robot, reaching out with her iron hand and gently placing it on Holly's.

"I'm very pleased to meet you," said Holly.

"My daughter has very nice friends," said Jane.

"Your daughter has a fourteen year old daughter Dawn as you might have heard," said Holly who pointed.

"Oh my, she is so beautiful," she said after Dawn stood up and waved.

"And at this very moment, your daughter is waiting for me to arrive over in California," said Holly.

"I wonder if they could come here," asked Jane.

"Oh, right, I should have mentioned this before, but when I was dispatched, Central said they knew where your other shuttle had landed so if I had to guess, I'd say they sent the Texas cowboys up there," said Janet.

130

"For what purpose?" asked Holly.

"To warn them not to leave the area," said Janet.

"Oh, no problem, Jane will totally ignore that if they tell her we're here," said Holly.

"She would?" asked Debra. "That sounds like something I'd do."

"Oh my god, are you kidding, if they tell her we're here in jail, she'll be down here as fast as she can get into her shuttle."

"Without directions?" asked Janet.

"She'll find us," said Holly with a shrug.

"That's my daughter!" said Jane with a very unusual laugh that sounded more like a fart.

"OK, well, hopefully, she'll arrive before Central does, if indeed Central comes," said Debra.

"I'm sorry that we created such a stir," said Holly.

"You did what I would have done, so we'll just deal with the fallout," said Debra.

"I still think it makes zero sense for them to have shot down your ship," said Janet. "Their primary goal is to ban weapons and curb violence..... period..... not shoot down spaceships."

"Well, it was happening, so we had to abandon ship," said Holly.

"But here's the thing, they've spent countless decades searching the world, destroying weapons, so when someone shows up blowing their stuff to shreds, they want to shut it down immediately and then deal with the offender," said Janet.

"I understand, but we just got here, so we had no idea what was going on, and besides, what they did to our ship is a lot more deadly than a weapon like Lian's," said Holly.

131

"If that's what they did, I have to agree," said Janet.

"Do they have jails in China?" asked Holly.

"They do," said Janet.

"Well, we do have a capable shuttle outside and another one in California, so we can run," said Holly.

"Where would you run to?" asked Debra.

"That's right, there's nowhere to go," said Janet.

"Eighty percent of the world's population is just gone, so there really isn't a whole lot out there but scattered survivors living in relatively primitive conditions," said Debra. "And survival on the surface is extremely difficult. We tried it, and here we are, still living in this cave. Recreating technology is extremely difficult, so it's a matter of resurrecting whatever old technology you can find and trying to make it work."

"I guess China is the only place that's anywhere near normal," said Holly.

"In reality, nothing is normal anymore, not even China," said Janet. "It remains a shadow of its former self according to reports I've read. When you start over, you not only have lost the hardware and software, you've lost much of the experience needed to put humpty dumpty back together again."

"Alright, so we'll just wait to see what they'll do," said Holly.

"That's really our only plan right now," said Janet.

"I never thought I'd say this, but I wonder if we'd be better off back on Eden," said Fan.

"Perhaps, but without our ship, that's out now," said Holly.

"So maybe it boils down to a discussion of your terms of surrender," said Debra.

"Surrender, now that's a depressing thought," said Holly.

Chapter Thirteen

"Where?" asked Jill as she piloted the shuttle in darkness over the barren landscape lit only by a partial moon.

"Straight ahead," Diedre pointed. "The radar shows what looks like a valley, and the shuttle's beacon seems to be in there somewhere."

"Over there!" Isaac pointed as they came over a valley.

"Yes, two aircraft on that ledge, and one is our shuttle," said Diedre after Jill had come to a hovering stop and flipped on the searchlight.

"That looks like the entrance to a cave next to that statue," said Jane.

"There's not enough room on that shelf, so I'll land down below and we'll walk up," said Jill as she carefully maneuvered the shuttle down into the valley.

"That statue looks more like a robot," said Isaac as the shuttle slowly settled to the ground in a field of sage brush and bunch grass.

"A light on its head just came on," said Diedre. "I wonder what we're dealing with here?"

"The cave entrance is behind it," said Isaac.

"Well, everyone is now inside the cave, so let's get up there," said Jane who had jumped to her feet and was on her way out the door.

"Wait, that could actually be a robot guard, not a statue, and it looks big," said Diedre.

"Why else would it be standing there," said Isaac.

"Look, everyone is inside and had to walk past it, so big deal, let's go," said Jane who was already halfway down the ladder.

"Maybe we should let someone know we're here first..... what do you think?" asked Ellen.

"I'm following Jane," said Virg who quickly disappeared out the door.

"Wait up," said Isaac as he followed Virg down the ladder.

The three of them began working their way up the rock fall on a path that had been crafted into the rocks. Jake and Sarah were next to pop out of the shuttle and follow. The others cautiously came out, one by one, and were strung out along the path. Jane was first to reach the top. She walked up to the metal giant and stopped a few feet away, looking up.

"I'm Jane, and I'm looking for Holly, Lian and a gang of teenagers," she said as she studied the metal giant.

"You're Jane's daughter," said Lucas.

"What do you mean?" asked Jane.

"Your mother is inside," said Lucas.

"My mother? What are you talking about?" asked Jane, who

blinked and then looked back at Isaac. Isaac shook his head.

"She's inside along with Holly and the rest of your party," said Lucas, pointing to the cave entrance.

"You're what, the jail guard?" asked Jane who was not much more than half the height of Lucas.

"No, I'm Lucas, and right now I'm just a decoration at the entrance," he replied. "Oh, and this is not a jail, it's just Debra's cave."

"Wait, you're THE Lucas of eternity block fame?" asked Jane.

"At your service," said Lucas.

"And you're inside that big piece of tin?" asked Jane.

"Just my mind," said Lucas. "Uhh..... big piece of tin?.... very good, Jane.....so who's that behind you?"

"I'm Jane's husband, Isaac."

"And I'm Virg, if you remember me from Shannon's immortality party," said Virg.

"Right, I wasn't at the party as you know, but I did meet everyone in Tucson," said Lucas.

"So, your mind is controlling that robot?" asked Jane, staring up at him for a moment.

"Yes, and your mom is a robot just like me," said Lucas.

"Oh she is......OK.....that's interesting," said Jane, again looking back at Isaac who just shook his head again.

"It's a long story," said Lucas.

"So can we go in?" asked Jane, pointing to the entrance.

"Yes, but before you disappear into the tunnel, Jane, you might want to let me know who these folks are," said Lucas, pointing to the trail of people just reaching the top. Jake and Sarah were the first to arrive.

"We're survivors from the area near your block northwest of San Francisco," said Luke who arrived next and overheard the question.

"I put Chandler at that block," said Lucas.

"Yes, but unfortunately Chandler met with tragedy a couple of years ago," said Luke.

"I'm sorry to hear that, but not surprised," said Lucas. "Look, I know your whole story, Jane. You have a daughter Dawn who is inside, and six of you lost your immortality when Shannon erased your chips."

"You have it," said Isaac as Diedre joined them with the rest of the group.

"This is Lucas of eternity block fame," said Jane once everyone was on the ledge.

"Diedre, yes, I know you, and I know Ellen, Brit, Lucinda, and I've already met Virg.... Shannon's people.....and Luke who was with Chandler.... but who are these two youngsters?" asked Lucas, waving his giant finger over the assembly, then pointing at Jake and Sarah.

"They're from Chandler's village," said Ellen. "Jake was the mastermind behind blowing up Chandler's lighthouse, as well as other crimes and misdemeaners."

"Misdemeaners?" whispered Jake. Sarah just put her finger to her lips.

"Wow..... village..... lighthouse, I look forward to hearing more about that whole episode," said Lucas.

"Some day you'll have to explain how you ended up a robot guarding a jail," said Ellen.

"It's not a jail, and I'm not really a guard," said Lucas. "But I did enlarge the entrance so robots my size could enter."

"Could you at least briefly clue us in on how you and my mom ended up in tin suits?" asked Jane.

"Well, first of all, your mom had been immortalized by Shannon as Ellen and the others here probably know," said Lucas.

"Her mom Jane is also a robot?" asked Ellen.

"Yes, so let me finish......your mom had asked to be assigned to one of my eternity blocks as a keeper. So when I came up from my cave I managed to get myself into trouble with the Chinese and went to her block to hide out. For reasons we can also discuss around a campfire someday, we decided to inter ourselves and later transfer our minds into these robots. Then we came out, and that's a lot more campfire tales to tell."

"I have a feeling that the campfire discussion could go on for a long time," said Jane.

"A very long time," said Lucas.

"OK, so why did you come out of the block?" asked Jane.

"To carry out a mission," he replied.

"What kind of mission?" asked Jane.

"Well, a group of military extremists that I had worked with in the past had the objective of destroying any enemy who might want to take over America."

"Like the Chinese," said Jane.

"Like the Chinese," Lucas repeated.

"So you stopped them."

"Well, sort of," he replied.

"Sort of doesn't sound very successful," said Jane.

"It wasn't, because they managed to launch a nuclear attack on China while we were trying to disarm them," he replied.

"Oh my god.....so your mission went to shit," said Jane turning to Isaac with raised eyebrows.

"Yes, but it gets worse," said Lucas.

"How could it get worse than that?" asked Jane.

"Because, in retaliation, the Chinese nuked Yellowstone and it erupted," said Lucas.

"So you're responsible for that too?" asked Jane.

"My list of sins would make the devil himself jealous," said Lucas. "And in line with Murphy's Law, the eruption from the volcano spewed miles and miles of lava and ash that covered the block your mother and I had put ourselves in. So we are now trapped in these tin suits forever."

"Nice going tin man," said Jane.

"But wait, in my defense, I aborted the missiles that were sent to China," said Lucas.

"And then the Chinese became the Controllers," said Isaac.

"Right.....I know, I didn't think about taking the blame for that too.... but yes, I guess I'm responsible for that too," said Lucas. "However, on the good side, their purpose is to prevent anything like the big war from happening again."

"So they've become a worldwide police force?" asked Isaac.

"Something like that," said Lucas.

"Two of those cops looked a bit disheveled when they came to warn us not to leave California," said Jane. "They looked like they were playing cowboy, and their attempted threat fell a little short."

"Those were the Texas Cowboys that Janet talks about," said Lucas.

"Other than the fact that they wore cowboy hats, and had

pearl handled cowboy guns, they weren't exactly what I would classify as a cowboy..... and, by the way, who is Janet?" asked Jane.

"She's the local Chinese cop who was after me way back when, and also the one who arrested Holly, so she's inside," said Lucas.

"Those cowboys said Holly and my colony were being detained, so I rushed over here," said Jane. "I just assumed that 'detained' meant jail."

"I'm glad you came, and actually, this in fact is Janet's official jail as far as the Chinese know, but it isn't really a jail, it's Debra's place," said Lucas.

"OK, I think I've got it, so can we go inside now?" asked Jane, pointing to the cave entrance.

"Of course, but first you should know a little about Holly's crime," said Lucas.

"Yes, please, I'd like to know about that," said Jane.

"Well, in retaliation for the apparent destruction of your spaceship, Holly decided to disable three of the Chinese light stations and shoot down six of their drones," said Lucas.

"Wait, wait, wait..... the Chinese destroyed our ship?" asked Jane, turning to Isaac.

"Son of a bitttttcchhhh!" said Isaac.

"Then she was justified in taking out their equipment and anything else," said Jane angrily.

"First of all, I have a hard time believing that your ship was destroyed by the Chinese," said Lucas. "However, I'm not sure if you want to take on these people."

"If they destroyed our ship, I'll definitely take them on," said Jane.

"Well, I've never seen them here before...... I mean ever, nor can I believe for a minute that they destroyed your ship, but they're 'the man' right now in what's left of the world," said Lucas. "So I suggest we just wait and see what they do, if anything."

"I hope you're right about our ship, but if you're not, believe me, it ain't over," said Jane.

"Look, Jane, you did the right thing by coming here and bringing everyone with you," said Lucas. "But of course all of you could be put in jail if they decide to show up and press charges. They do have laws about weapons and aggressive behavior."

"We have nowhere else to go, so perhaps jail is better than eating that grass down there," said Jane, pointing to the valley below. "But payback remains on the table."

"You even talk like my Jane," said Lucas.

"Can we go in now?" asked Jane.

"Of course, and just so you know, it's about a mile through the tunnel so it's a bit of a hike," said Lucas, standing aside. Jane nodded, then waved everyone to follow.

When they finally entered the greenhouse, they all just stood in the light mist and stared at the gigantic spectacle before them.

"Holy fucking shit..... this is paradise!" said Virg, walking forward and gawking. The others entered and were equally awed by the sight.

"I can understand how someone could live down here indefinitely," said Isaac.

"Yes, but a cave starts to feel confining after a few centuries," said Debra who overheard them as she emerged from the mist.

"Hi, I'm Jane, and you must be Debra," said Jane who stepped forward with her hand extended.

"Yes, you're Jane's daughter," said Debra who grasped Jane's hand, then grabbed her and hugged her.

"This is my husband Isaac, and, and, and," said Jane, pointing behind her.

"Right, we'll do introductions later, just follow me," said Debra who turned and started back into the mist. The others fell in line behind Jane who quickly caught up with Debra.

"So, you've been down here in this cave since the big war?" asked Jane as they walked out of the greenhouse and entered a long hallway.

"Yes, it's been two hundred years, with a visit to the surface a hundred and sixty years ago," said Debra. "That visit was cut short by the eruption. And finally, a trip to Shannon's cave ten years after that to get immortalized."

"Wow, that's a long time in a cave," said Jane.

"Too long," said Debra.

"I've been briefed on the current predicament with the downing of our ship and Holly's escapades," said Jane.

"We're discussing that right now, so if you have any ideas for what we can do, we need all the help we can get," said Debra.

"Look, we're just trying to get our feet wet since we just got here after spending twenty five years enroute from a planet far far away," said Jane.

"A bit of culture shock I'm sure," said Debra.

"To say the least, but our original purpose for returning to Earth was to find a way to reactivate our chips," said Jane.

"Well, Brady found Shannon's personal notebook and there are notes in there describing a portable device of some kind that might be what you're looking for," said Debra.

"Portable device....oh right, that has to be our so-called health machine, and it was up in the ship....so I guess that could be gone now," said Jane.

"The chips are activated by your nervous system, so they're always activated, but they can apparently be turned on or off using this machine that you may not have anymore," said Debra.

"Right, no ship, no health machine, no chip revival," said Jane.

"That's a real tragedy if indeed it happened," said Debra.

"Interestingly enough, even if we had that machine, Isaac and I have already decided not to reactivate our chips because of Dawn," said Jane.

"I understand, your child would grow old and you wouldn't," said Debra.

"And an immortal life without the feelings we now have is not something we want to experience again," said Jane as they entered the great hall.

Chapter Fourteen

"**T**hey're here!" came Lucas's voice over the loudspeaker in the great hall.

"Central?" asked Debra.

"I believe so, but it's dark, so I'm not sure," said Lucas. "However, the aircraft isn't one of those old helicopters, it looks fairly modern."

"Then it's not the Texas Cowboys," said Janet.

"I guess we'd better get up there," said Debra who turned to leave.

"They came for us, so we'll be the one's who face the music," said Jane, as she started for the exit and quickly caught up with Debra. Isaac was right behind her.

"Excuse me, I'm the local cop, so I have to be in the lead," said Janet who was already near the exit.

"No, this is our cave!" said Debra, now in full flight with Jane close behind. Brady was trying, but unable to keep up with the mass exodus.

"Let's not fight over who, how or why," said Jane, finally grabbing Debra by the shirt to slow her down. "It will be myself, Isaac, Janet and you."

"I'm the mother!" shouted Jane the robot from far behind.

"Wait for me Deb!" shouted Brady. "Remember, if they did destroy their ship, by their own standards, it's they who should be punished, not the other way around." But his words were not heard as they disappeared down the hall.

"Lucas will greet them if they get to the entrance before we do," said Debra a little while later as the four of them slowed to a fast walk in the tunnel.

When they arrived at the entrance to the cave, Lucas saw them and pointed. Below, a contingent of two women and two men stood at the foot of the rock fall, four abreast. A spotlight from their aircraft provided a backlight. Janet walked to the edge and waved for them to come up. Those down in the cave stood perfectly still, listening. There was very little chatter about what might be in store for them as they waited. For the colony from Eden, on a decimated planet they once called home and with their ship gone with no way to return, any hope of a peaceful life here on Earth could all be about to end.

When the Chinese contingent reached the top, they stood in front of them, again four abreast. Janet was in front with Jane slightly behind her but edging forward to finally stand next to her. Lucas towered behind. The Chinese were dressed in identical pale blue outfits. Janet bowed and Jane and the others followed her lead. The four Chinese did likewise.

"Our friends from the planet Eden interpreted your

destruction of their ship as an act of aggression, and that is why they disabled your light stations," said Janet. The woman on the end looked at the others with a confused expression before she took a step forward and spoke in broken English.

"We know that these visitors from the planet they called Eden are our youth who traveled there two hundred years ago in a stolen spacecraft," she said.

"Yes," said Janet with a nod. "Now, first of all, I am Janet, your regional police administrator, and this is Jane and Isaac, heads of the colony from Eden....and finally, this is Debra, the cave's owner."

"I am Chen," said the woman who then introduced the others in her contingent.

"Jane and Isaac are in fact two of the kidnapped teens, but their immortality was erased on Eden by Shannon, the person who stole your spacecraft," said Janet. "They both aged twenty-five years on their journey back to Earth."

"Twenty-three of our youth were taken," said Chen.

"The others are below in the cave and are all healthy and safe," said Janet.

"That is good news," said the woman, looking at her colleagues and nodding.

"We had thought that this immortality claim was just an American myth," said Chen.

"No, it's true as you will soon see," said Janet. "I have also been immortalized and am one hundred eighty six years of age."

"You are the same Janet?" asked the woman.

"I am the same Janet."

"You told us that the woman we sent here one hundred eighty

years ago was your mother," said Chen.

"I lied about that because I didn't think you would believe me, and I also lied to you about this cave being a jail," said Janet. "It's actually Debra's place."

"We have been aware that this was not your jail for some time now," said Chen who was clearly in charge of the contingent.

"Oh," said Janet with a smile.

"What about you, are you also immortal?" one of the men asked, pointing at Debra.

"Yes, I'm about the same age as Janet, and was immortalized when she was," Debra nodded.

"So our youth are over two hundred years old but appear as teenagers?" asked Chen.

"Except for two of them, and four others of our colony who were not Chinese," said Jane. "Those six had their devices erased by Shannon."

"Is this Shannon with you?" asked Chen.

"No, she was accidently killed on Eden," said Jane.

"That seems fair punishment," said the first woman. "Now, what is your pleasure Jane?"

"My pleasure? I don't understand?" asked Jane who looked to Janet for clarification. Janet just shook her head.

"Your people from Eden may return there if you wish, or you may choose to settle in peace somewhere here on Earth, including in our country where you will be quite welcome," said Chen.

"But you destroyed our spacecraft," said Jane.

"Destroyed? No, of course not, we would never do that, it would be an act of war, and war has been abolished on this planet for two centuries," said Chen.

146

"We simply placed it in a more stable orbit, and you apparently abandoned ship before we could explain," said one of the men. "Then, we were unable to contact your people to explain."

"So our ship is still up there?" asked Jane.

"Of course," said Chen.

"Oh my god, that's the best news I have ever heard," said Isaac. Jane turned to him and they hugged.

"Janet, can we go below so the delegation can meet our colony?" asked Jane who was speaking to her from Isaac's arms.

"Of course," said Janet, turning to Debra who nodded.

"Would you accept my humble invitation to come into my home," asked Debra, motioning for the Chinese contingent to enter.

"It would be our honor," Chen replied. The four stepped forward and were soon being led into the tunnel by Debra who began to chat with them as they made their way down the steps that Lucas had made in the rockfall down to the tunnel's level. The others fell in behind and by the time they reached the greenhouse the entire group was in loud conversation and laughing. Upon entering the greenhouse the Chinese contingent stopped to gape at the spectacle and a round of loud Chinese chatter echoed off the near wall.

"Our caves were more industrial, if that's the word," said one of the men.

"Compared to this they were ugly," said Chen to a round of laughter.

"Follow me," said Debra who led them to the great hall where a welcoming crowd waited. The room erupted into chamber-filling chatter as the Chinese delegation met with the Chinese youth from Eden. This was followed by a series of separate discussions with Ellen, Jane, Isaac and others as they went over what they wanted in their future.

"Have we pretty much given up on the idea of returning to Eden," said Jane as she stood with Holly and Isaac in a separate discussion.

"I think everyone was fairly emphatic about that when we left," said Isaac.

"If we did return to Eden we will have spent over one hundred years on that ship, and we'll be in our sixties when we get back," said Jane.

"Well, you're the ship's captain my dear, and you're the only person capable of getting us back there, so if the others decide to go back, we'll have to go back with them," said Isaac.

"In the innocence of youth, two hundred years ago, I eagerly learned how to fly that tin can, but in a million years I never imagined that it would end up like this..... the only one who can fly it," said Jane.

"They did essentially invite us to settle in China where living conditions are most likely fairly modern compared to anywhere else," said Isaac.

"That's right, so from a purely selfish standpoint, settling there would make a lot of sense," said Holly.

"Then there's Hotel Paradise," said Isaac.

"That would be very nice, but, a bit isolated in a wasteland of relatively primitive survivors," said Jane.

"Of course our colony is mostly Chinese, and many were born there and spent their youth there," said Isaac.

"OK, what's happening?" asked Fan who now joined them.

"We're discussing what to do next," said Isaac. "Chen invited us to live in China and we just came from Hotel Paradise, which are both options. Or, we could fly back to Eden."

"Eden, no thank you, I think we left there because we were through with it," said Fan.

"We agree," said Jane.

"So I guess it's between China and California," said Isaac.

"Whatever you choose for yourself and your family, we will follow," said Fan.

"You know that I love you and everyone in our colony," said Jane, a tear beginning to form in the corner of her eye. "And I could not bear to live apart from any of you, so I want everyone to be together wherever we decide to live. But I also want everyone to be in on this decision and be happy with it."

"I think the main thing is to stay together, wherever we settle," said Fan.

"That is the main thing," said Jane, nodding and looking at Isaac as if he could save her from her having to be the one who decides where they settle. He held out his arms and she very softly fell into them.

"What about Ellen, Debra, Luke and all those we've met here?" asked Holly.

"Has anyone asked them?" asked Isaac.

"I don't think so, but they almost begged to come with us to wherever we were going," said Jane.

"Alright, sweetheart, as we have been doing for two centuries, let me give you my input," said Isaac.

"It has always been so much more than input, Isaac," said Jane.

"I know, but I have always relied on your decisions, as has everyone in the colony," said Isaac. "So here's what I think. Most of our colony is Chinese, and China is probably the closest thing to what we have become accustomed to in terms of conveniences, so moving to China might be our best move. Let's face it, we've become entirely spoiled from our birth to now and from a purely selfish perspective, we all prefer to continue to be spoiled."

"I think I fall into that same category of spoiled people," said Janet who had overheard the conversation.

"So is Hotel Paradise in the same spoiled category as China?" asked Jane.

"Other than isolation in a sea of poverty and depravation," said Isaac.

"And we don't really know the people who live there, other than the little group who followed us here," said Jane.

"We don't know the people of China either, despite the fact that most of our colony was born there," said Isaac.

"So, to a greater or lesser degree, we'll be living in a strange land with strangers," said Jane.

"Well for our group that followed you here, we are essentially without a home," said Ellen who had just arrived with the others. "Now, myself, the girls and Luke wanted to follow you here because there was an almost magical connection between us. You are people like us, highly educated, centuries of experience, and looking for a home that has conveniences that we were used to before the war and desperately want again."

"I know, we felt the same strong connection, and we really like you guys and want to keep you as friends," said Jane, nodding.

"I can't speak for everyone in our colony but I'm fairly certain that either place would be great," said Fan. "Yes, many of us were born in China, but that was two hundred years ago and a lot has changed since then so we would still be strangers in a strange land."

"That's oh so true," said Jane. "So perhaps the most important thing is that we stay together wherever we settle."

By now, they were surrounded by everyone in the hall, including the Chinese delegation, and it had become remarkably quiet as everyone was trying to hear Jane speak.

"What was it like there on Eden?" asked Brady from somewhere in the crowd.

"It was a true paradise where we had built elaborate homes," said Isaac. "But it was complete and permanent isolation from our roots as an Earthbound species and society, and life there gradually became more and more primitive with regard to modern conveniences as our modern equipment slowly failed. The ability to manufacture new equipment was nonexistent, so we simply would have to adapt to an agrarian lifestyle, which we were either unwilling or unable to do."

"From that, I assume you'd never go back," said Debra.

"Never," said Jane shaking her head.

"Well, we here in this cave have discussed where we would prefer to live, and we're absolutely and totally through with cave life, so, Jane, we're following you to China or Hotel California, or anywhere else you choose," said Debra.

"It's Hotel Paradise not California," said Luke.

"I know, but in some ways it seems like Hotel California," said Debra.

"In more ways than one," said Isaac.

"What about you guys, Ellen?" asked Jane, looking around trying to spot her.

"Well, we're not going back to where we lived for two hundred years, so we're completely open to new adventures."

"What about Jake and Sarah?" asked Jane.

"Jake would have gone nuts if he thought he could travel to another planet in a spaceship, but that's out," said Sarah. "And to be honest, I think we are tired of the Hotel California area as well."

"Yes, I think China would make a very decent home," said Jake.

"So, I think I'm hearing a consensus......is it China?" asked Holly.

"Wait, will we still have to be the royal couple there?" asked Jane.

"That appointment was for life," said Fan.

"Perhaps it would not be legal in China," asked Jane.

"We honor royalty in China," said Chen.

"You'll always be my queen, no matter where we are," said Isaac.

"Oh crap, Isaac, how can I argue with that," she replied as she reached up and kissed him on the cheek.

Chapter Fifteen

"**H**i Jill," said Isaac as Jill reached the top of the steps to Isaac's and Jane's new home. Just then Jane appeared on the balcony above them.

"He's almost finished detailing, honest," said Jane.

"Well, it's nothing like his villa on Eden," said Jill.

"It's quite comfortable, but there's a certain sameness to everyone's house here, except yours is beginning to look way too polished," said Isaac.

"That's because Holly is even more of an anal retentive than you are," said Jill.

"But we're across from each other, just like on Eden," said Isaac.

"Isaac, we've been across from each other since we were five, and that's a very long time," said Jill.

"I know," said Isaac.

"I do miss being able to fully express our individuality in the overall design of our homes," said Jane.

"But those on Eden took decades to create, and here, the Chinese built ours for us, which was a very nice gesture," said Isaac.

"At least our interiors are all completely different," said Jane.

"The best part is, we're together as a community," said Jill.

"Yes, but explain to me again why everyone chose to turn off their immortality," said Isaac.

"I know, that's something I simply cannot understand," said Jane.

"Well, it's at least in part so they can be like the royal couple," said Jill.

"Royal couple.....no, Jill, there's obviously a lot more to it than that," said Isaac. "Because this is a very big deal. Giving up immortality is not like giving up Chocolate. It's accepting the fact that you will die some day when you know that you could have lived indefinitely if you chose to."

"It is a big deal, yes, but even though one would think that immortality is the universal wish of mankind, you really have to live it for a couple centuries in order to understand what it's like, and it's primarily why everyone chose to turn theirs off," said Jill.

"I'm sure there were different reasons that were personal to each individual," said Jane. "But you're right, we've had ample time to live it and have that backdrop compared to someone who is just thinking about how great it would be."

"In the end, we all followed you two down the same rabbit hole," said Jill.

"Isn't a rabbit hole a bad thing?" asked Isaac.

"Wonderland is never a really a bad thing, it's more like an exciting adventure," said Jill.

"Look, we never intended to affect anyone's life decisions in this way, Jill," said Jane.

"But seeing you two, and the happiness you had, made everyone begin to understand what normal life could be," said Jill. "And that's all good."

"Well, the upside is that everyone will now grow old together," said Jane. "And despite the fact that we can turn on our chips anytime we want to, I could never go back to the immortal side and lose even one minute of what I have now."

"I know," said Jill. "The universal dream of immortality has flipped for us, and became a universal passion to live a normal life."

"Unfortunately, Shannon's version of immortality was really a type of labotomy," said Jane. "We became both socially and physically sterile."

"But what if, when we're one hundred, if we live that long, we decide to turn our immortality chips back on?" asked Jill.

"Then, what..... we'll sit around in rocking chairs on our porches drinking lemonaid for the next hundred years?" asked Jane.

"Actually, I think that might be something to look forward to," said Isaac.

"I think I'll just stick with what we have for as long as it lasts," said Jane.

"Me too, and I think that would be another consensus among those here in the colony," said Jill.

"One thing I don't understand though," said Jane.

"And that is?" asked Jill.

155

"Why it didn't prevent Isaac and I from openly falling in love with each other long before we had the physical feelings to do so," said Jane.

"But Jane, we did fall in love," said Isaac. "We fell in love with the real us, the us without the other sensations we now have, and in the end, it's that real love that counts the most."

"Boom," said Jill, pointing up at Jane.

"That's why I love him so," said Jane.

"Another good thing about what's happened is that others are beginning to experience our kind of love too," said Isaac.

"And have started dating boys outside the compound, so I wonder if they'll assimilate into the population," said Jane.

"Actually, I'm not so sure they will," said Jill. "The Chinese boys like it here in our little pocket of diverse culture, so our colony may grow as a result, not the other way around."

"I guess that's due in part to the fact that we've been together as a colony for two hundred years, so in many ways, we're just one big and very close family," said Isaac. "Of course the family expanded a bit when the evacuation from California and Utah became a migration here to China."

"Including Janet and the two robots," said Isaac.

"When we decided to move here, I never really thought about how any of this would turn out, and I'm not sure if what we've created with this town is good or bad from China's perspective," said Isaac. "We're not just another neighborhood within a country, we're a separate community of people with a very different way of living."

"That may be true, but let's face it, coming here to China was really more about protecting our selfish interests than it was about seeking to assimilate with the population," said Jane. "The fact is, we're extremely old intellectually, and as a result we're set in our ways. These ways were largely established on a distant planet where we were isolated, selfish, and for the most part a bit lazy. So we're neither Western nor Eastern. We're totally unique. Debra's and Ellen's people were also intellectually old and isolated, so they fit in very nicely with us. In reality we're all just a bunch of nerd hermits with our own way of living!"

"Jake and Sarah are the exception to the nerd-hermit label since they lived in a primitive village," said Isaac.

"But Jake and Sarah are nerd-hermit-intellectual-wanabes that also fit nicely into our group as well as our way of life," said Jane.

"What about Luke, who was a teacher?" asked Jill.

"He came into this rodeo well educated and then lived by himself, except in summers when he was a teacher," said Jane.

"I guess he is really one of us," said Jill.

"So in many ways we're a rather homogeneous lot," said Jane. "And here we are, living in our comfortable little community, insulated from the outside world. But out there are the other survivors of this worldwide holocaust, many living in ignorance and in mostly primitive conditions."

"That's true, but we knew about that when we moved here, and in fact it's one of the reasons we did move here....... to live in comfort and safety, away from those we have few things in common with," said Isaac.

"Does knowing our blindness to reality mean that we must then simply continue to remain blind?" asked Jane.

"Well, I suppose we can condemn the Chinese for where we

are today in the world." said Isaac. "But that's 2020 hindsight by those who were not even here when it happened. Let's be fair, after the extent of destruction was known, China decided it had to protect its own interests. To do so, they chose to subdue survivors, most of whom were participants in the war that had resulted in laying the world bare. In China's process of forcefully removing weapons, stopping violence, and preventing survivors from acquiring the knowledge needed to advance as a potential enemy, these survivors had to live under stiff rules of behavior. The purpose was to prevent further violence. But over the decades, the Chinese have become increasingly soft in their enforcement of their rules. In fact, today there really is no effective enforcement, it's just the threat of enforcement."

"I'll grant you that, but any advancements among survivors are virtually impossible without access to mankind's knowledge base, the so-called 'extended brain' of the human race," said Jane.

"True, they can't access books or recorded knowledge, but it's not as if the Chinese are out there holding a gun to their heads," said Isaac.

"Threats have a way of achieving their own sense of normalcy," said Jane. "Yes, I suppose modern civilization could eventually return for some of these surviving groups. However, it's been two hundred years, and it looks like what the Chinese did initially continutes to have its impact on progress."

"But they were the only country to survive the devastation in any functioning form, and they were left with the responsibility to protect not only the future of their own people, but the future of the world," said Jill.

"I know, so who are we to second guess what they did?" asked

Jane.

"And to what end," said Jill.

"I suppose one could ask what we would have done in their shoes," said Jane. "Imagine how it must have looked: billions of bodies or body parts, and dying people wandering aimlessly about in the fire and radiation, scrounging for food and medical care. But there was no medical care. There were no food stores and only what you could find lying around to eat. No electricity, so no heat or lights. No sewer system, so you would have to poop in the bushes. No water system, so you couldn't find pure water. Little or no transportation so you couldn't travel very far on foot. Dark skies and descending cold with few places to seek adequate shelter from the cold. Desperate people competing with other desperate people over what was left. And to add insult to injury, pockets of aggressive war-minded survivors with guns still intent on fighting one another, sometimes just to survive, but more times than not, to establish control over what was left."

"Definitely a situation begging for some kind of order," said Jill.

"And, for a select few who stayed safely and securely away from the bombing and fallout in very special kinds of shelters with the most sophisticated equipment, they were able to survive to live another day," said Isaac.

"Like Debra, and who knows how many others who may or may not have survived if they eventually came to the surface," said Jane.

"How many survivors are out there?" asked Jill. "There is no census, so we have no idea. And, even today, China admits that they have no idea how many."

"Like Debra, survival on the surface for them was a non-starter, so I'm sure there are those who have remained underground," said Jane.

"And with potentially great technical and intellectual capability," said Isaac.

"Perhaps, but we have to go back to before the war started and ask how seemingly intelligent people could have let this happen in the first place." said Jane.

"I know, it was supposedly something that could never happen, but it happened," said Jill.

"Perhaps people had become numb to the threats and name calling, so they may have started to ignore what was going on," said Jane. "It was just another fact of modern life in a nuclear age. Except it wasn't JUST another fact. It was the world sitting on a powder keg with a number of hidden fuses. According to records here in China, there was an overwhelming amount of aggressive posturing by leaders. Most of it bluster, but hidden in the bluster was an element of seriousness. To the average citizen though, it was just headline news that was increasingly ignored, or considered an exaggeration and, of course, something that could never happen. The nuclear weapons were just there as a deterrent. Only a threat, not for actual use. And it had reached the brink many times in the past and nothing ever happened. So the shrill rhetoric was just a normal day in world news."

"Well, it had not led to a world war since World War II," said Jill.

"Yes, but now, this was nuclear war, with a ridiculously large number of competing nations armed to the teeth with the deadliest weapon ever conceived by man," said Isaac.

"Deadlier on an inconceivably grand scale," said Jane. "Two dozen countries had enormously large nuclear capabilities, and more than one of them, by themselves, possessed a million times more destructive power than existed in the entire world before 1945. Single countries could literally destroy the world by themselves. And meanwhile, most people thought they were safe at home behind their giant defense budgets, when the reality was that it was not possible to defend themselves against worldwide Armageddon. The home front was an exercise in flag waving by those who knew they would never have to be in combat because there was no draft in most countries. They could sit at home and pretend they were safe with their gun collections. In the past, the ultimate sacrifice had been dying in battle. Tweeting online, waving flags and saying thank you for your service is a far cry from the bravery and sacrifice of being on the battle field facing death. And now, in a nuclear war, there was no front line. No bullets ripped through your flesh. It was now a matter of pushing buttons from a cushy chair. The front line was the street outside your station, even though in a thousand years you could never imagine that it was anything other than just the street where you lived and worked. No bullets whizzed over your head. No bombs were bursting outside. You washed your shiny car on Sunday. You watched a game on Friday with your friends, or enjoyed a game of tennis at your club. Nobody was able to feel the sting of metal entering their bodies. But then, suddenly, a giant flash of light erased their life in a blink, or left them staggering in the street, now painfully aware of what nuclear war really meant."

"That was a key factor, wasn't it?" asked Jill. "A complete lack of personal contact with the incredible ugliness of war. War was a video game. Too many people had been protected from suffering the indescribable horrors of war. For far too long, most sat on the sidelines, safe, while their mercinary sons and daughters stood between them and the enemy. But now, in a nuclear war, there were no sidelines. No one could stand between you and the enemy. Everyone was at risk, but most were naively unaware of how deadly it really was. Nuclear war was literally beyond most people's comprehension to even imagine, and ultimately, beyond their ability to escape."

"According to the records, it happened so incredibly fast that there was no time to rethink what to do other than strike back, and strike back hard," said Isaac.

"The records describe how most major cities in America were the first to be vaporized in a mass attack of simultaneous flashes from bombs in a variety of forms, from trucks and submarines, to missles launched from everywhere, even within the country," said Jane. "And the ultimate revenge that followed triggered a hundred thousand exchanges, followed by countless attacks and bombings in the aftermath, until the destruction was complete."

"And this meant making the means for survival on the surface largely nonexistent," said Jill. "Those who lived past the flash, had no one to ask for help and nowhere to go as the world raged in fire, radiation and dark skies that lasted far too long."

"Obviously, many people were aware of the potential for this to happen, so it wasn't as if the possibility was a secret," said Jane. "But people just stood around like a pen of pigs waiting for the butcher to turn them into bacon."

"What could they do to stop it?" asked Isaac. "It was a surprise attack."

"That's right, it could have been triggered anywhere, not just America," said Jane. "There was an element of inevitability that it would happen."

"I suppose that's right, it was inevitable," said Jill.

"It was bound to happen given the species who built and held the bombs as weapons against fellow members of their own species," said Jane.

"But wasn't humanity too civilized for such thoughtless and ignorant behavior?" asked Jill. "In effect, they committed world suicide, an act by a mentally unstable person."

"Unfortunately, civility was not a badge of honor for everyone," said Jane. "Based on the history leading up to the war that I read, there were those who were quite prepared to push their agenda at any cost. Compromise had faded as a means of de-escalation between opposing ideologies. It was 'my way or nothing'. And once your enemy had been publically stereotyped as a demon, every man woman and child in your enemy's population was no longer seen as real people like you, but an evil that must be exterminated in order for your truth to prevail. That made the use of a nuke to vaporize every man, woman and child acceptable. A key ingredient that contributed to the end, was the belief by some that death for the cause was both honorable and a legitimate tactic for achieving some kind of moral or spiritual victory. In a world armed to the teeth with nuclear weapons, that belief was a fatal slogan."

"But what does it really matter to us now?" asked Jill. "It happened, and now we have to live with it."

"Of course we do, but, actually, the situation we just described sealed our fate long before the war finally ended it," said Jane.

"How so?" asked Jill.

"First of all, the development of the nuclear bomb with its demonstration of power in 1945 introduced the new, perhaps ultimate weapon of war," said Jane. "Several nations, including Germany were close to having it, so the fact that the US did it first was just a matter of who took the credit, and as we look back, the blame for doing it. And once the knowledge for making this ultimate people-killing weapon was embedded in our body of recorded knowledge, virtually everyone could eventually have the ability to build them to threaten others, or, if used on a massive scale, succeed in ending the existence of us all. Think of it, a single species with the intelligence and capability of destroying itself, yet lacking the intelligence, temperment and capability to eliminate it before it destroyed them."

"So, what you're saying is, we, as humans, never really had a chance to change our destiny once the bomb was on the table," said Jill.

"Yes, and I believe Einstein recognized that turning point when it happened, but, considering world politics at the time, could we have ever had the mutual commitment among competing nations to reverse course?" asked Jane. "The sad truth is no."

"So forget the hand written placards and the peace marches, because the end was already determined in that moment of time when nuclear weapons made their debut," said Jill.

"Pretty much," said Jane.

"But is this really the end of the line for the human race?" asked Isaac. "There are still several billion human survivors in various stages of existence. And we've been at the brink before

164

with far fewer survivors. As recently as seventy thousand years ago, our species dwindled to a few thousand, and from that collection of survivors we blossomed into a world of nine billion that reached every corner of the Earth."

"I know, but most of the survivors out there now live in conditions that are barely better than our ancestors of seventy thousand years ago," said Jane.

"Well, survival is a primal instinct, so I don't think we'll go extinct anytime soon," said Isaac.

"Maybe not, but some of this senseless aggression is in our genes, so it doesn't mean we won't try to commit suicide again," said Jane. "The seed of our fate is built into our evolutionary past, long before the bomb."

"You mean we're genetically destined to kill each other off?" asked Jill.

"Not intentionally," said Jane. "Self destruction is not in our genes, but tribal competition and the need to suceed, often at any cost, probably is, at least to some degree," said Jane. "It's survival of the fittest. So in a very real sense, what happened here was quite literally an act of nature."

"An act of nature?" asked Jill. "You mean this whole catastrophic event could have been an unintended consequence of our competition for food, women and territory?"

"I think one could definitely argue that," said Jane. "Actually, for reasons too complex to attach entirely to genetics, we evolved into an animal that was too smart. We became smart enough to create an almost miraculous world to live in, and at the same time invent increasingly more potent weapons designed EXCLUSIVELY for killing members of our own species! That fact alone is so shocking that it's difficult for me to even imagine that a presumably intelligent species could have done this! But we did! We, the naked ape, invented the ability to completely vaporize the entirety of our enemies, who, in reality are really ourselves. And in the process of doing that, we exterminated most of the other species in the world. And this super killing invention was incorporated into actual human plans for each selfish, paranoid, nationalistic country to defend themselves against other selfish, paranoid, nationlistic countries whose intentions could, of course, not be trusted, shared or tolerated. There was no real trust in the world. And of course we're talking about real people here. Our fellow human beings! Not rabbits. Not rats. Not cockroaches. Not faceless zombies. Real people...... us! Can we ever rationalize the idea that it is OK to vaporize ourselves, not just the loud mouthed leaders or intellectually deprived zealots, but every man woman and child, most of them entirely innocent? Yes, ourselves! Can you even imagine having the ability to vaporize everyone who doesn't believe as you do? These are human souls exactly like us. Souls that are not different than your cousin, or your neighbor, or your child. Should a human brain, not the reptilian brain of a partially evolved animal, allow this to happen?"

"Reptilian brain?" asked Isaac.

"A symbolic reference to when the genetic instincts from an earlier version of our species takes over from how we are capable of behaving as civilized humans," said Jane.

"You just made that reptilian brain thing up, didn't you sweetheart?" asked Isaac.

"I may have read about it, I don't remember," said Jane.

"So, this runaway urge to push things to the extreme and win at all cost is our reptilian brain taking over?" asked Jill.

"Symbolically..... it's obviously a bit more complicated than that," said Jane. "So maybe the necessity to win at all cost becomes the fatal flaw in our quest for survival as a species. Again, is the result we see now really just an act of nature? Or is it an implant to the mythical blank slate?"

"Wait.....blank slate?" asked Isaac.

"That's learned behavior added to what earlier researchers believed was our 'blank slate' brain," said Jane. "In other words, to them most of what we are is learned. As opposed to inherited behavior that is hard wired in our genes, often for the purpose of suviving in a world where only the fittest survive."

"And is war our reptilian brain's response to resolving disagreements?" asked Isaac.

"Look, war is very simply fellow human beings killing fellow human beings, because we are unable to effectively engage our unique ability as humans to reason and understand, or compromise," said Jane. "Is this a rational human resolving an issue with another rational human, or is it an animal flying into a rage to conquer another animal over a food source?"

"In other words we're unable to rise above our animal origins." said Isaac.

"Yes, and that failure is just a matter of survival of the fittest.....ergo, an act of nature?" asked Jill. "Well, I guess all mass extinctions are basically an act of nature too, right?"

"Yes they are, but not all of them are part of our evolution," said Jane.

"Nature gives and nature can also take away," said Jill.

"We can't change the fact that we're members of the animal kingdom and have animal instincts," said Isaac.

"It just comes down to a matter of whether we can recognize those instincts and control them as members of a species we have loosely defined as human," said Jane.

"But let's say war is our reptilian brain acting out the animal within us, and is an unintended consequence of who we are as animals," said Jill. "So our excuse for inhuman behavior is that we're just another animal? Then it's not really our fault because it's just an act of nature?"

"Well, I guess you could claim that, or you could also ask: do I have stupid written on my forehead?" said Jane.

"That's yet another excuse.....I didn't know because I'm just stupid'," said Isaac. "Perhaps that's the more accurate excuse for what happened."

"Good one, Isaac," said Jill. "But putting the unintended outcome of attempting humanaside and by destroying ourselves in a nuclear war aside....... we could still be destroyed by natural events that are outside of our ability to control. And that would also be another act of nature."

"That's true, it is an act of nature and a number of those have happened, like a mass extinction due to an asteroid collision with Earth," asked Isaac.

"We've had several mass extinctions since our beginning as a single cell three and a half billion years ago, and mankind did not cause them," said Jill. "Some things are outside of our control."

"In other words, we could eventually become extinct anyway, even if there was no fatal flaw in our DNA that caused us to commit nuclear suicide," said Jane.

"Well, mass extinctions are a fact in our planet's history," said Jill.

"So then is it fair game to go ahead and destroy ourselves since we'll eventually be destroyed anyway?" asked Jane.

"There's an element of truth to that, isn't there?" asked Jill with a little laugh.

"Convoluted truth," said Jane. "However, the fact is that human life on this planet is but a mere speck on the time line of Earth's history. Mass extinctions are far too rare on that time line to think of them as a threat to the continued existence of us as a species. No, as Pogo once said, 'we have found the enemy and he is us'."

"Who is Pogo?" asked Jill.

"She reads ancient comic strips," said Isaac.

"Comic strips, right, the light side of satire," said Jill.

"And to finish this comic satire...... it takes the ultimate thumb of world domination in order to keep the proverbial 'us' from finishing the job of attempted suicide on our species," said Jane.

"I'm trying to picture a giant thumb in a comic strip," said Isaac.

"Well, if the world has entered the new paradigm under the giant thumb scenario, yes, how would that graphic be drawn in the comic strip?" asked Jane.

"Fortunately or unfortunately, we do not live in a comic strip, we live in the here and now, and we have little chance of changing the scene we now find ourselves in," said Jill. "The giant thumb is a reality, so get over it."

"Perhaps on a future timeline which none of us will survive, the intelligence that made it possible for us to make ourselves the greatest species to ever live, and the only species capable of exterminating outselves and the world around us, will be the intelligence that will eventually allow us to live peacefully together like an actual human being might be capable of doing," said Jane. "That is, unless nature surprises us again."

"In the meantime, we just have to play the cards we were dealt," said Jill.

"I'm looking at a pair of deuces right now," said Isaac.

"Regardless of how bad our hand is, our collective consciences here in the colony must fade into numb acceptance, or we'll go batty," said Jane.

"So then, to rationalize this numb acceptance, we must look for excuses for why we have acquiesced to something we do not really like," said Isaac.

"Excuses.....perfect.....something our species is very good at coming up with to explain why we were not wrong about anything," said Jill. "Alright.....so here goes.....we can argue that China inherited an impossible situation, and to their credit they've destroyed all of the serious weapons they could find, including their own, stopped open aggression, and have only minimally impaired the world in their effort to recover. We don't actively support them, but we understand why it is the way it is."

"Sounds good.....so that will be our platform, Jill," said Isaac.

"You're all on the wrong track, it's men who need the excuses," said Jake who just walked in after standing outside and listening. "Because men have been the problem all along."

"Sorry, but he overheard a lot of this," said Sarah who came in right behind him.

"Jake, Sarah..... hi," said Isaac.

"How much is a lot?" asked Jane.

"Enough," said Sarah.

"OK, look, here's how I see it: from our earliest appearance in history as a species, men have been primarily responsible for wars," said Jake.

"One could certainly debate that, but you're suggesting that if the world had been ruled by women, we would not be in the situation we're in right now," said Jane.

"I think that's probably true, yes," said Jake.

"It's not really about who is ruling as much as it is about who we are as a species, and the fact that we've become smart enough to develop nuclear weapons," said Jane. "Our thirst for knowledge is insatiable, and that includes both men and women, and the atom bomb was a product of that. Once it was on the table as a weapon, it may not have mattered who was in charge. Religious, cultural and ideological beliefs are held by both sexes, and it was those beliefs, not gender, that drove nations to become blind to reason and dogmatically polarized in their values."

"But in your discussion, you talked about instincts and our animal origins," said Jake. "You said it was an act of nature I believe."

"That's right, it is, and if you're suggesting that it's primarily men who promote aggression and the win-at-all-cost drive for survival, you're wrong, women can be just as driven, even moreso," said Jane.

"But it was always men who led us from tribal battles into modern wars," said Jake. "Women entered the action late, and yes, they do participate, but I'm not at all sure whether they are as dangerous as men."

"What happened in the distant past did cast men and women into different roles when it came to fighting, with men carrying the spears, swords and firearms," said Jane. "But modern warfare allowed us to shed the body armor, and women quickly learned to kill just as efficiently as men. Some say even more efficiently."

"And once we had nukes, everyone became an equal opportunity killer," said Isaac.

"OK, but what does that mean for the future?" asked Jake.

"If the knowledge to build nukes still exists, it may not matter who is in charge if the beliefs are still polarized," said Jane. "Women can be just as tenacious as men in trying to jam their beliefs down someone else's throat or claiming that their belief is the exclusive truth."

"And we can be a good deal more shrill in doing so," said Jill.

"And here's the thing, and one you'll find difficult to accept, Jake: if we have any hope of survival, we must keep nukes off the table," said Jane. "To do that we must not allow unregulated research that can lead to their development. So freedom to study anything, as you have been doing, is something that will have to be regulated. In other words, in order to prevent the development of weapons that can kill us all, we will have to essentially limit the type of research we are allowed to study."

"Government controlled education?" asked Jake.

"Well, to some extent, that has always been the case," said Jane.

"In America?" asked Jake.

"Everywhere to a greater or lesser degree," said Jane. "But that's only half the problem. The other half relates to what is still out there. We have to first find then destroy any and all knowledge that exists about how to build a nuke. And that is likely to approach the impossible for a number of reasons."

"Didn't the war pretty much do that already?" asked Jake.

"No, I'm sure there are caves like Debras out there with records that include the appropriate instructions," said Jane. "Our ship, up in orbit, contains an extensive body of knowledge that also has enough information to allow for the eventual development of nukes."

"However, it takes extensive infrastructure to generate the material needed for these weapons," said Jake. "You can't build one in your living room."

"Of course not, but some, possibly many, survivors have the expertise, and it's also likely that some equipment survived," said Jane. "In other words, the means and the knowledge is likely still out there."

"But simply having the expertise, instructions and some equipment is far short of being able to build one," said Jake.

"We simply do not know how much infrastructure still exists out there, Jake," said Jane. "Some of that was deliberately placed in underground facilities before the war. And some of that is still likely to be intact. And remember, this is a worldwide phenomenon, not simply one country."

"Alright, but what you're suggesting with the government regulation of learning is draconian," said Jake. "Our forebearers spent centuries discovering, proving and documenting knowledge to pass on to the next generation, and you're suggesting that it should now be the function of the state to control what we can learn."

"I, more than anyone, would be appalled by such a condition, but logically, I don't think we have other options considering what just happened here on this planet," said Jane.

"Right now, any sort of government control means China," said Jake. "I know they already suppress knowledge, but they have become lax as time went on.....so do you think they could do this?"

"I'm not sure, because doing anything worldwide would be a real challenge," said Jane. "Right now, I would say no, they're not on the same page as I am and even if they were the likelihood of success would be minimal."

"They did destroy all of their nukes, but I suspect the knowledge still exists in their libraries and I'm sure some if not all of their infastructure could be revived," said Jill.

"Whatever they do in regard to this will be what they do," said Jane. "I'm just expressing my opinion about what might have to happen in order to erase our ability to repeat what happened."

"Well, I'm sure my library contains such information, so there would be a lot of book burning for me," said Jake.

"It's not your library, it's Ellen's," said Sarah.

"Whatever," said Jake.

"If China did implement such a program of censure, the books in your library would have to be carefully reviewed to make sure they were free of this type of information," said Jane.

"A blatant censure of knowledge," said Jake.

"Of course, and something that would be entirely unheard of in most countries of the past," said Jane. "The real problem, however, is not the books, but the electronic files, if they could even be found, and, of course, the nuclear physicists. Electronically, an entire library can be contained in a relatively small collection of chips, and every one of the two dozen combating nations would certainly have recorded detailed instructions for building nukes."

"That's true, they would have had to," said Jake.

"Finding the chips that survived the conflagration would be like looking for a whole lot of needles in a whole lot of haystacks," said Jane.

"So is there any hope of ever getting back to a safe place in our ability to develop and store knowledge?" asked Jake.

"It would be up to China to take that lead and that's a very big assumption," said Jane.

"Government control of what we are allowed to study would mean the curtailment of vital science, potentially of any science," said Jake. "We could slide back into a kind of intellectual dark ages under such controls."

"Or a sort of liberal arts age," said Jill.

"That's also possible, and something the world outside of China has already entered in a very primitive way," said Jane.

"Back to horses and buggies?" asked Isaac.

"We grew up in a village that was not much more advanced than in Biblical times," said Sarah. "And even at Ellen's place, they were living a relatively primitive lifestyle."

"Actually, despite the latest scientific advances in our spaceship, we walked everywhere on Eden, and even used smoke signals to communicate," said Jill.

"Of course we failed to become self-sufficient because of those food makers," said Isaac. "So we were blocked in achieving our peaceful nervana by modern technology."

"Look, I'm not going back to horse and buggy days after I

rode in that shuttle of yours!" said Jake.

"However, they have fallen back a century or so even here in China," said Jane. "Life here is far from where it was prior to the war."

"And the remainder of the world has fallen back to nearly prehistoric times," said Jill.

"Yes, but if you consider what is still hiding out there, like the knowledge to build nukes, and more cave dwellers like Debra, we could eventually see a re-emergence of modern technology and war machines..... even nukes if things are left unmonitored and unregulated," said Jane.

"Well, as long as women are in charge, we should be fine in the long run," said Jake.

"He's not through singing that chorus," said Sarah.

"Do you think a world ruled entirely by women would be more peaceful?" asked Jane looking down at Isaac with a smile.

"Well, I lived with you and thirty other women on Eden and in the ship for two hundred years and it was very peaceful," said Isaac.

"Yes, but you were a man, and on Eden, you were the Board Chair, so effectively you were the ruler," said Jane.

"Oh no, in reality, you made all of the decisions, I just rubber stamped them," said Isaac.

"I did not!.....did I?" asked Jane.

"Hello!?" said Jill with a little laugh. Isaac gave her a fist bump.

"It really depends on who the women are," said Isaac.

"That's true, because who is in charge is the universal question," said Jane. "But I'd like to know how the Chinese men

176

feel about the fact that women are mostly in charge here?"

"Or, if it took time to get used to it?" asked Isaac.

"Wait, by asking that question you're suggesting that men are naturally the ones who should be in charge because of their gender, and if women were in charge the men would have to get used to something that wasn't natural," said Jake. "In your own words, the issue is all about nature."

"We didn't actually say that...... did we?" asked Isaac, looking up at Jane who shrugged at first, but then nodded. "OK, fine, but let's look back into our evolutionary past and ask how this would have played out in hunter-gatherer tribes twenty thousand years ago,"

"You mean the hunter, protector and provider as the male role in the context of wandering the plains trying to survive while avoiding being eaten by predators or killed by your neighbors?" asked Jake.

"Well.....yes," said Isaac.

"Hold it!" said Jane. "So now you're comparing a hunter-gatherer man carrying a spear with a modern urban man having a nuke in the closet, and each man is out there protecting their woman?"

"Oh Jane, you have such a way with words," said Isaac.

"She's right, Isaac, my comparison isn't valid in a modern context," said Jake.

"That's right, compare slashing with a spear at an invading tribal warrior or saber toothed tiger to nuking a city of ten million," said Jane.

"Nonetheless, is the concept of the male as the protector still valid?" asked Jill.

"It may have been to our ancestors, but conditions have changed so much that the idea of a man as protector is no longer valid," said Jane.

"What about sexual dimorphism," said Jake.

"That was a product of role playing during our evolution," said Jane.

"Well, I don't know, aren't we just two legged animals off the plains that now find nukes far more effective than spears at destroying our enemies?" asked Jill.

"Probably, but let's picture this.....we no longer have the warrior in armor and sword out there on the battlefield....now it's both men and women sitting around a table shouting derogatory slogans about those we hate, and then sending our surrogates to their consoles to throw nukes at the filth we rant about," said Jane. "And believe me, in this scenario, women will be just as vocal and aggressive as men!"

"I'm not about to argue that point," said Isaac.

"So what you're saying is that without steel piercing flesh as in the past, women are just as determined as men to shut the mouths of those they either disagree with or, for whatever reason, hate with a passion," said Jake.

"That's what I'm saying," said Jane.

"I'll accept that amendment to my thesis," said Jake.

"You mean that women are just as guilty as men for what happened?" asked Jane.

"Yes, but not quite as guilty," said Jake.

"Should I feel at least somewhat exonerated by that caveat?" asked Isaac.

"Not completely, because I still think men started the whole thing, and deep down they are the real aggressors," said Jake.

"Some of what he suggests might be true..... maybe women in power will tone things down a bit," said Jill.

"Even with women in charge, we may have to castrate the men whose balls get too big," said Jake.

"Did he just say that?" asked Jane.

"He did, so I think someone needs to supervise his selection of books," said Sarah.

"Wow," said Isaac.

"Can we get back to our discussion?" asked Jane. "If I can remember what it was."

"Alright, here.....so the fundamental question seems to be..... do we have any possibility of returning to normalcy given the world that exists today," said Jake.

"Right, I suppose that is the question," said Jane. "Our truth in all of this is that we're here in China by choice because it's the only safe and secure place in the world with any semblance of the modern life to which we have become accustomed. And, in order to live here, we must live with the fact that everyone else out there is living in primitive ignorance."

"Which begs an underlying question: are we then, by default, accepting the fact that the giant thumb of China is necessary to keep an eye on the world, collect up weapons where they find them, suppress violence if they see it, and post threats of enforcement even if they never intend to enforce anything?" asked Jill.

"Add the eventual regulation of information content to that list," said Jake.

"By accepting that, does it render our verbal opposition to

this new paradigm moot?" asked Isaac.

"Of course," said Jane. "And therefore, whatever they're doing, I guess we have to accept, because that's what we chose to live in," said Jane. "And I'm not going back to Eden or live out there on the plain."

"What she says," said Isaac.

"OK then, that seems a fitting end to our philosophical debate for today," said Jill.

"Say good night Gracy," said Jane.

"Where did you dig that up from?" asked Isaac who looked up at Jane as he began to smile.

"I'm hungry," said Sarah, grabbing Jake's sleeve and pulling him toward the exit.

"You're always hungry," said Jake, shrugging as he was being dragged away.

Jane and Isaac continued to look at each other as the sun began to set over the wooded hills. It was peaceful in the little valley, and what went on beyond those trees was no longer of concern to them. They had each other, and all was well.